The Shaming of
Gwendoline C

The Shaming of
Gwendoline C

by Gwendoline

Gwendoline is a fictional character.
That is:
She is as real as you or I.
She is a Story
Such as those we tell ourselves
And those stories are
What we are.

TWIN RIVERS
PRODUCTIONS

Issued in print and electronic formats
ISBN 978-1-990255-07-6: *The Shaming of Gwendoline C:* Paperback
ISBN 978-1-990255-06-9: *The Shaming of Gwendoline C:* EPUB
ISBN 978-1-7771580-0-2: *The Shaming of Gwendoline C:* Kindle
ISBN 978-1-990255-05-2: *The Shaming of Gwendoline C:* Amazon paperback

Cover and text design by Counterpunch Inc./Linda Gustafson
Illustrations by Niki9door

Published by
Twin Rivers Productions
20 Bloor Street East
PO Box 75070
Toronto, Ontario, M4W 3T3

To receive a free book or novella, sign up at:
https://gilbertreid.com

CONTENTS

CAST OF CHARACTERS

Alcide Bianchi – James Hewett Spencer's chauffeur in Italy

Alfredo – Restaurant owner in Rome

Allison Hughes – Executive Assistant to James Hewett Spencer

Claudia Clermont – Gwendoline's grandmother

Cylla von Guttenberg – A German writer and journalist

Elena Bianchi – Alcide's wife

Father Berthollet SJ – expert on West African and Korean affairs

Georges Cuvier – French Nobel Laureate chemist

Giuseppe Esposito – concierge of Hewett Spencer's building in Rome

Gwendoline Clermont – mathematician, amateur actress

James Hewett Spencer – British millionaire venture capitalist

Kate Chastain-Pembroke – Gwendoline's housemate and friend

Lauren Lockhart – famous war photographer, journalist

Maria Esposito – concierge of Hewett Spencer's building in Rome

Martine Aubin – French actress

Matt Robinson – friend of Gwendoline, has a crush on her

Mrs. Neumann – Chair of the Williamson-Neumann Foundation

Nicole d'Artois – French sex expert, madam, courtesan

Philip d'Este – famous French-Italian film director

Professor Cynthia Parker – leading scholar of French literature

Professor Gerald Skinner – prominent English mathematician

Professor Harold Lehman – Professor of Medicine, Harvard

Professor Ho Chan Lee – famous Chinese-American mathematician

Professor Rupert Harrington-Smyth – University President

Stephen Clermont – Gwendoline's grandfather

PROLOGUE – IMPACT

"Don't worry, love, I've seen much worse."

The moment the man uttered these words, I gulped: I was helpless – the naked prisoner of a total stranger!

"Don't worry, love ..." His grin hovered closer. "I've seen so much worse. You can't imagine!"

Slimy, covered in sweat, half-conscious, naked, streaked with vomit and excrement, I trembled. Damnation!

I twisted. I turned. But ... My body collapsed – a puppet whose strings had been cut. I dissolved, and ...

He swept me up in his arms.

"Oh!" Choking back a flood of saliva, I gagged. The tiny part of my mind still capable of rational thought, spoke up: He had not taken off his expensive jacket or shirt or tie. My filth would spoil everything!

"I stink!" It was a child's voice, petulant, pouting. It echoed from far away, another universe.

It was my voice. Me – formidable, unflappable, brilliant Gwendoline! Saliva rose. I was going to throw up – again.

"Yes. You do stink, most definitely, truly dreadful." His voice smiled. The accent was decidedly classy, British.

"I'm sorry."

"Sorry? What for?" His dark eyes narrowed. His smile shone, diabolic, unbelievably beautiful.

I hiccupped. "You aren't some sort of, I mean ...?"

"Serial killer, rapist?" His voice came from the clouds, distant thunder, the voice of God.

"Yes," I slurred. My tongue slithered – a floppy hunk of meat. Saliva dribbled from my chin. I hiccupped. I belched. I farted. The world went blurry. I was fading. Oh, God!

I must focus!

Carrying me in his arms, he slipped sideways through a doorway. I was a limp, filthy rag, one arm dangling loose. A wall of plastic surged up, misty, steamy. It had black-and-yellow daisies. Bright yellow splashes, insolent smiling daisy faces. They grinned.

The shower curtain! It was the shower curtain! The cartoon daisy faces stared. Pluck, pluck – he loves me, he loves me not ... I wandered lonely as a cloud ... The man was carrying me into the shower.

"A serial killer? No, my dear, I am not a serial killer. I'm something much, much worse." Turning sideways, he edged his way, lifting me against the semi-transparent, crisp, plastic curtain. It fought back. It stuck to my feverish, hypersensitive backside. "A doctor will be here soon. But first –"

Whosh!

Water exploded. It was steaming hot and gushed, exploding, over my head and shoulders. Somehow, before carrying me here, he had turned on the shower. Or had he? When had he done it? Water splashed everywhere. In the middle of the shower, hammered with droplets, was the small, bright, varnished pine stool from Kate's room. When had he put it there?

I hiccupped. Time fell apart, pirouetting away into shards of light and darkness, bits and pieces, flotsam and jetsam of consciousness, separated by retching blackness. The man slid me out of his arms, lowered me onto the stool.

"You're going to get soaked," I gasped.

"I'm already soaked."

I burped.

"Hold on." His voice was level, serious, in control.

"I'm going to die." I was shaking like a leaf. I couldn't control it. "I'm totally utterly going to die." Clack, clack, clack! My teeth were chattering! They were going to break. Yikes! I'm going to bite off my tongue. I'm going to vomit blood. I'm going to shatter my incisors. I'll be toothless, tongueless, an ancient unloved hag!

I sank onto the stool, trying to make myself small, huddled, shivering in on myself, my fists squeezed tight between my trembling thighs. Water streamed everywhere.

"Stand, get up! On your feet!"

I glanced up. He stared down, a dark face, deeply tanned, commanding, in control. High forehead, thick, dark hair, wavy, combed back, a touch of gray at the temples.

I stood, or tried to. I wavered, almost fell. I grabbed his shoulder. I blinked. His jacket – Hugo Boss or something infinitely expensive like that – was totally soaked. I gurgled. I was a bleary-eyed, bedraggled mess. I managed to whisper, "I'm an ass."

"Yes, I would say that – an ass, you most certainly are!" His face was suddenly close. His midnight-dark eyes stared into mine. I closed my eyes, swirling down into vertigo. He began to sponge my back; then, he was shampooing my hair. I trembled – half-fever, half-sensual squirm – nobody had touched me this way, since … since when?

"Now, gently." He pushed my head under the showerhead, hot water pouring, a powerful gush, rivulets overflowing, rushing through my hair, down my face, over my shoulders, cascading, spraying, from my breasts. I was going to swoon.

He turned me toward him, pinched my chin, tilted my face up. I opened my eyes. Through the splashing, glittering water, I blinked. His eyes were narrowed, concerned.

"What did you eat?"

"Mussels." I looked down. "It must have been the mussels. Last night. Or the leftovers – potato salad. Today. From the fridge. I ate without looking at what I was eating. And I drank too much last night. Cheap wine, white wine."

"Good. Probably not fatal then."

"Fuck!"

"Tut, tut. Bad language!" He slapped me gently on the cheek. "Naughty girl, naughty!" I looked up. His eyes stared into mine. He was grinning. He had crinkle lines – from the sun I suppose and from smiling – and, yes, a touch of gray in his jet-black hair, just at the temples; his skin was tanned too, beautifully rugged. My vision faded. I closed my eyes but held onto him. I whispered, half to myself, "Naughty – that's a perverse word, a childish word. You're perverse."

"Of course, I am."

"As long as you know it."

"Shame can be an exciting sensation."

I was going to say, "Not right now, it isn't!" But I burped, opened my eyes wide, belched, and threw up – gushed all over his shirt and tie – a great gob of slimy stinking guck.

He smiled. "Naughty girl! Finished?"

"I ... d ... d ... don't know ..." A flush of shame flooded my face, my shoulders.

"A stutter?"

"Y ... y ... yes ..." My humiliation was complete. "Oh, boy, you are odious. I ... h ... h ... hate you."

"I'm sure you do."

Shame overwhelmed me, a warm hot inner flood of abasement,

pure abjection! What an ass I was! Diarrhea, vomit, nakedness, helplessness, and now the stutter. Goddamn! It added to everything else. Three years ago, my stutter had gone away – now it was back. The horror, oh, the horror!

The horrible stutter!

To get rid of the stutter, I'd taken up amateur acting with a local theater group. We did Shakespeare, Tennessee Williams, Albee, and Jean Genet. At first, it was pure torture. Then, it was a joy. It was a way of facing the challenge and overcoming it. Acting can be addictive. Often, I felt I was real only when I was playing a part, when I wasn't being me, wasn't being Gwendoline. Playing a part was like wearing a mask. It turned life into a carnival. Not being me, finally I was free.

In the last two years, I'd chased away all those old anxieties – my stutter, my teeth braces (now thankfully well in the past), my nerdish pedantic personality, the fact that at school the other kids had called me "robot," my vampire-like pallor, the slightly cross-eyed look that comes over me when I get tired, or really angry – or sick, like now.

"This is dangerous," I managed to whisper.

"Dangerous?"

"For you." I clung to him.

"Ah, yes, yes ... Of course. Dirty evil strange old man molests beautiful young woman, seizes her when she's helpless, strips her naked, despoils her of her innocence, and so on – you will be able to sue me for gazillions of pounds or euros – or, more likely, dollars. My reputation will be ruined, and I'll go to jail for a hundred years. Turn around."

I turned around, facing away from him. He was using the sponge, between my legs, down my backside, into the crack of my ass, deep and thorough; he was spreading me, soapsuds and water streaming – down my back, down my face. Delicious hot water running, rivulets, off my breasts. Oh, God ... His fingers under the sponge, then under the thin cloth, then just his hand, went everywhere: I was being sodomized! Well, almost, and gently, gently.

"Turn around."

"Yes, Master ..." With bowed head, I turned around, again facing him. I meant the "master" to be snarky, but it sounded submissive – and pathetic. "I ..." I looked up at him. "I think I'm going to ..." My voice faded to a lisp, my lips went numb, stars floated, flashing.

"You ... you're going to – what?" He was far away, at the far end of a long, dark, tapering tunnel. Eyes narrowing, he looked worried, serious. He dropped the sponge. His arms slipped under my arms.

The world went black. All the lights went out. I fell, collapsing like a castle of cards. My arms and legs, turned to jelly.

His arms, his chest, held me. I was falling, falling – falling endlessly. I was falling into him, onto him. Then I was rising. He lifted me up in his arms. Me – a tangle of loose-limbed flotsam, on a surging ocean wave.

I don't remember anything else.

So that was the beginning.

I didn't even know his name.

He was the most handsome, desirable man I'd ever seen, and I met him under the most humiliating circumstances I could imagine. That was the beginning. Not a great way for a romance to begin, but, then ... maybe it wasn't a romance.

And, then again, maybe it was, the greatest one of all.

∞

A few hours earlier, in the late afternoon of that beautiful, fateful, sultry summer day, I was sitting at my desk, tapping the eraser end of a freshly sharpened BH4 pencil on a blank white sheet of paper. I was fidgety, annoyed at myself.

The sky was bright – perfect blue! My desk looked out onto our second-floor deck. Beyond the deck, across a park, a hundred yards away, stood a thin line of poplars. They were sketches in green, white, and black, sleepy and fragile, shimmering in the brilliant summer sunlight.

I yawned, licked my lips, and looked down. I scribbled a few meaningless doodles on the blank paper. *Damn it! Get your act together, Gwendoline!* I squared my shoulders, took a deep breath, gritted my teeth, and began to fill out the mathematics fellowship form. It was the big prize: The Williamson-Neumann Fellowship!

Just looking at the form brought back all my insecurities, all the mockery, all the schoolyard bullying: What a hopeless nerd I was, and still am! What a freak! "Robot! Robot! Robot!" the kids at school shouted. "Vampire! Vampire!" I close my eyes. I hear their voices.

Sometimes, math professors, even at university, would throw up their hands, and turn the class over to me.

Pure math is an escape. It's a refuge from the world and from myself. It is a self-enclosed universe where I have total control. You just manipulate symbols on a page, or a computer, or maybe on a blackboard. It is beautifully reassuring. In the world of pure symbols, you can play God; the world of pure symbols has none of the messy undisciplined beauty and chaos of human relationships, none of the unforgiving unpredictability, none of the horror of loss, of absence, none of the terror of losing the person you love. None of the feverish midnight emotion.

Math is free of love and hate.

Oh, damnation!

I couldn't concentrate. And I knew why: I had just been abandoned by the person I love – Kate.

I forced myself to focus. I couldn't. I was antsy, irritated, utterly empty. Kate left only a few hours ago. But behind her, she left a sense nothing. Just me – a void.

I swore. I clenched my fists. My knuckles turned white: That's what I am – *a void*. I was in mourning. Kate had been my house-mate, my best friend, and, I have to admit, my lover.

≈

A few hours earlier, before the departure ...

Kate – Katherine Cynthia Chastain-Pembroke, to give Kate her full-blown highfalutin name – had come into my room. Kate is a budding epidemiologist. She studies how diseases and plagues spread, what patterns emerge, how you can predict where the deadly bug will go next. But she was a poet and a philosopher too, at least in my eyes.

Kate was barefoot, wearing ragged blue denim shorts, bleached beach-bum, threadbare white, a soft-knotted cream-col-ored sailor's rope for a belt, and a paint-splattered, black tank top.

She was in the midst of packing – about to leave for two months in Paris, France, at the École Nationale de Sciences Pol-itiques and at the Pasteur Institute, then a year, perhaps two, in West Africa – Senegal.

Kate is French on her mother's side; she went to French schools in France, and so she speaks the language as well as Eng-lish, maybe even better.

She came into my room to get her hairdryer, the one she had bought in Paris last summer, and which has the right plugs and voltage switches, apparently, for France and Senegal or anywhere else in the whole wide world.

The skimpy shorts and thin tank top gave her a castaway, roguish, little-boy look that was especially alluring, as always with Kate. She was alluring in whatever state she was – naked, dressed, in scratchy red long johns, in panties, or pajamas, or whatever. Alluring, that was the word for Kate.

The sun glared through the double French doors. It glittered in her coppery red, overflowing curls, held up by an emerald sweatband. In the blazing sunlight, her green eyes sparkled like blank windowpanes – she looked as if she were blind. And, it's strange for a person with green eyes and auburn air, but her skin is dark gold – with a few freckles across the nose – from sunning on our deck and from a recent week-long holiday on Cape Cod with her latest beau, a muscle-bound, beautiful – but, she claims, utterly boring – guy from Harvard. "Boring, darling, so totally boring! He treats me like a case study! He has a Harvard Business School, truly atrociously arid, MBA mentality! I felt like a poor little bean being counted – and found wanting!" Kate is totally mid-Atlantic, a touch archaic, and when acting up, she speaks in exclamation marks.

Standing just inside the doorway, she glanced around my room – math and philosophy books piled up against the walls, and tottering in towers on all the chairs, with some literature tossed in, and the powerful computer all lit up. She stared at me and wagged her finger. "You'll get yourself raped, you know."

"Raped?"

"That catsuit running outfit!" She pointed. "It is too damned sexy."

"Sexy? Really?" I raised an eyebrow.

"Yes, darling, a true fetishist's dream." She tilted her head to one side, and grinned, as she gazed at the fetish object. "Fess up, darling! You are a shameless exhibitionist."

"Really?" I feigned innocence. The running suit was brand new, never yet worn. With shivery pleasure, I had just spread it out on my bed. I stared at the thing. It was sleek, glossy-black, skin-tight, aerodynamic ... but was it sexy? Well, yes, maybe it was. Yes, on second thought, suddenly seeing myself – and the catsuit – through Kate's eyes, I realized that it certainly was sexy, provocative – and revealing, not only of my body, but of me.

Boy, can I deceive myself!

Sometimes you can know something and not know it at the same time. Particularly if it is something you want, but don't want, at the same time, if you see what I mean. Ambivalence, I believe they call it, and it used to be fashionable when people bandied psychoanalytic terms around, Doctors Freud and Jung and all that, quite a few decades ago. In any case, it was a matter of principle: I would wear whatever I damned well wanted to wear. It is a woman's inalienable right to dress – or undress – as she pleases.

"A sneaky perverse perv, you truly are!" Kate laughed. "The trouble with you, my dearest, is you don't have the slightest idea of the effect you have on people – particularly on people of the masculine persuasion."

She moved to the bed and patted the guilty catsuit, pinching the material between thumb and forefinger, stroking it. "Oh, slinky, slippery, oh, so kinky. Luscious! I rather think I should wear it! It would be utterly divine. I can just see myself. I would absolutely adore running around naked, painted in black latex! Perhaps we could do it together."

Kate's father is a famous English surgeon, Sir Alfred Pembroke – and Kate, being a prodigy, had received her Master of Philosophy in Epidemiology two years ago, age 19, from Cambridge University. She affects more than a touch of English irony; she often calls me darling, and she uses words like bloody and bugger and knackered and kinky and perv and randy and wanker and other terms which I found totally chic and cool. She sensed my awe and, when she wasn't doing the French thing, which came from her mother's side, she played up her Englishness.

Her insouciance, verbal daring, and Gallic mischievousness played havoc with the men we knew. To fevered male imaginations, her attitude promised wonders in bed, which, I was pretty sure – no, I was certain – I knew, first hand – she could deliver.

Her haughty cool detachment, too, seemed to put her above the daily whirl of judgment, taboo, and fashion – as if she were examining all of us, and even herself, from a lofty, comfortable distance, as if we were all in a Renaissance play, and laughing at it all – at us, at herself, at sex, at the whole Vanity Fair whirligig.

"You're a regular vamp!" she smiled, turning to me, coming up close, and running her fingers through my hair.

"Cruel wench!" I flared. "Your mockery knows no bounds!"

She put her hands on my shoulders. "Let us see, my dearest child. Shall we make an inventory? Shall we enumerate the ways in which thou art a vamp? Shall we detail your loveliness? Let us consider! There is the pure, classic, vampire look – chalk-white, perfectly unblemished skin … as if you have been dusted all over with powdery ivory."

"Ugh!"

"There's the jet-black hair, cut short, just a touch androgynous."

"Androgynous?" I frowned. "You really think so?"

"Oh, you're a boy, truly."

"Really?"

"Yes. A cabin boy on a pirate ship! With evil one-eyed pirates and threats of devilish mischief surging up all around you."

"Really? That sounds, ah, tempting."

"And that perfect nose."

"Too long, I think." I wiggled my nose. My gaze held hers.

"The most perfect pubic patch."

"Pubic patch? I'm not sure my pubic patch is …"

"A perfect, dense, coal-black triangle. Triangular. Geometric. Utterly adorable."

"Well, if you say so …"

"I do, I do. I am a true explorer. And it is indeed a lair of unsolved mysteries – the Heart of Darkness, your very own Bermuda Triangle, your secret treasure trove."

"Ah!" I sighed, protectively clutching myself.

"And those totally wicked eyebrows, dark and arched, and your eyes!"

"And what, dear Kate, what do you have to say about my utterly hypnotic eyes?"

"Dark, dark, dark – sinful and mischievous, full of smoldering fire, hidden lights, will-o'-the-wisp illusions, hints of perverse depths, as if you truly did have a soul."

"Whereas we know …"

"Whereas we know thou art but a mask, a carefully constructed personage, an artifact, a whirligig commedia dell'arte creation, a pure illusion conjured up out of nothing."

"That's a little too close for comfort …"

"Shush, child! No confessions or inconvenient truths allowed!" She pressed her finger against my lips. "And these lips, oh, these lips! Such gloriously full lips, high-colored, plum rich, but perfectly delineated, exquisitely precise, just like your adorable precise body and brilliantly precise mathematical mind are precise. You are self-contained neatness itself, even the way you move. It drives all the chaps crazy, and the girls too, and that little trick you have of looking up at people, you know, the little downward tilt of the head, then, false submissive and challenging too, looking up, jet-black eyebrows, jet-black eyelashes, and then that coal-black hair, cut short, with the chalk-white body! What a combo!"

"Whew!" I cast my eyes down and twisted the corners of my mouth into a pout. My role in our little dialogs was to play the clown.

"Oh, yes, darling, I so totally adore that mutinous little pout you put on, looking up from under your eyebrows, like a little boy caught robbing the cookie jar, and daring, just daring, somebody to punish you. To tell the truth, that look drives me crazy too. I want to take you in my arms, ravish you, and carry you off to a deserted beach where palm trees grow!"

"Maybe we should get married," I said, staring up at her. It wasn't an entirely ridiculous idea.

"Idiot!" She kissed me on the lips, a light kiss, but both of us let it linger, eyes wide open, our souls mingling, our tongues briefly flirting. "Yes," she breathed, "In truth, it's not a bad idea! Perhaps one day we shall."

"Oh," I said, "that is very nice."

"And there's the wonderful way you have of explaining everything, in extraordinary, analytic, pedantic detail!"

"I don't explain everything in extraordinary pedantic detail, not everything." I was piqued. But she did have a point; I do tend to lecture; if let loose, I am a total bore. And I do tend to think out loud: if A and B are the case, it then follows, as night follows day, that Z is the case, and, perhaps, Y too ...

"I do love you." She gave me a little parting peck and stood back. "And then there's the stutter, the marvelous stutter – you know the way you sometimes stutter if you're nervous."

She took my hand and led me out of my room and into hers.

"I don't stutter anymore," I pouted. Her hand was warm in mine. My heart was jittery, on edge, tears were in the offing. She was about to leave!

Kate's room! What a mess! Even worse than mine! She'd piled her clothes pell-mell on the bed. Books, an iPad, an Apple laptop computer, her cell phone, a little traveler's kit of different electric plugs, her documents in a plastic envelope: the letter from Science Po', the letter from the Pasteur Institute, the copies of degrees and diplomas, vaccination certificates, the burgundy-colored British passport, the dark blue French EU passport.

"Oh, come on, yes you do stutter! You do – every once in a while, an amusing modest little stutter."

"No, I don't ... well ..." I frowned. My stutter was a sore topic.

"Sometimes you do."

"Never up on stage."

"Yes, that's true. Never up on stage." She put the dryer down on the bed and put her arm around my waist, and I took her hand in mine. We danced, a few light steps, carrying us out of her room and back into mine; then she kissed me on the mouth, her lips cool and warm at the same time, and she recited.

Shall I compare thee to a summer's day?
Thou art more lovely and more temperate.
Rough winds do shake the darling buds of May ...

She repeated the kiss and I returned it. We were replaying a routine from a theater piece we had performed in the spring. We danced and recited a duet, using a choice of texts from Shakespeare and other Renaissance and 16th and 17th-century poets. We had improvised our own bridge material – dance and dialogs – to link the Shakespearean and other excerpts. We performed the whole song-and-dance on stage. It was, for me, delightfully ambiguous. I was the boy, Kate was the girl. We flirted, and danced, and kissed, and recited the bits and pieces of Renaissance poetry. We were quite lascivious. To have become outright lovers, literally, right there on stage, would have required, I think, just one extra dance step ... *et voilà!*

Theater had been part of my self-prescribed therapy – to act, to perform, and to play the clown, these were my ways of getting rid of my stutter forever, because out in front of three hundred people, five nights in a row, you can't stutter.

"Now promise me, darling, you'll behave when I'm gone."

"I'll behave." I bit my lip and gave her the mutinous look.

"Promise! Under that shy retiring demeanor, you are secretly very wicked, totally perverse, as you and I very well know." She held up incriminating object number one – the slinky black runner's catsuit.

I again gave her my special intimidating gaze from under the stormy eyebrows, then looked up, displaying wide-eyed innocence. "I promise, cross my heart, and hope to die."

≈

Kate was my first real friend. Her going away would leave an aching void in my heart and in my life. My parents were divorced, and my father had disappeared from my life so early that I had no real memories of him, though there were a few photographs, a handsome, muscular guy with a tousled lank of hair over his forehead, like some Hollywood hero from the 1930s.

"He just up and left," my mother used to say, and she repeated the refrain many times, "Walked out one night! Didn't say goodbye. And didn't care a shit about you. Actually, I think you, Gwendoline, were the problem. Yes, you were the problem, Gwendoline, most definitely." At this point, probably after the fifth glass, she'd slur her words. "He didn't like you. He really didn't like you at all." I wondered at it. How could I have been so objectionable? I was just a baby.

At that point, after the fifth or sixth glass, she'd become angry. "Go away. I hate you! You are a worthless ugly, charmless, little piece of shit."

Mother was beautiful, even when she was in an uncontrollable rage – dark hair, big tragic eyes, and the chalk-white skin I'd inherited. I wanted her to love me. But she hated me. While she screamed, I'd go to my room and lie on my bed and draw circles or squares or triangles.

I began to stutter. This made things worse. If my mother caught me stuttering, she'd slap me, over and over and over. "You don't even know how to talk! You stupid piece of shit!" And, a bit later. "I should have had an abortion!" Her anger made the stutter worse, so said the experts.

Mother had been an actress, and it had seemed at one point – people told me later – she would become a star. I saw the clippings: a secondary role in a horror film, where all the critics said she was outstanding, the "one redeeming feature of an otherwise mediocre and forgettable derivative bit of drivel." Then two or three leading roles – then ... nothing. "Too difficult to work with," said one fellow actor.

She would be ultra-affectionate one minute, smother me in kisses, take me with her everywhere, even out at night, even when she was drinking, or sniffing coke. And then, suddenly, she would tell me that I had ruined her life; that she had wanted to abort me, but that my father wouldn't let her; that she hated the sight of me; that seeing me reminded her of everything that had gone wrong in her life. In fact, I, Gwendoline, was what had gone wrong in her life – me. I had ruined her career; I had spoiled her looks. Sometimes, she'd slap me, hard.

I understood – but only later – that she had what was called a drug problem and a drinking problem, and soon my Grandmother Claudia – who lives in the country – convinced mother to go into rehab. Claudia took me to live with her, on the farm. There I often saw grandfather, who was divorced from grandmother, but they seemed really to like each other, often he came on visits. He is a well-known physicist. He taught me about math. His old studio in the farmhouse was full of math books. He'd take me for walks, and, while he joked and told me about the different kinds of plants and slapped at the trees with his riding crop, he'd ask me questions: "Define geometric progression."

Mother's rehab did not turn out so well. She tried to stab another woman, and she beat up one of the attendants so badly he was in the hospital for three weeks. Grandmother managed to have a psychiatric evaluation done – the diagnosis was paranoid schizophrenia. Grandmother had mother declared incompetent – a hard thing to do to your own daughter. Mother went to an asylum. I stayed with my grandmother on the farm in the country. Grandmother and grandfather are rich, very rich. They set up a trust fund for me. As a result, in a small way, I was – I am – rich. I really should not complain about anything. Money solves a hell of a lot of problems. People who have money have no idea how important it is, what a difference it makes. It becomes like the air you breathe. It can also make you feel you're important – and invulnerable, which is, of course, a dangerous mistake.

≈

Finally, Kate had her bags packed and changed into her traveling clothes. She was elegance itself – flat-heeled pumps, dark stockings, a dark pleated skirt, white blouse, and elegant slim black jacket. She had insisted I not accompany her to the airport. I hugged her and helped carry down her bags.

I suddenly realized I would have our house all to myself – emptiness!

Kate took one long look at me. "Look after yourself. And, darling, don't go running at night! Not alone, and not in that sleek catsuit – you look too irresistible. A goblin will gobble you up. You'll get into trouble!"

The cab was waiting. I slipped the suitcase into the trunk on top of the two other suitcases. The taxi driver was a handsome tall Sikh with a turban, fierce long beard, and big liquid eyes. He looked at me, smiled, and closed the trunk. I kissed Kate on both cheeks, held her by the shoulders. She threw herself into my arms and kissed me on the lips.

"I don't know if I can live without you," she said.

"Of course, you can," I said. "But I don't know what I'll do without you."

She gazed at me with those sharp green eyes, touched the edge of my cheek with the tip of her fingers, mimed a kiss with a pucker of her lips, and slipped into the cab. I closed the cab door carefully. It made a definitive chunk sound – a punctuation mark. Kate's face was behind glass. She rolled down the window. "I love you," she said.

"I love you," I shouted, as the cab pulled away.

As I watched the cab race off, I realized my eyes were wet. Everything went blurry: The poplars, shimmering green, white, and black, that lined the sleepy canal; the old crumbling asphalted towpath; and the row of drowsy red brick houses, stretching away toward the end of the street. The taxi turned the corner and was gone.

The street was suddenly empty, and sleepy in the bright sunlight. I stood there for almost a minute. It was a perfect summer day, warm with a gentle breeze, just a few clouds piling up, far away. But amidst the outer brightness, I was plunged into darkness. It all seemed ominous. A glorious period of my life had come to an end.

The empty house was unreal. I ran my fingers along the walls and curtains; I walked up and down the stairs. I sat down and stared at the pattern of the wood – curls of pine knots. I went out onto the second-floor deck, flopped into a deck chair, lay there, frowned, swore, stood up, walked around in circles, stopped, and watched a black squirrel jump from branch to branch. I wanted to talk to the squirrel, but decided not to.

I went back to my room. I sat down at the computer. The screen stared at me. I stared back. I had to finish the application for the Williamson-Neumann Fellowship, and I had to finish an article I was writing for The Journal of Philosophy and Theoretical Mathematics: *How do we know what think we know, and do we really know it? The role of axioms in modeling complex systems.*

Whew!

The night before, Kate and I gone out to celebrate her departure with some of her friends; it was a farewell banquet. I ate too much rich pub food, including very garlicky mussels. I drank too much too – a sweet heavy red wine. Then I switched to white, probably a mistake.

I'd never liked mussels, but Matt Robinson convinced me, mussels were just the thing, he said, mussels were entirely appropriate and very French. Matt was always poking at me, teasing me, and daring me to do things. He was a sort of star, football hero, I think, though I didn't pay attention to football and he knew that I didn't know and didn't care that he was Mister Touchdown or something. The fact that I could be so ignorant of what was essential in life piqued his interest, or so I presumed. I couldn't see any other reason he'd bother with me. A few weeks ago, we'd necked and "made out" in a clumsy inconclusive way. His car smelled of running shoes. I tried to be skillful, even enthusiastic, but I don't think I was very encouraging. And now, during the farewell banquet, he kept putting his hand on my shoulder, or in the small of my back, nothing particularly sexual, or at least that's what I thought, and I liked it, but ... But ... there was, for me, no ... excitement ... no danger ... no electricity.

Well, that was last night.

I yawned.

Right now, in the void, with Kate gone, I felt weirdly unsettled – sort of dizzy-empty. Maybe I had a fever. I put my hand on my forehead. There was a thin patina of sweat. Probably nothing. It was a warm day, the window was open, the air-conditioning was not on.

I focused on the computer and concentrated, and, with a supreme effort, I finished filling out the forms for the Williamson-Neumann Fellowship. I printed out the parts that had to be printed out. I folded up the pieces of paper. I checked and double-checked that I had included everything, that I had checked all the boxes, initialed and signed where I had to initial and sign, and then I put it all in the pre-addressed envelope. I checked all the sheets once more and then I sealed the envelope and propped it on my desk, beside the computer. It was done! There it was, the letter, the application. It seemed unreal.

On that little paper would depend my future. It had to be mailed tomorrow, at the latest. Filling it out and sealing the envelope brought a feeling of anticlimax. What do I do now?

The sun was low. It streamed through the window. I got up and pulled down the blinds, suddenly I was immersed in blue, striped shadows. I tried to concentrate. I couldn't. I felt like a ghost. The house was big and empty, silent and strangely pointless. It had lost its soul. I was restless, empty like the house, the void within staring back at me.

I forced myself to work – and I managed to lay out the solution to one problem for the article I had to write.

I'd already thought up the solution. Well, I'd intuited it, and now I had laid it out. It is funny how you can sort of "see" the solution to a problem, before knowing all the steps you need to take to get there.

My little niche of study is how mathematical models mesh – or don't mesh – with "reality" and how, sometimes, they should be used with caution. You have to be aware of limits. The quality and range of the assumptions you make are essential.

The work lies somewhere between science, methodology, and philosophy. Investors or economists might think a mathematical model tells them precisely what they need to know, but it might not. The same is true of models of weather, and climate, and, say, the spread of criminal or terrorist networks or traffic jams or of disease – that was how I met Kate, at a lecture on precisely that question: how does a plague or pandemic spread?

I stood up, stretched, and yawned. The computer screen was boring. I glanced out at the day. The blue sky outside was tempting. It was empty and perfect, not a cloud to be seen. It was one of those perfect days that make you feel you really ought to be happy. In fact, on such a beautiful day, you should be dancing in ecstasy. If you're not, you feel guilty, and thus begins a downward spiral. In such balmy perfection, there's no excuse not to be in bliss.

I got some leftovers out of the fridge – potato salad and part of a ham sandwich – and I gobbled them down.

I felt even weirder. I walked up and down. Outside, the blue faded. The sky turned pale, glowing with that milky light that is the first inkling of dusk. Soon it would be dark.

My stomach was weird too, empty, and nervous.

And – I was horny.

It must be psychological.

I could run a hot bath, lie back in bubbles, imagine something really exotic and exciting, and … satisfy myself …

No, not now, not today.

Maybe a run would be the ideal cure for the lonely horny paradise blues.

Yes, I'll go for a run. And I'll memorize some lines: Viola's soliloquy in Twelfth Night. Next week I was supposed to rehearse with some of the women in our drama group. As I'm sure you'll remember, Viola is a shipwrecked girl cast up on an alien shore.

She disguises herself as a boy, and, in the soliloquy scene, she has just met a beautiful widow, Olivia, who, thinking Voila is a young man, instantly falls in love with her. After Viola leaves, Olivia sends a servant after her with a ring she pretends Viola left behind; Viola wonders about the lady's subterfuge. Obviously, the lady wants to keep in touch. Has Viola's masculine disguise, God forbid, caused the lady to fall in love with her? What a pickle! I walked out onto the deck and paced up and down, working myself up, putting myself into the mood to play Viola, slipping myself into her skin. My shorts and T-shirt fitted the role, perhaps ... Androgynous, me? Hmm ... I am me, a young woman, playing a girl, who is playing a boy, and thus it is that I imagine myself: I am a strutting, impertinent, but timid pageboy – in reality a terrified girl – cast up upon a frightening foreign shore.

I left no ring with her. What means this lady?
Fortune forbid my outside have not charmed her!
She made good view of me, indeed so much
That sure methought her eyes had lost her tongue,
For she did speak in starts distractedly.
She loves me, sure!

My cellphone rang. I let it ring and then I went into my bedroom. The phone was lying on the bed. I picked it up.

"Hello?"

"Hey, you must be feeling terrible, kid, I mean, lonely, right – now Kate is gone." It was Matt. "Come on out for a beer. Some of the boys and I are going to ..."

I said no, as nicely as I could – I have a headache, I said, I just want to stay home, I said. Maybe later in the week, I said.

"Okay," he said. I knew he thought I was being a difficult snob, a neurotic bitch. There was a sudden touch of hardness in his voice, quick and curt. I was hurt, though I was the one doing the hurting. He wanted something from me – affection, sex, company, admiration, whatever – and I couldn't give it. I found him uninteresting: nice, but bland and flat as old rainwater. Maybe I'm too demanding, I thought, maybe I am a bitch. I stared at the phone. I almost picked it up to call him back and say, "Yes."

But I didn't.

I phoned Reanna Wilson, a friend of mine. Sometimes we ran together. But she had a "hot date" and couldn't come running.

I shouldn't go, I thought, it's getting dark already. No, I need the fresh air, it'll clear my head.

"Okay, damn it, I'll go – by myself."

I pulled on the sleek I-am-Catwoman catsuit, silky black, like night itself. Over it, I pulled a tight-fitting, black sweatshirt, with the big yellow glowing duck on the back, so I wouldn't get hit by a truck. Not that there were many trucks. It was an isolated, lonely, beautiful path, through the park, and along the canal. I laced up my scarlet-glow running shoes, sort of cute, and neon-bright. I put on the scarlet sweatband. I ran downstairs and then jogged in place for a moment, to get into the rhythm. I looked around. It was already dark – and foggy.

It looked like rain.

Where did that come from?

Oh, well, no matter.

I ran.

Running in the rain ... thoughts, sensuality, sights ...

I ran.

Fog moved in, gray and silver. It drifted between the trees; the bark and branches and leaves glowed, wet with fog; the air was heavy and sweet. Delicate smoky curls of mist rose off the stagnant surface of the canal. A man and woman ran past and nodded. I nodded back. I'd seen them several times, but we'd never spoken. I ran along the towpath bordering the canal, and then I ran up and across Gibbon's Hill, and then I headed down along canal drive.

I ran.

The rain began – a soft whispering rain.

I ran.

I kept running. It was good. I was light-headed, free, alone ...

Then, suddenly, I felt dizzy. I stopped. I did a few stretches. Under the spandex, my body was slick with sweat. Suddenly, I realized I was far away from everybody and everything. The path wound along the canal, beside the parkway road, which nobody seemed ever to use. The bushes and trees dripped water – silver droplets. Mist rose off the water. I leaned against a tree, my hand flat against the bark. It was cool and wet and sticky under my palm and fingertips. The metal railing along the canal gleamed, coal-black. The lamps on the canal shone bright, blurry, suddenly out of focus. Everything spun – slow at first, then fast.

It was deep night; darkness rushed in.

I heard an owl. Was it an owl?

The world was unreal. Was I hallucinating?

The world went double.

What was happening?

I was feverish, nauseous – flu coming on? Food poisoning? My stomach lurched. Cramps flashed, bolts of lightning tore through my belly. Explosions of pain. *Damnation!* I should have listened to Kate. Going running was a horrible idea!

I put my hand to my forehead.

Burning up!

Oh, God! I was going to throw up. Sphincter convulsing, losing control. Oh, boy! Diarrhea! The cramps rippled, tore through my gut. I leaned against the tree. I bent over. Oh! I want to curl up and die.

I was on my knees, retching. Oh, boy, oh boy! I threw up evil-smelling gruel, clots of something really ugly. My hair was soaked in sweat. Rivulets flooded the sweatband, ran down my forehead into my eyes. I was on fire.

On hands and knees, shaking uncontrollably, I looked up. I stared. Everything was blurry. A glare of headlights. A car had stopped. Very few cars came here, let alone stopped here.

I wanted to crawl away and die. *Damn it!* No one should see me like this. And I don't want to see anybody. I blinked, I wiped away the sweat and tears, I sniffled. The car was black, a Mercedes, its headlights making streaks of slanting white light in the rain. Heavy now, slashing down. *Damn it!* I don't want anybody to see me! I want to curl up and ...

A man got out of the Mercedes. He was a dark silhouette, walking toward me.

Ugh! I threw up.

I've got to run – I've got to run away ...

I got up. Took one step. Everything spun. I fell to my knees. A hot flush of shame overwhelmed me and I sank, shivering, to the ground.

I was on my hands and knees, retching, noisily, cough, cough, spewing stinky liquid; it splashed up; it drooled from my chin; it was all over my chest, all over the T-shirt; I coughed, I spewed more, horrible gobs of something. Ugh!

The man knelt next to me. "Here." He held out a handkerchief.

"Oh, God," I managed to say. I didn't accept the handkerchief. "I'll ruin it," I groaned.

"It doesn't matter." His hand was on my forehead. "You're burning up."

I turned my head. I looked at him.

"Oh, God," I choked. Another wave of nausea rushed at me like a freight train. I must be hallucinating. The guy looked too handsome to be true! Movie star handsome. Tanned. Dark. A scar across one cheek, as if he'd fought a duel or something. Expensive suit. Sumptuous tie. He looked like the Devil himself. Concern sparkled in his dark eyes.

I coughed, spewed again – a total explosion – and raised a hand to shield him from the spray – and sight – of vomit. Some of the vomit hit him square in the chest.

"I think, I think," I gulped ... "I've got horrible cramps, horrible, horrible – I think I'm going to shit myself ... I mean ... Oh, God!" I doubled up.

"A hospital is where you should be ..."

"No! No! No hospital – people die in hospitals!"

"A hospital, I think ..."

"No, no!" I almost screamed. "No hospital!" I burped and splashed more vomit. Oh, how awful! How shameful!

"That's all right. Where do you live? Come on, come on ..."

By this time, I was delirious, only half-conscious. Somehow, I gave him my address. Somehow, I told him how to get there. Talking was hard. It was beyond me. I tried to stand up, I just managed it. Then I fell.

He swept his arms under me and lifted me up.

"Hey, what are you doing?" It was barely a whisper. I lolled, filthy and retching, slippery and drooling, in his arms.

The cramps came in waves. My sphincter convulsed. "Oh, no! Oh, God!" None of this seemed to faze him.

I put my arm around his neck. "Oh, oh, oh," I moaned.

He carried me to the Mercedes, let me down gently, propping me against the car. The smooth cool metal came right through the fabric of the catsuit. Like I was naked. I trembled. My teeth chattered. I bent over in pure agony. He opened the door. He held out his hand. "Keys," he said, "Your keys."

It took me a second to understand.

I got the keys out and handed them to him.

I farted – a long rippling fart – and I shat myself. "Oh, God, I'm sorry," I moaned. Watery shit, dribbling slowly down my leg inside the skin-tight suit.

"What are you sorry for?" He was holding a plaid blanket in his hand. He must have gotten it out of the trunk. When did he do that? He spread it over the back seat. I was holding onto the car, trying not to fall.

"I'm sorry because ..." my voice faded. "I'm sorry because ... I'm sorry ... I'm sorry."

"That's idiotic."

"I'm sorry." I was whimpering. I wanted to cry, to bawl like a baby. I was ridiculous. I was stupid. I was sorry! The cramps came rushing again. "Oh, I'm going to shit ..."

"In you get, my love, easy does it." He lifted me up again, and slid me into the back seat of the car, onto the blanket. "Sit or curl up, whatever's easier."

"Yes." Vomit was rising.

The door chunked shut. He went around and got in the car. The motor started. He was talking on a phone. "Harry, glad I caught you! Sick young lady. Found her by the roadside. Yes, I'd say it's a bit of an emergency. Food poisoning, I suspect. Damsel in distress. Yes, charming situation. Retching, diarrhea, cramps, high fever. If you wouldn't mind. Yes, right away, if you can. It is a big favor, I realize. Otherwise, I'd take her to the hospital, but I think she would throw a fit if I did that and break something. Thank you, Harry. I'm infinitely in your debt. Yes, the address is ... Arrange for a nurse too, yes, a good one, the very best, thank you."

He hung up. The car was already moving.

"Who ... are ... a ... a ... are you ...? I'm ... m ... m ..."

"It doesn't matter who I am."

"No, I guess it doesn't," I muttered to myself. I could hardly breathe, let alone talk, I threw up again, trying to make sure the blanket got most of it. I closed my eyes. Time passed. I don't know how much time. Not much.

≈

He parked in front of the house. He got out of the car and came around to collect me. He opened the door, slid me out of the back seat, and held me up. All his actions were deliberate, precise, almost military. I tried to stand. My legs were like rubber.

"Oh, fuck! I shit myself! Again!" The shit was dribbling inside the catsuit. It was leaking out at my ankles. It smelled horrible!

"You're very productive, my dear. Manure all over the place." He leaned me against the brick wall of the house. I sagged. He held me up with one hand, and somehow opened the door. He hoisted me into his arms, sidled through the door, pulled the door shut, and carried me up the stairs. "Nobody here?"

"No ..."

"Good."

"Say, you're not some sort of serial killer, are you?"

"Not at the present moment I'm not. I'd better stay with you."

"Okay," I sighed, not really knowing what I was saying. I was burning up, lolling in his arms, limp as a drowned puppy. We got to the top of the stairs, went into Kate's bedroom, then into my bedroom. He looked around the room. Still carrying me, he glanced into the bathroom. He was very strong.

"I'm going to clean you up!"

"Oh, no, God, no! I've ..."

"Yes, you've shit yourself – again, but I think it may be over." There was a smile in his voice. "Naughty girl!"

"You're enjoying this."

"Yes, I do believe I am."

"You are terrible. I hate you!"

"Absolutely. You are quite right to hate me!"

"Oh, this is awful." I choked and drooled. Everything went extra blurry. Stars, drifting bright flashes, filled my eyes.

"Don't worry, love, I've seen far worse," he said, smiling. At least I think he was smiling. He held me up while he put two towels on the bed, and then he laid me down across them. His hand was on my forehead. It felt so cool, so strong.

"Don't worry. We'll soon have you squeaky clean." He was pulling off the sweatshirt. Now he was unzipping the catsuit.

"No, no, please ..." This was horrible. The catsuit was unzipped; he opened it up, and he levered my arms out of it, and he pulled it off my legs. It was tight; I was sweaty; it was not easy, but he peeled it away. I wiggled, protesting, kicking weakly, "No, no, no ..."

"Come on, hold still!"

He pulled my panties down my legs and held them up. "Well, look at this." They were soiled, visibly soiled, soaked, dripping shitty gruel.

"You are ... disgusting!" I managed to say, more a gurgling whisper than human speech.

"Well, then, here were go, my girl." He lifted me up and carried me, naked, wrapped in the towel, and slathered in sweat, vomit, and shit, into the bathroom. Yuk! The stench was overpowering. Yuk! He let me down. I tried to stand. I couldn't. I leaned against him.

He sat me in the shower, on a stool. It was the wooden stool from the corner of Kate's room. The one she piled books on. When had he put it there? Had he thrown the books on the floor? Kate would be so totally annoyed!

He held me so I wouldn't topple over, and he washed me. He was thorough, scrubbing every crevice, every orifice. I was dizzy, saying crazy stuff, like, "You can't do this! This is rape! This is disgusting! I am disgusting!"

"It's not rape. And you are not disgusting. You are actually extraordinarily beautiful and extremely charming. And I'm sure you have a mind, somewhere, though you seem, for the moment, to have misplaced it. You're a mathematician, I see, from the books. Some sort of child prodigy, I imagine."

The water streamed over me, and soapsuds and shampoo. Oh, it was so warm, so comforting. His shirt and jacket were soaked. His hands were everywhere. I leaned against his chest. I clung to his shoulder. He concentrated, using the sponge, the big blue sponge Kate was so fond of, and I was thinking he can't use the big blue sponge; he'll ruin the big blue sponge ... I have to tell him he can't use the big blue sponge, Kate's sponge.

"You ... you ... you ... can't ..." I tried to say, I gagged, and vomited and ...

"Well, well, well ..."

"Oh, God!"

"We'll have you all cleaned up in no time, right as rain, all sparkling and squeaky clean and ..."

His voice faded.

The world was gone. I was gone.

∞

I woke up drowsy and confused. What time was it? Where was I? Then I realized that I was in bed, in my room, and that it was raining. I could see streaks of rain against the window and I could hear the familiar pitter-patter of rain on the deck and the roof. A woman I didn't recognize was sitting close, watching me. She was knitting, and she was blond and cheery-looking and wearing a white smock and white stockings. I sat up. I discovered I was wearing elegant white silk pajamas that I had never seen before. Where had they come from? When had I put them on? "Who are you?"

"I'm Rose, I'm a nurse." She had a British accent.

"What are you doing here?"

"Mr. Hewitt Spencer asked me to stay, and Professor Harold Lehman."

"Who?

"Mr. James Hewitt Spencer and Professor Harold Lehman." She gave me a nice maternal smile that seemed to suggest that I was an idiot not to know who those two gentlemen were.

"Oh. Oh well, ah, that's very kind of them and of you; but I can't afford you." Actually, I probably could afford her; and I suddenly realized I was being mean and ungrateful. "I mean, thanks, and all, but I'm not sure I need ... What day is it?"

"It's Friday, almost five pm. Everything is paid for. Don't worry."

"Friday? The last thing I remember was Wednesday! Wednesday night!"

"Yes, you've been sleeping."

"Oh, my God, where is the envelope?" I suddenly saw the fellowship application envelope was not there where I had left it.

"The envelope that was there?"

"Yes."

"For the Williamson-Neumann Foundation?" She looked down at her knitting. The needles clicked away efficiently, almost automatically. It looked like a plaid turtleneck sweater.

"Yes." Sweat pearled on my forehead – maybe somebody had thrown the envelope out, or stored it away; maybe I had only imagined that I had filled out the forms; maybe everything was lost! Maybe I'd been delirious and destroyed it.

"Mr. James Hewitt Spencer took it," Rose smiled. "Would you like some tea?"

"Oh," my heart sank.

"He said to tell you that he would make sure it would be delivered immediately, that it would arrive on time."

"Oh, well, that's great, that's ..." I wondered. Could I trust him? Would he realize how important it was? Would it sit for weeks on the seat of his Mercedes? I knew nothing about this man except that he was gorgeous – and presumably rich, very rich. I got out of bed, and immediately felt light-headed. I sat down.

"You haven't eaten. I'll make some tea and toast, dear, and we'll get you right back on track. You'll be up and running in no time."

"Okay, thank you. And I apologize – that was very ungracious of me to say I couldn't afford you."

"That's quite alright, dear. I am rather expensive. But, as I said, it's all been looked after. Mr. Hewitt Spencer has been very generous. He and Professor Lehman were quite worried about you. I will stay as long as you want me or need me."

"Professor Lehman?" Was he the Professor Lehman that taught at Harvard? The one Kate had talked about? I stood up – felt faint – but managed to go to my computer and sit down. The silk pajamas were slinky and sleek and sensuously comfortable, an absolutely luxurious feeling. I was still light-headed; my tummy growled.

I turned on the computer.

Email – a pile of emails. A first note from Kate: She had landed safely in Paris and was already in her residence and had discovered a nice little restaurant I would love on the Left-Bank just down from the Pantheon. Another one from Kate: "Where are you, darling? Are you okay? This silence is disquieting." And then another: "Have you found a new lover? Is that why you are neglecting me?"

Then there was an email from the Williamson-Neumann Foundation. I stared at it for a moment, and then I took a deep breath and opened it.

"We have received your application. All the papers are in order. Thank you very much. You will be hearing from us in about a month."

I almost fainted with relief. I sat there, feeling weak, the spurt of terrified, nervous energy dissolving. Suddenly, I longed to be pampered. I lolled back, listening to the rain patter on the roof and on the deck; I could hear, downstairs, Rose puttering about in the kitchen. I sighed and stretched. I was alive! How nice!

Then, curious to know who my saviors were, I googled James Hewitt Spencer and Professor Harold Lehman. I sent an email to Kate – explaining my silence and detailing my adventure with the great and notorious James Hewitt Spencer. He did – or so it seemed from some of the online tabloids – have a dark and satanic reputation. He was a brilliant, but mysterious, investor millionaire; he was British ex-military; there were hints of work with the Special Air Service, of "black ops," hostage rescues, and connections in "intelligence." He was also known as a playboy who had wild and glamorous friends, and there were titillating hints of satanic mischief. Hmm, satanic ...?

≈

Rose was constantly cheerful, and I liked having her around; she seemed quite happy to be my keeper and insisted on staying for another two days just to make sure I was completely back in form. She reported continuously, she told me, to James Hewitt Spencer and to Professor Lehman.

Finally, Rose went. We hugged each other and promised to keep in touch, and she drove away, with one wave out the open window of her car. It was sad, suddenly to be in the house alone – once again.

James Hewitt Spencer. His business card gave addresses in

New York and London and Paris and Rome. His company was Sappho & Hera Venture Capital and Investments. An interesting name: a lesbian Greek poetess and a jealous Greek goddess. Maybe James Hewitt Spencer was a feminist.

I looked the company up. I hacked into its site, and I checked out some of its investments. Some of them were mysterious. But "mysterious" would not stop Gwendoline. I went deeper. There were a few suspicious-looking arms companies and defense contractors, and lots of small biotech companies doing interesting secret research, some power companies, and some pharmaceuticals and robotics companies, quite a few new technologies in telemedicine and nano-robots and nano-drones. They were mostly quirky outfits, doing cutting-edge research, as far as I could tell – in places like Germany, Spain, South Carolina, Italy, and France, Korea, Indonesia, and the UK. Hmm, so Mr. James Hewitt Spencer was an evil capitalist with quirky and sinful sidelines. Hmm. Gwendoline was intrigued.

Since I was going to go to New York next week to have lunch with grandmother Claudia, I decided I should visit the man and thank him – I was curious about my dark satanic savior. I sent him an email, A reply came, almost immediately, saying simply, "Come. Wednesday. 15:00 hours."

CHAPTER 1 – MANHATTAN

Grandmother Claudia was, as always, in excellent form. We ate at Balthazar's, an elegant noisy French bistro on Spring Street in SoHo. I had the chicken club sandwich, but hardly touched it.

Claudia, who is thin as a rail and as elegant and beautiful as a 1940s movie star, was wearing a charcoal Armani jacket, had large sunglasses tilted up on her sleek steel-gray hair, and two discreet strings of white pearls, and all of this was completed by a cream cashmere sweater. She chose the duck confit, with little caramelized onions and potatoes and mushrooms. As always, she ate with delicate, efficient gusto; she brimmed with health and good sense, and she washed it all down with several glasses of Chablis. "Well, then, darling, how are we really doing? Are we happy with life? Are you going to get the Williamson-Neumann Fellowship? Have you found a man? Whomever you find, darling, you will need someone challenging, and up to your standards, but you must not be too demanding, Gwendoline, you know very few people are as intelligent or as complicated as you are."

Claudia had this strange idea that I am complicated and perverse. She was – is – of course, right.

She knew a lot of things first-hand about my tastes and quirks.

When I was twelve, I had tried cutting myself – self-mutilation – and once I had arranged a noose, hung it from a timber beam in the barn, and tried to hang myself. The noose knot unraveled. I fell to the floor and banged and scraped my knees. Claudia found me with the unsuccessful noose still dangling from the beam and me sitting on the floor – amid horse dung and straw – swearing. It was totally humiliating. "You really must learn more about knots, darling," she said, as she knelt next to me. She took me in her arms and kissed me just about everywhere. Then she took me to the kitchen where she put iodine – how old-fashioned – on the scrapes, and served me a glass of wine, and, like two adults, we talked – about death and life – late into the night.

Claudia knew all about the suicidal yearnings, the self-mutilation, and the dark moods. Winston Churchill called them his "black dogs," she said, and she told me that melancholia used to be known as the poets' disease and often accompanied some forms of genius or creativity. She told me that if I really wanted to suffer, it should be carefully controlled suffering. "Really?" said I. Yes, it should be enjoyable suffering, sensuous, and intentional suffering, like a very hot shower or a very cold bath – preferably with ice cubes. "Ugh!" said I. Now, she explained, if we consider sex, and sex and suffering, it should be suffering at the hands of a rough, but sophisticated and caring fellow, who, she said, would satisfy my cravings for humiliation and – controlled – pain, but protect me from myself. You do not want someone who abuses you. He must give you what you want, not only what he wants. "Boy, oh, boy!" said I, "It sounds complicated." How do you fit two such complicated people's desires together? I was not sure I was up to the challenge or ready for all this enlightenment. "Never, if you can avoid it, do anything irredeemable," she said, "and killing yourself is fairly definitive; you might regret it later, and there's no going back." She took me to see a very nice lady shrink. Together the shrink and Claudia gave me back my life – them and mathematics. And grandfather – Steven Claremont – I have my mother's name – who was, as I have said, Claudia's ex-husband and probably her best friend; on his visits to the farm, he gave me puzzles to solve, mathematical concepts to conquer; he provided me with one challenge after another – they were signposts – a roadmap back to the land of the living.

Then, when I went away to university, there was Kate, who quickly became a favorite of Claudia's. Among other things, they shared fluency in French and a love of French culture, the paintings, and the literature – Voltaire, Balzac, Flaubert, Proust, and Jean-Paul Sartre and Albert Camus and Colette and Simone de Beauvoir. "You two are lucky to have found each other," Claudia said, "Kate is as complicated as you are, but I think in a much more serene and sunny way," Claudia gave me her bright, sly, friendly, all-knowing, all-forgiving Lauren Bacall smile, "And speaking of Kate, how is dear, delicious Kate?"

I reported that Kate loved being in Paris – it was her home in a way, or one of her homes, which Claudia knew, of course. Kate was bursting with energy and projects, already plunged into study and research, and busy preparing for Africa. Several new deadly epidemics were underway, and Kate was going to travel to the frontline to learn about the nitty-gritty of epidemiological detective work, testing, and how the information and statistics were gathered, trying to pin down how each particular pathogen spread from person to person, and country to country.

After lunch, I set off to see James Hewitt Spenser. Before leaving home, I had tortured myself – briefly – trying to decide how to dress. At first, I thought I would do business-like: An Armani type suit, dark pleated skirt, a simple white silk blouse or white silk T-shirt, black Armani jacket with fine 1940's shoulders, but then I thought, "No, I'll look like I'm applying for a job." I chose a black cotton T-shirt, no bra, a wide black leather belt, matte black belt buckle, black jeans, and black boots. It was a bit bohemian, old-style militant casual, but what the hell!

In my head, I went over what I knew about Mr. James Hewitt Spencer. He was British; he had military special ops experience, and probably intelligence experience, and certainly contacts in intelligence; he had worked in Hong Kong and Tokyo and Berlin – with a stint in Moscow. He spoke several languages – French, Italian, Spanish, and some Russian and German, a smattering of Arabic. He had served in various "operations" in the Middle East. He'd been to Cambridge and the London School of Economics and, briefly, at Columbia University. He was presumably as smart as he was handsome. How arrogant, I wondered, would he be?

It was a glorious New York early summer's day with a crisp blue sky and a gentle breeze moving down the long straight streets in the canyons between the buildings of Manhattan.

His office was just off 5th Avenue, a prestigious but discreet address.

I rode up in the elevator. I got off at the 11th floor and was shown into a small but luxuriously furnished waiting lounge, a marble floor, thick carpets, black leather-and-chromed-steel furniture, chalk-colored and steel-gray walls, and, along one wall, bookshelves. On the walls were paintings of half-naked women posing as pieces of furniture; and a painting of two muscular voluptuous legs encased in steel-gray latex or rubber. I recognized them as paintings by Allen Jones, a British pop painter – very fashionable in the 1960s and early 70s – who specialized in fetish themes, and whose paintings and sculptures had given me a sneaky thrill when I first saw them in a book Kate – subversive, diabolical Kate – had pushed under my nose.

A young woman came in, introduced herself as "James' personal assistant, Allison Hughes." She had straight long blond hair, a handsome narrow face, blue eyes, and was wearing black patent leather high heels, dark stockings, a pleated skirt, cream blouse, and charcoal jacket. I was glad I had come in jeans; otherwise, we would have looked like twins – or rivals. She held out her hand, and I shook it. "Gwendoline Clermont," I said, "Gwen, for short."

Allison served me strong English Breakfast tea, and she sat down next to me and had a cup herself. She like Mr. Hewitt Spencer was a Brit, a Londoner, South Kensington originally, she said; she'd studied in Cambridge – philosophy and English and French literature – and at the Courtauld Art Institute in London, and she had been working with James for four years, and it was challenging and very stimulating because his interests were vast, varied, and quite international.

"Not very politically correct," I nodded at the Allen Jones. I was wondering, not for the first time, what it would be like to be encased and sculpted in such a skin-tight rubbery outfit and to strut about in such stilettoes and be gazed upon by a lover or glared at by an anonymous crowd. I was wondering, too, why so many men found it arousing to look at such cartoonish forms. And I was wondering why I too found it exciting, imagining myself in those images, imagining myself captured in a painting or a drawing or a poster, like a naked artist's model in 19th Century Paris. What would it be like if I were that woman posing, on hands and knees, almost naked, as a coffee table or doubled up in an impossible position, exposed, serving as a lounge chair, feeling the gaze of other people – of men in particular but women too – on me? What would it be like to feel their lascivious fantasies – or their disdain and horror – define and sculpt me, to feel the titillating effects of shame and exposure, the interlocking dance of my fantasies with theirs?

"No, well, James is not very politically correct." Allison lifted the teacup to her lips.

"I didn't imagine he was."

Allison smiled. Her teeth were perfect, her skin flawless, and her lipstick precisely defined scarlet. She was like an illustration from Vogue. "He has quite a collection, actually, here and in Paris. Some of it is on loan to museums." She nodded at a thick volume of Erotic Art of the Ancient and Renaissance Worlds that was on the glass-topped coffee table.

I reached out and put my hand on it, caressing the smooth cover. "It looks interesting."

"Yes, it is, rather. Ah, here he comes, the devil himself."

"Oh, oh," I said. We stood up.

He walked straight toward us, glanced at me, and said, "What are you doing here?" He looked angry, this James Hewitt Spencer. He hovered over us, a dashing dark thundercloud of male beauty and energy – tanned, his black hair combed straight back, the scar across his cheek even darker, his teeth very white. They looked like they were going to bite. The better to eat you ... Yes, he was a wolf, and he didn't bother with the sheep's clothing. He stared at me with an expression that looked very much like hate.

He turned to Allison and said, "What is she doing here?"

"She had an appointment, James, and you asked her to come." Allison widened her eyes. She looked shocked – angry at his anger, her color rose, cheeks flushed. "The appointment was confirmed. I checked with you twice."

"Oh," he glanced at her, and then he glanced at me again; and again with what seemed to be seething anger. His eyes almost glowed. His lips trembled and tightened. "I ... I can't see you. I'm sorry. Not now. Go away. Wait somewhere."

At first, I didn't say anything: Damn it, I thought I don't have to stay, I don't have to wait for this arrogant asshole. Who does he think he is? "Don't worry," I said. "I'll go, and I'll go now." I was fuming. Who was he to treat me this way?

"Goodbye," I said. He stood there, looking pale under his

perfectly even tan, but said nothing. He didn't offer his hand; I didn't offer mine. I turned on my heels, and I walked out of the lounge and out of the office. The glass doors hissed shut behind me. Allison followed me. "Do come back, Gwendoline, please."

"No. It's clear he doesn't want to see me. This was a mistake." I pushed the elevator button.

"Well, then, please wait in the deli, Flo's Deli & Diner, turn right, and then just around the corner, on the right. He is sometimes like this. He talked about you. I know he wants to see you."

"It sure didn't sound like it," I said. "I think he regrets ever having met me." I pushed the button again. Why didn't the damn elevator come?

"No, I'm sure it's not that. Not exactly that."

"What is it, exactly?" I turned and stared at her.

"Well, it's … you'll find out."

"Like this is a mystery – a test of some sort?"

"In a way, perhaps it is. But, it's really more that."

"I'm pissed off, truly pissed off."

"I understand, Gwendoline. But just think about it." She laid her hand on my arm and gave me a very nice but sad smile. "Please, Gwen, please."

"Okay," I said, "I'll think about it."

The elevator arrived.

"Thank you."

"You've been very kind, Allison," I said. The elevator door opened. The elevator beckoned. I stepped into it, turned, and gave her a little wave.

"Goodbye, Gwendoline," she said, again using, as very few people did, my full name.

The door closed, and I fumed as the elevator whisked me downward; the elevator went "ding," the door opened. I was in the lobby. I walked out into the street. I was shaking and in a daze. I turned right. And, there it was, just around the corner: the deli. I said to myself, there is no way I am going to wait in that damned stupid deli for that stupid stuck-up arrogant Limey bastard.

But, then, as I passed the deli, I suddenly realized I was hungry, I guess from too much emotion and from merely nibbling at the sandwich during lunch with Claudia, and I wanted to sit down. A little sign indicated they had full Wi-Fi so I could eat and work at the same time, and then be gone and catch a train and go home and lick my wounds and maybe text Kate to report on the disaster or phone Matt and see if he wanted to go out. Even if I didn't find Matt interesting, he'd be a balm to my bruised ego, that is, if he wanted to see me, which he might not after the casual, brutal way I had brushed him off. I tried to imagine kissing him and …

No, I couldn't.

I frowned: I am really a bloody egoist, even thinking of exploiting poor Matt just to pour balm on my own hurt feelings!

I sat down in a booth in the deli

I ordered a double super-size hamburger with everything on it – double onions, tomato, bacon, cheddar cheese, gorgonzola, pickle, and lettuce – and with fries, coleslaw, and coffee. The waitress raised one eyebrow and said, with a smile and a touch of an English accent, her badge said, 'Sally.' "Famished today, are we?"

"Yes, we are, rather," I said, giving her a slightly snotty grin. What was it with these Limeys? They were bloody well turning up everywhere!

She winked and was gone.

I opened my netbook and linked it to the deli's Wi-Fi.

I opened my spiral notebook. I laid a black Paper Mate stick pen beside it.

I began to work: stochastic calculus applied to models for weather and climate, and dealing with the old question: how do we know what we know and what we don't know? How can we build conceptual and mathematical models of reality that are sufficiently simple – and therefore abstract – to be manageable, but also sufficiently "real" – matching the real patterns – to be useful?

I know, I know – boring and horrible, oh, most horrible, as Kate would say; but I liked it – and, to tell the truth, I am very, very good at it. I scribbled down one of the key equations in math, one of the Navier-Stokes equations, which are the equivalent of Newton's Second Law of motion, which states that the acceleration of an object is directly proportional to the net force applied to that object. Applied to fluids and not solids, Newton's seemingly simple idea poses almost insurmountable problems of feedbacks and complexity. There was a million-dollar prize for the person who could solve these problems.

$$\frac{\partial}{\partial t}(\rho \mathbf{u}) + \nabla \cdot (\rho \mathbf{u} \otimes \mathbf{u} + p\mathbf{I}) = \nabla \cdot \boldsymbol{\tau} + \rho \mathbf{g}$$

I frowned, turning some ideas around in my head. Well, I thought, I'm certainly not going to solve the million-dollar question today, so I'd better turn my attention to some solvable problems, some more immediately practical tasks. I flipped open a file on my netbook and began to type.

"Here we are, dear, a feast for the famished!" Sally beamed down at me. She was clearly pleased to be presenting such a mountain of food, such a comic monstrosity. The hamburger indeed had all the luscious trimmings. It was stacked so high it was impossible to eat without making an unholy mess, and so I made an unholy mess, and to hell with it, stuffing my mouth.

Soon I was lost in what I was doing. I was looking at some models for the climate and examining the logic of the statistical studies underlying them and what those statistical studies took for granted, what assumptions they were making, and how you could best eliminate the influence of chance or random events, or "static" – irrelevant "noise" – as they used to say. It is a bit like detective work and archeology – uncovering past worlds to understand the present and, if possible, to build up an idea of what the future might bring. The hamburger was yummy.

Somebody was standing next to my booth. I looked up. It was the man: Mr. James Hewitt Spencer.

"May I sit down?"

My mouth was full, overflowing. I wiped my mouth, tried to swallow, and had to gulp down half a glass of water.

"I don't know," I said. "Do you want to sit down?"

"Yes, I do, if you will allow me to."

"Like inviting Dracula into one's house, something like that? Once over the threshold, it is doomsday – and I get drained of all my blood and lose my soul and never regain it?"

"Yes," he smiled, "something like that. Precisely. Doomsday. You lose your soul – and you never get it back." He was looking down at me, that nice smile he had, the crinkles at the side of the eyes. Somewhere in my head, a little red light was blinking. It was shouting, Danger, danger, danger ...!

"Okay, suit yourself. Sit down." I stifled a burp. "And thank you, I suppose, for saving me. I guess you really were the knight in shining armor. And I am being perfectly ungracious."

"I wouldn't say that, Gwendoline." He slid into the seat opposite me.

"You were very stern up there. It looked like you hated me. I wanted to shrivel up. I was mad as hell too. I guess you do maybe – hate me, I mean. After all, you saw me at my worst – I probably ruined that suit – and I cost you a pile of money, and the nurse, Rose. All of which I'd like to repay, by the way."

"No, it's not that."

"Oh?" I opened my mouth very wide and took an offensively

humungous noisy bite out of the hamburger, and with my mouth full, and gooey gorgonzola dribbling out, I said, "What is it then?"

He tapped his fingers on the tabletop and looked down. "Have you ever looked at something you really wanted, but known that you really, really shouldn't want that thing – that you shouldn't even allow yourself to be tempted."

"Maybe," I said. This was, I thought, heading in an interesting – and dangerous – direction. I chewed in an exaggerated way; maybe I can make myself really totally disgusting, totally revolting, and then he will go away ...

"How old are you?"

"Just turned twenty," I answered, and going on twelve, I thought, and filled with unruly thoughts and unmentionable yearnings, though I no longer want to carve graffiti in my flesh or hang myself from a rafter in the stables. I took a bite out of the hamburger. I knew he already knew my age, and he knew I knew he knew.

"Twenty." He glanced at the menu. "And you've already got two undergraduate degrees and ..." The scar on his cheek caught the light.

"And part of a PhD," I said, chewing. "Math is a young bloke's game. It requires a quick empty mind. A girl has to move fast. And how old are you?"

"Forty-two," he said, and smiled wearily, looking up from the menu. His eyes were very dark, almost as dark, I figured, as mine. I noticed, once again, his tan, and the nice thought-lines, creases of wisdom, and smile lines at the edge of his eyes and flecks of gray at the temples of his thick black hair, and his high forehead. The scar on his cheek was intriguing. He had broad shoulders too, and a flat belly. Looking at him brought back the memory of what it felt like, being lifted up, carried, and held, by him, my body leaning into his. He knew I already knew how old he was, and he knew I knew he knew I knew.

"Whew! That's pretty ancient," I sighed, nodding, miming commiseration. I gave him the look, face tilted down, the sneaky, staring boyish pout from under my thick coal-black eyebrows – Oh, poor you! I licked my lips; some mustard or ketchup was on my chin, I could feel it, the stigmata of a slob. I wiped at it. He watched me and then looked down at the menu.

"What would you recommend?"

"Warmed up squishy easily digestible apple pie and vanilla ice cream. That's what my grandmother would have."

"I'd better take grandmother's advice then."

"Yes," I said, feeling stupid – and cruel. I really was being an ass. I wiped my mouth and decided that I would try to be a bit more gentle and genteel, at least until this ordeal was over. "Why all the Allen Jones?"

"Ah," his eyebrows went up ever so slightly. His eyes stared into mine. "What did you think?"

"I think that ... they are interesting." I held his gaze.

"Hmm, yes, well, it's a question of my personal taste – and they are, for me, a sort of statement."

Sally arrived and took his order. "Well, James, what will it be today?" She raised her eyebrows at the idea of apple pie and vanilla ice cream, glanced at me as if I were the culprit – which I was – and nodded and walked away.

"You were saying ...?"

"They are a kind of statement – I think we all have feelings that we rarely avow, that it is politically incorrect to avow, even dangerous to avow; and I think that it is healthier, better for everybody, if we can avow, and talk about those feelings – cruelty, power, fear, domination, submission. Even act them out, as it were."

I looked down and viciously speared a pair of innocent French fries. "So, objectifying, reifying, alienating, enslaving women, using girls as footstools, putting girls in chains, exhibiting

blindfolded girls, reveling in damsels in distress – the possessive fetishizing totem-like petrifying patriarchal imperialist
power-hungry power-anxious sadistic defensive male gaze in
action," I looked up and smiled my sweetest smile, "And so on,
and so on ... Those are the feelings?"

He was looking at me steadily, something that might be a
smile hovering on his lips. Without taking my eyes from his, I
stuck the French fries in my mouth and chewed sloppily, noisily.

"You are a very dangerous young woman."

"Oh?" I again gave him the look from under my eyebrows; the
look Kate said has the power of the Medusa. It can turn men to
stone, she said, or kill them dead outright, or drive them to drink.
She said it, late one night, when we were both drunk, sprawled
on my bed, lying on our sides facing each other; she was joking –
and stroking my thigh and tickling my belly, and I was running
my fingers through her hair, and kissing her earlobe and forehead,
then her lips, very carefully, very slowly.

"Yes. You are dangerous."

"Hmm." I chewed. "We all like to be looked at, I suppose. Well,
most of us, if the look is friendly. If it recognizes that you are
there, I mean, that you exist, that you are you."

"A subject, not an object."

"Yes. Precisely."

"I-thou."

"Yes, you got it."

"Authenticity."

"Absolutely. Two-way, mutual authenticity."

The apple pie arrived, with the big gob of vanilla. "That is an
unusual choice for you, James," said Sally. She knew him pretty
well, I could see, and from the smile and gentle slow way she put
the pie down and slid it in front of him, I could see she liked him
– a lot.

"Yes, Sally, special times, special measures!" He smiled at her.

She gave him a friendly, almost possessive, wink, glanced at me, allowed the wink to linger, and walked away.

He looked down and ate.

I looked down too, and speared some dripping coleslaw. I was displeased with myself – almost blushing. Admitting that I had noticed the Allen Jones paintings and that "we all like to be looked at" was maybe just a bit too transparent and dangerously revealing, though I had tried to recoup with the authenticity existentialist-theological I-thou routine and with reciting one of the post-modernist feminist mantras: "Thou shalt not be objectified." The terrible thing is that a few unguarded words of avowal can open a door. Then, in consequence, two other terrible things can happen. One, the door can be slammed shut in your face, and you are there, revealed, a supplicant, humiliated, locked outside, naked, perverse, all your pathetic desires and needs hanging out; or, two, the door remains open, wide open, and then you have to decide to go through it, and face the consequences, or to run like hell.

"This is good," he said, "Your grandmother has good taste."

"She also likes dry martinis," I said, chagrin at my puerile game-playing beginning to bite at me, "and Armani dresses and Glen Grant, she looks like Lauren Bacall, speaks three languages, has written six bestsellers, and plays a mean game of tennis."

"Tonight ..." He glanced at me, and paused. There was a flicker of hesitation and doubt in the depths of his eyes.

I nodded.

"If you are in New York ..."

"Hmm ..."

"Would you like to have dinner with me? And perhaps some other people?"

"Ah," I murmured, wondering about other people.

"The other people will be at a cocktail ... at the Met ... The Metropolitan Museum of Art ... We can dine afterward, maybe alone, maybe with another couple."

"Yes, I'd be honored," I said. "But," I frowned, "I don't have anything to wear. I came in jeans, and this T-shirt, and ... I was planning to go back to Boston tonight."

"We can solve that. We can find you clothes."

"Hmm, I don't want ..."

"It won't be a gift, if you don't want it, but ... you will make me very happy."

"Don't exaggerate."

"Okay, I won't exaggerate. Happy is too strong. But I'll be very pleased."

"Okay. Pleased is okay." My voice sounded a little husky. I picked up the coffee cup and drank. I looked up. "Pleased is nice," I said, and looked down.

"Good." He smiled.

"You have some ice cream on your chin, James," I said. I reached out with my serviette and wiped it off.

≈

When you take a step back and consider it, the Metropolitan Museum is an impressive awesome monster of a place. I got there early. Climbing up the steps and going under the arch and past the giant Corinthian columns, I felt like I was entering a temple – and I guess I was. It is a temple to the Gilded Age, to art, to money, to success, to creativity, to history, to humanity, to greed, to New York, to America, to ... everything. I wandered through the Great Hall and into the Gallery of European sculpture. I had a VIP ticket to the fund-raiser cocktail, so I was allowed to slip into the roped-off area for the reception. I was going to meet James there.

All those nudes and naked whirling bodies of gods and goddesses and heroes and heroines! I stopped in front of Degas's *The Little Fourteen-year-old Dancer*. She was so delicate, with her snotty, pinched, upturned face, and her legs at an angle, as if hesitating, frozen midway in movement, her arms – almost pinioned – behind her back.

I stopped in front of a small bronze statue, just under five feet tall, *Winter*, in English, or *La Frileuse* in French, which was more suggestive, implying many meanings: the shivering one, the frightened, vulnerable one, the over-sensitive one, the prickly one. It was by an 18th Century French sculptor: Jean-Antoine Houdon, and sculpted in 1787, just as the French Revolution was about to explode. A young woman, head down, her face almost entirely hidden by a hood, is naked except for a thick, draped shawl, that she has clutched around her shoulders, and which dangles down, clinging to her body, just enough to barely hide her sex. It was sleek and erotic; the sheen of the bronze on her thighs was for me electric, seductive, teasingly tactile. I wanted to touch her, embrace her, and comfort her.

The title, in French, indicated not only the freezing cold, a purely external sterile thing, about as sexy as a morning frost, I thought, but also the titillating inner shame of being naked, or almost naked, and of being seen to be naked, vulnerable, protected only by a shawl that could easily be torn away. Yes, it was another example of the "damsel in distress" trope, evoking a sexy, scary, and perversely arousing scenario. The English translation – rewriting the story according to the Hays Code – had naturally swept all those sensual creepy Gallic insinuations under the carpet. Hmm, I thought, each painting – or sculpture – is, potentially, a story, a story you tell yourself, often without even being aware of it, and people do like to control the stories we tell ourselves.

"Ah, there you are!" James was smiling. He had been observing my fascination with the statue. Oh, dear, another moment of revelation!

"You look marvelous," he said. He kissed me on the forehead. He was in a business suit, the same fine expensive suit he had been wearing earlier.

"Allison has good taste," I said. I was fitted out in black patent leather high heels, tailored black trousers that were, in places, skin-tight, a white silk T-shirt, and a black-and-white jacket with playful vertical stripes, and a cream handkerchief sprouting from the vest pocket – very dandy-like – and a black choker with an ivory cameo inlaid with Queen Victoria's profile. There was also, perched on top of my head, a Charlie Chaplin-style bowler hat Allison had insisted upon. I had tilted it at a rakish angle. I know! I know! I was being overly cute, intolerably androgynous, and insufferably pretentious.

Allison had taken me to a shop on a side street near the office. We browsed. She suggested one or two things. Then, finally, when we were putting the finishing touches on my "look," she had insisted on the Charlie Chaplin-like bowler. "No, no," I said. "Yes, yes, Gwendoline," she said. Then, even after we had chosen the evening ensemble, she made me try on different things. "This is fun," she said, "And it gets me away from the office."

It was interesting.

"He is taken by you," Allison said, looking at me in the mirror. I was trying on the jacket, turning this way and that.

"It's all a misunderstanding. We met under excessively auspicious circumstances."

"He, well, he did describe it."

"I'll bet he did." I squared my shoulders; I did like this jacket.

"Quite romantic, I think," Allison smiled.

"It didn't feel like it. I threw up all over him, and I had diarrhea

– I shat myself, true, stinky lumpy gruel and poop. I think a lot of it ended up on his suit. I farted too. Poop is not romantic."

She laughed. "But I can see how that would appeal to him."

"There's no accounting for ..."

"Taste," she laughed.

When we had made our choice, I said, "I can pay for these things." I ran a very strict budget, but I did not want to be in his debt, and, in fact, I could pay for them – they were in no way extraordinarily expensive. Money and credit cards are great props to one's dignity and identity. Allison made a bit of a show of trying to settle the bill with the company credit card, but when I insisted, she smiled and said, "I think in the end you and he will get on very well indeed."

"I hope so," I said.

"There is one thing though," Allison hesitated. "I'm not sure I should tell you. But he ..." she stopped.

"Go on. You can't stop now!"

"He doesn't want to fall in love."

"Oh, well, I wouldn't worry about that. I mean, I'm just ..."

"He's afraid."

"Ah."

"He's afraid of ... you."

≈

Now, at the Met, meeting all these people, almost all of them much older than I, and most of them famous and rich, very rich, and mostly knowing each other, bandying first names and bright smiles back and forth, I felt awkward. James was very attentive – as if I were a fragile work of art that might break easily. We walked past the buffet.

James got us two glasses of champagne – or Prosecco, I am not sure which. He toured me around, introducing me, and telling me who some of the luminaries were – the rich and the famous and the cultivated, usually with a funny little anecdote attached to each name, a neat memory device. He introduced me to Sir Charles Ryland and Lady Ryland, who were famous for their collection of Venetian Renaissance painting. Sir Charles talked to me about Piero Della Francesca, and, when he learned that I was a mathematician, he went on about a question of geometry, the invention of perspective in painting by somebody I had never heard of, Masolino da Panicale. I made a note to look this Panicale guy up.

I met various other people.

At one point, but just for a few minutes, James left me alone. He had to take an important call. He went off to the side, but even there, with his cellphone glued to his ear, he kept an eye on me and waved from time to time. I stood alone. Some of the men looked like they might like to come and talk to me, but they didn't dare, I think. So, feeling silly and out of place, I concentrated on looking at the art, in particular, a sculpture of a lady reclining naked on a sort of sofa or divan.

Then, when James came back, he said, "Perhaps we can get out of here and go to dinner." Several people, it seemed, wanted to dine with us. James was in demand.

"Do you want us to be alone?" he looked me in the eye.

"This is your show," I said, "These are your people, James. You decide."

"Well, then, splendid, we shall have company."

I was surprised, but I was pleased. He was not cutting me, the waif, the black sheep, out of the herd, isolating me, getting me alone for the kill. Not ready to feast on my blood, drain my soul away to the last drop – turning me into a lost soul, beyond redemption, at least, not yet.

≈

Dinner was by candlelight, and it was interesting – which was surprising. The very rich – and because of Claudia, I had met quite a few of them – are, for the most part, I find, stiflingly boring as conversationalists. We were dining with another couple. The man was a merchant banker with a London-based office. His wife, Anna, was an art dealer, both of them glossy with money and health. This is typical, I thought, this is going to be hideous; I don't belong here; I'm going to feel humiliated and misbehave and make an idiot of myself. I left the Charlie Chaplin bowler on when we sat down to dinner. I titled it to one side, then to the other, then down over my eyes. I suppose, child that I was, I was trying to make a statement, but, then, relenting, I finally took it off.

It turned out that Anna did know lots about art, and she loved it, not in a show-off snobbish way, but in a real, passionate, engaged way, and she knew what she was talking about. The banker was not the usual vulgar type. I had met a few of those during dinners at the farm or in Claudia's Manhattan flat. He had real financial projects – not will-o'-the-wisp short-term, computer-driven, testosterone-drunk, arbitrage, trading, and speculation in incomprehensible derivatives nonsense. He was talking about real shovel-in-the-ground, key-in-hand, developments, building bridges and container ports and public transport systems and how you calculate the feasibility of projects, and how you design the finance for such things.

This was all very mathematical, of course, and my ears perked up. I asked a few questions about the math they used and the mathematical models they adopted to calculate costs, returns, and risk. What about the risks, political risks, for example, or risks of certain kinds of natural disaster – for which clearly defined precedents, and therefore models, don't exist? After all, there is no guarantee, in some fields, strictly speaking in all fields, that the future will repeat the patterns of the past. What kinds of studies fed into the various models and so on?

The banker raised an eyebrow, gave a superficial answer, and then, when I quizzed him, he gave me increasingly technical answers. I asked more questions, and the conversation became detailed, back and forth, almost like I was cross-examining him. James was glancing at me while he was talking to the wife about the art market. They were discussing how low interest rates encourage speculation in contemporary works – and even in art from the past. How different schools of art from the past are re-evaluated periodically, often with an eye to the market, to create fads, including fads in scholarship, fads from which speculators and investors can profit by buying strategically, just as the trend of fashion is about to turn; and how the various schools and styles become objects of waves of speculation; how critics and curators become facilitators of speculation, as well as arbiters of taste; and how, as a consequence, economics and economic strategies act on the evolution of taste – what is chic and what isn't, what is "in" and what is "out." Corruption in the art market, they were saying, is rife, and they exchanged anecdotes of specific examples. Then they were talking about the surrealists from the beginning of the 20th Century, and then about British and American and Japanese Pop Art of the 50s and 60s. My ears were twitching, and both sides of my brain were working hard.

After, when we were out on the sidewalk in the sultry air, Anna kissed me on both cheeks and held me by the shoulders as we talked, her husband said that if I ever wanted a job, I should look him up. He gave me his business card. "We rely too blindly on models, sometimes," he said, "Bankers are often lemmings, all chasing the same fad at the same time. Stupidity is partly following the herd instinct. You asked all the right questions – and some of them I hadn't thought of myself, and think of myself as a pretty bright fellow!" I thanked him, with an androgynous little bow, a pageboy doing obeisance before a lord.

Then James and I were alone, on the sidewalk.

"Time for a drink?" He looked at me, his head titled to one side.

"Yes, I think so. Besides, I don't have anywhere to sleep. And – no pajamas, no toothpaste, no mouthwash, no ..."

"We can arrange for those things."

"That's good, because if you remember, dear sir, you said I would have a place to stay." I was thinking that if I phoned Claudia at this hour, I might wake her up, and I'd have to answer questions: "Did it go wrong?" she would ask. "Is he sufficiently intelligent and perverse for you?" she would ask. "No, Claudia, it was a disaster! Unfortunately, he didn't blindfold me and tie me up on our first date!"

"Indeed, I did. How could I forget?"

"Well, is the deal still on?" I raised my eyebrows. Perhaps I had failed the test; perhaps my performance had been lacking. Claudia had always advised me to find an interesting man – was this such a man? Was he the right sort of man? Was he "complex" enough? Was he sufficiently "perverse"?

"The deal is indeed on."

"So, we can have the drink at your place."

"That is an excellent plan," he said.

"Good!" I tilted the bowler back so he could see my eyes.

"I listened to you cross-examining de Villiers about his Indonesian and Kenyan projects. He was more than impressed. You're a prodigy."

"I'm a stick-in-the-mud extremely boring nerd," I said, but I was pleased.

We walked. It was a beautiful warm night.

We didn't say anything for a long time.

Strangely, I was not uncomfortable with the silence, not at all.

He took my hand. I felt it was natural, holding his hand. I was, in a small, tentative, guarded way, happy.

So, we arrived at his flat – well, flat was not the right word, it was a vast and palatial apartment in a very impressive building on Central Park South, not far from Claudia's, and up on the thirty-third floor. The apartment had a large entryway, a big studio living room, with a dining room attached to the right, with a terrace-balcony with plants and small trees, beyond some big sliding glass doors, and a central corridor with various rooms off to both sides. I don't know how many bedrooms it had.

He had to make a phone call or two. "It will just take about ten minutes."

He showed me a bedroom where I could, if I wished, settle in. It had its own balcony and its own bathroom, and it was equipped with toiletries. I brushed my teeth and gargled and splashed water on my face, and then I walked back into the hall and into the main studio that seemed to be a sort of giant living room.

There were rows and rows of books. I walked up and down, examining them, making an inventory. *The Story of O* in several editions in different languages; the Pléiade edition of the Marquis de Sade's works; *Dangerous Liaisons*; *Fetish: fashion and power*, by Valerie Steele, and more works by her, and Camille Paglia's *Sexual Personae*, and other books by Paglia, some Julia Kristeva and Melanie Klein, and much, much more ...

There were paintings too and drawings. It was more and more clear that he was into the coercive fetishist, dominance-submission, symbolic role-playing side of sex. Was it theater he needed, I wondered, or real violence? Was he dangerous, or was he just "complicated"?

I took a deep breath. There were posters of Josephine Baker, her hair slicked down, and wearing a clutch of bananas. There were reproductions of John Willie and Stanton drawings and other classics of the underground bondage and sadomasochistic canon.

There was the famous Japanese print of an octopus – or maybe two – making love to a woman, *The Dream of the Fisherman's Wife*, who is obviously in ecstasy. I wondered about the suggested multiplex delicate mouth of the octopus and all those tentacles that could touch a girl everywhere, with their slimy, sticky suckers.

There was a row of sumptuous photographs by Helmut Newton, a few drawings by the French artist Balthus of young girls in suggestive poses, and a few vintage pin-up photographs by Irving Klaw. In an alcove, were some vintage Alberto Vargas pin-up prints and a selection of opulent black-and-white Robert Mapplethorpe photographs, and, in the hall, were some more cool prints from Allen Jones.

No, James was not politically correct.

He came into the room.

He poured the drinks.

We sat down on the black leather divan and talked about life. I told him about growing up on the farm. I told him about my mother, about my last visit to her, in the insane asylum. I told him about my grandmother, Claudia, about my grandfather Stephen Clermont who was – well, is – a sort of mathematical genius, and who lives most of the time in Japan. I told him about Stephen's library, how I had invaded it as a kid, playing with its computers and iPads, and books of math. His library is still in Claudia's house, and, though they are divorced, he comes to visit once or twice a year, I told James about swimming in the swimming hole on the farm, about climbing the trees, about riding bareback, about wanting to be a boy, about my tomboy experiences. My grandmother did not believe in society very much. No private schools. Just public school and a home tutor. No clubs.

"She's a recluse?"

"No, Claudia's the opposite of a recluse. She has a pile of friends and comes to New York all the time. She has a flat here. But she thinks money, snobbism, and 'belonging' are dangerous – and boring. It encourages groupthink, she says, and superficiality."

"She's right." He put his glass down on the side table.

I leaned over and kissed him.

He kissed me back, very delicately very nicely.

He looked at me. "Too tempting ..."

I stood up and lifted off my jacket. The silk T-shirt was rather revealing. I sat down again and kissed him. "I'm an adult, more or less," I said.

"More or less ..."

"Yes." I kissed him again. I didn't know precisely what was getting into me – but ... I wondered: Did he put something in my drink?

A little later ...

His jacket was off, his tie was gone, his shirt was open, he was barefoot, and I was in the T-shirt, the tight black pants, and the high heels. We were dancing. It was sort of funny, and weird in a nice way, like from an old movie, dancing like that, the two of us, alone in the big room, on the smooth floor. It is strange, how you can feel nostalgia for the moods and sounds from a decade long before you were born. The soundtrack was very old-fashioned – big bands, swing, 1930s and 1940s sentimental movie songs, Cole Porter and Hoagy Carmichael. I guess, underneath, he was a nostalgic son-of-a-gun, with really precious and retro tastes; it was like he was his own great grandfather or something. Of course, he was British, so for him, all of this might be just a bit of American exotica. I like old stuff too, so it made me feel right at home. He was caressing my hair, and I was giving him affectionate little pecks on his chin; then I kissed him on the lips, and then I ran my fingers through his hair; and then I ran my fingers down his back, which was slender, and smooth and hard – he was in terrific shape. I began to unbutton the last few buttons of his shirt.

"I want you naked," I said, biting my lip and concentrating on the buttons. He kissed me on the forehead. I kept unbuttoning his shirt. I opened it up and pulled it out of his trousers, and he let me pull it off.

"You are in great shape for an old man." I kissed his chest.

"Thank you," he said, "you are a very kind and gracious young woman."

He kissed me. I closed my eyes and kissed him back – the warmth of his kiss swept me up and dissolved me into some other place. Soon I might see stars. I stroked his chest.

"You smell very nice," I said.

"And so do you," he said.

"Not like the last time."

"No, not like the last time."

He had turned off most of the lights. The glow of the city was reflected in the high-ceilinged room, and the music still played, very quiet and low. Manhattan from up high, and at night, is a magical place. There are so many cities with lots of glittering sky-scrapers, but I think there is still something magical about New York. Here all the glitter has a history; it's like ancient Rome; all the stones tell stories – pioneering days, the Gilded Age, the Roaring Twenties, the Depression Thirties, the Booming Fifties and Sixties, the Troubled Seventies, Madison Avenue, Broadway, and Mad Men, and ... Just dancing in the dark – well, almost dark – high over Manhattan was like breathing in the glamor of it all, the history, the things that had happened here.

"Take off your shoes," he said.

"You take them off for me."

"Of course." He knelt and lifted off the shoes and placed them neatly side by side next to the floor-to-ceiling bookshelf. Barefoot, I felt much smaller, more vulnerable. A few minutes later, I had taken off my trousers and folded them on the divan, and I was in the T-shirt and panties and the choker. He was in boxer shorts, vertical stripes, black and gold, and rather neat, I thought.

We danced and kissed. Then we were sitting on the divan, again, talking, and necking, and smooching. It was like being a kid again. He was like Kate. I felt I could tell him everything and anything. After all, he had seen me naked. I had vomited and shat all over him. I felt that we had already been truly intimate. He had a small scar on his chest, on the left side. It looked like a teardrop. "What's that?"

"Moscow," he said. "Competition. They didn't like what I was doing. I asked too many questions about a particular company."

"So ..."

"One night, just outside my office. I didn't see it coming. A man leaning against a car. And then, he stepped forward and gifted me with a nine-millimeter bullet."

I leaned over and kissed it.

We got up, still talking, and began to dance again.

"I want to try something," he said.

"Okay, what?"

"Twist your arms behind your back."

"Hmm, okay ... Like this?"

"Yes. And now I'll hold you like that."

I licked my lips and gave him the look, and I said, "Okay."

"If you want me to stop, tell me."

"Okay. I'll bite you if I don't like it. If I'm okay, you get a kiss."

He smiled and clasped my wrists tight, pinioning my arms

behind my back. The pressure twisted my shoulders back, just a bit, and thrust my breasts forward. We moved, and I felt my breasts pressing through the silk T-shirt against his chest. I kissed him.

"I like it," I said. "I like it when you hold me, when you have me ... in your power."

He kissed me. It was a rapid, sudden, ravishing kiss. He let go of my wrists, and I flung my arms around him. We twirled around. He lifted me up. We plunged back down onto the divan. I was astraddle him, on my knees, looking down on him, breathless.

"Lift it off," he said.

"You lift it off," I said. I bowed, and he pulled the silk T-shirt over my head, leaving it halfway off for just a minute, and masking my face. He kissed me on the forehead through the silk. His lips pressed on my lips, and I hungrily tried to kiss, but I was a prisoner of the silk, and then, slowly, he pulled the T-shirt off my head, and my lips were free, and our lips met, and we kissed, a deep, free warm, liquid kiss. I was melting into him.

His hands went up and down my back, sweeping, exploring, pressing, and caressing. He kissed my breasts, slowly, licking and biting each nipple.

"Oh, now," I said, "it's your turn."

"You do it," he said.

"Me? Okay, I'll do it." I levered myself up and hooked my fingers under his boxer shorts, and slowly, slowly, I pulled them down. His erection sprang free, well almost. It made a very nice tent pole.

"Oh, boy," I said, "Now this is splendid. This is just what a naughty girl wants for Christmas."

He laughed and reached up and tousled my hair and then smoothed it down and pulled me to him, so that we kissed, and I slowly pulled back and finished untangling his shorts from his erection and pulled them down his legs and then I stood up and held them out and looked at them. I tossed them over to a side table – they landed neatly, without overturning anything.

The golden light from the lamp rippled over his body – tanned everywhere with just the slightest of pale marks at his hips. He was on his knees now, next to the divan. I stood in front of him. He kissed my belly, twirling his kiss around my belly button. Then he pulled gently at my panties and slid them down my legs. I stepped out of them and put my hands on his shoulders. He stayed on his knees, kissed my thighs, and muzzled my sex, very slightly a light caressing kiss.

"Very neat, very beautiful," he said, "darkness itself."

"Kate says so. My little Bermuda Triangle, she says."

"Kate?"

I explained about Kate, a mixture of London and Paris and southwestern France, the wine and oyster country, vast Atlantic beaches and sand dunes, near Bordeaux, my dear Kate, a wild, beautiful, funny egghead.

"Ah, she sounds interesting. The copies of *The Story of O*, the Pléiade edition of the Marquis de Sade, I presume they were hers."

"Yes, that's her." Hmm, I felt a tinge of jealousy. I had read them too. "Kate is very, very fine, and quite perverse in an elegant French sort of way. You are going to make me jealous," I said. Put it all out on the table – and "bite the bullet" – Claudia had always told me: Don't wait for life to hit you, hit it first, but nicely, gently, and with irony if possible, with humor.

"No need for jealousy, no danger." He stood up and kissed me, a very sweet surface-of-the-lips soft kiss. His hands were on my shoulders, then went down my arms, pinning my arms to my sides, pinioning me, and, as I felt the dawning thrill of helplessness and possession, he kissed me, rougher this time, but still sweet, still tentative.

I was naked except for the choker.

The lights were low.

The city lights were tempting. He saw me glance at them, and he turned and looked, and he said, "Outside?"

"Yes," I said.

We walked out onto the terrace.

He said, "I shall leave you here, and I'll be back in a moment. I'll bring some wine."

"Okay." I wondered at this game.

"I'm going to lock you out here. That is, if you do not object."

"Hmm ..." The tip of my tongue ran along my lip, and I felt a tiny thrill of fear. Was this the beginning of something dangerous?

"I won't do it if you don't want to feel it – the feeling of being locked out here, alone, in the night."

"Okay, hmm, but not all night ... I might want to pee. I'd have to pee in one of your pots." I nodded at some large potted plants.

"No, just a few minutes."

"Okay. If this is a game, I'm game."

He closed the door. He locked it.

Well, well, now I'm in for it. I stretched. In truth, I liked being naked. Kate did too. Often, in the house, we didn't wear clothes, or maybe just panties. It was very risqué, of course, in a minimal naughty girlish sort of way. I think she and I had fun skating around just on the edge of what was possible, kissing, caressing, playing. It made for some fine and delicate electricity. The charm was in the trust, and in the lightness and the temptation, in the frontiers we flirted with, danced along, and sometimes crossed. Now, I was alone, naked, outside, on a romantic sultry midsummer's night, in the middle of Manhattan, at the mercy and pleasure of a man I barely knew. I felt a tiny little frisson of fear, a tiny little tingle of pleasure. Oh, but this was naughty! Well, sort of ...

The moon shines bright ... but there is no moon.
The moon shines bright. In such a night as this
When the sweet wind did gently kiss the trees.
And they did methinks make no noise ...

"Hmm ..." I chewed delicately at my knuckles. If James were truly wicked, really a seriously bad boy – a true sadist – well, it could be dangerous. I could be in trouble; I could find myself out here all night – or worse! I could find myself hogtied and locked away naked and blindfolded in one of his cupboards! I shivered and licked my lips. A ticklish feeling stirred in my belly, and rippled, radiating up, and down. I went to the edge of the balustrade, leaned my elbows on the friendly grainy damp stone, and looked over. Cars were streaming far below, their headlights gleaming on the pavement. Music – a sentimental tune – came from somewhere far away. I could see Central Park and caught a glimpse of what was probably the Metropolitan Museum. The reflected light from inside the apartment turned me chalk-white, painted with zebra stripes of gold. I was a ghost, a happy ghost, with that nervous ticklish ripple trembling in my tummy. I was invisible and free. I touched the choker and caressed with my fingertips its little ivory cameo and its comforting profile of Queen Victoria. It was a warm night, and damp. A breeze rose up and tickled its way, with nervous light fingertips, over my skin.

Yes, I was chalk-white, except for the famous jet-black, perfectly geometric pubic patch. My Bermuda Triangle ... Maybe he would leave me out here all night. Hmm! Let's see! I'd have to climb my way down to Central Park. I looked around. There were no ropes or chains, not that I could see, no mountain climbing gear, and it was a long way down. I peered over the edge. I could see myself, naked, down on the street, dodging between potted plants, if I could find any potted plants, a stark-naked fugitive, ducking this way and that on the sidewalk, hunted and despised, an outcast from civilization, a savage, an animal.

I'd probably get myself arrested. Naked mad girl collared by Cops in Central Park South! But I might evade capture, slip into the park, and live in a cave; I'd pretend I was in a jungle in some deep dark and utterly undiscovered continent. There I'd be – castaway. I'd regress to total savagery, I'd forget how to speak, I'd never bathe, and I'd live off berries and nuts and roots and pizza crusts.

There was a balcony terrace next door. I tiptoed up to the dividing wall and pulled over an iron garden chair, so I could climb up and look over the wall. I heard voices. People were having a dinner party on their terrace. Six people were seated at a table. Candles lit up their faces – luminous masks of gold. I was hidden by the wall and by a large hedge. This was exciting. A man stood up. He was serving the wine. He was in a tuxedo and black tie. A woman – she was deeply tanned, had a plunging neckline, a black bodice, and a pearl necklace – was saying something like, "Well, the mayor really should do something about it." The man who was pouring the wine said, "Of course he should, darling, but he won't." He had a self-satisfied all-knowing smirk on his face. "Well, the mayor means well, but I think the complexities of the job are beyond him," said one of the other men. Several of the guests nodded sagely, and one of the women displayed a bright, beautiful, open smile that made her look like an idiot. I, for some reason, liked her: She is playing a role, I thought, and she's bored, she's too intelligent for this crowd – or for some reason doesn't belong with them – but she's bravely making the best of it. She'd rather be far away, running around naked, a girl werewolf, in the midsummer moonlight – though tonight as yet there was no moon. I had a brief fantasy of leaping over the wall, kidnapping the beautiful creature, and carrying her off, over my shoulder, or hand in hand, to a life of wild, wordless, girl-on-girl debauchery. I watched for a minute, then I climbed down and put the chair back, just as he came out the door.

"You're an accomplished voyeur, I see."

"Just exploring." I gave him that mutinous from under the eyebrows little boy glance.

"That choker is very attractive," he said.

I put my finger to it and caressed it and said nothing.

He was carrying two glasses and a bottle of chilled white wine – very dry – Chateau la Tour, I saw on the bottle.

We lay back on the two deck chairs.

Then he took the thin mattress off one of them, and put it on the terrace pavement. We sat on it cross-legged, and we drank. The cool white wine was delicious – and very easy to drink. Both of us were naked, and it seemed completely natural. The huge city buzzed gently around us.

I got onto my hands and knees and kissed him. Then I knelt, holding his face in my hands.

"Dangerous girl," he said.

"You think so?"

"Most definitely."

He kissed me; and gently eased me around, and down, onto the mattress so I was lying on my back, looking up at him and at the mottled red and black sky where the lights of the city reflected in the humidity. One aircraft, its lights blinking bright white flashes, passed overhead. Then, gently, he was on top of me. Then he was holding my arms stretched above my head, my wrists pressed against the warm damp stone, as if he were crucifying me on a tall narrow cross. He kissed my breasts and my shoulders, and he kissed my mouth. Then he let my arms go and kissed my belly. His fingers slowly massaged my lower belly. With his fingers on my hips, holding me, controlling me, he nuzzled downward and kissed the inward slope of my tummy. His fingers pressed upon me, gently massaging. The excitement was rising everywhere – in my tummy and right across my belly, down my legs, and up to the tips of my breasts. He was kissing the inside of my thighs now, soft, easy kisses. Then, slowly, delicately, he opened me, his gentle liquid fingers so savvy, so knowing. He kissed me again, a light feathery kiss. He kissed and licked his way inward, kissing just with the point of his tongue, and began to explore the Heart of Darkness, the Bermuda Triangle ...

Oh, boy ... I shuddered ...

I gripped him between my thighs. I wanted him to be my prisoner and my slave, and I wanted him to be violent and quick and rough, and I wanted him to be soft and slow and gentle, oh, so slow, so very, very slow. My fingers grasped and clutched at his hair. I let out a gasp.

His lips were so tender and his tongue so soft, so attentive, so precise, exactly where I wanted it to be – so precise I didn't even know how it could be done with this ... ah ... precision. The clitoris, of course, he found with ease, and it seemed suddenly to become the very center of me, of what and who I was, I was everywhere and nowhere – in an instant. Oh, I clutched at his hair, "Oh, you, you, you!"

"Goddess," he whispered, "Little goddess."

"Oh, oh, oh ..." I could feel the excitement, the tension rising, and I wanted to control it, to stop it, to prolong the pleasure, but I couldn't ...

I shuddered, and arching up, I came, in one convulsive, agonizing, utterly wonderful, obliterating explosion.

"Oh, oh, oh ..." I cried out. My whole body seemed to be vibrating. "Oh," he was still at it, and I was convulsing, and, "Oh, oh ..."

"Oh ..." it went on and on and on ...

"Stop," I whispered, "please stop," I begged. I wanted him to stop, and I didn't want him to stop.

I came, and I came, and I came ...

He had not even entered me.

"Come, come into me," I said, I was holding his head in my hands and whispering, desperately, whispering. "Come, come into me."

"You're sure?"

"Yes, yes, I'm sure."

He kissed me on the mouth, an earthy echo and taste of me. Then he kissed his way down my body – breasts and belly. Then, suddenly, he plunged down, opened me up. Once again, I was liquid, melted liquid. He entered me, and he kissed me again, on the mouth, and, with my arms stretched above my head, he was in me, and it seemed so large, so immense, I thought I would explode.

"Oh, darling," I whispered, "Oh, darling!"

He released my arms, and I held him. I wanted to consume him, all of him; I wanted to possess him, all of him, and I wanted him to possess and to consume me, all of me. My legs were up around him, scissor-like, enclosing him.

We both came, in one shuddering moment. He cried out. I cried out. "Oh, oh, oh ..."

It went on, and on, and on ...

≈

Later, and it seemed like hours later, we went back into the apartment, leaving behind the lights and gentle breeze of Manhattan. His hand was on my bum. "Now, let's have a shower." He slapped my backside, a gentle affection slap.

"Yes," I said, looking over my shoulder.

"I have a little adornment here." He held it up.

"A blindfold?"

"Indeed."

I looked at it. A black rubber padded blindfold with four rib-bon-like strings to snap it on around my head. He handed it to me. I felt it. It was delightfully sensuous, a smooth skin-like ma-terial. Blind, I would be putty in his hands.

"Okay," I said.

"That's a good girl."

He smoothed it over my eyes and fixed it, tight around my head. I was plunged into darkness. I stretched out my hands. They met his chest. He led me into the bathroom and to the shower.

"Oh, this is nice," I said, as he shampooed my hair, and gently massaged my scalp as the water poured down over my shoulders. It was another all-over, no-holds-barred, intimate, in-depth wash-ing. It reminded me of that first night, that first shower, but this time it was an exquisitely sweet invasion and conquest. He knew all of me, every opening, every orifice, well, he knew me, all of me, on the surface, at least, but beneath the surface ...?

He dried me, using a big fluffy warm towel and a hair-drier.

"Spread your legs."

"Yes."

"Bend over."

"Okay."

"Stand still."

"I'll try." I had to giggle. He was tickling me. All the time, I could see nothing, just silky darkness. I could feel only his hands, his lips, and hear his voice.

With both of us now completely dry, he led me, still blind-folded, out of the bathroom and into the bedroom; and he led to me to the bed, sat me on the edge of the bed, and he massaged my back, very gently, very slowly, and said things like: "You have the most beautiful backbone. I adore your shoulder blades. I am indeed partial to this little valley behind your knee, and the two dimples, on either side, in the small of your back – delicious." His touch matched his words. He was numbering the ways – it re-minded me of Kate.

Then he was silent, and I, blindfolded, imprisoned in darkness, could see nothing; but I could feel his hands, his fingers, their pres-sure, here, there, everywhere. Again, the yearning rose. I turned to him. I felt his face. I held his face between my hands. I kissed him and, sensing he had an erection, feeling it against my belly, I bent over him as he lay down and I caressed it and held it and licked it and kissed it, and, for a time, I swallowed it and I licked and sucked, my hunger knowing no bounds. Luscious, luscious, yum, yum!

Strange that this is so exciting!

I wondered at it.

I felt a yearning to possess him, possess him fully; I slid up onto him, and sat astraddle his midriff. I lowered myself down, and, blindly, in total darkness, I felt him slide into me; his hands were on my breasts; then his hands were pulling my hips into him; then he bent me down toward him and kissed me. All the while, he was bigger and bigger within me, commanding, enor-mous. I rode him. I kissed him. I touched him. I shuddered in pleasure.

Afterward, he held me, and I held him and kissed him, over, and over, and over.

≈

It was already light when I woke up. I was alone. James was gone. Draped over the bed, on my side, was a black silk nightgown; it was semi-transparent, and at the side of the bed, on the floor, were two very high-heeled black mules. Well, then: The theater didn't end at dawn!

I went into the bathroom and brushed my teeth, and gargled, and spit, and gargled again, and I looked at myself in the mirror. "Well," I said, "well, well ..." No bruises, no dark circles under the eyes, not yet.

There was a bidet.

I squatted on the bidet and washed, thoroughly. I dried myself, and I sighed and stretched, and, turning around, watching myself in the mirror, I sighed again: "Gwendoline, Gwendoline, Oh, Gwendoline!"

I slipped into the black silk nightgown. It was so delicate I felt I was bathing in talcum powder, vaporous and caressing; it wafted like a silken breeze around me. There was no way to close it; it floated open, a diaphanous sheen. I might as well be naked.

Okay, well, that's the way it is.

I wondered if there were servants in the apartment. Well, we shall just see, Gwendoline, won't we?

I slipped into the mules and, with the nightgown drifting around me, tickling, caressing, stroking my buttocks and breasts, I walked out to see what I would find.

"Ah, Princess," James said. He was standing there, in a business suit, as if he had been waiting for me.

He kissed me on the forehead and put his arms around me – again, with the nightgown, it felt as if I were more naked than naked, and the high-heeled mules lent me a particular self-consciously piquant, sinful gait and posture.

He led me out onto the terrace where breakfast was gloriously laid out on a table: waffles, eggs and bacon, toast, various jams, fruit and granola, coffee and tea, luscious curls of butter, and cream, and milk in jugs. *The New York Times* and *The Financial Times* were lying on a side table. He asked me if I wanted one of them. "Yes, *The New York Times*," I said.

I was famished.

As I ate, he sipped his coffee and watched me.

I glanced at the *Times*, but I didn't pick it up.

"You look very beautiful this morning," he said.

"So do you, James," I was buttering a piece of toast. "Would you like one?" I asked, holding it up.

"Ah, sweet youth, so dangerous, so unaware of its power."

"Maybe not completely unaware," I said.

≈

Later I pulled on my clothes – the Charlie Chaplin outfit, including the bowler and the choker – from the night before. We left his building together. Then we stood for a moment, awkward, on the sidewalk.

"Goodbye," he said.

"Goodbye," I said. I leaned up and kissed him.

I took the 2 pm Amtrak back to Boston and a taxi home. I felt very fine wearing the bowler hat and the striped jacket. It was a brilliant summer day. On the train, a very nice girl tried to pick me up. I was tempted. The bowler hat, the nifty jacket, and the black choker worked wonders. Allison, I decided, was a genius.

CHAPTER 2 – THE WAITING GAME

So I was back in Cambridge, and I found I could work and work hard. I cleaned up my room. I was bursting with energy. Matt wanted to take me to a movie. I let him, and strangely I was all bright and talkative, and I think charming. He seemed very happy to be with me.

When we parted, on my doorstep, I gave him a chaste peck and said, "Goodnight."

I think Matt was not at all upset that I didn't invite him in. I think he was relieved, because I think he did have the vague idea – not entirely mistaken – that Gwendoline Clermont is not the simplest of girls and that, perhaps, had he wanted to spend the night, or merely do some heavy doorway sex, it would have been complicated and unpredictable, and perhaps – how horrible! – it would have been embarrassing. Once you open some doors, it's hard to close them.

And, of course, I waited for the phone call.

Is that not what girls have done since the beginning of time?

I waited.

And, of course, I was annoyed at myself for waiting. I called myself an idiot. I was an idiot. I value my independence; I do not like to be distracted.

≈

In the end, I didn't have to wait long. Four days after the great event, I got an email. It was rather business-like. "Could we talk on the telephone tonight? Phone me at 6:00 pm if you can." It gave his cell number.

Oh! Oh! He wanted to break it off.

Allison had warned me. He was afraid, she said, afraid of me, afraid of commitment, afraid of love, and I suppose his little games, the mildly kinky rituals – and I certainly shared his taste for them – were a mask, a shield, a way of dealing with his fears. Such games imply complicated agendas, conflicted and interesting psyches, divided selves, ambivalent feelings. They are tactics for getting close, and, at the same time, not getting close.

And when you get too close, you run away.

I should know.

I had written to Kate about my little adventure. I had told her how I was smitten by a forty-two-year-old British millionaire who had seen me naked and covered in shit and who liked to see me naked and blindfolded and locked out of doors in the Manhattan starlight. I told her how he was super-effective in bed, how he was efficiently muscular, pinning me down on a divan or a rug, and how he gave me a neat, completely invasive, all-over soaping down and shampoo massage.

Kate sent a short email: "He sounds luscious, darling, I like the games; they sound positively perfectly titillating, but keep your defenses up. You know men like that – well, they live in a fantasy world: you are a player, an element, in the fantasy. The demoiselle in the drama may not really be the real you. Such men, I suspect, are eternal adolescents or children, puer aeternus I believe Father Jung called them, eternal Peter Pans; they do tend to flit away on their little wings and move on. Am I being cruel?"

I answered: "Yes, my love, you are being cruel. But, darling, I need to know the truth, and you are my best friend, my sister soul, my love. I am glad you told me what you think – it matches my own diagnosis."

She answered: "Big hug, darling, and be brave. Enjoy the sunshine while it lasts. Carpe diem! Seize the day!"

I tried to work, but it was difficult. The email from James had totally upset my Olympian calm and detachment – and shattered my concentration. So I went for a run. The same sleek, skin-tight black catsuit, thoroughly cleaned and restored. I didn't bother wearing the T-shirt. I was a sleek panther, and I didn't give a damn. I was shameless now.

Sweaty and breathless, I got back home. I showered, and I ate some chocolate, and I tried to work, but I was waiting for 6:00 pm, eager for it to come, eager to put the ghosts and fears and hopes to rest.

Finally, I rang the number. I held my breath. He didn't answer right away. It rang and rang and rang. I was waiting for voice mail to kick in; if it kicks in, I thought, I will hang up.

"Hello," he said.

"Hello," I said.

"So. It's you."

"Yes. It's me," I cleared my throat. "I said I'd call. So I'm calling."

"How is your work going?"

"It is going very well, thank you." I thought I would scream. "It is kind of you to ask."

"You can work more or less anywhere, can't you?"

"Yes, I can." I waited. He said nothing. I couldn't stand the empty silence, so I added, "All I need is a powerful laptop and a good Internet connection and maybe a few of my notebooks. I can access virtually anything I need online."

"Good." Then silence – he didn't say anything.

"Well," I said, in an even tone, "it does make it easier, sometimes." I took a deep breath. I wanted to hang up. He was breaking it off. He'd come to his senses; he realized it was crazy; I was young and insignificant, and he was old and important and too busy, but he didn't want to be cruel; so all this empty chitchat was a polite way of working up to the fact that it had been a one-night stand, great maybe, terrific possibly, but ...

"Next week I'm leaving for a month in Rome, then three weeks in Paris. It's quite hot in Rome at this time of year. I have a rather large apartment there."

"Oh ... It sounds nice." So he's going away.

"I was wondering if ..." He hesitated again. How could a man who was so unhesitating in making love, who was so elegant, so sure of himself, so masterly in social situations – and I'd seen it at the Metropolitan Museum when he'd talked with fluid ease to all the people he seemed to know, and he seemed to know everybody, and to each of them he was utterly charming, adopting precisely the right tone, talking about precisely the right things, making every person he talked to feel good about themselves – how could such a man be such a perfectly pathetic jerk when he wanted to say goodbye? All he had to say was, "Look, kid, it was great, but you're a kid, you don't know anything, and I'm a grown-up and sophisticated, and we'd look ridiculous, and besides, I'm very busy and important and an international personage, an ultra-rich VIP, so ... goodbye!"

"I was wondering if you'd like to come – for the month I mean, to Rome. We might go to Paris after that, for the three weeks. I also have an apartment on the Left-Bank, close to Place Saint Germain des Près, and ..."

"What?"

"What?" He sounded startled.

"What did you say?"

"I want you, adorable Minx, dangerous perverse little personage, hypnotic, barefoot mathematical genius, to come to Rome and Paris with me. That's what I'm saying. For two months, yes, almost two months, maybe more ..."

I frowned. This was a total reversal from where I thought the conversation was going. Did I want to go to Rome and Paris with this man I hardly knew? Could I go to Rome and Paris? Well, I didn't have a cat or a dog or babies. The house could pretty much look after itself, the neighbors had the keys, and they knew what to do if there was an emergency, the bills could be paid automatically, I just had to set it up. I could in fact work from anywhere, and ... Grandmother would not object.

"Yes," I said.

"Good. Bring whatever you need – traveling light preferably – and be at my office next Tuesday, at noon. Allison will have prepared everything else. Do you have your passport? Is it up to date? Any medical issues? I'll provide insurance."

"I have travel insurance," I said.

"Well, I'll provide double," he said. "I'll be working during the day, most days, when we are in Rome and Paris, so you'll have time to work."

"Great."

"And you will be ready to play ... some games?"

"Games, yes," I took a deep breath, "Yes, games. Yes, James, I'm ready for games."

"You are an angel," he said, and he hung up.

I held the phone to my ear for a bit longer. I put it down. I stared at it. What a diabolical instrument! What had I just agreed to? What was I getting myself into? In a daze, I undressed and took another shower – steaming hot, then icy cold. I needed a shock to absorb the shock. Brrr!

Wrapped in a big, extra-fluffy, black Turkish bath towel, I went out onto the deck and walked around in a circle. So, now I am a concubine. Me? I'm going to play games? What sort of games? I'll bet he's got complicated new games in mind. Hmm ...

I sent an email to Kate and described, what had happened – if she were still in Paris, I might see her there. Kate said, "Marvelous! Darling, do be a concubine or a mistress. It will be a marvelous, pampered experience. You will have some wonderful stories to tell!"

≈

Grandmother Claudia said that James Hewitt Spencer sounded sufficiently complicated to keep me going, but that, if he turned out to be a regular Marquis de Sade, I'd better be careful. "Put my number on speed dial," she said.

"Right," I said.

"The age difference should make him intelligent and experienced enough to handle you," Claudia's smile was audible over the phone. "And, if you are being perverse, Gwendoline, just make sure you don't get carried away and get hurt. And, darling, try not to hurt him."

Hurt him? It had never occurred to me that I could hurt him. He was rich, powerful, in his prime, sophisticated, and he was the one who would almost certainly define all the games we were going to play.

"You don't realize your power, Gwendoline. You are certainly capable of hurting people, even when you don't know you are doing it." Claudia paused. "And, if you get into the slightest bit of trouble, Gwendoline, you are to push the button and phone me immediately! I'll come and get you in Paris or Rome or anywhere you might be – even Antarctica."

CHAPTER 3 – ROME

Foolish naïve me! I expected that we would be traveling together, that we would fly together, but when I entered the office, all excited and not a little afraid, Allison told me that James had already left. That he had had to fly to Moscow, it was a last-minute thing.

I stood there like an idiot, my mouth hanging open.

"It's not so tragic, Gwendoline," Allison said, "It happens all the time."

"Right," I said, squaring my shoulders.

My plane would be leaving at 5 pm, and I would be arriving in Rome alone early in the morning; and so I thought, well, okay, and I can pay for the flight, which I insisted on doing, though Allison was stubborn about that one. It had already been purchased, she said – a done deal. She called a cab. And off I went.

The seat was in business class.

I downgraded to tourist and paid for the ticket. After a bit of haggling, I managed to have the refund for the original ticket sent to James' company.

I sat in a window seat, so I could look at the clouds, and I was next to a woman who did crossword puzzles the whole time. I was sneaky and watched. She was very good at it. Then I watched a movie. It was an old movie with the English actress Kate

Beckinsale looking luscious in black leather as a vampire heroine. When the movie was over, I had time to think: This was like a fairy-tale, and I was Little Red Riding Hood setting off into the Big Bad Wolf's lair. Passion and love, I mused, are like fairy-tales and initiation rites; there are stages, there are tests, there are symbols and thresholds, and, when it is suddenly over, you are no longer yourself, and your life is not what it was before, but it has become something else.

Who and what would I become?

Would this plunge into the unknown bring freedom – or slavery?

I got to Rome airport at about nine in the morning. The sun was already bright over the Mediterranean and over the beaches and small seaside towns. After getting my luggage, I intended to take a taxi to the city, but a handsome, distinguished-looking man, with silver-gray hair and a mustache, was standing there with a sign with my name on it. So I went up to him, and he told me that his name was Alcide – which he pronounced "Al-chee-day" – and that he was Mr. Hewitt Spencer's chauffeur in Rome, and in Italy generally, if, say, we decided to go to Milan or Venice or Florence. He would take me to the apartment and see that I was properly installed, in comfort, and with everything I needed. He was not sure when Mr. Hewitt Spencer would be arriving – perhaps tomorrow, perhaps the day after, or the day after that. But my arriving early would give me time to get to know the neighborhood. Alcide or his wife would show me around, or the concierge Maria or her husband, Giuseppe. "Okay," I said, "that is very nice and very generous of you. Thank you, Alcide."

I watched the scenery go by, the Tiber, and the EUR, or Esposizione Universale Roma, a satellite city Mussolini had planned to build between Rome and the sea, and then we were in downtown, central Rome, with its little winding, cobblestoned streets, and the car, apparently, had a special badge which allowed it to go into pedestrian areas. So there I was. I was in Rome.

"Your apartment is just a few steps away from the Tiber," Alcide said, as he opened the trunk. He insisted on carrying my two suitcases.

The entry to the building – an arched gateway large enough for a Mack truck to enter – loomed up darkly and looked rather gloomy. There was a little porter's lodge over to the side with a glass-paneled wooden door. Alcide knocked, and a very handsome middle-aged woman came out. She had a broad face, lively eyes, and clear fine-grained olive skin. I saw she had the television on, and she was cooking – a wonderful smell of garlic and tomato sauce wafted out around her – and there were newspapers spread out on what looked like the kitchen table. Alcide presented me to her.

"This is Mr. Hewitt Spencer's friend, he said, Signorina Gwendoline Clermont."

"Very pleased to meet you, Signorina," said the woman, "I'm Maria."

"Il piacere è mio," I said, mobilizing some of the Italian I knew.

My accent must have been okay, so she went on in Italian, but I caught the gist; if I had any problems, I was to come to her; she or her husband Giuseppe would solve any and all my problems. She gave me a card with her email and home phone and cell phone.

There was a little old wood-paneled elevator and a broad old stone staircase that probably dated back 500 years. The staircase had been designed, Alcide told me, so horses could gallop up it, and so they could carry heavy coffins down.

"That sounds promising," I said.

Alcide responded with a very nice smile. "Many, many generations have lived and died here, lots of history." His eyes twinkled.

We went up in the creaky elevator, rather squeezed together. There was just enough room for me, Alcide, and my luggage. The elevator was in a sort of metal frame tower, loosely linked to the stairs; it swayed and rattled as we rose upwards. I was glad I don't get seasick.

We came out on a landing. It was very broad, with a dark patterned marble floor, dark marble walls, and gray dusty-looking busts of ancient worthies, some bearded and some clean-shaven, perched in large dark niches.

Alcide took out the keys and opened the door to the apartment. Suddenly we were in a different world – a total contrast to the gloomy ancient gray staircase – the apartment was full of light. It was ultra-modern, with walls of white, with beautiful modern furniture, a fireplace, and contemporary and modern paintings here and there, all of it luminous as if one were bathing in pure light.

"Wow," I said. "This is – extraordinary!"

Alcide smiled. "The apartment is the only one on this floor, it ensures total privacy, and it includes the top two floors of the building and has a big terrace," Alcide put down my suitcases, "and you can order food from the restaurant just down the street, if you don't want to cook."

"I am occasionally very lazy," I said.

"Well, Maria or Giuseppe will introduce you to the owner, Alfredo. The phone number is beside the main phone in the kitchen. The market on Campo de' Fiori is about a three- or four-minute walk. Every morning they sell fruit and vegetables and fish from outdoor stands, until early afternoon. There are little cafés and wine bars on the Campo you might enjoy. Good places to watch people or to work if you like working in a café. You must watch out for purse-snatchers."

"I will." I'd read about how they bump into you and say they are

sorry, and zip, your purse or wallet is gone, or how they come gliding silently up behind you on a Vespa and speed away with your
purse or camera or computer. It is important to keep your purse
or shoulder bag between you and your partner, or between you
and the wall or the parked cars, so the Vespa or purse-snatcher
has no room to squeeze in for a surprise attack. I took note.

"We are close to the French Embassy, which is in a palace once
owned by the Farnese family. Michelangelo designed the façade
of the palazzo, and the interior is spectacular too. There are a
couple of nice restaurants on the Piazza Farnese in front of the
Embassy. So you can sit eating spaghetti arrabbiata, drinking
Chianti, and appreciate Michelangelo's art."

"Sounds luscious," I said. Already, I was feeling hungry.

After showing me around the flat, and answering lots of my
questions, Alcide said his wife, Elena, would come by at nine
o'clock the next morning to show me the neighborhood. And,
then, with a big smile, he gave me the keys and left.

≈

So now I was alone in a strange flat in a strange city waiting for
whatever would happen and whoever would turn up – James the
gallant gentleman and skilled lover, or James, the bad-tempered
neurotic ogre who would gruffly ask me who the hell I was and
what the hell I was doing here in his flat and send me packing?

I walked around. Everything was ultra-modern. There were
several spacious bedrooms. There was a large studio living room
with modern furniture and a fireplace. There was an outside terrace with a blue-and-white striped canvas awning over part of
it, with trees and plants, and stone benches and a stone balustrade. There was a spiral staircase leading up to a sort of studio
loft on the top floor, and it had its own little terrace and kitchen,
and there was, in the main flat, a large very modern kitchen that

looked like it was a set for a photoshoot in a cooking and fashion magazine. The view from the terrace was spectacular. There was a hill to the west, toward the beaches on the Tyrrhenian Sea and overlooking what I took to be the Trastevere, the "across the Tiber" side of Rome. Trastevere, I had read, is a sort of bohemian tangle of small streets and squares snuggled in a curve in the river. On the top of the hill, I could see a statue – if I remembered from the guidebook I had read on the flight, it was probably Giuseppe Garibaldi – one of the liberators of Rome and unifiers of Italy. There were also some large square buildings clinging to the slope.

I set up my computer in one corner of the studio living room.

Alcide had given me the Wi-Fi password.

I checked that I had a connection.

Yes, miracle, it all worked. There was also, for more secure use, a cable connection.

I sent a text to Kate. "I'm all alone, in a spooky old building, in the lap of luxury, in a huge modernist flat. There's a charming chauffeur. There's a huge terrace, and I'm drinking a home-made espresso and looking out over the rooftops of Rome."

She replied. "Right this instant, I am turning bright green!"

Using the street number, I looked up the building on the Internet. It was historic and bore the name of one of the old princely families of Rome. More than five hundred years – half a millennium – of births, deaths, love affairs, and murders had taken place in these rooms, and on the staircase. It gave me the shivers; the place was full of ghosts, all those passions, all that happiness and suffering, all gathered here.

I yawned.

I took a shower. The bathroom – and there were several – was a marvel of efficiency and beauty. It had a bidet, a large walk-in shower, and a recessed walk-in bathtub that seemed designed for an orgy or two, maybe more. I explored. A note lay on the kitchen table. "Set yourself up. The blue bedroom, or the red bedroom."

Hmm ...

I decided on red.

I was exhausted. I finished drying myself, slipped out of the towel I had wrapped around my waist and lay down naked on the bed, and stared at the ceiling. I will lie here and think deep poetic thoughts, I told myself. I fell asleep. I must have slept for many hours.

A bell was ringing.

Oh, the doorbell.

At first, I didn't know where I was.

The room was getting dark; it was coming on night. How long had I slept? All day? Had I missed a whole day of my life? I sat up, rubbed my eyes, and got out of bed.

I pulled on a black silk bathrobe that had been hanging in the bathroom and went to the door.

"Compliments of Alfredo," said the handsome, eager, tanned young man, who was standing there, on the shadowy landing, grinning at me. He was wearing a T-shirt that said "Alfredo" and black trousers, and he said his name was Beppe, short for Giuseppe. Another Giuseppe! Italians don't have that many proper names, I discovered. Beppe was bearing an offering, food, a fully prepared meal from the restaurant down the street. I thanked him, asked him to come in, and he laid the meal out on the terrace as if he were very familiar with the flat. "And, Signorina Gwendoline, there is a bottle of chilled Chablis," he said, "in the refrigerator."

Beppe left, and I sat alone, in splendor, in the bathrobe, in the gathering twilight on the terrace listening to the birds twittering and screaming as they gathered to nest for the night. When the birds went silent, calm descended, and a vast murmuring emanated from the Eternal City. I had the feeling that I had tumbled into some sort of weird paradise.

I slept a dreamless sleep.

≈

The next morning Alcide's wife Elena arrived precisely at nine. She was a slender, handsome woman, tanned, and with jet-black hair, and as distinguished as her husband. "This will be very informal," she warned me. "Exactly what I want," I said, "I want to feel like I live here."

It was a bright sunny day, ideal for sightseeing. Elena took me on a tour of the little streets in the neighborhood and told me some of their history and mysteries. There were layers and layers, going back more than two thousand years. She showed me via Giulia and Via Monserrato. We walked through Piazza Farnese and Campo de' Fiori. We went over the little pedestrian bridge, Ponte Sisto, which took us to the other side of the Tiber. There we explored Trastevere, Rome's "Left-Bank," a tangle of higgledy-piggledy little streets; and, then, back on "our" side of the Tiber, she showed me Piazza Navona, a large oblong piazza, shaped like a miniature racecourse, which was like everybody's living room and which had in fact been an ancient Roman racecourse. In the Renaissance, the Romans sometimes filled the piazza with water and fought mock naval battles. It was a favorite place, too, Elena explained, for rallies and demonstrations and for making political speeches.

While we drank espressos, standing at a bar in Campo de' Fiori, I tried to store away all the colorful details she was giving me.

After Elena left – her 10-year-old daughter had a dentist's appointment – I bought some fruit and vegetables in the market in Campo de' Fiori and filled up the refrigerator.

From the first day, I adopted as my preferred hangout one of the cafés in a corner of Campo de' Fiori where I found it was quite pleasant to work, scribbling notes, and watching the life of the market, the shoppers and tourists strolling by, the vendors calling out their wares. The market closed at two pm, the fruits and vegetables and fish were all packed away and carted off, the stands were folded up and stacked out of sight, and the Campo was hosed down; and from then on, it was just a cobblestone piazza like any other little piazza, but with an intense life of its own. This is home, I told myself, this is home. One evening, and once for lunch, I ate at Alfredo's, which was just off via Monserrato, and, since I had an introduction from Maria and her husband Giuseppe, I was immediately treated by the owner Alfredo, and by the waiters, as "one of the family." For three days, I developed a routine. I really was beginning to feel at home; I was surprised at how fast it happened.

≈

About seven-thirty, on the third evening, the doorbell rang, and thinking it was Maria or Giuseppe, I went to the door and opened it. James was standing there.

"Oh, it's you," I said. My heart leaped.

"It is indeed me." He came in and shut the door behind him and stood there, looking around. Then he looked at me, and his dark eyes seemed to flash as if with tiny bolts of lightning. "So here you are," he said, putting down his suitcase.

"Here I am."

"Let me see you. Turn around."

I turned around.

"Even more beautiful than I remembered."

"Your flattery will definitely go to a girl's head, dear sir," I bowed.

He opened his arms, I rushed into them, and he kissed me. I kissed him back, at first timid, then hungry, hungry for more.

"Let me have a shower, and then let's go out for dinner, and let's see what you want to do and how you want to do it."

He disappeared into his bedroom and showered.

I waited. I walked up and down. I had been anticipating this. But what "this" would be exactly, I had no idea. He came out of the shower, dripping wet, and steamy, and naked, toweling himself, and I felt a sudden hungry yearning for him, for his skin, his body, his dark energy, his smell, his touch, his voice. He smiled at me, crinkling his eyes, looking me up and down. I was dressed in shorts, a T-shirt, and sandals; I was dressed; he was naked, not I; somehow, I was pleased that he was naked and not I. He was the concubine, not I.

"Do you want to towel me down?" He winked. The man winked!

"Yes," I licked my lips. Lascivious wench!

I began to towel him vigorously, rubbing and rubbing.

"Oh, that is fine."

"I'm delighted to serve you."

"Ah, Gwendoline, you are truly good to me."

I soon had him crisp and dry – though it was a warm and humid night. He said, "Now we go out to dinner, just down the street, there is a very nice restaurant. I reserved from the airport."

"Da Alfredo?"

"Precisely."

He laid out what he intended to wear. "Do you approve?"

"Most definitely," I said.

I watched as he got dressed, in black jeans, with a thick black leather belt, an open black shirt, and black leather sandals. He eyed me up and down. "Hmm ..."

"Do you want me to change?"

"No, let's start off natural – then we shall slowly transform you into a true creature ... a thing of wonder."

"Transform me into a true creature?"

"Yes, a true creature."

"Hmm," I bit my lip, and narrowed my eyes, trying to envisage what this might possibly mean.

I was, of course, already a familiar at Alfredo's – "part of the family" as Alfredo put it. It was a very glamorous but unpretentious place on a small intimate cobblestoned piazza abutting on via Monserrato, and not far from the market square Campo de' Fiori and even closer to Piazza Farnese. Film stars and models and soccer players, and sometimes even Italian politicians, tanned and wearing very expensive suits, came to sit at the tables outside, on the terrace. Vines tumbled down the warm ochre walls of the miniature palazzo on the opposite side of the piazza, giving the whole place a warm, intimate feel, cozy as if it were inside, not outside, and as if it were bathed, even at night, in sunlight.

Usually, I had gone to Alfredo's in simple jeans and a T-shirt, and I had watched in awe the glamorous, sexy people who sashayed around the place. One woman I saw one evening was in skin-tight gold tights, another in black slinky tights; one girl was wearing a thin, skimpy leather dress and almost certainly nothing underneath. It was hot, even late at night, so I could understand that people would not wear too much – and I liked to look at them, seeing how daring, how naked, they could be, and still look impeccably stylish.

Alone in the apartment, I had usually walked around in panties or naked or at best in a towel or the black bathrobe. In the cool of the evening, wearing a T-shirt and jeans, I would work with my computer out on the terrace, though I did feel I should really be out in the city doing something wild. But then I would plunge into whatever work I was doing, and forget everything – where I was, what time it was, what was going on around me.

James was, of course, a regular at the restaurant. Alfredo

himself came out to greet us, and he ushered us to a good table from which we could easily watch the stylish parade. We commented on what we saw: a girl with a dress slit down one side; a well-known male model; a fabulous – and famous – black model in a simple outfit of black jeans and black T-shirt; an older woman in a shimmering figure-molding sequined dress; two Punk-Goth girls in hot pants. James, I noticed, had a very precise and discerning eye for different styles of female beauty. Then James asked me about my work. These turned out not to be perfunctory questions or disguised small talk, but profound, probing questions. He knew more than enough about mathematics and about the philosophy and history of science to know precisely what I was doing and why I was doing it. Only Kate, and occasionally grandfather, asked such pertinent searching questions. Claudia admitted that my mathematical, scientific side was beyond her.

"So, you really are interested," I said.

"I really am interested," he said.

"In me and in my work."

"In you and in your work."

"I-thou," I said.

"I-thou." He raised his glass.

≈

James was busy for two days with business, though we did go out one night with a well-known priest, a Father Berthollet S J, from the Vatican who was an expert on French Africa and on Korea – where he had served for a number of years; James wanted to learn what Father Berthollet knew. The priest was very suave and jovial. He told us a great many things about tribes, clans, guerrilla warfare, corruption networks, terrorist and jihadist groups, the health catastrophe, conflicts between nomads in the Sahel, and about human trafficking and people smuggling across the

Sahara and in the Mediterranean; and we ate in a very nice restaurant close to Piazza Navona.

The priest shook my hand when we parted. A dark limousine with Vatican license plates had come to pick him up. He offered us a ride, but we were happy to walk. We strolled back through Piazza Navona, and we sat down in a café opposite Bernini's Fountain of Four Rivers and Borromini's Sant'Angese in Agone church. We ate sorbets – lemon and strawberry.

"You are not Catholic?" I thought I'd better ask. It had never occurred to me that James was religious, but I figured I'd better check. Perhaps he was secretly preparing me for a nunnery, and I would have to take a vow of silence, wear sackcloth, cover myself in ashes, and pray on my bare knees through the long gloomy gray winter nights in a damp unheated stone cell and recite a gazillion Hail-Marys.

"Not at all."

"A believer?"

"Not at all."

"So – you are truly diabolic."

"Absolutely. And you?" He leaned forward and kissed me.

"Nothing, I believe in nothing," I said, "I am happy to be nothing, and to be in your arms."

We finished our sorbets, licked our lips, and stood up. We kissed, our lips still cool, and flavored with lemon and strawberry; we walked through Piazza Navona to the small L-shaped alleyway that leads out to one of the main thoroughfares, Corso Vittorio Emanuele II. Then we made our way onward to Campo de' Fiori and through a tangle of little cobblestoned laneways to what I was beginning to consider home.

We showered and went to bed, and we made love – very tender love, just love, lots of exploring, lots of touching, lots of kissing, lots of caressing, and then the delicious act itself – la petite mort

– the small death, as the French call it. Then I fell sound asleep and I think James did too.

≈

The next afternoon I came back early from working in a café – just sitting with my computer in a corner on a terrace in Campo de' Fiori. It was easy to concentrate with the buzz of activity around me; and when I wanted a distraction from my work, or just to loosen up my ideas, I only had to look up, and there was always entertainment: kids bouncing a ball, teenagers hanging out, delivery wagons coming to the restaurants, strolling tourists.

When I got home, James had just arrived, and he said, "Let us have a shower, and then ... let us play."

"Play?"

"Yes, play."

"As you wish, James, let us play."

We showered, and then he said, "You may go out to the terrace, goddess, and I shall follow you."

"Yes, I shall wait for you."

Wrapped in a giant white bath towel – it went down almost to my ankles – I walked through the bedroom and then the living room – with its fireplace and deep carpet and wonderful sleek modernist furniture – and out onto the terrace. The smooth yellow and blue Sicilian tiles were bright and cool under the soles of my feet. In the setting sun, everything seemed almost too vivid, hyper-real – the semi-tropical plants in large ceramic and terracotta vases, the brilliant red geraniums, the cream-colored wood-frame deckchairs. Overhead, reaching partway out onto a corner of the terrace, was the striped white-and-blue awning that, stirred by the light warm breeze, made a gentle rippling sound. I walked to the balustrade, put my hand on the warm, weathered railing of grainy stone, and looked down.

Below me was a narrow, deep, cobblestoned street that wound its canyon-like way toward Campo de' Fiori. Already, it was filled with dark shadows. Down there, night had come, while up here, it was just on the edge of dusk. As I watched, the street lamps down below went on, making circles of golden light in the thickening gloom. The sultry air was absolutely still, everything suspended in quietness. Time seemed to have stopped.

Below me, on a rooftop two buildings away, a barefoot boy in brown shorts – he was probably about 10 or 11 – was watering some geraniums; the splashing stream of water from the hose sparkled rich amber in the light of the setting sun; the boy's skin shone like warm smooth toffee. He looked up, and I waved.

"Ciaò, Signora," he shouted and waved back.

I blew him a kiss. "Ciaò, ragazzo bello!"

He grinned, stuck out his tongue in the nicest way, bowed a sweeping low theatrical pageboy bow, almost bending in two and swinging his arm under his waist; he straightened up and waved again, and went back to his geraniums. I turned my face to a just perceptible breeze I felt rising, a touch of moving air.

The sun was setting over the Janiculum, which is the name of the hill on the west side of Rome, on the other side of the Tiber. Going down in all its glory, the sun tinted everything red. Up on the Janiculum, I could see, silhouetted by the bright western sky, the statue of Garibaldi, the Liberator of Rome, up on his pedestal, and the block-like building of the Spanish Academy, perched on the very edge of the hill. They were far away.

I looked around. Nobody could see me here; there were no buildings nearby as high as our building, and steep tile roofs protected the terrace on both sides. It was an invisible and very private place. I licked my lips. It would be nice, very nice, adventurous and romantic and daring, to make love here, in the open air, maybe when the stars were up.

I looked up at the sky. It was a clear, deep, crisp, darkening blue, almost night, yet the air was warm, and the gentle sea breeze smelled of cedar and pine and of burning grass. The wet evaporated from my skin with a tingling sensation. A tiny breeze sufficed. I ran my fingers through my hair and turned my face up to the sun, now just disappearing, flaring out, and sinking behind the hill.

"The ponentino," James said, coming out onto the terrace, his tanned body glowed dark and steamy; the white towel around his waist, tinted rose by the last reflections of the sun, looked like a centurion's skirt; his tummy rippled, flat and hard. I gulped. I wanted to leap on the man. I wanted to run my hands down those muscles. I wanted to scratch his glowing skin with my nails, leave my red bloody adoring mark, I wanted to brand him and make him mine.

"Ponentino?"

"An evening breeze from the west, from the sea, it comes up just at dusk."

"Ah, of course," I visualized it. "During the day the land heats up faster than the sea, so the temperature of the air over the land heats up, the air rises, and draws the cooler air from over the water inland, and so we get this cooling breeze ... But is this right? It could be the reverse. Let me see ..." I couldn't help myself.

"Dear beautiful budding scientist, exquisite math egghead!" He grinned. "Drop that goddamn towel."

"Here? Now?" I clutched the towel closer. I looked around, suddenly feeling timid and exposed. Nearby were terracotta burnt sienna tiled rooftops, and rooftops lower than ours, farther away were a few steeples and church towers, and, in the distance, Garibaldi, and the Spanish Academy, shadows now, up on the crest of the hill, silhouetted against the fading light of the western sky, yellow and aquamarine and rose. If I dropped the towel, there was nobody close to see – but what if they did? What if some-body got a photo and sent it out on the Net, all over the world?

"Here? Now?" He echoed. His imitation of my timid shocked voice was precise and amused, quizzical, not cruel. "Yes. Here, now. I want to look at you – all of you."

"Ah!" I looked down at myself, at the thick towel clutched to my collarbone. I looked up at him. I raised my chin and narrowed my eyes in a sign of pride and resistance. But it was only for show. With a tingle of fear and – like *la Frileuse* in the Met– a frisson of vulnerability – I knew I was destined to surrender.

"Okeydokey." I stuck out my tongue.

I opened the towel and threw it, carefully, onto the back of a deck chair.

He stared at me, a smile on his face, his head tilted to one side. The light had turned cooler, a faint rose mingled with gathering bluish shadows. Out of the corner of my eye, I noticed a bright single star, it must be Venus, I thought. It was just above where the sun had disappeared and where a yellow and emerald glow, aqueous and subtly shifting, traced the horizon, as if we were underwater.

"Turn around," he said.

"Yes." I turned around twice, then faced him and bowed.

"Tiptoes, arms stretched up, again."

"If you so desire." I turned twice, then faced him, and again bowed.

He gave me an amused appraising glance. It was very lofty. I felt doubly naked, totally exposed, standing before him. Mr. James Hewitt Spencer was becoming a god, and I was being transformed into a female acolyte or pageboy supplicant. Or per-haps James was a Roman emperor or centurion, and I was an apprentice concubine – or catamite. I wondered what it would be like – to be a smooth-skinned slave girl or slave boy, recently acquired in some distant clamorous North African or Middle Eastern market, slipping softly into the arms of a weary emperor-warrior, at court in Rome or far away on some distant snowy barbarian frontier.

Part of me still wanted to be a boy, a real boy, a Peter Pan, androgynous, innocent, forever young, climbing the apple tree, jumping into the river's swimming hole, where the water swirled around and was so dark and deep, shaded by the high cliff of crumbling warm clay and whispering poplars. I wet my lips and took a step toward him.

"Tonight, you will be naked." He was still smiling.

"Oh," I said.

"No clothes allowed." He put his hands on my shoulders.

"Oh."

"And we shall play some games, if you agree." He lifted my chin and kissed me. "It may involve some equipment."

"Equipment? Oh." My tummy flickered and trembled. I licked my lips. Branding irons? Chains? The rack? Crucifixion? A trickle ran down my spine – from my wet hair? Or was it sweat from fear and trembling? Or wet pearls of anticipation? "You are so commanding, so decisive, I think I must call you 'master.' Do I have your permission to call you 'master'?"

"Yes, you have my permission."

"And, Master, we are to play now, you say – and with equipment?"

"Yes." He opened his towel, pulled me gently toward him and wrapped the towel around our waists so we were held together, naked, locked together in fluffy warm intimacy, bound, as if we could dissolve into one body. He pressed himself against me. He was hard – Oh, boy! Already hard! I looked up into his eyes. I felt I wanted to melt into him, merge with him, and be one with him.

Going up on tiptoe, I kissed him.

"No clothes, Slave," he said.

"Yes, Master," I whispered, "I shall wear no clothes." I am generally very independent – and in many ways a feminist – but uttering the word "master" and hearing him use the word "slave" gave me a shivery thrill, a catch in the breath, almost goosebumps.

"I shall keep you with me," he whispered, "naked."

"Yes, Master. Barefoot and naked – in the kitchen." I wet my lips. "Slaving over a steamy stove, cooking an omelet, or a soufflé." I blinked, touched his lips with mine, and gave him my best, most intense mutinous look.

"A soufflé," he whispered, half closing his eyes, and he kissed me. I kissed him back, biting his lip. His kiss hesitated, drew back slightly, then attacked, wild, savage, and deep.

His grip on me tightened. Each finger was a claw of steel. I melted. We merged. Every fiber of his being penetrated me, consumed me, sculpting me, every nerve end tingled, every inch of my body glowed. I shivered. "Oh!"

"Perhaps with a collar." He leaned back – giving me a calculating look.

"A collar." I half-closed my eyes and saw it: Me, naked, in a collar. "A collar, Master. I see."

"Yes, a collar, thick, made of leather and steel, with a ring of iron. A leash, perhaps."

"A leash? Like a dog?"

"Yes." He kissed me on the forehead, "like a dog."

"And I will be attached to something solid, I suppose – a radiator, the balustrade, a potted plant?"

"That is a very good idea."

"Can I have a computer?"

"Oh, yes."

"As long as I can do math ... and recite Shakespeare." I nuzzled and kissed his chest, such smooth skin, such hard muscles; my mouth moved along his chest, kissed his nipples; the warm wet chest hair tickled my lips; my hands all on their own became curious and explored the small of his back, it was so tight, lean, and strong.

"Yes, your mind will be free. You can invent a new theory of relativity if you so desire – and perform every role in every play and read the sonnets and poems ... as long as you like."

"Naked."

"Yes, barefoot, and naked."

"And I'd be yours."

"Yes, mine, forever mine."

"Oh, Master, this is crazy, and I'm crazy, you know." I breathed it out, almost under my breath, like a dirty secret. I reached up and stroked the side of his face.

He peeled the towel that imprisoned us away and let it fall. I felt it slide softly off my backside, and I felt, too, his rising excitement, hard, erect, pressing against me.

My nipples were erect, straining, aching, pressed against his strong warm damp chest, the tangle and pattern of his hair. He was a beast, an animal. My excitement was rising again, to match his. It was as if my heart were about to burst or to flip flop, breathless, into a dark abyss.

"Of course, you are crazy, my darling, but, then, so am I." He kissed me and his oh-so-clever hands seized my waist, tightening, and then sneaking up my backside, pulling me, pressing me closer, into him. He kissed me again, and his lips moved down my neck to my shoulder and then to my breasts.

"Oh," I said, "Oh."

He bent over me, kissing my collarbone and then my breasts, carefully, slowly, his hands traveling down my back, and over my backside; suddenly, he was on his knees, kissing the whorl of my belly button; then he was forcing me open, gently, gently, his tongue exploring caressing, devouring ...

"Oh ..." I exhaled a deep, shuddering breath. I tipped on the very edge. He bit me, gently. Oooooh!

He pulled in the reins, the bit and bridle, of the frisky frothing filly that I had become; this sudden halt made me wilder, crazier; then, once again, he brought me, trembling, up to the very, very edge of the cliff – of orgasm, of loss of self.

Then he pulled me back. I blinked and trembled. Around the two of us, there was a whole world, a whole universe. It seemed too vivid to be real, like the backdrop in an opera. Venus was brighter and lower now. The sky had turned deep indigo. One by one, stars appeared.

My fingers clutched his hair, caressed the side of his head. "Don't stop," I whispered.

Still on his knees, he kissed me, the very heart of me, deeper and deeper; he took me higher and higher, and once again to the very knife-edge.

He eased back, eased away, gently, gently, kissing his way down my thighs, and then returning, messaging me deeply, his touch was so gentle, so strong ... I teetered and tottered again on the very edge. "Oh, oh, oh!" He was being cruel, so cruel.

"You are like silk and vanilla and lavender," he said.

"Vanilla and lavender?"

"You taste like dessert," he said, still on his knees, looking up at me, his hair tangled over his eyes, his hands locked on my waist. I smoothed his hair back. He grinned. His eyes sparkled – diabolical!

"Oh, cruel, cruel, Master!" I whispered. I wanted him to finish what he had started, to take me to the edge of the cliff, and toss me over. I felt I was on the verge of the biggest, most anticipated, most slow-motion, most roller-coaster, most teasing twisting frustrating damned orgasm of my whole life ... but ...

He laughed, and after a last carefully prolonged – teasing, twisting, rolling – lick and twirl of his tongue, he withdrew from my poor eager panting "Heart of Darkness" and kissed his way slowly down my thighs, up my belly, between my breasts, taking time to concentrate at each little stop, at each station on his pilgrimage.

He stood up, kissed me on the mouth, lifted me – it was so swift and sudden, just one smooth movement, sweeping me up into his arms, I didn't have time to cry out, "Hey!" And he carried me through the French doors into the apartment.

The night breeze from the sea with its smells of cedar and pine and burning grass – a sort of wild perfume – drifted into the room. The lamps were on low. They sent a golden glow over the thick carpet where he lowered me down in front of the fireplace, which, despite the warm evening, was burning with a low crackling fire. "You, Master, are the devil," I said.

"Oh? How so," he smiled and went down on his knees. He took my face between his hands and held me that way, cupped between his warm, strong hands. He lifted me up, and – suddenly – he was under me. He lay there, looking up at me, and caressing me, touching my breasts with the most teasing wicked little pinches and soft swirling caresses. I closed my eyes. I wanted to howl. Then, somehow, I found myself on all fours; he was facing me, staring into my eyes – I was wet, soaked with desire, a bitch in heat, trembling in near-hysterical anticipation. He kissed me, almost primly, stroked the side of my face, ruffled my hair, and stood up. "I shall get dressed now, but not you. Okay?"

"What?" I was shocked.

"I, your Master, will get dressed, but, you, darling, will not."

"As you wish, Master." I stuck out my lip in a pout.

A bottle was by the fireplace, in an ice bucket, and two glasses were beside it. I didn't remember seeing them there. He must have put them there eons ago, while I was out on the terrace flirting with the toffee-colored boy who was watering the geraniums. It was white wine – and undoubtedly very expensive.

My Master poured a glass and handed it to me. I swiveled around, and sitting cross-legged on the floor, I drank, looking up at him. For some reason my eyes were wet

"Wait here," he said, and disappeared.

"Yes, Master." I licked my lips and drank. This was strong, delicate stuff – dry and smoky with a hint of sulfur, and it was delicious, cool and edgy. I gulped it down. What was he going to do now? I refilled my glass and lay down on my belly. I took another sip, and stared at the flames in the fire; they made a relaxing pattern; but I was all wired up, caught in an inchoate tangle of images and desires, raring to go, and ready, too, to curl up and sleep, drowsy and horny, all at the same time. What a mixture of feelings – it was a storm of emotions; I was tempest-tossed, a sleek clipper trapped in a typhoon, battered this way and that, the crew in a panic, and about to capsize.

My Master came back into the room, barefoot, in black jeans, and a black shirt open down to his waist.

"Now, whenever you want to stop, you just have to tell me."

"Okay." I bit my lip and gave him the look I'd practiced in the mirror, the fiery glance from under the eyebrows, subservient, mistrustful, mutinous. Dark eyelashes and coal-black eyebrows help – I'm a study in black-and-white, as Kate has often told me, chalk-white skin, and jet-black hair, and a precise little anthracite triangle, like a cache-sex or a G-string. Now I was naked, and he wasn't, and I wasn't playing a role – or was I? Physically, I was naked – and psychologically, I was exposed. By arousing me to a pitch, then stepping away, my Master – and he was rapidly becoming just that, my Master – was stripping me of all pretense, of all defense, laying me bare. I felt a catch in my breath – fear. Fear and desire.

As my Master came toward me, the light from the fire and the candles shimmered on his chest, on the thick black leather belt, and on the wide embossed dark metal buckle. I felt a thrilling fearful feeling of shame, and goosebumps on my arms. Would he take the belt off and whip me? Did I deserve – did I desire – a spanking? I briefly glimpsed, in my mind, the images.

He bowed gallantly. "Would you permit me – this dance ...?"

I gulped, blinked at him, and, carefully, stood up. "Yes, Master," I said, and I moved into his arms.

"Close your eyes."

"Yes, Master." I closed my eyes.

Music began. *You must remember this; a kiss is still a kiss ...*

He held me in his arms. We danced.

"Let us make things a bit more complicated."

"Okay ... May I open my eyes?"

"Yes."

I opened my eyes.

"I think I'd like to have you at my mercy."

"You already have, sort of ..."

"Yes ... but ... let's have a look." He went to a sideboard, opened a drawer, and lifted out something that looked a bit like a complicated device to control a donkey or pony. It was a highly polished thick black leather collar, studded, and with a large steel ring, and with something that looked like a harness attached to it.

"Here, take it," he said.

"You are truly equipped, Master, and prepared for all eventualities." I gave him the dark mutinous look, but with a grin – yes, he was truly equipped, as I had truly and repeatedly discovered. I wished to discover more. There was a definite hard bulge in his jeans.

"Yes," he whispered. The tips of his fingers touched my chin, and then ran down my throat; it was a soft yet strong caress – as if in an instant he could strangle me or break my neck – which he certainly could.

"So, this is the collar." I took the collar in my hands and turned it over. It smelled nice, fresh leather and polished, gleaming steel. "But it's more than a collar."

"Oh, yes, it's more than a collar."

"Hmm ..." I looked him in the eye. I leaned forward and kissed him lightly. He kissed back. My breasts, pressing through his shirt, touched his chest, muscular, warm, inviting, luxurious ... I leaned back. "Do it," I said.

"You trust me?"

"I trust you."

"If you want me to stop at any time ..."

"I'll tell you, Master, I'll tell you."

"If you whinny twice, in quick succession. That will mean stop." His hand was on my left buttock, and he gave me a slight, quick slap.

"Whinny? Like a pony?"

"It might come to that."

"Do I have to draw a cart or something?"

"It might well come to that, too, my dear. In fact, that does sound like a splendid idea." His hand moved across my buttocks, caressed my flank, and curved along my haunch, with a series of slight slaps, tender teasing caresses, and deep, kneading strokes that tingled in every nerve, every millimeter of skin.

"Okay, Master. I shall whinny, if I must whinny." I licked my lips. I took a deep breath. My heart was beating fast. My gaze held his gaze. His eyes were wicked and smiling. I wondered if I was sufficiently wicked and sufficiently daring to enter fully into his world. Above all, I didn't want to disappoint him. My heart performed little flip-flops. An intense and diabolic light burned, like scarlet embers, in his dark eyes, but his mouth was still smiling.

"You may want to pee first," he said, "Afterwards, you won't be able to."

"Hmm." I squared my shoulders. Hmm, I wouldn't be able to pee. Hmm! Well, that was interesting. I was going to be a brave little soldier. "Okay, Pee, yes, Okay, Master, I'll pee."

I went into the bathroom, sat on the toilet, and looked around at all the civilized and civilizing things. There they were: the thick fluffy towels neatly aligned in their heated metal racks, the soaps and lotions, the large mirror that was quite flattering, the large shower with its smoky glass door and the separate step-in tub, made for two, at least two, for bathing, most assuredly by candlelight in foam-filled perfumed water. I finished peeing, wiped myself carefully, and walked out to meet my destiny.

My master was standing there, his back turned to me, looking out at the night beyond the French doors; the sky was turquoise, deepening to black. Again, I caught a whiff of that wild smell – cedar, pine, burning grass.

"Master, I am yours," I said.

He turned and smiled. "Let us begin."

He fastened the collar around my neck; it clicked and locked into place. It was high and rigid and tight, something I hadn't realized before, not fully; it forced me to hold my neck erect. I wiggled my shoulders.

He kissed me on the forehead. "Turn around," he said.

I obeyed.

"Put your arms behind your back – straight – like this."

"Yes, Master, like this?"

"Yes. that is perfect!" I felt him attach the harness-like thing to the collar. Then he slipped it around my arms; it was a sort of leather tube, with thick laces to tighten it. He began to pull the laces. As he tightened the laces, they squeezed my arms close together, twisting my shoulders back. My breasts suddenly felt the tension. "Tighter, Master, tighter," I said. My voice sounded husky.

"Don't worry." He laced my arms tighter and tighter, bending my shoulders back, tensing my breasts and nipples. I took a deep breath.

High heels came next, black patent stilettos, with straps and a lock. He sat me down, perching me on the edge of a chrome and leather chair, so that he could slip my feet into the shoes, and snap the locks shut.

"Stand up," he said.

Wearing high heels, I have learned, has a radical effect on posture and on the female body; calves and thighs are tightened, the muscles strained, the pelvis thrust forward, and buttocks pushed outward, and breasts tightened and pushed forward. It made me very self-conscious of my body, which was, I suppose, part of the charm. Here, at least, the stilettos were not clicking on a hard cement or marble pavement – that might be just too much.

"Let us dance." He bowed.

"Yes, Master."

He took me in his arms, and we danced. From time to time, he gave me sips of wine. If I spilled some, he licked my lips for me. I felt every inch of my body straining toward him.

"Tell me, my darling, how is it you became so interested in math?"

"I doodled," I whispered into his shoulder.

"Doodled?"

"Yes. Doodling was an escape." I whispered to him as if it were a shameful secret; I pressed myself tighter against him; he held me closer. His erection pressed through the jeans. I wanted it, I wanted it, I wanted it, and I realized how wet I was, and open, and eager. "I doodled, and I wondered if I could describe the doodle with a formula."

"Ah ..." His lips brushed mine; his hands were on my buttocks. "You doodled – and you wanted to find a formula for the doodle."

"Yes. Descartes invented the Cartesian coordinates – you know the x, y, z coordinates thing, where you plot algebraic formulas, when he was lying lazily in bed watching a fly buzz around his room. The fly looped around, this way and that. Descartes realized he could locate the exact position of the fly in space, in three-dimensional space, at any given moment, with three numbers, three coordinates, horizontal, vertical, and in-depth, height, length, width, three dimensions – x, y, and z."

"Descartes did that, did he?" His lips brushed my forehead.

"Yes." I blushed. "I beg forgiveness, Master. I'm giving a lecture." I felt a warm rush of shame. I truly am an idiot. A flush crept up my back, spread to my cheeks.

"That Cartesian fly should have gotten a Nobel Prize," whispered my master, closing my mouth with a kiss. It was a warm, hungry kiss. His hands suddenly seemed to be everywhere, cupping my bum, shimmying down my belly, his fingers feeling their way into me. His fingers, shiny with liquid – shiny with my excitement – came up to his face, and he smiled at me – the musky smell. "Sugar and spice," he said, "and everything nice." He offered me his fingers, and I licked them, and he kissed me.

We danced and the candles burned, the fire crackled, the music played.

"Now we'll put on a mask," he said. "Do you mind?"

"No." I was panting, dying for him to touch me, to take me.

He lifted the mask out of the same side drawer. It was like a hood, of black rubber or latex.

"That's not a mask, Master. It's a hood." I was standing, manacled, and teetering on the stilettos, in the middle of the room.

"Why so it is!" He held it up, his eyes widening, as in surprise.

The hood, I saw, had no holes for the eyes, just tiny nostrils and a hole for the mouth.

I trembled. "It's going to muss up my hair." I gulped, a catch in my breath. "I'll have to shampoo." My hair was short enough that the hood wouldn't mess up anything, but I had to say something. I was playing for time.

"We'll have a shower – another shower."

"Good ... Squeaky clean we'll be, then, Master." I swallowed.

"Yes, squeaky clean." He looked at me closely. "Are you happy?"

"Yes, Master, I am exceedingly happy," I said; I wanted to say, "Yes, you fool. I'm happy, but I'm horny as hell, and I'm dying for you to grab me and take me and possess me and ..." But I didn't dare. I wet my lips. Inside I was wet, dripping, dying with desire.

He slipped the hood smoothly over my head, tightened it, and locked it to the collar. The world went black. The hood pressed my eyes shut and left only my mouth and my nostrils free. "You are very evil, Master," I whispered.

"Yes. Yes, I am." He kissed me, lightly, his hands closing tight, squeezing my waist. "Hmm," he said, his voice muffled by the tight hood that pressed down on my ears.

"Hmm," I echoed.

The music began again, muted now by the hood. I was wrapped in a feathery, silken sheen of darkness, sight gone, hearing muffled. As we danced, he held me extra tight, pressing against me. I couldn't respond and hold him, and I couldn't touch him except by pressing my hips and breasts and lips against him. That was what I had become, a mouth and a body, all I was becoming – just a body: lips, tongue, teeth, nipples, breasts, skin, hips, belly.

We kissed.

Buried in the deepest of nights, I swirled down into darkness without end. My world contained no moon, no stars, just empty dark plunging space. I could feel every surface of my body, skin glowing, beaded with sweat. His body too, I could feel, warm, and close, as if his body were part of mine, his skin close on my skin, everywhere, his muscles, so smooth and hard, pressing in, the flatness of his stomach, tense like a weapon, his belt, his jeans, his erection.

His hands, seeming to melt and meld into my body, moved everywhere, sliding down my back, cupping my backside, sculpting my ass, oh, oh, oh ... I was breathless, helpless, and yearning – for more.

The high heels, dancing softly on the deep carpet, and the warmth of the fire, licking along my skin, made me feel as if I were coated in gold. The whole world was a caress. I felt I might easily suffer an attack of vertigo, and fall, and fall, and fall, spinning downwards, but his strong arms held me; his kisses locked my body into his, protecting me, absorbing me, devouring me ...

I pressed into him. I kissed him, a deep kiss, as deep as I could manage.

"Ah," he sighed, and kissed me back.

"Wow," I breathed, his chest was pressing me, strong muscles, smooth hot skin, my breasts were on fire. I wished, I wished ... "Now," I whispered, "now ..." I wanted him to lie down, so I could straddle him, blind and bound, but lowering myself onto him, taking him into me, and ... and ... and ...

The doorbell rang.

"Oh, we have guests." His hand moved across my backside, a quick, artful, stroking, caress. There was a tone of amused surprise in his voice.

"What?"

"Don't worry." He kissed my breasts. "You look beautiful."

"I can't ..."

"I think you need a gag, so you won't be recognizable. Your

mouth is too beautiful, uniquely beautiful, and if you were to utter a word, they would know ..."

"What? What?" What was he going to do? My heart flip-flopped; my breath quickened; beads of sweat broke out everywhere.

"Don't worry!" He kissed me.

"Who is it?"

"We'll see – guests, special guests."

"This is ... outrageous!"

"We wouldn't want the slave talking out of turn, now, would we?"

"A gag? I'm not sure ... A gag? You are very, very wicked, Master, you can't do this."

"Do you want me not to gag you?"

I took a deep breath – I only had words now, no glance, and no expression. I was a mask, not even a mask. But I had come this far. I was not going to retreat. I swallowed and whispered, "Do with me what you will, then, Master, my body, my life, my destiny are in your hands." Boy, I thought, dear Gwendoline, now you are really asking for it!

"Open your mouth," he said.

"What? How wide?" He stopped me in mid-phrase by slipping a rubber ball into my mouth, forcing my jaws wide open. The ball pressed down on my tongue. My teeth clamped down onto the rubber – it was a strangely voluptuous sensation – almost like bending over him and ... The ball seemed to be attached to a thick strap on either side of my mouth. I felt the strap wrap around the hood, and I heard it click into place, joining the hood and the collar. With my mouth forced entirely open, I was breathless, and humiliated because I was sure I'd slobbered onto the ball as he slipped it into my mouth; I was going to drool; I was excited – and afraid.

I wanted to say "I trust you" – but all that came out was a soft grunt. That's me? I wondered at it. I tried again; it came out like a whinny, deep in my throat.

He kissed my breasts. My nipples ached, engorged, ultra-tight, erect, and straining with tension from the way my shoulders were pulled back by my pinioned arms.

The doorbell rang again.

"I'll hide you in the bedroom."

I grunted, whinnied. I couldn't give him the look from under my eyebrows; I couldn't do the witty Lauren Bacall wisecrack. I couldn't do anything. He guided me. I followed blindly, a tethered blinkered pony. Stilettoes and pinioned arms do strange things to a girl's body and to posture – this is doubly effective if you can't see, and can only feel, and if you are walking on a deep plush carpet.

The doorbell rang again. Who would it be? Who were the mysterious guests he spoke of? The police? The neighbors? Maria? Giuseppe? Oh, my God, I realized how humiliating this could be!

He guided me by the hand, with one hand on the small of my back, then caressing my backside, gently, firmly, as if carving me out of clay, as if creating me anew, a sculpted creation and slave. Then he slapped my backside, lightly, something between a caress and a teasing slap.

I wanted to protest, but, of course, I couldn't. Oh, my God! I could do nothing! Who were these guests? Maybe James was going to sell me into slavery in some weird market in some godforsaken desert or jungle kingdom where I would be a slave-concubine to a sex-mad infinitely perverse desert monarch or filthy rich kinky Texan oil billionaire. Fearful fantasies ran riot, delicious, and horrifying. I saw myself sealed in a container in a container ship; I was a special delivery package being sent ... where? Should I whinny, and whinny twice? No, I'd be damned before I'd whinny twice! Gwendoline is not going to give up!

He steered me to the edge of the bed, and guided me as I sat down, my backside perched on the edge of the bed, unable to hang on, just perched, like a doll or a puppet.

"Now, the leash."

"Glumph!" A muffled, drooling snort was all I could manage. What was this about a lash? Was he going to parade me through the streets?

He attached the leash. It was a chain. The cool metal links dangled between my breasts, hung down my belly, and coiled between my thighs. Am I going to be led around like an animal in a pen?

"Glumph!" I tried to growl. "Glumph!"

He pinched my nipples, giving each of them a soft, gentle twist, and then I felt him kneel in front of me. He kissed my breasts, he licked and kissed my nipples, softly, nibbling, licking, and then his hand slid along the inner side of my thigh, wet, satin shiny with moisture, warm. Oh, I wanted to leap up and throw my arms around him and kiss him – but I was a bound statue, rigid, erect, and blind.

The doorbell rang again; this time, it was a long, insistent ring.

"I'll be right back, darling," he whispered, and I heard the muffled sound of the door to the bedroom closing.

I sat on the edge of the bed, stiff, exited, and scared.

I heard the front door open or thought I did. And muffled voices. A man and a woman, or at least I thought so. Who were these people? The owners of a bordello? Business partners of James'? Traders from some barbaric mythical country where women tourists and innocent girl mathematicians were kidnapped, bound up, and sold into slavery? Was he going to sell me? These fantasies flooded into my mind. I was feverish, excited, breaking out in a sweat.

How did I get myself in this fix? I tugged at the arm harness. No give, no flex, no escape. It was inflexible and tight, the rigid high collar too, and the skin-tight hood. The metal chain swayed, cool and hard, between my breasts, it was smooth and metallic, and it coiled, insidious and chilly, between my hot damp thighs, a serpent ready to strike. My body was beaded in blossoms of sweat; every millimeter of skin sparkled.

The French doors were open to the bedroom balcony, exposing me to the whole city. A car, far away, honked; an airplane was passing somewhere overhead; in the far distance, a siren wailed, plaintive, and rhythmically repeated. A drop of sweat trickled, wandering down my spine, under my pinioned arms. It tickled. I wiggled. From the living room, I heard more muffled conversation – impossible to distinguish the words – and laughter.

Okay, well, whatever happens, he won't hurt me.

I'm sure he won't hurt me.

I'm pretty sure he won't hurt me.

I don't think he'd hurt me.

A woman laughed; she laughed again, and then the hushed voices continued.

Then there was nothing but silence. I waited. I wanted to stand up and bang my head against the door.

I growled – out came a muffled gurgle. "Galumph!" It gave me a weird thrill – being so helpless and yet sounding like a caged wild beast. Tiger, tiger, burning bright ...

The cool chain leash with its fine metal links swayed between my breasts, tickled my belly, and weighed lightly, coiled cruelly between my legs, on my thigh. Maybe I belong in a zoo, I thought. Or a freak show. I certainly am a freak! A thrill of shame rippled up my spine, a hot, sweaty flush of abasement spread to my tummy and beasts. Maybe I was going to be displayed in some shop window in Paris or Amsterdam.

Maybe in a few minutes, I would feel the delicious horrible irredeemable sensation of being publicly shamed, paraded, naked, and bound, gagged, and blindfolded. He would swing the door open, come in, take the leash, and make me stand up, and parade me in front of his guests. I would never forgive him. Or would I? Warm sweat trickled down my spine. I saw myself being led down the stairs, or into the elevator, and down the cobblestoned streets, perhaps to the Campo de' Fiori market, to be displayed, all eyes upon me, and all I would be able to do was whinny!

Then I heard the door to the bedroom open.

"So, here she is!" His voice declaimed.

"Oh, God," I thought. I took a deep breath, held myself even more stiffly erect. If I were going to go down in flames of shame, then I would go down with a stiff upper lip, with whatever dignity I could muster. I would brazen it out. I would walk stiffly, blindly, led on a leash, a proud pony. Perhaps the man and woman would bid for me, as in an auction. Perhaps my master would lead me to Alfredo's to be displayed on the piazza, all the diners turning to look, the whole terrace falling silent. A weird trembling excitement rose, a fiery liquid tide.

"So, this is the magic creature," he said. His hands were on my thighs and in my utter blindness, I sensed that he was on his knees, and he gently pushed my legs apart and lifted the coiled metal chain away. He kissed the inside of my thighs, and he kissed and licked gently – working his way along the inside of my thighs, and he pushed me back gently, placing a pillow under my head, with my body arched up because my pinioned arms were under me. He kissed my breasts, and then he kissed me between my legs, slowly, slowly, licking, touching softly, softy, going deep within me. I felt his legs and hips, and he leaned into me, on his knees, and I realized he was naked. He was kissing sweetly, delicately, moving into me, deeper, deeper, then stopping ...

Were we putting on a show for paying guests?

My mouth, filled with the rubber ball, overflowed with saliva. Oh, don't do that, stop, don't stop, stop, don't stop! Stop! No! Don't stop! I wanted to shout out, seize his hair, and pull him deeper into me: but I couldn't say a word; I merely grunted and groaned and gurgled. Oh, oh, and he was closer and deeper now, into the very heart of me ... and ... a rush, a tidal wave swept over me, and over, and over, and over ...

≈

He slipped the gag out of my mouth, unclicked it, and, before I could say anything or even gasp, he kissed me, he kissed my mouth, slick and overflowing with saliva and dribbling, dripping onto my chin and breasts.

"Oh," I managed, blindly. I had forgotten how to talk.

He turned me over, so I was suddenly on top of him, a blind and bound rider. He guided me as I lowered myself down onto him. I was so wet he slid into me easily, slowly, slowly, holding me steady; he let me ride him, and ride him, and ride him, and I was saying, Oh, oh, oh, oh – and even to me it sounded ridiculous – Oh, oh, oh ... And, with a rush of breathless excitement, I came.

I shuddered and screamed.

I bent down and kissed him.

"Oh, God," I whispered, and I remained there, holding him between my thighs, my hooded head pressed against him, my arms cantilevered, pinioned behind my back.

"Ah, princess," he nibbled my lips and kissed me.

I gurgled, kissed him back, and licked my lips.

"Now I must free you," he said, and he helped me off the bed, and stood me up on the tottering stilettoes. I was dizzy and thought I would fall, bound and blind as I was, into his arms.

"Steady there." His hand was on my shoulder.

"Yes, Master," I whispered.

I just managed to avoid falling flat on my face – or on my butt. He unlaced the arm harness and lifted it off. Whew! I was still hooded and blind, but my arms were free, and I wrapped them around him and held him as tight as I could. We moved around the floor, like a dance. Suddenly, he lifted me up, in his arms – Whoops! – carried me into the living room, and plunked me down on a chair. As I perched, trembling, on the edge of the seat, I could hear the crackling in the fireplace, and I could hear traffic out beyond the terrace. I wondered, still caught in my fantasy of being sold into servitude, if the two "buyers" were sitting there. Had they been watching the show? Was I being displayed, put through my paces?

He unlaced and opened the hood, lifting it away, just leaving the high stiff leather collar, and the fine metal leash.

I blinked. Everything was blurry. I felt the hot shame and sweat cooling on my face.

The table was set.

There was no one else in the room.

"Waiters?" I raised an eyebrow and gave him the look.

"Yes, room service from Alfredo's," his smile was a bit crooked, as if he were rehearsing a grin. "They set the table, and they left."

"You bastard!" I had to laugh.

"Yes."

"You, Master, are truly evil."

"And you, my little princess, are truly brave," he said.

"I was caught between cold fury and utter terror," I bit my lip, "I was excited. Despite myself, I was excited." My heart was still trembling. Saliva flooded up. I licked it back and swallowed. Confessing the feeling was bolder than the feeling itself.

"Good. That is good. So, you will be prepared for what might come next."

"Prepared for what comes next?"

"Yes."

"Oh, I see – Ceremonies and rituals and tests?"

"Yes, ceremonies and rituals and tests – and displays."

"Displays?" I frowned: this was intriguing. Part of me wondered how far I was willing to go – though it was a bit late for that. Where was all this going?Ceremonies and rituals and tests and displays? Hmm! The idea of display was exciting – me in a shop window, frozen in place, displayed as a plastic mannequin, wearing lingerie or – nothing.

"Show business," he said, smiling. His hands were on my backside, cupping and pressing me, and then, seizing my waist and arching his back, he bent me back, and, bending over me, he swung me around, as if we were dancing a tango, and kissed me full on the mouth and then a full French kiss, deep and earthy. My arms were around him. I slid my hands down his sides. I seized him between the legs and squeezed; his arousal stiffened, but his kiss didn't stop; it went on and on, and then, coming up for breath, he whispered, his voice husky and choked, "Naughty girl."

I bit his lip, and looked into his eyes, "Anything you can do ..."

"I can do better," he smiled, it was a devilish grin, his eyes shone, his teeth gleamed; he was pressed into me. I adjusted my stance, I was liquid, totally now, and for some reason I noticed how bright and merry the fire was, just as he entered me, plunging straight in, like a sword.

"No, you can't ... do better ..." I whispered. I was about to swoon. He had taken me right up to the promise of orgasm, the moment just before orgasm. I was at the altar, consumed by the rising tension, rippling upwards, and I was trembling uncontrollably. He was deep inside me. It was as if we were one creature, welded together with superglue, a hybrid animal, male and female, two in one; I caressed his hair at the temples, the adorable little bits of gray, flecks, my fingers were moving in his hair.

We lowered ourselves to the rug. Now I was on top of him. The fire in the fireplace was close and hot – burning like a primitive sacrificial fire in the sultry air drifting in from outside.

"You have lines, nice little lines here, and here," I licked them and kissed them, "right at the edges of your eyes, as if you were squinting into the sun."

"Age," he said.

"Your eyes are dark and have lots of little gold specks." I lifted myself up so I could focus on them.

"Your eyes, Princess, are divine." His smile seemed almost sad, "Your eyes are darkness itself."

We were moving slowly now, bonded to each other, dreamily and crazily. He was deep inside me, enormous. I was breathless, the excitement again rising, and rising, and rising ...

"Oh, Oh, Oh ..." I shuddered.

I screamed. I jerked back and forth. It was like being electro-cuted. I clenched my teeth, and I screamed again. "Oh, oh, oh, oh, yes, yes, yes ..." Then I sobbed and shook all over, and he still moved inside me, still hard, still a giant, moving more slowly now, more gently.

I bit him. "You are selfish," I whispered. I licked his shoulder.

"Hmm, how so?"

"You make me come, and come, but you won't come ..."

"Give me time – I want to prolong this."

"It makes me feel ... ridiculous, silly ..."

"You are beautifully silly. Very beautiful when you come! Trembling and covered in sweat and saliva. Exquisite."

"Ugh!"

"Sublime."

"Hmm, it's a power trip, I'll bet ..."

"Hmm," he nodded, the wise professor waiting for the preco-cious student to explain.

"You are a phallic narcissist," I muttered. I'd read the expres-sion somewhere in an essay on psychoanalysis; it seemed to apply perfectly. He was using his cock, his prick, his sword and scimitar to control me – as a weapon and totem and instrument of his masculine glory and power, as a demonstration of his self-control, and his mastery over me. "I am a poor lamb, a sacrifice to your vanity." I pouted.

"Am I so transparent?" He pouted back and raised an eyebrow.

"Hmm, yes," I nuzzled against his forehead. "Let's try again, big boy! Let's see who can outlast whom."

"The girl becomes bold ... she becomes brazen."

"Yes."

"Well, then, we must satisfy her desire, we must obey." The tip of his tongue was licking my lips now, just the tip, just playfully. We were both cross-eyed, being so close, concentrating so hard, intent on gazing into each other's eyes. Who would blink first? I wanted to capture his soul and eat it.

"You are delicious," I said.

"Ah."

"You are yummy."

"Ah."

"I want to eat you."

"Little Miss Cannibal, and yet so refined.'

"I'm not refined," I sighed. My thighs were slick with cum and sweat.

I wrapped myself around him and squeezed my legs together; then, I shifted strategy and put both my legs between his, so I could squeeze the living daylights out of him. He was going to come if it took me all the way to dawn's early light! I was going to force him to come. I would subdue him; I would force him to orgasm. I kissed him slowly, and I withdrew, and then I rose up, and I came down. Each time I made it slower, withdrawing to the very slippery limit, even though I wanted to plunge down, imprison him inside me, and keep him prisoner, locked in, keep him in me forever; but I was determined to tease him to the limit, slowly rising, slowly falling, leaning low and kissing him, and watching his reactions. Oh! Oh! I was reacting faster than I planned. The more I tried to control him, the more I realized I was losing control of myself.

"Oh, God! Oh, God! Oh, God!" I was swept away. I fought it, I fought it, I fought it. No, no, no! I shuddered, arched my back, and cried out. He was plunging deep into me – again, and again, and again – and I was in total ecstasy and utterly mortified. People blocks away, people on the other side of the Tiber, could hear my screams, I was sure, and the Pope in the Vatican heard them! But I didn't care, I didn't care at all. The aftershocks echoed, and echoed ...

He was still moving in me, still hard, still immense.

Oh, oh, oh, oh ...

As the wave of my excitement receded, he was smiling a slightly distracted smile, and he held my head, his fingers burying themselves in my hair. He jerked my head down, and he kissed me – and it was the most violent deep kiss I had ever experienced, hungry and biting, licking, sucking, consuming, bruising, mauling. My whole body was aquiver, slathered in sweat. My mind and senses opened up. My ego ceased to be. *Poof!* I was gone. I no longer existed. Drifting in from the terrace came the bitter fecund earthy perfume of the geraniums, and all around us was the musky smell of sex, of my sex; I was slathered in it, coated in it, liquefied in it, glowing with it, bathing in it, and I was that musky smell, I was sex, my sex, I was nothing but sex. I was liquid, shimmering, and trembling and ... non-existent.

I had ceased.

Gwendoline was gone.

His fingers were everywhere; his hands slipped, grasped, held, kneaded, sculpted; his lips kissed me everywhere; his thighs were locked onto me, and Oh!

Oh!

Oh!

I was on the knife-edge and then sliding over it, and, again, the shuddering came, involuntary, sweeping over me, and I wanted to cry out, I wanted to bawl, I wanted ... I wanted ... I wanted ... and I came again ...

Oh!

Oh!

I came.

And he came. He came! Finally, he came!

Oh!

Oh!

∞

The curtains were drawn shut, but still, somehow, the sun got in. Stripes of golden sunlight flashed and flickered on the wall, just above the burnished white dresser.

"Whew! Oh, boy!" I sat up in bed.

James was still asleep, or so I thought. Then, with his eyes still shut, he reached out and touched my thigh, and he said, "Love in the morning is a wonderful thing, don't you think?"

I wanted to pee and brush my teeth and gargle and shower and drink a cup of dark coffee, but I sighed, "Yes."

I turned over, so my body was against him, and I slid up onto him – both our bodies sticky, and I thought it would be off-putting and disgusting, but it was excitingly nice in a gluey disgusting sort of intensely intimate way. I kissed him and he kissed me back. He was already erect, and I felt myself getting excited already. He turned me over on my back, and he began, slowly at first and gently, to caress me. I think part of me was still half-asleep in that half-dream half-awake erotic zone and still aroused maybe from the night before. In a few seconds, I was fully aroused and ready for him, and I slid back up onto him, and brushing my breasts against his chest and kissing him, I helped him guide himself into me.

I rode him gently. "Oh, oh, oh ..."

He seemed gigantic.

"Oh, oh, oh ..."

I wanted to say something witty, but I couldn't say anything.

We both came – simultaneous.

After a long gliding series of aftershocks, I slowly detached myself, and I lay curled against him.

"Ah, Princess," he sighed.

The sun behind the curtains slowly brightened. The stripes on the wall were glowing – a lighter, paler gold.

"Today, we should go exploring," he said. "What about a long walk – perhaps on the Appian Way?"

"Great." I yawned. "I'll make breakfast." I didn't move.

He didn't say anything, his hand was caressing my hair, and his other hand was caressing my right breast, playing hide-and-seek with the nipple, pinching it, twirling around it, letting it go, teasing it, holding it. Finally, he cleared his throat. "Okay, my sweet Princess, you have a shower, then you can make breakfast while I shower. Is that a deal?"

"It's a deal, Master." I kissed him, slid out of bed, and headed for the bathroom. A quick pee and a relaxing well-structured healthy poop, and a quick deep and very thorough shower, and I was right as rain and eager for a coffee. I walked out, still dripping wet, wrapped in a towel, and headed straight for the kitchen.

I love kitchens. They are like laboratories or workshops. All sorts of shiny instruments, tools, and little tasks you can break down into simple segments and simple steps, almost like math.

I made breakfast. Fresh coffee and heated-up croissants, bacon, eggs, and toast with jam and orange juice. It was an excellent breakfast, I thought. I had enjoyed shopping for the ingredients.

He padded his way out in a bathrobe to the terrace where I had set things out. We both had iPads. We commented on the news of the day. I thought, this is like an old married couple in a cartoon in The New Yorker. I was still dressed only in the towel, but it was tucked up demurely under my armpits and above my breasts. I also had laid out, next to my bacon and eggs, a guide to Rome. I was reading about the Appian Way that we were going to explore.

"So, I suppose you know all about the Appian Way," I said, while absent-mindedly buttering a piece of toast.

"No, Princess, I don't. I know nothing about the Appian Way. Enlighten me."

"Ah, you risk unleashing the dusty pedant in me, dear sir."

He looked over his coffee cup. "I'll take that risk, Goddess."

"Well, then, the Appian Way is a military road, essentially, and the first section was finished in the year 312 BCE. It had been ordered built, or the building was overseen, by a Roman politician called Appius, and that is why they call it the Appian Way."

"Ah, ah," said James. "My world is already richer."

I raised an eyebrow and gave him the look. "At that time – and this was before the Roman Empire – Rome was a republic. It was expanding south along the coastal plain toward the Bay of Naples, and it had made an alliance with the city of Capua, which is just north of Naples. But opposing Rome's advance southwards and the link with Capua were some mountain folk, the Samnite tribes, who lived in the Apennine Mountains, the mountain spine that runs down Italy, parallel to the coast." I stopped to catch my breath.

"Most interesting," James smiled and nodded. He forked some egg and bacon. "Go on, Princess."

"Well, these hill folk, the Samnites, were horseback riders, and good fighters, and by trickery they had already trapped a Roman army, surrounding it in a mountain pass and forced it to surrender nine years before the Appian Way was built. This defeat happened in 321 BC. The Romans were annoyed. They did not take kindly to being beaten. So, they decided to up the pressure on the Samnite tribes. To do this, they needed mobility and quick transport for their armies. There were swamps and hills between Rome and Capua, and no good roads. There was one road, a winding, and twisty road, which went along the jagged coast from Rome's port of Ostia to Naples. It was too narrow, indirect, and vulnerable to ambush and attack. And there was another road that went inland and wiggled its way along the foothills of the inland mountains that overlooked the plain; this road had the same problems – It was vulnerable to attack. Neither road was ideal. The Romans decided they needed a straight road, going southeast, parallel to the Tyrrhenian coast, so they could quickly transport troops and supplies to the battlefield. That is why they built the Appian Way, to cover the 132 miles – or 212 kilometers – from Rome to Capua. It goes south, just past the Alban Hills, old volcanoes where the Pope has his summer residence in Castel Gandolfo, and, farther south, the road skirts the old swamps that lie along the seashore and have now been drained. They are known as the Pontine Marshes; they extend for about forty-five kilometers along the coast between the coastal towns of Anzio and Terracina. Now, these mountain tribes ..." I glanced up.

James was watching me closely, fire in his eyes.

I had been concentrating on reading and summarizing, and I hadn't noticed that the towel had totally slipped away, and now hung from the side of my chair. I was naked. "Oh," I said. I glanced around. No one, I thought, could see us here. I let the towel stay where it was.

"Continue, dear naked Professor." James took a bite out of his toast, "I am all ears."

"Your wish, Master, is my command." I rattled off more facts about the Samnite tribes and how the Romans fought three wars against them over fifty years – between 340 BCE and 290 BCE – and how the Romans finally beat them and obliterated them from history. Virtually nobody nowadays has heard of the Samnites. Then I told him, since I had read up on it, about how the Romans built their roads. "So, James, now listen carefully! The roads consisted of four layers, and these layers were up to five feet deep, and in one of the layers, the Romans used concrete, a Roman invention, made from mixing fine gravel with sand and lime and water, as a ..."

He stood up, came over, lifted me up, and kissed me. "My dear wonderful Princess, if we are going to see this Appian Way you know so much about, we'd better get going."

"How do you wish me to be attired, Master?"

"Walking shoes, socks, shorts, suntan oil, a broad-brimmed hat, and a T-shirt, something easy and light and cool. And a water bottle and some dark chocolate!"

"Yes, Master, indeed, Master, I shall so equip myself."

We left the flat and walked along the Tiber; we cut through the old Jewish ghetto, past the Synagogue, past the kosher restaurants; we took a shortcut over the Capitoline Hill, with its beautiful broad, gentle ascending stairs designed by Michelangelo and the magnificent statue of the warrior-philosopher, Emperor Marcus Aurelius, on horseback. We skirted the Roman Forum, going along the Avenue of the Imperial Forums, and past the gigantic pine-shaded ruins of the Baths of Caracalla, huge brick walls and arches soaring up, and we went out the Saint Sebastian Gate. Then, finally, we were on the Appia Antica. I felt I was bathing in history. Ghosts of centurions and slaves were marching all around us in the brilliant sunlight and gentle breeze.

"If necessary, Alcide will rescue us at the end of this," James said.

The sun blazed down.

We walked and walked.

The paving stones of the Appia Antica are enormous uneven bocks of black basalt.

We walked between thick hedgerows and ancient walls of powdery red brick.

We walked past shadowy umbrella pines and cypress trees.

We walked past ancient tombs.

We walked past open fields, with the wheat waving and shimmering in the breeze. The sun was brighter and hotter. I was lucky I had the broad-brimmed hat. An ancient aqueduct ran parallel to the road.

"It's like we are centurions of ancient Rome," I said.

"Or like slaves," he put his arm over my shoulder.

"Yes, like slaves, Master," I said.

"And perhaps I am taking you to market."

"To sell me to some stranger?"

"Yes." He looked sage, superior – a true cruel ancient Roman.

"Oh, Master, I do not want to be sold." I took off my hat and wiped my brow. "I want to remain with you. You are the best possible master in the whole wide world!" I tilted my chin upwards and kissed him.

He returned my kiss, and we kept walking, sometimes hand in hand, sometimes with a few feet separating us. The breeze was soft and, as the afternoon waned, the light turned to gold.

We were, it seemed, walking into the sun, into the purity of light, toward the distant mountains, toward the sky. The mountains drifted like blue shadows. The big flat and curved black stones of the ancient Roman road were hot and glowed under our feet.

The aqueduct stretched off across the fields, the fields were ripe, and the wheat was long and golden, leaning slightly, rustling, and glimmering in the sun. A light tingling breeze from the sea perhaps, or from the mountains, danced on our skin. Finally, we left the Appia Antica and cut across country, following a rutted farmer's lane, where tractors had left deep imprints in the dry dust and powdery mud. We came to a paved road where we found a rustic inn with a restaurant. It was too late for lunch, but the waiters were very friendly and let us sit outside on the terrace in the shade and drink white wine and eat a frittata.

≈

James had a piece of frittata speared on his fork; he looked over at me. "Alcide will come to pick us up. Or we can take the local bus into town, you decide."

"Let's do the bus." I was savoring the cool, dry wine, so exhilarating and perfect after such a long walk.

James called Alcide and told him not to bother coming, if that was not inconvenient. Alcide was absolutely fine with it. He said his wife had prepared a barbecue, and we were invited to join them if we got back to town in time.

We finished the frittata, had a salad, and drank another glass of the cool white wine. The inn's terrace was shaded with vines growing up and over a wooden trellis. We were not too far from the Alban Hills, and the Pope's summer residence at Castel Gandolfo.

"So, Professor," James captured with his fingertip a dribble of wine that was on my lips, "Tell me about the Alban Hills."

"Really?"

"Yes, I want another peek into that remarkably well-stocked mind of yours."

"Okay, dear Master, you asked for it!" And I told him what I had

picked up. In the three days I was alone – before James arrived
– I had decided to find out what I could about Rome and some
of the places around it. I knew Roman roads helped keep the
Roman Empire together – and it and the Roman Repubic lasted
maybe 600 to 800 years – so I'd looked into Roman roads, and
then I wondered about those hills that I could see on the horizon. Their peaked shape made them look like old volcanoes, so
that got me to researching about the Alban Hills, and the Pope's
summer residence, which is perched over Lake Albano, which is
a water-filled caldera, the collapsed remains of two ancient volcanic craters. So that got me to thinking about why there were
volcanoes here, close to Rome. It turns out that Italy sits on the
frontier between the Euro-Asian continental plate, and the African continental plate. The African continental plate is nudging
its way northwards, and bits and pieces at its ragged edge are
pushing in deep, sliding under the edge of the Euro-Asian continental plate, that is, under Italy. As these fragments plunge under
the Euro-Asian plate, they enter into the hotter strata, and so
they melt, creating liquid magma, which magma, being lighter
than the surrounding rock, rises upwards and fuels volcanoes;
and, separately, the buildup of friction and stress between the
two colliding plates causes earthquakes. It also pushes up the
crust of the earth and folds it over, creating mountains. So Italy
is rich in volcanoes and fold-up mountains – the Apennines and
the Alps – and earthquakes.

"Well, well," said James, primly wiping his mouth with his nap-
kin, "I have truly acquired an encyclopedia!"

"I am sorry, Master." I hung my head in mock shame.

He stood up, seized me around the waist, picked me up, and
kissed me. "Adorable, you are adorable."

I took a deep breath, and kissed him back, and I believe I was
blushing; but Kate has told me that my blushes never show; that

my skin always remains perfect vampire chalk-white, so perhaps I was not blushing. Maybe an invisible blush is not a blush. I must ask Kate; I am sure she could clarify this thorny question. Oh, I did miss her; I missed having a girlfriend, someone to whom I could confess everything, but, then, James – my Master – was almost like having a girlfriend. I felt I could tell him everything, well, almost everything.

As we stood there, kissing, in the cool shade of the inn's terrace, under the trellis and the vines, I wanted to tell James I loved him, but I remembered Allison's warning; I knew he was frightened of love, and so I bit my tongue and kissed him again, and took his hand and held it.

≈

The bus came, and we went back to Rome.

The next few days were calm. James worked at home but did go out for a few meetings in the city or just outside Rome in the EUR, which was to have housed the 1942 World's Fair, but which was canceled because of the war. EUR is now a sort of business and residential suburb of Rome. I worked at home, with my computer, or out at a café on Piazza Navona or in Campo de' Fiori, with my notebooks, and sometimes with my iPad.

We ate dinner at Alfredo's or at home – I cooked, and James was sous-chef. Sometimes we reversed the roles, James cooked, and I was sous-chef. James, I discovered, was an excellent and talented cook. He was one of those annoying people who do a great many things very well and who always look perfect, perfectly groomed, perfectly composed. I had fallen for a dream.

∞

One morning, James folded the paper, put it down, and said, "I think we should be serious, before we get playful."

"Oh, what does that mean?"

"Tonight we have a dinner."

"Oh?" I was lying in a deckchair with oversized sunglasses and shorts and a T-shirt and making notes on my iPad. I was reading a book about the relationship between the scientific revolution of the 17th, 18th, 19th, and 20th Centuries, and the changes in political theory over those same centuries. A bit of light relief from pure math! Funny, but I find the mind is calm after lovemaking, and in that calm, it is easy to fall asleep, but, if there is any energy left, it is also easy to think. James glanced down at the book. "May I?"

"Of course, Master, what's mine is yours," I looked up at him with what he called my ironic smirk. He weighed the book, and glanced at the title: Philosophies of Society and Science, from Plato and Aristotle to Milton Friedman and John Maynard Keynes.

"Hobbes," he said, "now what did Hobbes think of society?"

Clearly, this was exam time, and I was to perform. I rather liked performing for my Master. I cleared my throat, and assumed a pompous professorial voice. "Left to themselves, Thomas Hobbes thought humans would revert to savagery, a war of everybody against everybody, total civil war, and life would be nasty, brutish, and short ..."

"Of course, Hobbes had witnessed the English Civil War." James flipped a few pages.

"Yes, and he had seen – or was aware of – the recent religious wars in France and Germany ... Millions of dead ..."

"And what was Hobbes' answer to this threatening chaos and anarchy?"

"Yes, Master. Well, Hobbes thought one sovereign, one master, should rule over society. This sovereign should have absolute undivided power, and protect people from each other, and from those beyond the frontiers. The sovereignty should be absolute, not divided, as it could be, between, say, the Monarch and Parliament. If sovereignty was divided, it was not sovereignty."

"Ah, yes," said James. "I saw some graffiti on the Tiber's embankment: *Un Duce, un Popolo, una Volontà.*"

I sat up, sideways, on the edge of the deckchair. I raised my arms, and James knelt beside me and lifted off my T-shirt. "One Boss, One Will, One People," I translated. "*Volontà* doesn't translate easily into English," I said, thinking I really am excessively pedantic and professorial today! My mouth really does run out of control. What an asshole I am!

"You are right. It doesn't translate easily, my dear." His eyes twinkled. "Bluestocking," he whispered, his breath cool on my nipples. "I believe such creatures as you were once called bluestockings." He brushed my breasts with his lips, kissing the nipples, which were already quite perky, and eager to play.

"Oh, Master!" I stood up and wiggled out of my shorts.

James looked up at me. "So Hobbes had seen what happens when society breaks down – and he thought that was the natural state of society – chaos."

"Yes," I said.

"So the Hobbes was the opposite of Rousseau." James was still on his knees; he ran his hands up my belly to my breasts, and teased the nipples. His mouth was on my belly.

I shuddered in pleasure. "Yes," I gulped.

James hooked one finger under my panties, and tugged at them, slowly pulling them down until they were just above my knees.

"So, Rousseau ..." James looked up at me. "You were saying?"

"Yes, Rousseau," I licked my lips, and swallowed, "Man is born free, but everywhere he is in chains."

"So the state of nature – before society, before rules and laws, and without any sovereign – would be paradise, the garden of Eden, not the brutish, short, violent, homicidal hell portrayed by Hobbes."

"Yes," I breathed, "Hobbes and Rousseau were opposites on this particular point." I swallowed again and licked my lips. The panties, halfway down my legs, made me knock-kneed.

James stood up and kissed me. "How shall we dress tonight?"

"Dress?"

"Dress?" He ran his finger down the side of my face, earlobe, cheekbone, jawline, and then he tilted my face up to his.

I bit his lip, closing my teeth on his lip and pulling, just a bit. He smiled and murmured. "Hmm, a cruel wench!"

"Yes, Master, I am cruel." I stroked the side of his face; sometimes, I saw a sadness in his eyes, a sadness I yearned to cure.

"It's a rather formal event," he said.

"This is an occasion for my little black dress?"

"No, not the little black dress. That will be for later."

"Well, then, Master, what shall I wear?"

"I have arranged a fitting."

"A fitting?"

"Yes, I've chosen something for you. I think you'll like it."

≈

As James was busy the rest of the day with meetings, I was to head off to the fitting all by myself. I slipped into jeans and a T-shirt and sandals and, with my purse slung around my neck, I walked down to Campo de' Fiori and then up through Piazza Navona and then to Via Condotti and into the chic little side street where the dressmaker had her shop.

It was a high fashion place. I was early. The rooms were modern, minimalist, and luxurious. An elegant young woman served me coffee. I sat down and looked at catalogs; I flipped through *Vogue Italia*, and then I took out my notebook and began to scribble down some mathematical ideas.

Sex, I was beginning to discover, has for me an unexpected liberating side effect – suddenly ideas were flowing like a broad, easy river; maybe it's because sex exhausts the physique and it opens possibilities in the mind, like a long walk or a hot bath, both body and mind become fluid.

Of course, sex can be enslaving too, and addictive. Jealousy and anxiety and obsession – especially, addiction – are dangers! As well as sexually transmitted diseases, of course. Well, the world is full of ambushes! Nothing ventured, nothing gained, as my grandmother Claudia likes to say. I scribbled some ideas on the complexity of models built on probabilistic theories concerning future events.

A young woman came up to me. "Gwendoline? Gwendoline Clermont?"

"Yes, that's me." I stood up, and the young woman, who said her name was Adrianna, led me into a fitting room.

I expected something daring, maybe even indecent, a sort of trial run for the "creature" I was to become. I was in for a surprise. The dress was formal but not too formal – it had a period feel, classic 1950s fashion. The black bodice was tight, slinky black velvet, with a plunging off-the-shoulder V neckline, and with a tight, almost wasp waist. The skirt was mid-calf, a full flaring skirt of white chiffon tulle.

I put it on.

The instant I caught a glimpse of myself in the mirror, I understood what James had done.

"Wow!" I wanted to twirl round and round.

Adrianna was stroking her chin, examining the effect. "It looks like it was designed just for you. Let's try the belt."

The belt was wide, black patent leather, and the high-heeled shoes were also black patent leather.

"Here, put on these white pearls."

The ensemble was complete.

I phoned James. Without saying hello, I said, "Grace Kelly in *Rear Window*, adapted to today."

"Yes, the Edith Head creation."

"You ... How did you?"

"I saw it on your wall – the poster."

"Oh, of course."

"You were sleeping. I stayed until Harold – Professor Lehman – assured me you would be fine and until Rose – the nurse – was set up and organized and told me she could handle the situation."

"Oh, boy, yes. You are my knight in shining armor!"

"See you later, Princess."

"Yes, Master, till later."

Adrianna said that I was ideal; that the ensemble was a perfect fit. "The black bodice against your chalk-white skin, and your jet-black hair, it will be absolutely divine. The tulle dress, shorter than in the original Grace Kelly model, will be a perfect foil for your complexion. You have wonderful legs, Signorina Gwendoline."

"Thank you, Adrianna," I said.

They would deliver it, Adrianna told me.

And so they did.

≈

Back in the flat, I showered, dried myself by walking around the apartment, and out onto the terrace, naked, flapping my arms like an overweight bird trying to take off.

Then I dressed, carefully, in my own separate bedroom, which I rarely visited except, occasionally, for an afternoon nap.

"G-string panties over the garter belt," I had been instructed. "Yes, of course, Master, so be it," I had said.

≈

James knocked, and, when I invited him in, he entered my room, stopped, and stared. "Astounding!" he said. He was wearing a tuxedo and looked like my very own James Bond.

"You like it?" I curtsied.

"You and that dress are made for each other." He seized my waist, twirled me around, lifted me up, and kissed me.

"So, Master, where are we going?"

"It's a surprise."

≈

So it was that, dressed in splendor, we walked through the narrow cobblestoned streets, creating our own tiny little ephemeral sensation. Romans in the old "historic center" are not shy about commenting on people's looks, or clothes, or attitudes. I felt like James and I were making a royal procession, in miniature of course. Smiles lit up and voices rang out. Che bella! What a beautiful dress! What a beautiful couple! Ciaò bella! Ciaò bellissima!

Then we were there, on Piazza Farnese. All the windows of Palazzo Farnese, the French Embassy, which fills one whole side of the piazza with its enormous façade, were lit up, and though the piazza is normally a pedestrian area, limousines and taxis were delivering their cargo of Very Important People right to the door.

"The French Embassy?"

"Yes."

"Who's it for?"

"The Nobel Prize winner, the chemist Georges Cuvier."

"Ah! His work is very interesting."

≈

When he presented our invitations at the large gate, James was immediately recognized. "Bonsoir, Monsieur James," the guard saluted, "Bonsoir, Mademoiselle."

We went up the long gradual staircase. They had designed the staircase, a gentleman told me, like the staircase in our very own palazzo, so that horses could gallop or trot up to the second and third floors. I wondered about the horse flapdoodles or little knotty piles of steaming dung. Maybe they trained the horses to be polite and not to shit inside, but I imagined not. Servants probably had to rush along behind the horses, and sweep up all the dung, and cart it off to fertilize the palazzo's gardens.

"Yes, that's probably what happened with the horse dung," said James, who had caught the drift of my musings. He did seem to be able to read my mind.

On the ceilings, which soared above us, there were paintings and frescoes. We came to a huge reception hall where we stood around, with hundreds of other people, and drank champagne. Above us, the chandeliers sparkled. It was for me all a blur of long gowns, tuxedos, and cupids cavorting on high ceilings, with the story of Hercules on one ceiling, and a vast splash of ceiling and wall panels, the Love of the Gods, in another huge room. Then we were standing among milling people, all looking rich and glamorous, and holding slender glasses of champagne. James left me alone for a moment as he went over to talk to someone with whom he had some urgent business dealings. I sagely sipped my champagne and hoped that nobody would talk to me. I am a total disaster in terms of small talk. I never know what to say, and so I always say idiotic things. I am sure that insincerity oozes out of my pores. I tried to look serious and self-absorbed, to discourage any approaches. But –

"Hello, my dear," a woman whispered like a conspirator, into my ear.

I turned around to face her. She looked like a model, with sharp ice-blue eyes, tanned golden skin, full lips, and wonderful cheekbones; her hair was platinum; her dress was a clinging sequined silver affair that revealed a lean, athletic, but voluptuous figure. I took her age to be forty-something.

"Oh, hello," I said. I reached out my hand.

She took it and held it, and she said, "You and James Hewitt Spencer make a beautiful couple."

"Thank you."

"So you are spring, and he is autumn."

"Is it so obvious?" I gave her my best fiercest smile.

"I love the 1950s retro fashion look," she said. "So, my dear, who are you?" She had a very precise, clipped way of speaking; her accent sounded German.

"Gwendoline Clermont. And, you, who are you?"

"Cylla von Guttenberg," she said, letting go of my hand. "You must be all of 16 years old."

I took a careful sip of champagne, and adopted my best mid-Atlantic sophisticate's pseudo-British accent. "A bit older, actually."

"And you have captured the most handsome man in the room – James Hewitt Spencer is famous and –"

"Well ..." I shrugged. I had no idea where this was going. I was wondering if James would come back and rescue me.

"Or did he capture you?"

"It was mutual, I believe, mutual capture," I said, evenly, narrowing my eyes, staring with my dark, dark eyes into her beautiful, ice-blue Nordic eyes. "Let me think about it."

"Mutual, ah, ah, and dramatic, I suppose." She took a sly sip of champagne, and smiled. She did have a glorious smile.

"Yes, rather dramatic, actually." I caught a flash image of me, naked, throwing up, thrashing about, covered in shit.

"I see. And what are you, Gwendoline Clermont, other than young and beautiful?"

"A mathematician."

She recoiled as if stung. "My God! Beauty and brains! They used to punish us for that! All of the patriarchs utterly abhor brainy women, particularly if the woman dares display her brains."

"Finishing my PhD."

"I see. So, did James Hewitt Spencer fish you out of some dim, dank library or some dusty hall, where, covered in a thick cloud of chalk dust, you were scribbling an endless equation on a black-board to awe-struck students – and wave his magic wand and turn you into a princess."

I laughed. "Yes. He gave me a glass slipper. But at midnight, we both turn into pumpkins." I gave her the look. "And what are you, other than beautiful?"

"Touché, my dear. You are too kind." She gave me a warm smile, and took my arm as if we were the oldest of friends. "I write novels – in German – and I write for a German newspaper, *Die Zeit*."

"Ah," I said.

"Well, I think you and James have been lucky to capture each other, I must say. Many, many years ago, I once set my sights on Mr. Hewitt Spencer, but he didn't succumb to my icy Teutonic charm."

"Oh." I raised an eyebrow.

"Don't worry. I've recovered. Do you know Cardinal Milano? Let me present you to him."

She took me over to meet the Cardinal, and the three of us talked about the weather and then about the frescoes on the ceilings. I discovered I rather liked Cylla von Guttenberg – she teased the Cardinal, and he accepted her teasing. Then someone called her away and there I was, alone, just for a moment, with the Cardinal. She had told him I was a mathematician, and he said that I should probably meet some of the mathematicians working in Rome, there were several Jesuits, he said, who were doing very advanced work. He nodded toward Cylla and said, "She is quite a lively woman, I must say, a very critical mind, and, you know, she is a quite likely nomination for the Nobel Prize in Literature."

"Really," I said.

"It has been most pleasant meeting, Ms. Clermont, do talk to some of those Jesuits I mentioned," he said, as he was hustled away by his assistants who told him there were other people he must speak to before the dinner began.

I talked to a few more people, one of whom was a very interesting chemist, and to my great surprise, I found I was having a good time. Maybe it was the champagne, maybe it was the dress, in any case, James returned, and I was delighted – and relieved – not to be navigating the jungle on my own.

≈

We were ushered into a dining room, and there, again under soaring ceilings with cupids and cavorting whatnots, beautiful food was laid out and served beautifully. In the seating plan, James and I found ourselves once again separated.

"Oh, horror, oh, the horror," I whispered. He squeezed my hand and puckered his lips slightly, miming the kiss that would be my reward – our reward – once the ordeal was over.

It may be that touch of dyslexia – one of my dark little secrets – but I have always found it difficult to sort out which knife and fork and spoon are used for what. To compound matters, I had been made to understand that the exact order of knives and forks and spoons differs from country to country, so I cast sneaky glances at my neighbors to see what they were doing.

One of the guests sitting opposite me was a famous blond French actress who was in her 70s at least. She saw what I was doing and carefully held up one little fork and wiggled it and winked, so I was relieved and made a little bow of my head signaling my thanks.

Then the conversation began and, again, surprisingly, it was very interesting: I found myself sitting next to a writer and a filmmaker. The writer was finishing a book on the Mafia. He explained the differences between the Sicilian Mafia or Cosa Nostra, and the Calabrian Mafia – which has an impossible name, 'Ndrangheta, which is possibly Greek in origin – and the difference between those two and the Mafia in and around Naples, which is known as the Camorra.

The actress asked me what I did, and I told her I was a mathematician. "Oh, you are destroying all my stereotypes regarding mathematicians," she said. "It is terrible to have one's certainties overturned at my age!"

There were some speeches, and I discovered that one of the people I had been talking to during the cocktail before the dinner was the man being honored, the chemist Georges Cuvier. When he was giving his speech, he looked around the room, and he caught my eye and smiled and nodded, for just a second.

When I was talking to him, I had no idea who he was. He had seemed very nice, and I think I avoided making a fool of myself, because I had said something about how interesting Cuvier's work was, not knowing I was talking to the man himself, and how he'd applied some very sophisticated mathematics from what I could tell. "Oh, and in what way were they sophisticated?" he asked, with a twinkle in his eye.

I gave him my quick summary of what I thought was unique, from the mathematical point of view, about the work of George Cuvier. I quickly added, "I'm not a chemist, of course, and I've only read about his work. I've never met him or studied with him."

"Maybe one day you will," he said, "And in fact, I hope you do." Then somebody tapped him on the shoulder, and he was taken away to meet other people, but not before he said, "Au revoir, Mademoiselle. I hope we meet again."

"Moi aussi," I said, and gave him a little wave, rather gauchely I must admit.

≈

"You have made several conquests, I see," said James after the ceremonies and as we descended the grand staircase.

"You too. I noticed you flirting with that Italian actress."

"Ah, is my princess jealous?"

"She might be. I spoke to Cylla von Guttenberg."

"Ah, Cylla. She didn't bite, I hope."

"No, she just nipped and growled a bit. Then she turned all puppyish and licked my hand and introduced me to a Cardinal. She said you were the most handsome man in the room. She has a very good eye."

"Ah, Cylla. She was wild, a true revolutionary. Now she is famous, and a pillar of the establishment. Time flies, does it not?"

"Indeed it does, Master." I took his hand – we were now outside on the piazza just in front of the embassy – and I kissed him. He kissed me back, and it was a nice ferocious kiss, which lasted much longer than perhaps decorum on the doorstep of an embassy and with a crowd in attendance would decree. Cars were picking up VIPs; other elegant couples just seemed to be drifting off into the night.

We walked, hand in hand, back toward home. Already, after

only a few days and nights, it had become, in my mind, "home." We human beings are vagabonds, and all our roots are fragile. We pick up our rags, our few belongings, then we move on, and yet we desperately try to give to our brief encampments all the attributes of permanence, of eternity, as if we were going to live forever, just as we are.

It was a sultry overcast night. Thunder rumbled in the distance, and in the air, there was a hint of rain. I felt, in the Grace Kelly dress, like a princess in a fairy-tale, and James was my attentive and gallant prince. We stopped from time to time to admire little details, shop windows, ancient bits of stone, or strange patterns made by the old plaster or stucco on burnt sienna and ochre walls, or the effect of the lamplight on the humid cobblestones. A man came down the street, whistling a tune. It was from Verdi, I think – *La donna è mobile*. He was brilliant. He had the tempo, little pauses, trills, and the whole works, as if we were at the opera! We stopped and listened. He smiled and nodded as he passed, without interrupting his performance.

Finally, we were "home."

We went through the big gate, past the porter's lodge, and we began to walk up the broad, dark, and shadowy stairs. James kissed me and the kiss didn't stop, not for a second, as we climbed the stairs, James was still kissing me and holding me, and it was as if we were waltzing, turning around and around, waltzing, and I could almost hear the music, it was enchanting, and I thought, I'm drunk, I must be drunk.

"There, my darling," he said. We were suddenly inside the apartment. James took my hand and led me toward the living room that looked out on our terrace. A bottle of Cognac stood on the table.

"I shall help you disrobe, Mademoiselle," he said. He was very adept at it, at undressing me, and the beautiful Grace Kelly ensemble was soon stored happily and carefully away in the wardrobe. I was naked, except, since he had insisted on it, for the stockings, garter belt, and high heels. He was still in a tuxedo. This, I thought, was very neat. I was free; he was still imprisoned.

"Will you serve?" He held the bottle of Cognac out to me.

"Yes, Master," I bowing and took the bottle.

He smiled, put his finger under my chin, tilted my face up, and kissed me. It was a quick, ferocious, hungry kiss. I almost dropped the bottle. He drew back, and grinned.

"You are unbearably beautiful." He cast off his jacket and began unbuttoning his shirt.

I filled the two glasses, classic brandy glasses, sniffers I think they call them, which seemed to me to be pretentious and silly; I was about to laugh.

His chest was beautiful. He seemed to glow in the dim lights we had left on. Holding out the glass, like an offering, I approached him.

He had already taken off his shoes and socks, and now he tossed his shirt to the white leather divan. He took the offered glass and said, "Will you open my belt, please, my darling?"

"Yes, Master," I put my glass carefully on the side table.

"Are you my slave?"

"Of course, Master, absolutely – I am indeed your slave." I knelt in front of him, and unbuckled and opened the belt. Blood was throbbing in my temple. I could hear my heart and my pulse, going bump, bump, bump. I slid his pants down his legs carefully. He stepped out of them.

"Now I shall hang them up, Master," I said.

"Yes," he followed me as I went to the wardrobe. His hand was on my back, and he slid it slowly down my back as I placed the trousers, carefully, and straightened them, preserving the crease, on the hanger. Next to his tuxedo was the glorious Grace Kelly dress. The mirror on the back of the door swung back, giving me a glimpse of my body and his body: I – vulnerable and pale chalk-white, like a cool marble statue, and he – tanned dark, curly black hair on his chest. "Oh my God, you are beautiful," I said.

"Say, Master," he said. He was smiling.

I smiled back. "Yes, Master," I said. "Oh, my God, you are beautiful, Master."

He raised his glass. Our glasses clicked. We drank.

The room flashed blue.

Lightning.

"Ah," he said. "I think the storm has come."

"Yes, Master," I said, "I believe the storm has come." I was now becoming that nymph-like spirit Echo, mentally imprisoned, passively, repeating my master's words.

Again, the room flashed blue.

Suddenly, in a rush, rain slashed against the plate glass door that led to the terrace.

"Barefoot," he said.

"Yes, Master," I said. I stepped out of the high heels.

"Put them in their place."

"Yes, Master." I placed the shoes in their special place in the main wardrobe, kneeling to do so. He was close to me now, barefoot and naked, except for shorts.

When I stood up, he knelt in front of me. He began to unclip the garter belt. "My goddess," he said, "my little goddess."

I caressed his hair, stroking his temples, touching the distinguished flecks of gray. He opened the garter belt and freed the stockings, slowly unpeeling them, caressing my thighs, and then the back of my thighs, down past the knees, touching the little cup between the tendons at the back of my knee. He put the stockings and the garter belt aside, laying them carefully on the white divan.

He stood up and brought the thick leather collar out of its hiding place in the sideboard. He held it up, smiled, and closed it carefully around my neck, locking it in place. I bowed my head in obeisance. "Master," I whispered. I felt a subtle thrill as if he were branding me: I was marked; I was his.

I was naked except for the leather collar.

"These must go," I said, hooking my fingers under his underpants.

"Yes, Princess."

I slid them down his legs.

"Oh, Princess!" He knelt and buried himself in me. He kissed and caressed, and opened me with his tongue, slowly, slowly, delicately, and slowly, oh, so slowly, caressed and kissed and licked, and Oh, God, I put my fingers in his hair, tightening them, and I held on, and I trembled. I whispered, Oh, God, breathless, and Oh, God, and Oh, God!

I shuddered and cried out. My fingers tightened, locking around him. I leaned back. I shuttered, and again, and again!

Then he was standing, his lips on my mouth, and his fingers inside me. As we kissed, he danced me around, around, and around.

I hung limp in his arms, letting him carry me where he would, penetrate me how he would, take me whichever way he would. My heart was beating like crazy. With a movement of one hand, he slid the glass doors open.

Suddenly we were outside, on the terrace, in the dark, under the rain, twirling around in a sort of waltz, turning and turning and turning. I closed my eyes. The rain was warm. It washed over us. Then we were standing still, both naked, glistening with rain, sheltered under the awning, our hearts beating in unison, with the deluge thundering down around us. He kissed me. "Wait here." He disappeared inside the flat and came back out with the two brandy sniffers.

"How are you, my goddess?"

"I am well, indeed well, Master," I said. I was soaking wet and trembling. I took the glass.

He put his arm around me. We left the shelter of the awning. We went to the balustrade and looked out over the city. The rain thundered down. We both drank. My heart was still beating like crazy. I was dripping wet, not only from the rain.

"Well, my slave boy, what do we do now?" he said. With the one word "boy" and adopting the imperious master-servant tone, my Master unsexed me, transformed me into his catamite. I had been repurposed, no longer female but now male: I was his page-boy slave, and he was my master, and we were no longer in 21st Century Rome, but he had transported us to ancient Rome, the Rome of the Caesars.

"We do what you will, Master." I bowed, as a boy would bow.

He put his finger in the ring of the collar and tilted my face upwards. He pulled me close. As my breasts brushed against his chest, he kissed me.

"Come," he said, the rain pounding on his face, bouncing off his shoulders. We were utterly soaked. I wondered if anyone could see us. He led me to the far end of the terrace, and there was the silk-smooth, waterproof deckchair mattress, laid out on a stone bench just under the terrace balustrade.

"Hands and knees," he said.

"Hands and knees?" I looked at him. He nodded.

I took a deep sip of brandy, handed the glass to him, and I got down on the mattress on my hands and knees, and waited. The rain splashed down, bouncing, reflecting on the mattress.

"Stay there, just like that," he said.

"Are you sure, Master?" I felt exposed, as if on display.

"Yes." He ran his hand along my flank, and curved under and touched my nipple and squeezed it, very gently.

Then he was gone.

I looked around. Was anyone looking? Could anyone see me? In a way, if there had been a witness, I would, perhaps have been pleased. The shame and the shamelessness of it mingled with a weird sense of freedom, of casting off convention. The situation was theatrical, or perhaps sculptural. This, I thought, is a new role: All the world's a stage, and all the men and women are players ...

There were two flashes. Photographs! He had taken photographs of me naked, on my hands and knees, in the rain, for just a second I was furious, I flushed, but I didn't move; I kept my pose. He put away the camera and knelt beside me.

"Now you truly own me, Master," I said, thinking that some primitive tribes – who perhaps see deeper than we do – believe that once your picture is taken, your soul has been possessed and enslaved.

He didn't answer. He stroked my hair, which, like the rest of me, was soaked. The downpour pummeled both of us. He stared into my eyes. His smile seemed to be a sad smile. It made me want to reach out and comfort him, but the implicit rules would not allow me to reach out, so I looked sideways and said something bold, something I should perhaps never have said. I said, "I love you."

He smiled, a happier smile now, and kissed me through streams of water. The rain was a torrent.

He came behind me; his body curved over me; he reached under me; he caressed my nipples, my belly, and my shoulders. His hands and lips, like the rain, seemed to be everywhere at once. My body was one tingling singing ringing surface of sensation; his hands touched me, and his fingers opened me, wider and wider, and then he entered me. "Oh!" I shuddered. I gripped the mattress; water splashed all around us; my eyes went blurry, my eyelashes dripped water; I licked my lips; the mattress faded to a dim white shape; then, lightning struck, somewhere, an enormous blue flash. I hardly noticed.

"Oh, oh, Master," I whispered. In the tumult, I don't know if he heard me, and I didn't care. I was in such a place of pleasure that I didn't know who I was, or who he was, or who we were, or where we were, or – even – what we were doing. He was so strong and so gentle, so slow, so fast, then slower, then rapid. I was on the very edge of orgasm; then he led me away, just a touch, back into a sort of suspended painful bliss that was pure exquisite torture, then, again, he took me to the edge, and again, and again.

"Beast," I cried.

"Animal," he whispered.

"Lion," I shouted.

"Tigress," he bit me on the ear and whispered, "You are an animal, my animal, a brilliant animal on all fours. Growl!"

I growled.

"Again!"

I growled.

He entered deeper now, harder now, hard and harder, and Oh, I thought, Oh, I am going to burst! I am going to be split wide open. His fingers explored everywhere; his chest, the hairs slick and thick and dripping wet, pressed against my back.

I came. "Oh, oh, oh, oh!"

I came. Again, I echoed, "Oh, oh, oh, oh!"

The rain roared. The thunder echoed. Brilliant flashes of lightning lit up the terrace, and they seemed to merge into one long continuous flickering blaze of bluish-white fire.

"Oh, oh, oh." I was shuddering.

I had ceased to exist.

I was a beast, a lion, a tiger, an animal; I was ...

Then – I don't know how it happened – I was astride him,

looking down. He was lying on his back, looking up at me. I bent down, my breasts brushing his chest, the rain pouring all over us; he was still inside me, as hard as a rock; we swayed locked together like this in the thunder and the rain; I wondered if other people knew such pleasure, such annihilation, the way we knew it, the way I knew it. This was a silly thought. Of course! People had known such pleasure since the beginning of time, since before humans were humans, since before there were human words to speak human thoughts.

Prolonging the pleasure was something James did very well.

I rode him, and rode him, and then, again, a wave of pleasure overwhelmed me, and I felt him come too, together, with me, finally – Oh, finally!

At last, we ceased, and we lay together, facing each other, our arms wrapped around each other, with the warm rain thundering down on us.

Then, we wandered inside; we showered together, and we crawled into bed, lay in each other's arms, and fell asleep.

≈

Two days later.

James was out all day – meeting with some Italian pharmaceutical company. I stayed at home working. It was geeky, wonky work. I was trying to develop a series of formulas to compensate for the weaknesses of some predictive models in criminology, traffic control, and epidemics, to sort out meaningless "static" from real relevant information. I had developed a little Artificial Intelligence app that could fill in gaps in information and predict what might next be relevant, where we, the AI and I, should go looking.

The humidity had built up. Dark clouds were piling up in the sky. I made myself a sandwich for lunch. Then I went down to have an espresso at the corner bar. I needed to get out and see other people. In the narrow street, the sky seemed even darker, more menacing.

"Signorina," the barmen knew me; I was a regular.

"Ciaò, Pino," I stood at the bar, munching on a chocolate biscotto.

"How is work going?"

"Good, slow, but good." I went outside and sat down at one of the little tables on the sidewalk and watched the people go by. Suddenly it began to rain – a semi-tropical deluge. Within seconds, my T-shirt and shorts were soaked. I sheltered under the café awning with a couple of other customers and passers-by.

I decided to walk home through the rain. It was so warm! It was like being in an African shower or waterfall. I tilted my face up to greet and celebrate it. I let it pour over me. It was ecstasy!

I wished James were with me. I could see us, running, kissing, making love, under the downpour. I walked along, quite happy, and lost in my reveries. By now, my T-shirt and shorts were transparent. My scarlet flip-flops made a squishy sound. The rain pounded on the cobblestones. Lightning flashed at the end of the street. A Vespa putt-putted by and the rider shouted,

"Brava, Signorina!"

"Grazie!" I called out.

As he sped away, the water bounced off his shoulders.

I was deliriously happy.

I got to our building absolutely soaked. "Ah, Signorina Gwendoline, you are a sight." Maria was standing just sheltered in the large shadowy gateway, right at the edge of the flood, with a few dark splashes on her dress. She shook her head at my naughty insouciance. What a little girl this little girl is, I could see her thinking. "Come in," she said, "I will get a towel, or I shall bring the towel here? I think you like it, the rain."

"Yes, I do. I do like it," I said, but she had already disappeared.

I stood just beyond the rain. Then I stepped back out into the downpour, hugged myself with glee, and then stepped back into the shelter. "Oh, you are a child, Signorina Gwendoline, a real child!" Maria began toweling my head.

"I do like it," I admitted.

"Ah, just a child you are!"

I thanked her and had another espresso – which she offered me, and we drank standing watching the silver rain pour down, a Niagara, just a few feet away from us. The cobblestones were overwhelmed, flooded, overflowing with glittering water. The air was a glossy perfumed silver-gray.

"Well, I must do some chores."

"Me too," I said. I kissed her and thanked her. My extravagant kiss surprised Maria, but she seemed very pleased and gave me her biggest smile.

With my scarlet flip-flops making a delightful squish-squish, I walked up the monumental staircase.

I took off my clothes, which were soaked, entirely soaked, and put them in the washer. Then I walked out onto the terrace, sat down naked on a garden chair, and let the rain just rain itself all over me.

James called to say he would be a bit late. He asked if we could eat at home.

"Yes," I said.

I felt lazy, so I ordered a meal from Alfredo's.

They would deliver it at nine o'clock, or if I wished, I could come by and pick it up. I said, "I'll come by."

James came back, and I said, "I'm going out to pick up the food at Alfredo's. Do you want to come?"

"Hmm," he said. "If you are going there, why don't we eat there?"

"Great!" I was in jeans now, and a blouse, a wide leather belt, and high-heeled pumps. He was in jeans and an open shirt.

I phoned and warned Alfredo.

"No problem, Signorina Gwen," he said.

The rain had ended; it was now a dry, crisp, warm evening – the air cleansed and fresh from the beating it had taken.

We ate on the terrace at Alfredo's, and James told me about his day and described some of his meetings. His descriptions were hilarious; he could mimic accents and personalities, and he had a wonderful sense of the ridiculous. But there was a serious theme too. He had discovered that some of the companies he was interested in had some uncomfortable silent – or invisible – partners: these were Mafia connections, and they were, apparently, various forms of Mafia, not just Sicilian or Italian.

We got home. It was already late. The night was deliciously warm, perfumed, and dry. "We might go out to have a drink," said James.

"Oh, yes, that would be nice," said I, thinking of a pleasant drink on a café terrace, watching the passers-by.

"You might change."

"Oh. I see. Are we doing something interesting?"

"Yes, perhaps." He opened a package that had been leaning against the wall, and that had already piqued my curiosity.

"Try this on."

"What is it?"

He held it up.

"Oh," I said. "Oh."

It was a shiny black latex catsuit – no holes for hands or feet, more or less a total thing.

"Okay. Hmm…" The suit was shimmering, perfectly black, with a high gloss and sheen, and very, very thin.

"Maybe a bit of heavy Goth makeup would go with this," I said. I could see myself, lush streaks of mascara over my eyes, purple-black lips, maybe a nose ring – a false nose ring if I could improvise one – maybe a few tattoos, yes, I could be the tattooed lady in the circus. How interesting.

"No. You won't need makeup. There is also, dear Gwendoline, a hood and mask."

"Hmm ... I don't know about a mask. How do I put this on?"

"The instructions are right here." James handed me a little booklet.

I read. So I had to turn the catsuit inside out and sprinkle the whole inside with talcum powder, and, of course, it was better if I wore nothing underneath, which was what I would do. This looked like fun, but also like hard work – and where could I go in this thing? I'd probably be arrested.

I turned the catsuit inside out and laid it out on top of a big towel, out on the terrace. I could hear music from Piazza Farnese. They were putting on an outdoor concert. It was getting late, so they were probably winding down.

"It has no holes for feet or hands."

"No, it has fingers – see. And feet."

"Ah, yes, I see – total enclosure."

"Yes."

I got down on hands and knees and spread talcum powder all over inside of the suit. I turned it over, and sprinkled and smoothed talcum powder on the other side. "Hmm, looks ready."

"Maybe this will make it even smoother."

"What's that?"

"A sort of spray talcum powder."

"Oh, oh."

"Turn around."

I turned around, and he sprayed the stuff all over my body.

"Now, my hands are all slushy powdery."

"Don't worry. I'll clean and polish the suit once you are in it."

I began to pull on one leg. I had to make sure it went on, that it was tight over my right foot. "This is tricky."

"It's got to be smooth." He stood back, rubbing his chin.

"I know, I know."

"If you put this on, you won't be able to pee."

"Right, so I'll pee now." I disengaged my foot from its latex prison, went off to the bathroom, and peed. Luckily, at Alfredo's I hadn't drunk or eaten very much. I looked at myself in the mirror. No belly bulge, just the right amount of roundness. The silvery sheen of the full-body baby powder treatment made my skin sparkle.

I walked back onto the terrace.

James insisted on more powder spray. While he covered me in sparkling foam, I turned around and around, spinning like a top. "This is sadism," I grunted.

"Yes, it is."

"You're having fun; you're like a little boy smearing his mother's lipstick all over her face."

"Yes, exactly. I once did that."

"You did?"

"I made her look like a clown."

"So, your sadism started early."

"Yes, it did, trouble from the womb onwards."

"Well, ambivalence takes many forms, I guess. Love and hate, desire and fear, parody, and self-parody."

"You really are a dangerous girl." He sprayed more of the silky-slimy stuff. Soon I could swim in it.

"Thank you, James. I believe that, coming from you, it is a compliment – being considered dangerous."

"It is." He grinned. "And I put toothpaste in her hair, almost a whole tube, while she was getting ready to go out. I was standing on the makeup bench, next to her. She didn't notice."

"Until it was too late." I blinked at him with my trademark mutinous look.

"Yes, until it was too late."

He kept spraying the stuff, and the air filled with a fine mist of it. Finally, he stopped.

I looked down. My perfect coal-black pubic patch, my proud Bermuda Triangle, was now a wedge of frosted wedding cake, and my whole body looked like marzipan.

"You look good enough to eat," he said.

"Yeah, definitely." I tilted down my head and again gave him the mulish look.

"Okay, now the tricky part." He held out the suit.

I took hold of it and balanced on one foot, and tried to pull it over the other foot. "Boy, this thing is tight. I need help."

"Here," he said, "sit down. I'll do it."

I sat on the very edge of a metal garden chair, over by the terrace balustrade. The night air was cool against my powdered skin. "It makes a crinkly sound." I licked my lips. "Like cellophane."

"Crinklier, snappier, than cellophane."

"Like a rubber band, maybe."

"Yes."

Mummified in rubber – well, as they say, there is no accounting for taste. I took a deep breath. This was exciting. The latex snapped and crinkled. Boy, was it tight! Inside, with all that spray-on baby powder, it was slinky and oily.

I helped him by pulling as hard as I could. "The thing is you've got to roll it up, and then unroll it, I think." I concentrated.

He was on his knees and had one of my feet snuggly inserted, and he was pulling that leg tight and smoothing it, which was nice as he caressed and smoothed it. Then we got the other foot inserted, and the other leg snapped into place.

"Whew!" I stood up.

Then, somehow, both legs and most of my torso were inside the thing. It felt slimy and smooth, like an all-over total mud massage. James pulled it up over my breasts. Under the latex, I was awash in liquid powder. It was like swimming in painted-on cold cream. I felt all slinky all over! "Oh!"

"You like it?"

"Yes, but this stuff is hard work." Getting the hands and arms in was almost as tricky as pulling on the legs. "I think the zipper's in the back," I said, reaching around to try to get at it.

"I'll do it." He zipped it up, right up to my neck. Now, the catsuit enclosed everything below my neck. It went high up my neck, almost to my chin.

"How does it feel?" He stood back, like an artist contemplating his work, which I guess he was. This image was his creation.

I went up on tiptoes. I walked around. It was so thin, the latex, like a second skin, that it was like walking in bare feet.

"What does it feel like? It feels smooth." I pirouetted. "The talcum powder makes it feel, hmm, like I'm slathered in butter or olive oil."

I turned around several times, walked to the edge of the terrace, and looked out at the night. It was weird, naked, and not yet naked; I was revving up. I wanted to jump on my Master, and jump into bed, or make love here on the terrace, but with my body encased in this sheen of latex, I couldn't do anything. "It's really late," I said.

"Yes." He ran his hands down my body. Each pore, each nerve responded to his fingertips. Yes, it was truly as if I were wearing nothing. I kissed him, and we exchanged a nice lazy long friendly kiss. Arousal was rising like a night tide, a warm inner flood. There was a slight breeze, that famous breeze from the sea, but crisper, drier. I wanted to see myself in a mirror. I was curious – what did I look like in this thing.

"We have to finish you up."

"Finish me up? Sounds like killing me off?"

"Not killing you, changing your self-definition."

"Sounds like brainwashing."

"Oh, you might like it."

"Let's see," I bit my lip. "Let's see if I like it." I was in a riptide of desire. I wanted action, and I wanted it now, but I decided I must play my role – and see what happened next.

He opened a box and pulled out the equipment – a hood, a collar, stiletto shoes, and a leash.

"Okay, Master, what do we do with all these toys?"

"The hood, plus scarlet lips, I think, Gwendoline, will be ideal."

"Oh, are you ordering me, Master, to wear the hood?"

"Yes, I am ordering you, Princess, to wear the hood."

"Hmm," I bowed, and he handed me the hood. Pulling on the hood I discovered was complicated. I folded it up, and then I pulled it over my face, then I stretched it over my head. It pushed my hair down tight. I reached behind, groped for the invisible zipper, and zippered it shut, and it snapped tight, into place, like a second skin. Only my mouth was free. I could breathe, but I had no nose. I could see, but I had no eyes. My nostrils had little invisible holes for breathing, and my eyes seem to have holes, invisible holes: they must have consisted of some kind of one-way material, for seeing. My eyes could see out, but nobody could see in. It was as if I had no eyes.

"Now, the shoes." He held up some adorable fetishist black patent leather stilettoes with overlapping black straps and little locks at the back.

He knelt. I looked down, caressed his hair with my latex fingers, and inserted one latex foot into one of the shoes, and then the other into the other shoe, and James locked me into both. These were true needle-like stilettos, designed to sculpt and cantilever a girl's posture into a strutting parody of sexuality. James had turned me into an Allen Jones lithograph.

"Now, the collar."

"Oh, yes, of course, Master, the collar. And I suppose it comes equipped with that cute little leash you've been dangling and swinging in your hand."

"Why, yes, indeed, so it does." He mimed surprise, grinned, closed the collar around my neck, snapped it shut, and locked it.

"It's tight," I swallowed.

"Yes."

"And it's high."

"Right – chin up!"

"Yes," I mimed a sigh. "Chin up!" In fact, I couldn't have lowered my chin if I wanted to. I did begin to feel like a prancing pony.

"Now, lipstick," he said, offering me a lipstick tube.

"Scarlet?" It was so bright it glowed.

"Yes, and non-smear."

"You really are an expert." I turned toward him, intending to flash an ironic glance, but I couldn't use my eyes. My eyes were invisible. My challenging, powerful, reifying, masterful, objectifying female feminist gaze had been neutered, veiled, and utterly extinguished.

"Ah, darling!" He held me and kissed me.

He led me into the bathroom. I stared at myself in the mirror. My face was a black featureless satin-like oval, no hair, no eyes, no ears, no nose, just a suggestion of nostrils, only a mouth. The one-way eye material was very effective.

I licked my lips; it was strange. The mouth seemed to belong to no one, just to be there – all by itself.

I stepped back to inspect the effect in the full-length mirror. The suit was so tight and the latex so thin that it molded every detail of my body perfectly; it looked like I was naked, but lacquered in shiny black paint; every muscle, tendon, and curve sculpted to perfection. It was like being a statue; it evoked, too, those dreams about walking around the city naked; but those are dreams, not reality. James silently watched me studying myself, the new me, the "creature."

I figured we would remain at home, have a few drinks, and I would strut around for him, and that would be it.

I applied the lipstick carefully. I almost never wear makeup, but when doing Shakespeare and other drama with Kate, I had become an amateur makeup artist, learning how to put on mascara, and lipstick, and foundation, and ... I stared at the mirror. It was weird.

"I look like Spiderman," I said.

"You look better than Spiderman," he said, "Much better." His hands were stroking my rump.

I leaned forward, concentrating on the lipstick. "It's not really me. I mean, not the old me." Not seeing my eyes, nose, hair, ears, I really did feel I was no longer the Gwendoline I had known. A frisson tickled my belly, electric excitement rippled tremors of liquid fire sparking down my thighs and up my sides, a little storm of shivery goosebumps. This was titillating. I was a statue, I was an animal, I was anonymous; I was no longer me, I was no longer Gwendoline Clermont; I was, as my Master had decreed, a "creature."

I applied the last touch of lipstick. All that I could see now were bright scarlet lips. They seemed much larger and fuller than my lips really were. I wondered: this must be some sort of optical illusion.

"I need to polish you," he said.

"Polish? Oh, yes, of course, Master, polish." That sounded interesting. I was a statue in a museum. I was going to be polished.

We went back out onto the terrace. "Polish away, Master."

He sprayed on the oil-like polish – I felt the cool of the spray land on the latex skin as if it was landing directly on my skin – and he began rubbing the surface of the catsuit – which felt like he was giving me a very intimate massage. I turned around like a little merry-go-round pony to make it easier for him.

"There," he said. "I think we are done." He stood back. "Turn around," he said.

I turned around.

"Perfect," he said, "Let's trot you around a bit, and try your paces."

As we walked back and forth, around the terrace, the stilettos made a satisfying pony-like click-click-click on the tiles. It was unbearably sensual, the oily latex and slimy talcum pressing against me: each millimeter of my body teased and caressed and vividly aware of itself.

Well, this has been all very exciting, I thought, but now that I was aroused and horny, it was time to undress, to shower, and to make love, and then to fall asleep in each other's arms. "All dressed up and nowhere to go," I said, brightly, clicking back and forth on the stilettos.

"Oh, there is somewhere we can go," he said.

"Oh?"

"Yes."

"Like this?" I looked down at myself.

"Scared?"

"A little," I sighed. "You really are a monster!"

"Yes. Of course, I am!" He slid his hand down my sides, slick and slippery, and slapped my bum.

I took a deep breath. I had, yes, willingly, eagerly, embarked on this little adventure, but now it was taking me farther, perhaps, than I had reckoned, and in directions I had not foreseen. I looked around at the rooftops. Rome was asleep. I couldn't hear any traffic sounds. I went to the parapet, put a shiny black latex hand on the balustrade, and looked down. The little cobblestoned street was empty – not a single soul to be seen. Probably all the other streets were empty or almost empty; there might be just a few night owls, night prowlers.

We would be night prowlers. I felt like Catwoman setting out on a mission, or like a panther, escaping from the zoo. It was a bit confusing – was I in a position of submission or mastery?

Both, I figured.

Girls often forget – or underestimate – the power they have.

"Okay, Master," I said, "It's your party. Let's go."

He hooked the leash to the collar.

"Well, well ..."

"To make sure you don't escape."

"Of course. Am I allowed to whinny?"

"Whenever you think it appropriate, whinny to your heart's content."

He led me to the door and opened it, and we exited the flat. He locked the door behind us. There we were, out on the landing. I hesitated and then took a few steps to get used to the stilettos on the pavement. Unlike the marble and the tiles of the flat and the terrace, which were utterly smooth, the pavement on the landing was ancient and uneven. Click, click, click, I went, back and forth, click, click, click. The heels did make me sound like a pony prancing on a stage.

"I'm ready," I said.

We went down the large, broad stairs built so horses could ride up them. My heels made a loud and neatly precise echoing click-click-click as I trotted down the staircase. I sounded something like an old-fashioned typewriter. There was a think tank, "Global Studies for Progressive Economic Policy," on the third floor, the floor below us, but, thank God, none of the thinkers were hanging about gossiping on the staircase. It was far too late for thinking. I pictured them all at home, snoring and dreaming ponderous thoughts. After all, it was just after midnight, the witching hour. I was terrified that Maria might suddenly come out of her lodge. I might have a bit of explaining to do. But maybe I could blame it all on James. That would be fun!

"High heels and cobblestones! Ugh!"

"You'll get used to it." He slapped me on the bum. The slap echoed.

"I will, will I?" I intended to give him the dark eyebrows suspicious-submissive look, but of course, I couldn't give him any look at all. I just turned the featureless latex oval mask toward him.

He laughed. "Oh, darling, you are wonderful!"

We exited the palazzo and found ourselves in the street. This was interesting. What would happen now? The street was empty. The street lamps, poetic-looking gas lamps, gave a glossy dull glow to the cobblestones, and some of the cobblestones still had a humid glimmer from the rain earlier in the day. I had to keep my chin up and my head high, looking straight ahead, because of the stiff collar. As we walked along, I felt the leash, its little chain links, hanging slack, against my breasts and against my side, a cool tickling sensation. We went past the little corner café, and past the convenience shop. From time to time, my Master put his hand on my backside, caressing me or giving me gentle little buttock slaps. "Is this the ponygirl thing?" I asked. "I mean, am I your pony?"

"That would be nice," he said. "But you'd need hooves, and bit and bridle, and a swishy tail – and perhaps a very tight corset."

"Oh, there's a whole science to this, I see."

"Indeed there is, Princess."

"Stages of initiation."

"Absolutely."

"Like a religious order."

"Absolutely."

"Or like joining the Masons or Rotary or something?"

"Quite." He rattled my chain and slapped me on the rump. It was a nice strong slap. It echoed, and flooded my buttocks with stinging tingling warmth, that traveled down my thighs and around my belly, and into the heart of me. "More, Master, more," I wanted to say, "More, please, more!" But I managed to control myself.

We came into a crooked, cobblestoned little piazza, a sort of triangular space, just off the Tiber, where three people, two men and a woman, very elegant looking, were sitting under the dim light of a gas lamp at an unvarnished wooden picnic table; they were drinking white wine from simple water glasses and a large glass wine flask.

They looked up. "Cazzo (fuck!)," said one of the men.

The woman shouted, "Ciaò bella." She waved.

I turned, so from behind my latex veil, I could see her clearly. I waved and said, "Ciaò bella!"

"Cazzo," said the other man.

"Exactly," said James; he tugged on my leash. "Cazzo!" he said.

All three laughed and went back to their drinking. "If you're thirsty later, and we're still here, come and join us," one of the men shouted.

"Thank you, perhaps we will," said James, and gave me a friendly little slap on the round curve of the right buttock. It made a smooth reverberating whack.

"Oh," said the woman, "How wonderful!"

We left them behind, turned into a small side alley, and came out onto a large boulevard, just opposite a small square, really a triangle, decorated with a few skimpy trees and stone benches, and where, facing us, were the towering facades of two 16th and 17th Century churches, the Chiesa Nuova, and the Oratorio de Filippini. We looked both ways. There were no cars.

"Come, pony!"

"Weehugghaa!" I tried on my best imitation of a whinnying pony. "Weehugghaa!"

"Excellent pony!" My Master patted my rump, tightened the leash, looked both ways, and led me across the boulevard. Clip-clop, clip-clop, clip-clop. The high heels and the high collar, I noticed, did make me lift my legs in a special, knees-high, strutting stride, perhaps a bit like a pony. Maybe the pony-like gait, clop, clop, clop, was part of the appeal of high heels, for men who watched, and for women who walked. A black Mercedes surged out of a side street and roared past us. I glimpsed white faces turning in amazement.

"Now I know what a freak in a freak show feels like," I said.

"Interesting sensation, isn't it."

"Well, I think this is not the same thing, to be honest." I slid my arm under his as we stepped up onto the sidewalk.

"No, it isn't, my dear Gwendoline. This is reversible, and this is by choice, your choice as well as mine."

"You are, of course, right, dear Master."

We walked arm in arm along the side of Francesco Borromini's 17th Century Oratorio, down a narrow cobblestoned street, via dei Filippini. The lamplight glowed. A black cat appeared from somewhere and walked along beside us but didn't cross our path. It looked up at me several times and meowed. I think it thought I was a distant relative, a fellow feline.

My heels made an uneven click-click sound on the bumpy cobblestones; the sound echoed – reverberated, amplified, in the narrow street. I was afraid I might wake someone. Children in fluffy white 19th Century nightgowns might suddenly appear at windows to stare down at the human pony trotting by. The high heels and the collar forced me into what was becoming almost second nature – an erect, almost military posture, buttocks out, tummy in, breasts out – clip-clop, clip-clop.

On we went, me making high-steps, more and more self-conscious, more and more the prancing pony, melting into the role, absolutely exposed, every millimeter of my body sculpted in lacquered three-dimensional relief; it was all skin-tight black latex, every detail, and it was me, my body, constrained – and caressed – and self-aware, slathered all over in hot silky-slimy talcum butter. It was yummy and shivery, all at once.

We went up another narrow street, came out on a little piazza, and then entered another very long, straight cobblestoned street. The city was like a ghostly lamp-lit labyrinth. Antique shops and art galleries – all closed – lined the street, and the long cobblestone vista was empty of people. Good! No witnesses! I was invisible!

Oops! We suddenly came upon one antique shop where all the lights were shining. The door was open. The owner was probably inside, doing inventory. We stopped. "You want to have a look?" said James.

"Yes, Master, of course," I said, thinking, this will be interesting.

I turned my blank latex-sculpted face toward the shop and caught a fleeting glimpse, through the half-open door, and beyond a clutter of piled up paintings and furniture, of an exceptionally handsome woman. She was wearing black jeans and a black T-shirt. She was probably in her fifties or sixties, deeply tanned with steel-gray hair cut short and wearing large circular brass-colored earrings that went almost to her shoulders. She had a catalog in one hand and was staring, looking a bit dazed and perplexed, at the piles and piles of objects. Since the door was open, we just walked in.

"Well, James Hewitt Spencer, a sight for sore eyes," said the woman, as she turned toward him, and then she saw me and focused her intense blue-eyed gaze on me, as if studying a newly acquired work of art. She tilted her head to one side. "This is a new one for you, James! Who are you torturing now?"

"This is Gwendoline," he said, "she's a mathematician, one of the best."

"Hello," I said. I held out my latex hand, and she shook it, "I'm Julia," she smiled, "This is my shop." She didn't let go of my hand. "You're really a mathematician?"

"Yes," I said, "I'm finishing my PhD."

"Well, perhaps you'd be interested in this," she said, letting my hand go, with a last squeeze and seemingly with regret. "It's not what I usually carry, but when it was offered to me, I couldn't resist. It's Brother Luca Pacioli's book on arithmetic, geometry, and bookkeeping. He worked with Leonardo da Vinci, and he laid down the principles of accounting. It's an early 16th Century edition."

"Oh, yes," I said. "He was one of the first, if not the first, if I remember correctly, to introduce plus and minus signs. The invention of double-entry bookkeeping was very important; Pacioli helped popularize it. It was fundamental to the development of large-scale enterprises and capitalism."

Julia gave me a look, patted and stroked my arm, and handed the book to me. I turned over the pages carefully. The latex hands were as sensitive as real hands – a second skin, a second me.

"Here, you can see the quality of the paper," she said.

"It's very fine," I said.

James' arm was around my waist. "Perhaps we should buy it, darling." He pressed his hand on the small of my back, caressed me.

"It must be very expensive."

Julia named the price.

"I think you should twice think about this, James," I said.

"I think that is very wise, Gwendoline," said Julia. "I do not intend to sell it right away, so it will be here if you want to look at it again. Meantime, have a look at the shop. I have a nice bottle of prosecco in the back. I'll get it."

I looked around. The shop was piled high with ornate brass and gilt lamps, brocaded chairs, gilded frames, paintings, mirrors, boxes, poufs, and ottomans. There were gilt chandeliers, stacks of china, boxes of silver, place settings, marble busts, architectural drawings of Paris, and drawings of gothic-looking houses, and sketches and paintings of the streets and houses Baron Haussmann had designed for Paris in the 1850s and 60s. It looked like French Second Empire stuff, Napoleon III, furniture and knickknacks. I was lost in contemplation when, in a gilded full-length mirror, I caught a glimpse of myself, a shiny black faceless long-legged creature, attached by a high stiff collar to a sparkling silver chain; and there was my Master holding the chain nonchalantly twisted around his wrist. Suddenly I saw myself as others would seeing me. I can be seen, I realized fully and for the first time, but I can't glance or gaze back; I can see them, but my face is a non-face, no expression, no visible nostrils, no eyes, just full scarlet lips, and bright teeth. It took getting used to.

Julia returned with a bottle and several glasses. She put them down on a tabletop – the table had curved legs of varnished mahogany, and a gilt floral design.

"You specialize in Second Empire?" I nodded toward the table.

"Yes, my dear. As I said, my specialty is not the Renaissance, and it is definitely not mathematics textbooks. As you recognized, this is a fine Second Empire table, and this chair and this divan are both Second Empire. Here, sit down on the divan, lounge on it. May I take a photograph of you?"

"I don't see why not," I said.

"Certainly," James bowed.

Julia shot a picture of me reclining on the Second Empire divan.

She showed it to me.

"Wow," I said.

It was a weird juxtaposition. My legs seemed much longer than normal, the stilettos were like punctuation marks, and the contrast between the classic Napoleon III divan and the faceless fetish model, sculpted in satiny reflections of glossy anthracite, was stark.

"Very provocative," said James.

"I think I will put an enlargement of this in the window," Julia said, "with your permission, of course. It will stimulate customer curiosity."

"I'm honored, and I have no objection," I said. "James?"

"Absolutely none." He bowed, kissed my hand.

Julia showed us some of her favorite pieces.

"I like the malachite inkwell," I said, and I reached out a latex arm and hand and felt its smooth surface. "Is it a Tahan?"

"Yes, it's a favorite of mine."

"Gwendoline's an encyclopedia of specialized and arcane knowledge," said James. He seemed to be almost bursting with pride. Tut-tut, I thought, my master is showing off his pony. All is vanity in this world, mere vanity. I squeezed his arm.

"She's more than that, I think," Julia said, stroking my arm.

"Absolutely," James beamed at us both. He was in danger of becoming fatuous. I pinched him. He winked and crossed his eyes, and stuck out his tongue. So he knew he was fatuous, he was fatuous on purpose; Kate's idiom was more appropriate than mine is for such behavior – so, inwardly, I adopted her tone: the devious bugger! I growled a perfect panther-like growl. I wanted to bite him, right there, right then, grab him, throw him down on the floor, and make love.

"Don't worry, Gwendoline. As we both know, men are irredeemably silly. James is just trying to live up to the stereotype," Julia sighed, her hand still on my arm, and stroking it. "You must bring Gwendoline back, James. I think she and I would have much to talk about."

"You two alone together, that would be the sum of all my fears," said James. "But, yes, I'm sure Gwen would like that."

"Yes," I said. "I'd like that." I turned my blank face to Julia. "In any case, I do wander around by myself – without a leash and without my Lord and Master in tow. So I could just drop in – just me, all by myself."

"That would be wonderful. I'm usually here. You and I will have sherry or tea and gossip about James. But when you come, you will have to tell me who you are because I have no idea what you look like."

"Yes, that's true," I said, and for some reason, I licked my lips.

Before leaving, we drank a glass of the chilled prosecco. It was delicious; just the pick-me-up I needed to give me stamina for a night out on the town.

I shook hands with Julia. She leaned forward and kissed me on both latex cheeks and whispered, "You look stunning, Gwendoline, but don't let him yank that leash."

≈

We were out in the street. The night was warmer, more humid. Again, I was conscious of how the high heels made me stand very erect. I really was becoming a prancing show pony. There were little pots of plants and flowers along the narrow street, and the gas lamps cast a glamorous sheen over everything – potted plants, cobblestones, storefronts and facades, and tables left out in front of cafés.

Nobody else in the street. I turned to James and kissed him. "She was very nice and friendly," I said. "Have you brought other ponies to her shop?"

"No," he said, "you are the only pony. I've never done this before."

"You are very cute, James."

"You think so?"

"Yes, I do, I really do. Give us a kiss, then, little boy."

He kissed me, and I kissed him back, gently, and he stroked my sides and my belly and gave me a friendly slap on the bum. I kissed him again. I did feel like whinnying – Weehugghaa! Weehugghaa! Part of me wanted to assume fully the role he had assigned to me. But I thought I would hold my newly acquired whinnying talent in reserve, for future use, when I became a real pony, with hooves and a swishing tail, and perhaps chewing on a bit. I might even learn to neigh.

≈

The bar was on the corner of a minuscule alleyway. It was tiny and empty except for two guys and girl in a corner – and the barmaid who I saw was actually a bar guy, and rather cute, slender and fragile, with pale ivory skin, freckles, and a red curly mop of hair and big kohl-circled eyes, and a soulful pout printed in glowing scarlet lipstick. She was acting as a she. Maybe she was already a she; or maybe she was on the way to becoming a she. I thought of her, in any case, as a she; or maybe, it just occurred to me, she was a she on the way to becoming a he. No. That was surely not right; she was surely a he getting rid of the last annoying vestiges of masculinity, plunging into the adorable voluptuous female consciousness of being a total she. Yes, that must be it.

She blinked her long lashes at James. "Good evening, James. I see you have brought an extraordinary creature with you this evening." She blinked at me. "We are honored with your presence, beautiful divine creature. What would you like this evening?"

James glanced at me. "Cognac?"

"Cognac, Master, yes, Cognac."

We sat at the bar, perched on high leather stools thankfully equipped with backs, which made it more restful. Perched there, I felt, well, as if I was truly naked, totally exposed; but that was okay. My Master was with me. A silver glitter ball hanging from the ceiling turned round and round, casting shifting colors, red and blue and white, glitzy dark sequined shards of light, over everything, turning us into hieratic figures in an ancient stained glass window.

The barmaid poured the Cognac into the sniffers – very generous portions.

"Thank you," I said.

"Thank you, Marilyn," said James.

"You are welcome, divine creature. You are welcome, James." She favored us with the bright pouting smile, flapping her eyelashes. I saw an echo of my own pout in her expression and wondered at it. Now that I had no face for other people to react to, their expressions seemed to be strangely naked, exposed. How could people go about with such exposed faces that other people saw, all the time, and could interpret? What nakedness, what vulnerability! Now I began, for the first time, to understand some of the sneaky subversive charms of the niqab. I am not advising it, mind you! As Marilyn turned away, I noticed how beautiful her back was – so slender, so pure, so bare, and sculpted with blue shadows and sparkling reflections, so fragile, suspended between male and female, such delicate promise, such tantalizing loss.

"So, now, Panther Goddess," James said, "what's on your mind?"

I turned to face him, stroked his hair, and slid my hand under his shirt and felt his chest. "I'm looking for your heart."

"Oh." He raised an eyebrow.

"I want to make sure you have one. I want to check. Do you have one? Is it still beating? Or have you risen, a heartless vampire, from the dead, a prince charming, a zombie Dracula, to ravish me, and carry me away to the underworld and turn me into a featureless nocturnal wanderer, a soulless creature of darkness?"

"Oh, Panther Goddess," he sipped from the sniffer, but stared across it at me and laid his hand on my thigh and stroked it. "You are dangerous, Goddess, you are letting me play all my games. I may lose my heart to you."

"Maybe they're my games too."

"I hope they are, Panther Goddess; I hope they are ..."

I kissed him. "Yes, they are. This is fun; really, it is." It was true. My master was reinventing me. I was becoming a "creature" – his creature. I liked it. I was allowing myself to melt and merge into his desires. I kissed him, sipped some brandy, and kissed him again, and our mouths seemed to merge, and we two were one.

≈

The rest of that night in the bar dissolved into a series of impressions.

A little man, a cute blonde with heavy makeup, a blonde wig, and his body poured into a tight scarlet sequined dress, was telling me, in Italian, which I just managed to follow, that the good old days were gone forever. "Everything has changed," he sighed, "Sin is no longer sin. Anybody can do anything. The pleasures of transgression are no longer what they once were. Being risqué is no longer risqué. Now that anything is allowed, the young will never know the ecstasies and forbidden thrills and transgressions of yesteryear." I nodded my featureless face sagely and said, "Yes, things certainly change." The little man tugged at his tight red sequined dress, and sighed, "Well, you, my dear, are unique, I can see that you understand – for you are truly an exotic being, a creature of the night, a slave of passion, a tiger, a panther, yes, and you are an outlaw." He puckered up and blew me a kiss and put the palm of his hand against my latex cheek, and stroked it gently, and then he climbed up on the bar and began to strut up and down, wiggling his hips, and singing old songs, songs once sung by Edith Piaf and Marilyn Monroe.

Then …

"He beats me up," said the large, muscular, heavily made-up girl, who was suddenly sitting next to me. Oh, you are not a girl, or not yet, I realized. "He beats me up all the time," the girl who was not a girl repeated. She pointed at her boyfriend, who was sitting in the corner. The boyfriend was a small skinny fellow. He had a wicked black mustache, and a nose ring, and unshaven cheeks, and long sideburns and a brown leather vest with nothing under it but his hairy chest, and a leather collar; he looked like a Neapolitan gangster from an old film, and the flashing lights made him look like a leering gargoyle, peeking from some cathedral roof.

"Why don't you beat him up? You look strong, and you are much bigger than he is."

"I love him. I just can't face beating him up. And if I did, beat him up, I mean, I'd spoil his looks, and I love, oh, I love, the way he looks."

"He certainly is cute." I took a sip of my drink, thinking: people are confessing to me because I'm in a mask. I'm not a person. It's like being a priest behind the screen in a confessional. Or a stranger on a train to whom you can tell all your most dreadful stories.

Another woman – I wasn't at first sure it was a woman – was leaning against the bar and kept glaring at us. Finally, she came over and sat down next to me. She told me how difficult it was to be a classic prostitute working the streets, since there was so much competition from transsexuals and transvestites from Eastern Europe and Africa and Brazil. "Oh, the Brazilians are the worst, darling," her hand was on my arm, "You see they have all this fabulous and very expensive work done. Who can compete with that? I mean, they are more real than real! Well, darling, I must get back to work." She patted my thigh and got up and went to the door, turned and saluted everybody. "Toodles, all," she said, and was gone.

≈

In an alcove off to the side, a glow was radiating up from the floor. I stared at it. What could it be? "What's that?"

"I'll show you," said James. He took my arm, and we went to look.

"Oh, look at that!" I exclaimed, tightening my hold on James' arm.

"Wonderland, in a way," said James.

One section of the floor of the bar consisted of transparent glass. Below our feet was a whole world in miniature, a city street, with cafés and a merry-go-round, and little streetlights, and it was a world entirely peopled by little dolls. It was a perfect toy town, created for a mischievous and perverse child. It could have been put under any Christmas tree except that many of the dolls were hardly dressed at all, some were in tights, and some were tied up on crosses, or down on their hands and knees, bottoms bared, being spanked by evil-looking lady dolls clad in leather. Some of the dolls were dancing, tango style, skirts flaring out, others were doing what looked like a waltz. A toy train went through the town; then it disappeared, and then it came back through the town, and then again disappeared.

"I love it!" I pressed myself against James.

He laid his hand firmly on his pony's right buttock and tapped out a gentle little tune. In response, his pony swayed in rhythm.

≈

We left the bar and walked back home by a slightly different route, along a straight street that was full of shops that were closed, with all the metal shutters pulled down and locked.

It was now three-thirty in the morning

The click-click-click and the clop-clop-clop of my heels echoed in the sultry emptiness. It seemed even warmer, more humid.

Just off via Coronari, we came upon an interesting shop window, an elaborate flower display, where the flowers depicted a woman pouring water out of a vase. Real water was flowing from the vase. We stopped. I put my hands on James' shoulders and kissed him. "I'm a panther," I said, "Now I'm a panther."

"Yes, you are," he tugged on the leash, reeled me in, and held me close.

"I want you naked," I whispered.

"Hmm," he said; he kissed me and released the leash.

We walked on, hand in hand now. The leash dangled loosely between my breasts, swinging between my legs, stroking and tickling my belly and the inner curve of my thighs. Through the ultra-thin latex, it felt like a priceless long pearl necklace, or like a snake-like lover, a serpent, with a mind of its own. I gave my hips an extra little sway to accentuate the experience.

Two police officers were coming toward us. They were Carabinieri, members of Italy's special military-style police. I recognized the two officers; I knew them because they often passed by Alfredo's restaurant and seemed to have offices or a station nearby.

"Good evening, Professor," said one of them, and he added, "Good evening, Signorina."

"Good evening, Colonel," said James.

"Good evening, Colonel," I said, and added, "Good evening, Lieutenant."

"It is a fine night, is it not?"

"It certainly is, Colonel," I said.

They grinned and bowed as they passed, and then I heard the colonel explain in Italian, "There's a special club down there near Piazza Navona. They must have been ..."

"Lucky man," said the lieutenant.

"Yes, but I'm sure she's a handful, has a mind of her own, as you may have noticed. Not to be toyed with, you know, and ..." Their voices faded.

"Professor," I said, "They call you Professor."

Water ran gurgling along the gutter from an open drain, and then disappeared back down underground through a small round hole in the curbstone. The cobblestones shone darkly. Humidity glowed everywhere. The heat was building up for another storm.

"Yes," James had turned to me and was running his hand over my ass, sculpting both cheeks, curving them, shaping them; affectionately, he patted my pony rump. It was as if his hand was on my naked skin. I made a hoarse, gurgling sound, deep in my throat. The cool chain leash dangled, swaying, between my legs.

"And I'm a handful," I said. "So says the colonel."

"Your Italian is fast becoming excellent." James kissed me. He had an erection under his black jeans. It looked quite nice, appetizing, very promising. I was dying to take advantage of it, here, there, anywhere, in the street, in the piazza, in the middle of a gushing fountain; but of course, I was encased, and sealed, slimy and wet and excited, trapped in my glistening latex panther skin – which was also feeling excellent, and very, very arousing. What is the word? *Empowering*, it was strangely empowering.

We came to the entrance to our palazzo. It was a massive gate of the kind that vehicles and carriages and mounted gentlemen and retainers could enter. In the middle of the big wooden gate, was a little Alice-in-Wonderland door, for Lilliput humans. James turned, gave me a knowing glance, and unlocked the little door. Suddenly we were in the dimly lit, musty interior, silvery grayness flooding all around us. The courtyard and the monumental staircase beckoned.

"So, Professor," I said, "I want you naked, a bit at a time."

"Oh, really?" he said.

"Yes, give me your T-shirt."

He bent his head, and I pulled his T-shirt off. I kissed him, pressing myself against him. "Trousers and sandals at the next landing," I said.

"Really?"

"I am a panther," I said, "and I am a handful."

We got to the next landing. "Okay," I said.

"Yes, Mistress." He rolled his eyes.

I unbuckled his belt. He kicked off his sandals, and I pulled down his trousers. "Oh, oh, what do we have here?" His underpants, skimpy underpants, were bulging. I kissed the bulge. Then I kissed his chest. Then I kissed him on the lips.

We got to our landing. I had his trousers – and the keys to the apartment. "Okay, Professor. Let's see."

"Really, Gwendoline!"

"Fess up and strip down, Professor."

He kissed me. "Well, I shall do it, if I have to."

"Yes, you absolutely must do whatever the Panther and Ms. Handful decree, and do it perfectly, and in exquisite detail, and completely."

"Oh," he said; he looked adorable, dark, lean, strong, all energy and muscle, the ripples of muscles, the swelling of muscles, and the dark currents of chest hair. The bulge in his underpants was outstanding, very distinguished; I wanted to fondle it and kiss it.

I knelt before him, and pulled down his underpants. He lifted one foot, then the other, and there he was, naked, except for his wristwatch. I gave his erection a soft little peck of a kiss and a soft little bite.

"Ouch!"

This erection was splendidly elastic, deliciously resilient.

I stood up. "Now you kiss me," I said, "a nice long kiss, and you hold me, and you caress me."

"Oh, Gwendoline," he sighed. He kissed me, and he kissed my latex coated breasts. He knelt naked before me, and he kissed my latex belly and thighs, and he held me and buried his face against me. His hands caressed the small of my back, and my buttocks, and my thighs, and then he stood up and kissed me on the lips. His erection was increasingly tempting, and seemed even harder if possible than before, magnificent, really, and I thought, this is the tiller of a ship I shall certainly enjoy steering.

There were echoes of the big gates opening below. Someone was coming. "Oh, how fortuitous, how timely, how nice, we have visitors," I said. I kissed him. "I wonder who is coming to visit us. They will certainly enjoy this sight of the Professor in all his glory."

"Gwen ..." he smiled.

Whoever it was, summoned the elevator; it began to move downwards, making that familiar creaky echoing whining sound; the cables vibrated and hummed in the trembling elevator tower. This is thrilling. I was holding my Master's trousers, with his keys in the pocket, behind my back.

"I wish I had you on a leash, oh, Professor."

He was grinning in exasperation. "Gwen ..."

"Oh, one more kiss, Professor."

"Yes, oh, Panther Goddess." He kissed me. It was a long wonderful liquid hungry overwhelming kiss. His erection pressed against my eager but, alas, totally imprisoned latex belly, such a warm possessive intimate feeling, so close yet so far – lovers Heloise and Abelard whispering desperately through a chink in a wall.

The elevator reached the bottom. The doors clanged open. People were entering it. Muffled voices echoed. The doors clanged shut. The elevator lurched into motion and began to creak its way upward. We were on the top floor, so it probably would not come all the way up here, but who knew? Would the startled – traumatized – witnesses call the police? Would they arrest us? Would James, be exposed as a naked slave to the Panther Goddess, and cease to be "Professor"?

I licked my lips. "One more kiss, my darling," I said, "I am hungry for you. I want to eat you up!"

He shook his head, laughed, and kissed me; he was excited – I know he was excited – as excited, perhaps, as I was.

The elevator was slowly creaking its way upwards. Voices – male and female – were arguing in Italian. "The report was supposed to be ready on Monday!" "Well, nobody told me that!" "You're supposed to be able to figure it out yourself, idiot!" All this was clear as a bell. Yes, my Italian was getting much better.

"I shall take pity on you, Master," I whispered, brushing my lips against his.

"Oh, thank you, Goddess."

I took out the keys and opened the door; I bowed and allowed him to enter first, and, finally, we were inside the apartment. "You stay naked," I said.

"Yes, Goddess." He was grinning, and he looked adorably ridiculous and manly, with that outstanding erection.

"Here, slave, follow me," I said. I gave his erection a little tug, and I pushed the music button – and the sound system began to play Shostakovich's "The Second Waltz" – and, holding his erection, I led and steered my master out onto the terrace. There were stars overhead, romantic stars, dimmed by the rising humidity.

"Let us dance." I put my arms around him. We danced. I pressed my naked latex-lacquered body against his. As we twirled around the terrace, I kissed him. I kissed him again and again; I felt every inch of him, and I yearned for every inch of him; finally, at the end of three sweeping turns around the dance floor, I said, "Sit down, Master."

He sat down on the stone bench, just under the balustrade. I knelt before him. I made obeisance. I kissed his erection, the very head and point of it, and as I licked, he was literally bursting, straining to the very limits. "Lie back," I said, and I stood up and lowered myself down onto him, kissing him, and then rubbing myself against him.

"Oh, Gwen!" he said, it was a sigh.

"They should make little gateways in these things," I said, "little zippers or flap doors so the dog or cat can come in and go out."

"A gateway to the Heart of Darkness," he murmured; his eyes were closed, his head bent back.

"Yes, a gateway to the Bermuda Triangle." I intended to master him totally, and make him come. I rode him, pressing down on the erection, sliding along it, kissing him, touching him every-where, every inch of his body, with my latex-doll body, every muscle and tendon in my own body strained and wiggled and twisted against him; and I kissed him and I licked him, and I kissed him.

"Oh, Gwen, Oh, Goddess," he groaned, his eyes flickering, as if he were having a fit.

I was down on my knees. I took him in my mouth, and I licked and bit and sucked and sucked, and I tightened my grip, and with my latex fingers I twisted his nipples, and twisted the root of his erection, my mouth overflowing now, with saliva dripping, I sucked and sucked and sucked and licked, and nipped and …

James groaned, and groaned, and twisted, and twisted, and he clutched his hand over my head, pressing down, holding me where I was – though I didn't need holding – and he groaned, and he cried out and –

He came in a great shuddering splash and gush.

I licked and slurped. I was in ecstasy. I had tamed him. I was the Master and the Mistress. I was the Panther Goddess.

Now – Urgently – I wanted him inside me.

He was groaning and bending back, he was still in my mouth, and I shuddered, and, almost, I thought, I'm going to bite it off! I licked some more, cum overflowing, running from my lips splash and dribble and flow.

Slowly I withdrew, giving his erection a final, playful, little farewell lick.

I was utterly soaked, wet, and eager, and I thought, this thing really does need a flap door, but now I shall make him work for his pleasure – and mine. After all, I had just done something for him and with him that I had never done before, not fully, not for anybody, or with anybody.

I stood up slowly, and my mouth still wet, still dribbling cum, I kissed him, and he kissed and licked back, our tastes mingling. He was trembling, and so was I. I was the plastic goddess, and he was my naked man, my worshiper.

"Okay, now, my darling Slave," I said.

"Yes, Goddess."

"You must undress me, slowly, and then we make love."

"Yes, my creature."

"First, Slave, kneel, and kiss my tummy."

He did.

My latex fingers pulled on his hair. I caressed him softly and pressed him to me.

The first sensations of dawn were by now in the air – a brightening pale milky light, a fresh damp cool breathable beauty, and, from somewhere nearby the twittering of birds.

He ran his fingers up and down my thighs. Then he seized the cheeks of my butt, and he nuzzled and kissed me, burrowing deep into me, through the ultra-thin latex. He worked his way up – to my breasts, my collarbone, and my shoulders, and again he kissed me on the mouth, a salty, primordial, fecund kiss: turned to fluid, we mingled as if we were one.

He cupped my face, bringing me to him and kissed me, licking my latex chin and my swollen scarlet lips. He unhooked the leash from my collar and laid it in a coil on the glass-topped wrought-iron terrace table where there were still large trembling silver drops of rain.

I was breathing fast and heavy. I yearned to whinny or growl. I kissed him and bit his lip, not hard, but I held it, delicately imprisoned, between my teeth.

His eyes were laughing. I let him go. He unlocked and opened the collar and placed it carefully on the table next to the leash. Then, he knelt, down on his knees again, and clicked open the shoes, and released my feet.

He stood up and reached around, unzipped the zipper that ran down my back, and peeled the latex off my shoulders and down to my waist. I was covered in a sheen and slather of creamy, oily powder, almost bubbly. The air was cool on my skin. He knelt again and peeled the latex from my legs. I was free.

"Now," he said, "Now, you are mine."

"Yes," I said, "Yes, Master, I am your catamite, or your concubine, whatever you wish, take me."

I lay down on the thin mattress that covered the stone bench;

I was slippery as an eel in a barrel of oil. He knelt above me, pressed me down, holding my arms outstretched above my head, crucified, and he began to suck my breasts, first one, then the other, and "Oh, oh, oh!" He still had that erection, that magnificent hard erection. I could feel it between my legs.

"Come, come," I whispered.

He kissed me, to silence me perhaps. The kiss was long, as if our lips, like our bodies, were now glued together, prisoners. He slid into me as easily as a sword sliding through half-melted butter. He filled me; I yearned for him to fill all of me: my mouth, my vagina, and my anus. Yes, he should take me as an emperor would take his catamite; I wished for all of this at once; I wished to be possessed totally, torn apart, ripped into little ribbons of fluttering, sizzling sensation.

The long liquid kiss went on and on. He slid back and forth inside me. I twisted my hips and squeezed my thighs to trap and keep him. Our mouths were dripping from the kisses, overflowing and shameless. He moved back and forth, gently; my hands, released from crucifixion, were clutched in his hair, grasping, my fists closed, pulling. I was kissing him deeper, licking, and kissing; our mouths submerged in one long kiss; our two mouths had become one. I closed my eyes and then opened them. I tightened my thighs in one supreme effort, one supreme spasm. He tensed.

"Yes, oh, yes," I whispered. Every muscle of his body was straining to the very limit. I was teetering on a knife-edge, about to come, and then, in one spasm, and long series of rippling spasms, we came, both of us, in the same instant.

"Oh, oh, oh!"

"Oh, oh, oh!"

On and on it went.

"Oh, my God!"

On and on ...

"Whew! Oh, my God!"

On and on ...

"Oh, oh, oh!" Slowly it subsided. I bit him. He kissed me, and then he smoothed my hair, and caressed me, held me, and comforted me, taking onto him all of my slippery slathered body, reeking of sex and talcum powder and perfume and saliva.

We lay still. I was sprawled on top of him; I was a drowned sailor cast up by a tidal wave and flopped down, inert, on a glorious sandy beach.

His hands were in my hair, all sticky, caressing my hair.

"We'll get one with a flap," he said.

"Definitely," I yawned.

"But not a zipper."

"No, not there, not a zipper. A zipper might hurt the little emperor." I took the little emperor – somewhat limp by now – in my hand and slithered my way up and down along his body, wiggling back and forth, zigzagging like a serpent, and bit his lip. "I don't want to hurt you or your little emperor."

"I think I'll take you to Alfredo's dressed like you were tonight and perhaps even in something more interesting, or we could go to Dal Bolognese on Piazza del Popolo. Famous people frequent the place, actors and politicians and fashionistas, and also strippers and sex artists. You will be worshiped."

"So, you shall parade me, then, Master, hooded and faceless, a latex statue, in high heels, and on a leash. A symbol of your macho masculine mastery at hunting and stalking your prey, at domesticating your very own panther, and demonstrating to all and sundry and the assembled multitude your patriarchal phallic totem-like guy-power so all the other Neanderthal hunters will fall on their knees before you."

"Oh, Gwendoline, you do speak the truth, like the oracles of old, and you are truly a dangerous girl."

I was by now astraddle his midriff, looking down. I licked my lips and sighed. "You are the most beautiful naked creature I have ever seen."

"And you, Gwendoline, are too beautiful. No words can convey, no thoughts can measure, no –"

"Oh, Master, no words!" I put my finger to his lips. "No words now. Just sacred, worshipful silence." I clenched my knees around his midriff and lowered my breasts to his mouth. "Suck," I said, "suckle and suck."

He put his lips to my breast. I caressed his hair while he licked and sucked and nibbled. I groaned. My nipples were erect and straining against their limits, and I wished my breasts were heavy with milk so I could feel my life pulsing into him. He was hard again – my master must take drugs, I thought – but he swore later that it was not so – and I wanted him to suck and suckle forever. I wanted him to be a mountain of strength, a true man, and I wanted him to be a suckling child, a baby, clinging to me forever, hungrily, hanging at my breasts. I wanted him to take sustenance from me, me – the fecund and earthy goddess he had created out of clay, and me, the ethereal impertinent boyish nymph he worshiped, the water sprite, light and quick as air, and the source, for him, of all life and nourishment and desire.

Later ...

"Perhaps, my love, we should take a shower." His hands were working their way up and down my sweat, sex, and powder slathered body. His body, too, was streaked and sweaty now.

"No," I said, "let's stay dirty."

"Ah, of course, the goddess has spoken. Let us reek and wallow in our true natures."

"You got it. That's it, precisely," I said.

"Well, I am your humble servant," he said.

"I'll make breakfast, and I'll bring it to you here. You wait out here on the terrace. No clothes," I said, "clothes are forbidden."

"Yes, Gwendoline," he said. He was smiling.

The sky was pale blue; it was dawn.

∞

We finally did get that shower – late in the morning – and we slept and lay in bed and fooled around and talked and then went out to eat at a little bistro – a wine-and-cheese place – just off Piazza Navona.

The next few days were restful, the calm after the storm. James worked in the flat and often went to meetings. If he and I were both home, I would cook, or we would cook together. He was a very good chef and an excellent sous-chef. When we cooked at home, he liked me to be naked, or wearing just a cooking apron. He had also bought me a rather fancy garter belt and some black silk stockings.

"Just the thing a girl cook should wear," I said.

"I hadn't thought of that," he said.

"Really?"

Following my own fancy, I sometimes cooked in nothing but the garter belt and the dark silk stockings and black satin, high-heeled, slip-in pumps. Sometimes I livened up this minimalist outfit with eye shadow and a black velvet Edwardian choker – with ivory cameo – I had picked up in the Rome flea market at Porto Portese.

One night, we went to Alfredo's, and the colonel and his faithful lieutenant strolled by. James signaled to them, and they came over, sat with us, and had a drink. They were not in uniform and were not on service, so they could accept a glass or two. The young lieutenant kept staring at me. I winked at him. I looked a bit different from the last time he'd seen me.

He said, "So you're a mathematician."

"Yes," I said. He asked for more details, and I told him. It turned out he had done a degree in mathematics and was an expert in statistical analysis applied to crime. He and I had something to talk about while James and the colonel got into a deep discussion about organized crime – and in particular about people and arms smuggling and the Russian Mafia.

The young lieutenant was, I think, in some measure smitten by me, well, not by me exactly, but by the idea of me. There is nothing more exciting for a man, I think, than seeing a woman – someone else's woman – displayed as a fetish object, an accessory, a projection of that other man's power. For each male, such display must be an implicit challenge to his own status and hunting ability. If one man desires such a woman – or shiny automobile – then I'll bet other men feel impelled to desire her – or the Maserati. But, in truth, what do I know? I must study this subject in depth.

CHAPTER 4 – REMOTE CONTROL

One day, James took the train to Milan. He was going to stay there for four nights. I was left to my own devices, which meant working, and some tourism, and having lunch and dinner at Alfredo's.

When I got back from dinner the first night, James called me on a video link. As we talked, I did a striptease, totally dedicated, of course, to him, carrying the laptop and its camera around with me, and out onto the terrace.

I lifted off my T-shirt. Then I knelt, and took off my sandals, one at a time, dangling each one from a fingertip, while I let my tongue hang out in what I thought must be a very alluring manner, but I suspect I looked more like an eager spaniel than an accomplished Las Vegas stripper. I sashayed around the terrace, wiggling my hips, and, then, setting the laptop on a table, I squirmed, very slowly, out of my shorts, and then twirled the shorts, and let them drop, while I undulated and twisted my hips this way and that. After all, this was what I had seen done in the movies. I put my fingers under my panties and pressed down on my pubis. Slowly, I stretched the panties, and slowly, slowly, slipped them down my thighs, adopting for a moment the panicked little girl knock-kneed Marilyn Monroe-Betty Boop look, bending over, pushing the panties past my knees, and then I held them out, dangling from one toe and kicked them away.

So there I was, Gwendoline, just Gwendoline, out on the terrace with the gentle breeze reminding me that it was Rome; that it was night; that it was summer; and that the pine and cedar forests and the Mediterranean were not far away.

"But you have to strip too," I said, leaning back against the parapet and sticking my tongue out at the screen.

He did. He was pretty damned good at it too; it was a parody of my little act, but it was also really macho, and very dark and sexy, and – in the nicest way possible – threatening. He was a monster of primal energy, and he seemed to desire one thing in the world – me!

Whew!

"Hurry home, Master."

"I think we may have inaugurated a tradition," he said.

"Yes," I said. I licked my lips.

And, so, we said goodnight.

≈

The next night we played a relaxed game of strip poker. It was a sultry night in Rome, and I walked around the flat as we played – it involved flipping coins – and I won. James was naked. I ended up still wearing panties, which was a definite anticlimax. Carrying the laptop, I walked around the flat and around the terrace. Then I slipped out of my panties and sat down in a chair in the kitchen; James was sitting on a chair in his hotel room, and we talked, just as if we were sitting across from each other at the dinner table, covering a whole variety of subjects, including some of the difficulties of his business negotiations in Milan.

At one point, James asked me what I thought of masturbation. I said, "What is there to think about?"

"You are getting sassy," he said.

"I know. It's the bad influence."

"A spanking will be in order."

"Ah, a spanking, well, we shall see about that, Master. How shall it be done?"

"I'll design it carefully," he said.

"I'm sure you will. You'll do it when you get back?"

"I certainly will."

"In the meantime, Master, to wrap up tonight's proceedings, I think a bubble bath would be nice."

"Indeed," came the echo from Milan, "Proceed, then, Princess. Make yourself a bubble bath. Cavort, enjoy, splash about."

I lit some candles. I placed the camera so he could watch me in the bubble bath. I cavorted in the bubbles, making a great show of my legs and my breasts and caressing more or less every part of me, and at certain points, following James' instructions as to which part of my anatomy needed immediate attention and what sort of attention.

Finally, I rose out of the bubble bath covered in bubbles and foam, letting the bubbles flow down over my body and undulating and caressing myself in the most visible way possible. I think the dim golden light made this apparition particularly flattering.

"Very pleasing," said James.

"I am delighted you are pleased, Master." I curtsied.

"Like Aphrodite rising from the sea," he said.

"Oh, Master, you are too kind."

While I dried, James had to take a conference call; but he left me connected, so I could listen in. I walked around the terrace carrying the laptop and eavesdropping, with the towel over my shoulder, just letting the subtle movement of the night air dry my skin, and with little snaky sneaky rivulets, like the curls and serpentine strands of a Medusa, running down my back from my hair. I put the towel on the stone bench, and sat down on it, naked, and just listened.

James and his associates were talking about some difficulties they were having with the Russian competition. The Russians were tough, and they had worked out an alliance with some even tougher Georgians. It was pleasant to be naked – and invisible – in the evening breeze listening to these intimate insider discussions of high affairs of state and business. Life should always be like this!

One thought did occur to me – some of the deals James was involved in were very dangerous; I had better do some hacking and research, to protect James from himself by finding out what I could find out. I was about to open a terrifying Pandora's Box, but I didn't know it at the time.

When James finished with his call, we discussed the next night's program. I was sitting on the stone bench, naked, with the little eye of the computer aimed straight at me.

"Self-stimulation would be nice," James said.

"How euphemistic of you, Master!"

"Well, Goddess, I am timid, you know."

"No, I hadn't noticed, to tell the truth."

"Touch your left nipple, please."

I obliged and licked my fingers and touched my left nipple. I teased it. I twisted it and caressed it. The nipple did not need any encouraging. It rose to the occasion, stiff, engorged, and feeling ultra-sensitive. I felt vaguely humiliated, enslaved, and excited, so openly demonstrating the overly responsive, trigger-happy sensuality of my body. It really does have a mind of its own.

I licked my lips and stuck out my tongue. "So this self-stimulation thing, Master, what do you mean by that? Do you want me to masturbate for you? Is that it? Or do you want to masturbate for me? Or should we both try to masturbate together?"

"In unison, if you wish, Gwendoline."

"I wish."

"So, then, until tomorrow."

"Yes, until tomorrow, Master. Meantime, sweet dreams, Master."

"Sweet dreams, Gwendoline."

≈

For that third night, I decided that a striptease contest should precede the main act and the climax. I had to prepare. If you are going to do a striptease, the one precondition is that you have to be wearing something to start with. This forced me to do some thinking.

"Let's see. What shall I wear? A swimsuit? A business suit? A ball-gown, worker's overalls, a catsuit? Hmm?" I held up some samples and considered them. "Ah, yes, a teddy, yes." I had fished it out of a box of supplies that James had bought and which I had not yet tried on – a purple silk teddy.

"So," I said, "Okay, we do a striptease, and see who gets there first. Is that okay? "What are you wearing?"

"Shorts and a T-shirt and socks," he said.

"I'm wearing a teddy and panties."

"Okay, so the socks won't count."

"Yes, take the socks off. Socks? How could you wear socks? Socks are absolutely unsexy! Master! I'm ashamed of you!"

I flipped the coin, and he had to take off his T-shirt. Then I had to take off my teddy. Then I had to take off my panties.

"Let's do this slow-motion. Leave your panties on," he said, "but start to wiggle out of them, to pull them, to twist them, to ..."

"Ah, you want the indirect, suggestive, poetic approach."

"Yes." My Master's face smiled from the computer screen.

"Your merest wish is my command, Master." I began to undulate and wiggle my hips and ass in front of the screen. "You too,

Master, it is only fair. Wiggle your hips! Stroke yourself. Nurture that erection! Help it grow and prosper! Put your heart into it!"

"Yes, Gwendoline," he said.

"Someday, Master, I'm going to paint you in sequins."

"Really?"

"Yes, really." I was swaying back and forth, and, preparing for the main scene in this drama, I was applying lube and stroking my clitoris, the little chap – or is the clitoris a girl? – seemed absolutely to adore the experience, the soft but accelerating sideways diagonal circular strokes, particularly with my Master looking on, albeit from a certain distance, like 600 kilometers. I wondered. Is my clitoris an exhibitionist? "Master, do you think an orgasm is purely physical, or is it an idea, the result of a thought or a concept?"

"An idea?"

"What triggers an orgasm? Is there a concept, a tag line, a scenario, a situation? Does it involve psychological triggers or just pure physical stimulus?"

"Well, darling Gwendoline, I think it is both – sexual excitement is physical, but it's also an idea, a scenario as you say – a concept. When I feel, when I think, my darling Gwendoline, that I have become truly one with you, well, then, in that moment, in that epiphany of unity, or merging, of being one, I ..."

"Then you come ..."

"Yes, that's the bottom line. Psychic unity, psychic identity, which is an idea, is the climax of the story."

"That is interesting, Master, for it is when I feel you have consumed me, taken me, possessed me, become one with me, when I have devoured you, consumed you, and made you one with me, and me one with you, that is when I come."

"It is splendid and most interesting that we agree on this vital scenario, Gwendoline."

"So, dear Master, we need a high-concept screenplay to consummate our union." I paced up and down, trying to imagine myself in a Hollywood story meeting with impatient bottom-line executives hounding me. "Let's see. Get down on your knees, Master."

He got down on his knees and adjusted his laptop so I could see him. From what I could see, he was at the foot of his bed in the hotel room. In the background, I could see an ornate dresser. He was staying in a classy joint.

"Okay," I said, "now you are bowing before me."

"Okay ..." My Master put on an appropriately devoted expression and looked sufficiently worshipful, in a lustful sort of way.

I frowned and concentrated. "Let's see I am offering myself to you and you are kissing me and licking me, first my tummy, and then the Heart of Darkness and – My right hand will have to play you, as a stand-in. Is that okay?"

"Absolutely, Gwendoline, your right hand is me."

"Let's see, this will have to be both of us, doing it to each other. Oral sex, then?"

"Yes, darling. Of course."

"Okay. You imagine me, leaning over you, and you are kissing me, and touching with your tongue and fingers my poor sex that you have captured, and excited to the point of a frothing tizzy, and made your own."

"Yes, yes ..."

And so we did it. I caressed myself. I talked him through the scenario. My fingers worked away, sliding on my labia, twirling my clitoris, teasing it in every possible way I could imagine. I twisted my nipples too, and I licked my lips, and I tossed my head back and opened my legs, and then scissored them together. I let the saliva run. I lubricated with oily lubricant my belly and my labia and my clitoris, until I was liquid, engorged, excited, tottering, and tipping on the edge. And, as I was describing to him what he was doing to me, with his mouth and lips and tongue, and what I was doing to him, taking him into me, sucking, licking, biting, caressing, twisting, we both ended up closing our eyes – and oh, oh, oh – we came! We both came in the same instant, and then we floated down, in silence.

"Oh, Master," I sighed

"Oh, Gwendoline," he groaned.

≈

The next night was different. I had thought about it, from time to time, during the day, between dabbling in differential equations and stochastic processes, and I had come up with a new concept. Sex, I had decided, is show business. I dressed in baggy, creased, scruffy trousers, with an old second-hand leather belt, and, over a ragged half-open shirt, an old leather vest.

We made our video connection.

"Good evening, Gwendoline." My master was in jeans and an open shirt.

"Good evening, Master."

"You look exceptionally alluring this evening, Gwendoline."

"Yes, Master, well, Master, I have prepared for this."

"Let us begin, then, Gwendoline."

"Okay, Master, tonight, you are a pirate."

"I'm a pirate?"

"Yes, Master, you are a pirate. And I, Gwendoline, your obedient princess, am a cabin boy on an old Spanish galleon merchant ship bearing gold and you, Master, evil pirate that you are, have captured the Spanish merchant ship and have taken me for your own."

"This sounds perfect, Gwendoline."

"Isn't it great that I'm a cabin boy? Isn't it what you've always wanted? To have your very own cabin boy?"

"Absolutely, my lad, absolutely!"

"I wonder," I frowned. "Is it a three-mast merchantman?"

My master was opening his shirt and taking it off. He closed his eyes. "It's a galleon – a three-mast galleon," he said.

"A galleon, a ...?" I licked my lips. Excitement was rising. "Three-mast, you say, Oh, Master, oh how totally wonderful – three masts! Three masts are so totally cool! A galleon – Oh, boy!"

"So, then, boy, off with your clothes."

"Really, sir? Me, sir? Do I have to, sir?" I shrank back in horror.

"Yes, indeed, boy, and you'll enjoy this!"

"I will, sir?"

"Indeed, you will!"

"Oh, sir! I'm not so sure I will, sir!"

"No matter, boy! When destiny calls, do not hesitate! Off with that canvas jacket! Good! Off with that smelly undershirt! Good! Off with those trousers! Off with that last remaining rag! Now, let me look at you, boy. Turn around."

"Oh, sir!" I turned around, now despoiled of all my raiment – totally naked – and absolutely abashed, a boy prisoner of the dreadful wicked English pirate.

"Let me take you in my arms, boy!"

"Oh, Sir!"

"Oh this is delicious, sir, you are touching my chest, sir. Why are you touching my chest? And you are patting my bum, sir! Have I done anything wrong that you would want to pat my bum?"

"No, boy, on the contrary! Now, boy, with my magic wand, I transform you into a girl!"

"Oh, Sir, oh, what is happening, sir? Oh, Sir, oh, where did my wee-wee go, sir? Oh, what have you done, sir? Where is my wee-wee? What have you done with my wee-wee?"

"Don't worry, boy – what you have now, though it's invisible and well concealed, is much better than any wee-wee yet conceived, I know it, and you'd better believe it!"

"And what are these, what are these little mountains?"

"They are paradise, boy, and you'd better get used to it!"

"Oh, sir, have I truly become a girl?"

"Yes, indeed, boy, it looks like you are no longer a boy."

"Oh, woe, woe is me!"

"So, now, down on your hands and knees, girl, and I'll show you what pirates do!"

"Girl, sir, girl? Are you talking to me, sir?"

"Yes, for that is what you have become, boy! Have you forgotten? You are now a girl!"

"Oh, woe is me! That such a thing should come to pass! I am a girl! Oh, horrible, most horrible!"

And so it was that I, Gwendoline, alone in Rome, was down on my hands and knees, and while I was playing me, the girl, ex-boy, I was also, with my right hand, playing the pirate, him, James, my Master. Such acrobatic scripts can get complicated.

"Oh, sir, oh! You are touching me, and your tongue is in the strangest and most forbidden places, sir, and what are you doing with your fingers, and are you trying to milk me, sir? I am not a cow, sir, at least I don't think I am a cow ... Oh, oh, oh ... Oh, how can you do this to poor innocent me, Master Pirate. Oh, my breasts, and my new found pubis, unmanned as I am, Oh, Master Pirate! Oh, delicious manly pirate man! Oh!"

≈

James had the strange idea too that licking liquid Swiss chocolate from my breasts and perhaps from the Heart of Darkness might be fun. He was in Venice. I was in Rome. We were on WhatsApp.

"It has to be Swiss?"

"Absolutely."

"Liquid chocolate, thick, gooey, dark liquid chocolate?"

"Absolutely."

"It can't be Belgian?"

"No, absolutely not."

"Hmm. What if it covers all of me, every inch, that's a lot of chocolate; wouldn't you get tummy trouble licking it all off?"

"Any sacrifice is worth it, Princess."

≈

Another idea he had was a paper-thin black plastic raincoat.

"A plastic raincoat?" I perched the computer on the coffee table and let the computer's beady little eye stare at me. I was naked, wearing only the thick leather collar, and lying on the living room divan, my feet up on one end of it, and slurping a homemade chocolate milkshake.

"Yes, a cheap, thin, off-the-shelf of a discount Dollar Store, flimsy, black plastic raincoat, and you are wearing nothing under it, totally naked, and we go to the movies in a big downtown cinema and then perhaps out to dinner at some very fashionable restaurant where a lot of important politicians and cardinals –"

"Cardinals?"

"Cardinals of the Catholic Church, Vatican Cardinals, not bird cardinals, they hang out there, the church ones I mean, at the restaurant, not the bird ones."

"Yummy." I slurped some milkshake, "Transgression."

"I thought you'd like it."

"Is it a sultry dark thundery night?"

"Yes."

"Traces of recent rain reflect on the cobblestones?"

"Yes, definitely, and the cobblestones reflect your long, chalk-white, virginal, naked legs."

"Virginal?"

"Virginal."

"Okay, if you say so, Master. Virginal. And I'm not wearing anything except the little flimsy plastic thing."

"Yes."

"And I'm wearing very high heels."

"Yes, you are wearing ultra-high, cheap, stiletto pumps bought in some sex shop, when we went shopping the day before, you barefoot and dressed in a black plastic garbage bag, and –"

"Yummy!" I slurped a big gob of milkshake, stood up, and stretched. "A black plastic garbage bag! Wow! That's terrific! You are by my side and will protect me, right? And when I'm wrapped in the raincoat, we smuggle a bottle of whiskey or Cognac into the movie theater and drink it out of straws going, slurp, slurp, slurp!"

"Yes."

"Peachy," I yawned.

I carried the laptop out to the terrace while we were discussing this screenplay, and I lay down on the mattress on the stone bench just below the balustrade. "Let us go back, Master, if you permit, to the Swiss chocolate caper."

"Yes, of course, Gwendoline."

"Describe, dear sir, the chocolate. Are you licking me, are you kissing me?"

And so it came to pass that my Master went into exquisite detail about the chocolate. He told me what it looked like, what it felt like on my skin, and under his tongue. He told me where it was on my body, how it dripped, how it drooled, how it dribbled and flowed, its consistency, its sumptuous glimmering sheen, its color, and, seeing it all, in the vividness of his description, in the warmth of his voice, feeling it all, I responded as only a bad girl can. "Oh, yes .... Do it again, do it again, Oh, play it again, Master, play it again ..."

All alone, by the sheer force of his voice telling me what he was doing to me, how he was doing it, well, I blush to admit it, Father, but I came! I came, gloriously and fully I came, lying there on the stone bench, splayed open under the Roman night, wet with feverish, yearning, lonely, mystic desire, I came, all by myself, I came.

"You are most eloquent, dear sir," I gasped.

"Thank you, Goddess."

"Come back to me, fast, come back, dear sir."

After that little episode, I walked around the flat and back out onto the terrace and let the sultry Roman night wrap itself around me. I was sleepy, but restless too. Solitary sex – shared via Skype or WhatsApp or Whatever – can be wonderful, but it does have its incomplete, inconsequential side. Having James here would be better, much better. I ran my hand along the rough, grainy stone surface of the terrace balustrade, and I sighed.

CHAPTER 5 – TRANSFORMATION

Three days after the Swiss chocolate caper, James got back to Rome. Several days after that, we both took the day off – it was a Saturday – and we had lunch, a very light lunch, at Fortunato al Pantheon, a small restaurant that is on a side street close to the Pantheon and the Senate and the Chamber of Deputies, and frequented by many of Italy's top politicians. The wine was delicious, a sharp white, a Chablis, I think. The waiters were very attentive.

Following my Master's instructions, I was in a classic and demure mode, wearing the simple low-heeled shoes, the black tailored slacks, and the little white and black striped jacket from the evening at the Metropolitan Museum back in New York a lifetime ago. The Charlie Chaplin hat I had left at home. Rome, in a strange way, is a serious city; in certain questions of taste, and depending very much on context, it imposes a severe sense of decorum.

There were politicians and lots of certified VIPs, writers, TV personalities, and business tycoons, all around us. Some of them James knew, and some of them I had met. They waved, and several stopped at our table. Two of them bowed and kissed my hand.

James and I spoke of his business. He'd asked me my opinion of some of the mathematical models a company used to estimate its future profits. It was mostly math, but of course, garbage in, garbage out, and so I asked a bunch of questions about where the information came from, who provided it and why, and how inclusive or representative it was. How long the various time-series were and how homogeneous they were, and whether any underlying conditions had changed in the meantime, which would impact on the relevance and accuracy of the inputs, the parameters, the correlations, and the models. He argued with me all the way, posing counter-questions.

Then we discussed local politics – the Italian Government was in crisis and perhaps about to fall – and we watched the various VIPs and politicians greet each other and do that incredibly warm exuberant lunchtime schmoozing Italian business people are so good at. You would think that everybody was in love with everybody else. And, yet, often, the knives were already out. After James had paid the bill, and as we lingered over our espressos, James leaned back and gazed at me and said, "Today I think is the day for a true transformation."

"Oh?" I raised an eyebrow.

"Yes, today, you shall, if you agree of course, become a naked, lacquered, painted, pagan goddess, to be displayed to the multitude."

"Really?"

"Yes."

"Well, that sounds, ah, yummy, Master."

"It will be a metamorphosis, a change."

"Ah, okay, Master, today I am to become your tailor-made monster. How do we effect this transformation, this transmogrification?"

"Follow me." He stood up.

"Always, Master." I stood up and took his hand.

We walked up a few bright sun-filled streets, savoring the smell of coffee and chocolate. We walked past the Chamber of Deputies and past the Prime Minister's Office in Palazzo Chigi. We walked through a high-ceilinged glass-covered 19th Century shopping Arcade, and out into some crowded pedestrian streets and then up a very chic cobblestoned street lined with houses of high fashion: Prada, Gucci, Bulgari, Ferragamo, La Perla, Valentino, Louis Vuitton, Dior, Cavalli, Missoni, and on and on. The place reeked of status, and sex, and beauty and power and money, and, I thought, musing on it all, that it represented a quest for a sort of immortality and invulnerability – fashion as armor and religion. This fear and anxiety seemed to me to underlie so much of fashion. Don't get me wrong – I love fashion!

We came to a small elegant boutique that sold perfumes, nail polish, and mascara and such-like things. "Hmm," I said.

We stopped outside the door. We were on a narrow little pedestrian street – no cars, but with lots of people going by on foot. The other shops were all fashion boutiques, some big names, and some, lesser-known, but even more exclusive. Down at the corner, was a café with tables set outside on the cobblestones. People were sitting, gossiping, talking, reading newspapers or magazines, or bent over iPads and Smart Phones.

All around us were ordinary lives, the surface of ordinary lives, and here I was, about to be transformed into a goddess – probably a painted whore of Babylon.

I had an instant image of me, naked, totally shaved, garishly painted, from head to toe, in brilliant psychedelic colors. I am sitting in the lotus position, and receiving burnt offerings, amid clouds of incense and sandalwood, from peasants wearing loincloths, while my warrior guardian, James, my Master, also in a skimpy, revealing loincloth, stands, very erect, at my side, holding a spear, to protect me from any attempt upon my divine virtue.

Looking around, I suddenly felt as if, in playing at our intimate little games, we had separated ourselves from all the mundane surface activity of all the other people. I suddenly felt as if, in our erotic frivolity and mischief, we were attaining heights and depths no one else had ever attained, as if nobody else, in the history of the universe, had ever played at being naughty. Still, however silly or obscene it may be, sex is, potentially, an entry into the sublime – and into the underworld. Maybe the two – Heaven and Hell – are not so far apart. This is a fact that the old gods knew quite well, but the new gods do not, or so it seemed to me. Then, of course, wherever these games led, I was privileged, uniquely privileged, I could experiment: I had money, I had all-understanding grandmother Claudia, I had frisky Kate, and I had James. I was young. I was healthy. I had math – if a catastrophe were to happen, I could walk away from anything – well, almost anything.

"I love your little pubic patch."

"I am delighted you love my little pubic patch. It is indeed pleased that you love it."

"I think though it should have a little holiday."

"Oh." For a moment, I didn't say anything. I tried to absorb this, to decipher it, to visualize it. "You mean a temporary holiday?"

"Oh, yes, of course, temporary."

A little frisson of fear rippled up my spine. My Master wanted me smooth, naked, and defenseless as a newborn babe. Is not mystery part of woman's power? What if my adorable little patch was taken from me never to return? What if it came back all unruly and revolutionary and imperial, lolling around, spreading this way and that, like an untended garden? Kate, who said she worshiped it, would not recognize me. She might repudiate me. Me, with no Bermuda Triangle, would I be me? Oh, dear! "So, you want me smooth."

"Yes," he kissed me and held me very tight, "Totally, absolutely, totally smooth, darling. "

I put my finger to my chin, and I stuck out one leg as a Renaissance courtier, or offhand spoiled first son dithering prince might do, and I declaimed. "Why, look you now, Master, how unworthy a thing you make of me! You, Master, would pluck out from me the heart of my mystery. Oh, yes, you would!"

I walked back and forth and then stood defiantly before him, my hands on my hips. "You, Master, would play upon me naked, and, knowing all the naked, exposed stops of my precious little flute, you would sound me, Master, from my lowest note to the top of my compass."

I looked down at myself and put my hand, modestly, protectively, on my pubis. I looked up and appealed to his mercy. "And there is much music, excellent voice, in this little organ – and, oh, how you know how to make it speak and sing!"

He stood for a minute, a smile hovering on his lips. He was a powerful prince in all his grandeur. He took me into his arms and kissed me. "So you played Hamlet."

"Yes, and in tights too, Master, which I am sure would have pleased you mightily, and a small, narrow-waist doublet, and I had a hat with a feather on it, cocked at just the right angle." I kissed him, put my hand to the side of his face, and sighed. "We only did a few scenes. Kate was Horatio – my wise philosopher friend, who counseled skepticism, while I countered with belief in and submission to the invisible mysteries of the universe. There are more things in Heaven and Earth, Horatio, than are dreamt of in your philosophy."

"So, you intend to oppose and refuse me, then, Princess."

"No, Master, I have decided to submit to your will, to bow to your caprice."

"Ah, you are my goddess!" He took me in his arms and kissed me.

"Won't it be prickly?"

"No, they tell me this method leaves you smooth and soft."

"Smooth and soft ... ah ..."

"Yes."

"Okay," I said, "I mean ... Hmm." I had thought I would have time to think this out – perhaps sleep on it.

"Splendid!" He grinned. "Well, here we are, then."

"Already?"

"Yes, already." He pushed open the door of the shop, and I found myself in a very exclusive looking little salon, with one or two young women waiting, perched on gilded Louis XV chairs. It seemed I had an appointment.

"Shall I leave you alone, darling?"

"Ah, yes, I guess so."

"I'll be at the corner café, out on the terrace. Scream if you need me."

I gave him the mutinous look from under my eyebrows, wondering if, were I all-smooth, shaved, punk-like, with no eyebrows or topknot, would I be able to give him any look at all? Perhaps that would be the next thing he would require of me – total all-over smooth and hairless, and then locked faceless inside a mask of latex. The idea was intriguing. I took a deep breath, closed my eyes, and kissed him. "Yes, I'll scream," I said, "I will most certainly scream."

And then he was gone.

A young woman came out from behind a curtain. "Gwendoline? Gwendoline Clermont?"

"That's me."

I was ushered into a little room that was lit up like an operating theater, but there was music playing, soft music, almost subliminal, soporific, and reassuringly cozy. Suddenly, I was alone with a young woman who had marvelous cheekbones, a voluptuous mouth, perfectly tanned skin, and very blond hair;

she was dressed in a transparent-looking white smock – I imagined her naked and lustful under the smock. She ordered me to undress, which I did, and she ordered me to lie down in a reclining chair, which I did; and she set quickly set to work. She used creams, wax, and various magic lotions. It was like having a gynecological examination, or maybe more like having a pubic and vaginal massage. "The skin has to be very tight, stretched tight," she said. She ordered me to lie on my stomach on a sort of operating take. I stood up, and then lay down on my tummy, one arm under my cheek, and one arm straight down by my side. The woman examined me.

"Spread your legs," she said.

"Okay," I mumbled. I was beginning to feel drowsy.

"You are amazing," she said.

"Why amazing?"

"Hairless, absolutely hairless, except for that little triangle."

"Yes, I know," I said, "It's one of the few things that make me unique."

"And I've gone and taken it away," she said, with mock commiseration.

"Exactly," I said, sighing. "Its name is Bermuda Triangle. Or Heart of Darkness. My girlfriend prefers Heart of Darkness."

"Oh, that is so sweet!"

It took about half an hour, and at the end, I looked at myself in the mirror, and it looked like I had hardly any sex at all – just a tiny, discreet little slit, hardly visible. I felt it – it was all silky smooth. "This will grow back?" I gulped.

"Oh, yes," she said, "but if you decide on permanence, we have the best laser service in the city."

"We'll see," I said.

≈

When I came out of the little shop, I could see James seated at a table on the terrace of the café down at the street corner. He was reading The Financial Times. The sun was lower and shining down at an angle, and most of the street was in shadow.

I stood for a moment, feeling shy and newly exposed, and observed James. He was truly a handsome specimen of humankind. My heart warmed, just looking at him.

Feeling self-conscious, and suddenly naked in a new and unfamiliar way, I walked toward the café and the person who, for the moment at least, was "my man" – my Master. The space between my legs seemed breezy; it was as if the wind were caressing and tickling my labia, though there was no wind.

James, glanced at me from under his eyebrows, folded his paper, and stood up. "How do you feel," he said. "Do you hate me?"

"You will suffer shortly," I said, and kissed him. In truth, I liked doing things for him. I would strip naked here on this fashionable street in Rome, crowded with shoppers, and crawl on all fours, if it pleased him. Of course, I would make him pay for it – afterward.

"Ah, ah," he said, "I look forward to suffering at your hands."

"I'm sure you will enjoy it. I promise you your punishment will be exquisite – and exemplary."

"Would you like a coffee?"

"No, I think I'm ready for the next stage – whatever that is."

"Well, darling Gwendoline, then we just go down this little side ally here, and through this doorway here, and then into this rather private courtyard, right here." He led me by the hand, and I followed, a willing schoolgirl. I was Little Red Riding Hood, being led to the slaughterhouse by the handsome wicked wolf.

The courtyard was an enclosed small cobblestoned space, which for some reason, looked and felt more like Paris than Rome. The facades were white. A few large, very leafy plants overflowed from oversized terracotta vases. There was a porter's lodge beside one entrance. There was *La Fontaine des Mystères*, a dealer in antique books, mostly occult and mystical it seemed, with a scattering of vintage erotica, including ancient postcards, old dusty volumes were piled up behind the shop window. On the opposite side of the courtyard, there was a small shop, *La Petite Boutique Rouge*, with two smallish shop windows, displaying lingerie – black and red and white lingerie, corsets, stockings, and chokers with cameos and, discreetly, in one corner, a black leather cat o' nine tails, with a red handle. You could see through the display, dimly, into the interior. It looked like someone's boudoir. I examined the whip. It was quite pretty, intricately woven tresses of red and black leather.

"Am I to be whipped, Master?"

"Not now, not today, and never, Gwendoline, unless you desire it."

I leaned against him. "So, we are to enter here?"

"We are to enter here."

We entered.

A little bell tinkled.

The shop was empty. It truly did look like an 18th Century boudoir. There were gilt Louis XV chairs, with armrests; there were two full-length mirrors with gilt frames; and there was a Louis XV dresser, cream-colored with ornate gilded handles. Above the dresser, was a reproduction of some 18th Century French painting, a naked nymph type thing, and then, beside it, a reproduction of Fragonard's *The Happy Lovers*. Thick cream-colored velvet curtains masked the back of the shop. The effect was intimate and personal, something like a lady's boudoir. There were newspapers in a rack, and magazines, Vogue, Harpers, The Economist, Le Monde, the Frankfurter Allgemeine Zeitung, Corriere della Sera, and so on.

A very elegant woman, in her forties, I guessed, with short black hair and sharp and classic, fine features, an exquisite beauty really, came out from behind the curtains, pushing them gently aside. She was dressed in a charcoal black Armani broad-shouldered jacket, and short pleated skirt, dark stockings and low-heeled pumps. "Hello, James," she said.

"Hello, Nicole," he said. "I'd like you to meet my mathematical prodigy friend, Gwendoline – Gwendoline Clermont."

"Greetings, Gwendoline." Nicole and I shook hands. Nicole's handshake was warm, dry, and friendly and applied just the right degree of pressure. I noticed she had a French accent.

"Well, what happens now?" I looked around.

"James has shared some ideas with me, Gwendoline," Nicole kept the friendly smile on her face, "And perhaps you and I could try them out and see if we can make them work – and of course we can then decide if we like what we are doing – or not."

"Okeydokey." I squared my shoulders and wondered where precisely this little adventure might be leading me.

"I will wait here," James said. "There's an interesting report on Hungary." He held up The Economist.

"I think the government will fall," I said. I had just read all about it, early in the morning and, foolishly, I wanted show off and establish my creds: I am not just his bimbo; I really am an important, really intelligent young woman and ...

Also, aside from that particular petty little defensive move, I am, in general, a know-it-all blabbermouth, and I like to impress people, particularly people I find attractive. I couldn't help myself.

"Oh, how so?" James raised an eyebrow.

"The trade unions are threatening a strike. And Nagy, the Secretary-General of the ..."

"Oh, yes, I see your point. Nagy, of course, he's a wild card."

"I'm sorry ..." I looked down; I was being a pedantic nerd know-it-all-show-off; my gambit had backfired, at least in my own eyes.

James grinned. "You see, Nicole, I told you. Gwendoline is a prodigy and an encyclopedia." He turned to me, put his hands on my shoulders, and kissed me on the forehead. "The more expert you become on everything, dear Gwendoline, the more enchanting and sexy you are. There is nothing to be sorry about."

James, my Master, could see right through me. I sighed and turned to Nicole, and I couldn't help but wonder how many times James had done this, how many times he had connived with Nicole to transform some young innocent, such as myself, into a bejeweled naked goddess or a tattooed slave or whatever I was destined to become.

Nicole saw the drift of my thought. "James came to see me last week. It was the first time he and I met. He told me about you, and he explained he had a little project which you and I could work on together." She gave me the warmest of smiles. "Also, I have the items you asked for, Monsieur James."

Nicole disappeared behind the cream-colored curtain, and reappeared with a large package and put it down on the dresser and invited me to open it.

It turned out the package contained a latex catsuit with a little flap opening at the crotch. I held it up. "Oh, how nice," I gave James a look. "And I see it doesn't have a zipper! How thoughtful!"

There was also another catsuit, not of latex, but of elastic black velvet. This, James explained, would be for around the house or for going to Alfredo's. Matching the black velvet catsuit, were long black velvet gloves. Slinky. There were a few G-string looking things too. Hmm. I was truly destined to become a circus performer.

Nicole turned to James. "Now, Monsieur James, do you want me to close the shop?"

"No, no, I think such beauty is to be seen, is it not?"

"Yes," she smiled.

Oh, oh, I thought.

"Well, Gwendoline, shall we begin?" Nicole turned to me.

"Yes, I guess we shall." I took a deep breath.

I preceded Nicole through the thick cream curtains, and then through another velvet curtain into a rather luxurious dressing room. "Undress here," Nicole said. There was a mirror with a warm light. I looked, well, I looked great, maybe a bit pale. There was a glass of red wine. Nicole nodded toward it. "It's for you." She left the room. I took a sip. I began to undress.

James peeked in, between the curtains, looked me up and down.

"Everything," he said.

"Everything?"

"Yes."

"Okay," I swallowed. This was maybe more than I bargained for. I took off everything.

Nicole came in and stood beside me. "Let us go into the back room," she said, and opened yet another curtain.

"Okeydokey." I preceded her.

This room had a makeup table and cabinets that looked like they might be at home in a pharmacy or a medical office. Whisks and whips were hanging on the walls, and ceiling-to-floor closets, and several full-length mirrors.

Nicole took one of the whisks from the wall.

"Let us examine you, Gwendoline," she said. "Turn around."

"Yes, ma'am."

"Excellent deportment," she said, running the stiff sparkling whisk down my backside, flipping it back and forth, then over

my belly, then down my thighs. It tickled and whispered dangerous insinuations to each nerve ending. Little sparkles of nervous electricity moved up and down my skin. She whipped me
with the whisk, but gently – something between a tickle and a
sting.

"The erogenous zones are multiple, and it is good to be sure
we have sensitized them; but I think you know this already," she
said, stroking my belly with the whisk and then tilting my chin
upwards with two fingers, and then cupping my face with both
hands. Her hands were warm and dry.

"Take the delicacy of the earlobe," she said, and she stroked the
outer edge of my ear, and tugged gently. "We could pierce these,
for example, and hang a quite nice large circular ring from it. Or
we could enlarge the lobe, as some body artists do, to contain, say,
a two-inch brass or ceramic ring."

"Yes," I swallowed. She was stroking the earlobe and the edge
of my ear. Her breath was perfumed, close against my skin. She
kissed my ear. Her lips were ultra-soft and smooth. She nibbled,
with her lips, then with her teeth, at the earlobe. I took a slow
breath. Was I supposed to grope back? No, I don't think I was.
The wispy strands of hair at the nape of my neck seemed elec-
trified, moving, standing up. I swallowed. I was tempted to say
something, but didn't.

She touched my lips with her fingertips, running them back
and forth, and then she kissed me. "The lips too can be redesigned," she said, "made fuller, more voluptuous, or even more
radical interventions can be undertaken. I imagine you've seen
those girls in Africa with the lip plates – or body artists who imi-
tate them."

"Yes, I have," I said, swallowing. "But I don't think I'm quite
ready for the ..."

Nicole held up her hand. "Of course not, of course not." She favored me with a radiant smile and stood back. "We shall not transform you beyond recognition. He loves you very much – just as you are. I am jealous. Rather envious, I must admit. He seems a good man. I would like to be in the position you are in."

"Yes, he is good, a good man," I said, thinking, and he's rich and handsome and virile as a stallion and funny and knows a hell of a lot of things.

"And that is very nice," she said, indicating my naked look, no sign whatsoever the Bermuda Triangle had ever existed. I looked at myself in the mirror: *La Frileuse*, totally naked.

"Yes," I said.

"He suggested it, I believe." She put her hand there, and then stroked my nakedness, just touching my labia. Her fingers were soft, but strong, no hesitation – just possession, as if it were the most natural gesture in the world.

"Yes," I said, "It was his idea."

"Now, let's try this on," she said and handed me a garter belt. It was slender, elastic, and black, and it went around my waist. "Here," she said, "It has clasps at the back. I'll clip it shut for you." She did. Again, her hands were warm and caressing. Each touch was soothing yet electric

"Now the silk stockings," she said, "these are the very best." She rolled the stockings up my legs. Then she clipped the stockings into place. They were magnificent, sheer dark perfection.

"These shoes are just your size." They were black, patent leather stilettoes, true stilettoes. I took a deep breath. She slipped the shoes onto my feet.

She was kneeling in front of me as she did this. She stroked my calf and my ankles and looking up at me, as if she were worshiping an idol – or calculating, in the friendliest way possible, my worth, my willingness to surrender, and my degree of compliance.

She let her hand rest on my leg, and then she moved it upwards, along the inner side of my thigh, to the top of the stocking. She let her hand rest there, and asked, "How does it feel?"

"Ah, good," I breathed, thinking what a stupid, insipid thing to say.

She smiled and licked her lips. Her hand continued up the inside of my thigh, which was damp now. I held my breath. She reached out with her other hand and took a gob of cream – what looked like cream – from a small open vase of white ceramic I had not even noticed – and her hand continued upward and then she caressed me.

It was a weird sensation, being so smooth, so naked, not even a hint of pubic hair. She placed the gob of cream on my labia, and began, slowly, to massage and open my lips.

"Is this really …?" I looked down.

"Shush little baby," she said, "You and I are together in this."

Little baby? How dare she?

Oh, well, by now, she could dare anything. I was an idiot.

The cream – whatever it was – warmed me, and I felt a rising excitement. She put more cream and more, caressing deeper and deeper. I was wet now and almost trembling. "I'm not usually called baby," I said.

"I know." She smiled.

She went to a built-in set of side drawers, opened one, considered for a moment, took out one jar, put it back; she took out another small jar and a makeup brush. "This is very delicate," she said, "It shouldn't irritate your skin."

She crouched in front of me, dipped the brush in the jar, and, frowning in concentration, began to work. A cool and then a warm sensation spread across my lower belly.

I looked down: she was painting my pubis in sparkling gold.

"Oh, boy," I said.

"Yes, oh boy," she said, not looking up, dipping the brush in the jar, and again applying paint, with light feathery strokes. "Oh, boy is quite appropriate."

Soon the former home of my late lamented Dark Triangle had become a glittering naked gold triangle.

"Good, that looks good." She licked her lips in satisfaction, stood up, smiled, kissed me lightly on the lips, and then held my naked shoulders, stared into my eyes, and said, "Well, now, a little makeup."

"I never wear makeup, or hardly ever."

"Yes, you certainly don't need it. But now you shall wear it – we are inventing a different look, a different you, something entirely new." She kissed me on the lips, and then she slid open another drawer and took out a full makeup kit.

I frowned.

"So," she said, "this is a matter of taste. I think you are perfect the way you are. But, we are here to please. Are we not?"

I nodded. I felt my eyes were becoming glossy, a little blurry. She turned to me and ran her hand over my ass – her touch was smoothly sensual, intimate, easy, and warm. My nipples, I noticed, were erect, begging to be touched, to be licked, and to be sucked. Inside – hidden by my stoic outer calm – I was wet, hot, eager, trembling. I wanted Nicole to seize me, touch me, take me; and I wanted to grab her, kiss her, and rip that elegant jacket and all her clothes, rip every stitch from her beautiful fragrant body; I wanted to make her as naked and exposed as I was; and I wanted her down on her knees, worshipping me, licking, kissing, searching, exploring me. Whew! What was happening to me? Well, I knew quite well what was happening to me, damn it! I was getting lusty, horny as hell, very unladylike. Gwendoline, calm down!

Nicole gazed into my eyes and winked. She had understood every thought, every feeling running through my feverish and addled brain. Gazing back at her, I noticed, that she had little flakes of gold in her dark iris and pupil; she had, too, the finest looking eyelashes, long, thick, jet-black, like mine, and as if tipped with silver.

She set to work. She concentrated, a true artist, painting my face, lying down a thick and complete foundation, taking her time, sculpting, studying, sculpting, adding a touch here and there; she stood back, and let the tip of her tongue run along her lips. "You are delicious," she said, "A perfect mask."

"Thank you, I think."

She kissed my shoulder and lightly brushed my right nipple, letting her fingers linger for just an instant.

She began to apply mascara and eye shadow; I could feel it; the design was being filled in. My face was beginning to take on the stiff hieratic look of a ceramic doll. Finally, she applied lipstick, a brilliant glowing red shade. She held up a small mirror; it just showed my lips.

"Boy," I whispered.

"Yes," she said, "The lipstick is non-smear. Here, I'll show you." She kissed me, forcing my lips open, and just allowing her tongue to brush mine.

"Now, let's have a look," she said.

I turned and looked at myself in the bigger mirror she held up.

It was startling. I looked like a cover of Vogue, one of those schematic, perfect, highlighted faces that are unreal, unbelievable. There was a suggestion, in my bright scarlet lips, of a cupid's bow. My eyelids were heavy shadowy turquoise. My eyebrows arched up in quizzical surprising form, coal-black, with touches of turquoise and silver. My cheekbones displayed a bright, circular rose-like blush. Oh, boy! I did look like a ceramic doll, or a clown on a movie poster. My eyes had never seemed darker – almost coal-black – as if the irises and pupils had completely merged.

"Now!" She put down the mirror, stood back, and contemplated her creation. She stepped forward and brushed my nipples and areolae with a sort of scarlet lacquer. It evaporated, with a cooling, astringent effect. My nipples tightened, even more erect. I had never felt such a sensation in my breasts before – not like this. It was a strange mixture of pinching pain, engorgement and swelling, and soft almost nostalgic yearning. I feverishly craved for her to squeeze my nipples, twist them; I wanted Nicole to put her lips to them and suck and suckle.

"Exciting, no?" She winked, again as if she had divined my thoughts – and she applied yet more lacquer – it was cool, then hot. My nipples, burning pleasantly now, frozen erect, straining to be touched, yearning to be touched, to be twisted, squeezed, and sucked. The bright scarlet nipples and areolae were startling against my chalk-white skin.

I cleared my throat and licked my lips.

She stood back and looked at me. "Turn around," she said.

I turned around, catching a glimpse of myself in a full-length mirror. The stilettoes thrust out my ass and pulled in my tummy. I looked like a painted doll or toy soldier, standing at attention.

I took a deep breath. I felt that I hadn't taken a breath, not for a long time. I was liquid with desire. I was coated in a thin, invisible patina of lustful sweat.

"Now," she said, "a finishing touch, my dear." She knelt in front of me. She took out what looked like a tube of lipstick – and she painted my labia – a ruby glow. Oh, my God!

"Special, non-smear," she said. "The color will resist, even get brighter."

"This is ..." I was going to say, and did say, "outrageous."

"Yes, it is, isn't it?" She stood up, moved away, and contemplated her work. "Well, Gwendoline, I for one am pleased."

I turned and looked at myself in the full-length mirror.

"Holy Moly," I breathed.

Nicole draped a thin white silk sheet over my shoulders and wrapped it around me. I held it against my body.

"Now, let us see," she said, "let us see what effect we have."

≈

James was sitting in one of the gilt Louis XV chairs, reading a newspaper, now it was the French Le Monde.

He looked so perfectly poised, so handsome, with the crisp jeans, the impeccable blue shirt, the casual sandals, and his tan, and dark, perfect hair, there he was, the lean body, coiled dark energy!

Nicole nodded. I bowed my head and let go of the silk sheet; it slipped off my shoulders, wafted away from my breasts, slithering off me like a satin-slippery skin sliding away from the newly naked body of a reborn serpent. I was unveiled. Truly, now, I was a slave girl in a slave market on the coast of Barbary. But, in its own way, this was not a fantasy; this was real. I held my breath; I didn't move.

James was silent. I swallowed.

"Turn around," he said. His stare was intense, almost hard.

I turned around. The stilettoes made every move, every muscle, and every tendon self-conscious. Nicole had sculpted me in naked flesh, just for him. I was his, a chalk-white, breathing marble statue. My body, my flesh, my skin – existed only for him. This was even worse, even better, than the latex – Oh, the latex panther cat girl-look! She was so sweet, so pure, so long ago!

I felt James' eyes moving on me, like electricity, like a caress; his gaze made me feel as if his fingertips and lips were moving over me, exploring, probing, defining me, mapping every millimeter, recreating me out of fresh wet clay, a creature of his masterly and manly imagination, his gaze flowing over me like invisible fire.

This was truly the reifying, defining, objectifying, male gaze. I was living it, in its true unadulterated splendor. But, at the same time, strangely, I was not only me, I was also him; I saw myself through his eyes; this double conscience gave me an extra thrill – I was me, and not me.

James stood up, came over, and kissed me on the lips.

"You are a goddess," he said. He moved back, and considered me again. "Perhaps more gold," he said.

"Yes, Monsieur," Nicole said. She disappeared.

James put his hands on my shoulders and kissed me again.

Now, I was standing, naked except for the thin garter belt and stockings; I thought for just an instant about precisely where I was – in the middle of this strange shop, La Petite Boutique Rouge, in the false Louis XV boudoir; visible to anybody who happened to come in, or to anybody who peered through the windows. Through the gauzy curtain, I could see the courtyard. A couple was walking across it. The woman had a dog on a leash.

James handed me the silk sheet and draped it over my shoulders. "But leave it open," he said, "Don't cover yourself."

"Yes, Master." I gave him a quick smirk, and bowed in a brief pageboy obeisance. Bending over, caused the silk sheet to slide from one of my shoulders; I pulled it back, just a little bit; it covered my back down to my knees, but in front, I was naked except for the garter belt, the silk stockings, and the stilettos. My crimson labia, gold pubis, and scarlet nipples and areolae were all offered, fully in view.

The door opened, the little bell tinkled, and a couple entered. The man looked at me and looked at James. "Ah, should we ...?"

"No, no, not at all, come in." James bowed slightly, displaying his most gracious and welcoming manner.

My instinct was to clutch the silk sheet around me and scurry for shelter, but James shook his head: No. So I left it there, non-chalantly, wafting open, draping only my shoulders.

Nicole came out with a small bowl and a brush and glanced at the couple. "Yes, we are open. Please do make yourselves at home. Stay, look around."

This is a performance, I thought, or maybe like a piece of performance art. I am an illustration. I am a circus animal. Soon I will jump through hoops. I glanced at the windows. Outside it was getting darker; already, it was late afternoon, intimations in the air of a long, sultry, Roman summer evening. My inner thighs were damp.

The young woman looked at me, blinked, smiled a shy smile, and turned away. She began to examine a turquoise and scarlet corset on a mannequin torso by the entrance.

Nicole knelt before me, and she began to brush my lips and, delicately, to add more paint to the area around my labia, an extra, sequin-like, feathery brushing of gold, snaking up my stomach to my bellybutton.

The girl glanced sideways at me. She smiled and hazarded a small wave. I nodded curtly and blinked. Then I smiled. Her smile was open and friendly, a smile of complicity, as if we shared a secret. I had seen her somewhere. She had a face of stunning classic beauty, perfectly symmetrical, with full lips, blue eyes, a golden tan, blond hair, stark black eyebrows, and thick black eyelashes. I tried to think where I might have seen her. It almost made me forget, for an instant, that I was naked, and everyone else was dressed.

"She is very beautiful," said the man, in French, nodding toward me, but pretending to examine the scarlet and turquoise corset that was mounted on the mannequin.

"Yes, she is," said the girl.

"I'd like you to try this," said the man, again in French,

indicating a black-and-red topless corset mounted on the wall.

"Breasts too," said James, pointing at me, "and the cheeks of her ass."

At the mention of my "ass," I frowned, "Grrhh!"

James winked and smiled, delighting in my allergy to vulgar language. He stood up, came over, and touched the tip of my left nipple with his finger.

The nipple was lacquered, scarlet, and rigid, but it responded to his touch as if to an electric shock. It has a life of its own – utter desire. Again, I yearned to kiss him, devour him, to eat him, to merge into him.

I could sense everything about him. The texture and smell of his clothes, the crisp, clean jeans, the denim shirt, the lingering smell of sunlight and salt on his skin. His pure physical presence overwhelmed me.

He squeezed the rigid nipple, and twisted. His touch was like lightning. I almost groaned. I almost said, "No, please ..."

"Yes, James, the breasts and the cheeks of her ass." Nicole lifted the silk sheet off my shoulders and folded it over a chair. She turned to examine me. Narrowing her eyes, she tilted her head, and like the true artist that she undoubtedly was, she set to work. The brush fluttered over my breasts, laying down a satin patina of sparkling gold around the scarlet nipple and areolae. The same golden treatment she would now apply to the cheeks of my ass.

The French girl was holding at arm's length the black-and-red corset, looking at it, but also glancing at me.

"Now, walk, back, and forth." James was rubbing his chin, as if considering a difficult choice of wines, or whether or not to buy a pony. I was the circus pony, or perhaps I was a red Ferrari or a bottle of Châteauneuf-du-Pape.

All of them were looking at me now, and I felt the moisture rising.

"Mademoiselle," Nicole turned to the young French woman, and said, in French, "You may change if you wish. I shall join you in a minute. It is best, Mademoiselle, if you and Monsieur agree, that you remove all your clothes."

"I agree, I certainly agree," said the man, again in French.

The girl looked at him, blinked, smiled a crafty smile, and stuck out her tongue: it was a damp, pink tongue; it flickered between her full lips, and disappeared, leaving just a trace of glowing saliva. She winked at me and, carrying the black-and-red corset, pushed through the thick curtains into the changing rooms.

Nicole returned to painting my backside, the inner side of the cheeks. The brush tickled, it felt feathery, and cool, and, at the same time, it burned as if with each touch of the sparkly gold Nicole was branding me with a mark of shame and eternal lust.

James sat down in one of the Louis XV chairs and motioned to the Frenchman. The Frenchman nodded and sat down beside him. The two men, comfortably seated in regal chairs, gazed at me. I pretended to ignore them. The Frenchman had long, thick black hair, big sensitive eyes, and strong features. Everything was perfect. He looked like an actor or film director. His shirt was open on his tanned chest – lots of black curly hair and a glow from a patina of sweat. It was hot outside. In here, it was cool. I could vaguely see, through the window display, people going by; a few of them stopped to look in the window; some of them, I am certain, noticed me.

"Now, Gwendoline, walk up and down," Nicole said.

I walked up and down, I turned around, and I turned around again. I glanced at myself in the full-length mirror. The two men watched me.

"What do you think about gold?" James said. He was smiling. He had folded up Le Monde and laid it in his lap.

"Gold?" I thought of my pubis, sequined gold, of my breasts, brightly lacquered and shadowed with gold, and my backside, sculpted and painted in gold. James was looking at me, staring me straight in the eye. James was asking what I thought about the market for gold! The idiot! The bloody idiot!

Rising to the bait and like a good little wind-up clock, I decided to perform. "Well, Master, the price of gold will depend on supply and demand, and on certain short-term purely speculative factors based on expectations about the price of gold, which makes the whole thing a bit circular, an example of reflexivity, as George Soros would say, in other words, of feedback loops. The demand for gold in India will depend partly on the Monsoon, which will depend in part on the La Nina-el Nino cycle. The La Nina-el Nino cycle will depend on the pattern and prevalence of the trade winds; the Monsoon will determine harvests in India, and therefore the amount of money that Indian farmers and families can invest in gold, or, if the harvest is really bad, the amount of money they must draw down by selling gold." I cleared my throat. "In rich countries, where gold is seen as a hedge against inflation, the demand for gold will be influenced by expectations about inflation. Inflation expectations can be judged from the level of interest rates and the yield curve linking short-term interest rates with longer-term interest rates, since the farther out in future time they are, the farther interest rates have to compensate, by being higher, for the perceived risk of price rises, in other words, inflation. Some central banks, being very reactionary, and mistrusting the reserve currencies, in particular, the US dollar, may decide to purchase gold and as backup and insurance against a decline in the value of the dollar. Now, if interest rates, or yields, on other assets are high, then the cost of holding gold, which pays no interest, is high, and that can discourage holding gold. But the price depends too, at the margin of supply, on many supply factors – political trouble in gold-producing countries, for example, and on your time-horizon, short-term, or long-term, and … and … so on. In short, it is all very complicated, depends on speculations about the future – the future which is unknowable, as John Maynard Keynes pointed out – and on the lemming-like psychology of markets and investors." I curtsied.

The Frenchman who had been closely watching this little performance raised his eyebrows. James smiled – his cute fatuous smile.

I frowned: I am a trained monkey, a circus monkey, or maybe I'm a parrot. I should squawk "Pretty Polly" to earn a biscuit. I was sorely tempted to recite "Pretty Polly! Pretty Polly!" But I didn't.

The young French woman came out from behind the curtain. She was wearing the tight-waisted strapless topless corset. It was black and red, with elaborate filigree work, spiraling down both sides, and red ruffles flaring out just below her breasts and red ruffles at the bottom and with dangling garter belts that hung down her naked thighs. She wasn't wearing stockings, or panties.

No one was looking at me, so I allowed myself the luxury of giving her the once-over. She was barefoot, slender, and blond, with golden skin, a golden, all-over tan, and no pubic hair, perhaps just a suggestion of gold stipples, but that may have been an effect of the light, or perhaps she had tried out the little bottle of gold spray Nicole had left behind.

I wanted to touch her pubis to see if she was perfectly smooth like I was or if there was a little sandpapery feel. I wanted to establish a sisterhood of nakedness. Somehow, seeing her wearing the corset, made me feel even more naked.

Nicole turned her attention back to me and contemplated her creation. "Well, Gwendoline, we can choose your clothes now.

Please wait for me in the change room. Oh, and leave the silk sheet here, please."

I left the silk sheet folded up on the chair. I narrowed my eyes and stuck the tip of my tongue out at James, and I sashayed, rather boldly, I thought, back into the change room. I looked at myself in the full-length mirror. Is that me? That person in the full-length mirror with the scarlet lips, the heavy eye shadow, the white ceramic mask for a face, and the scarlet nipples and areolae – and the golden naked pubis with the scarlet labia. Was that really me?

Nicole entered and began to add more lacquer to my nipples and areolae.

"Aren't you overdoing it?"

"We can never have too much of a good thing, Gwendoline," she said, pursing her lips, and adopting a mock pedantic schoolmarm voice, a bit straight-laced and puritan, and giving me a neat slap on the bum. "You may have a long night ahead of you. We must be prepared."

"Have you ever used that cat o' nine tails, the red and black one that's hanging in the window?"

"Oh, Gwendoline, how inquisitive you are!! Well, yes, I did once or twice use not that particular one, but one just like it, on several gentlemen, and I did have occasion to use it several times on a rather naughty and quite eager young woman."

"Hmm, did you enjoy it?"

"Yes, I did, but not as much as my victims did, I'm afraid."

The French girl, still wearing the frilly topless corset, entered the change room. Who invited her? I was about to object, but then I realized that I didn't mind, really, the more, the merrier. She smiled, and I smiled back.

"This will feel like nipple-clamps," Nicole said, "A very sensual form of pain and constriction." She painted on more lacquer.

"Ouch!" I bit my lip as the thicker scarlet lacquer tightened.

"Now, a little refresher."

The French girl watched as Nicole took a plastic tube, knelt in front of me, and injected a large gob of cream between my labia. I whispered, half-mocking myself – the innocent abroad. "Oh, God, what is that?"

"It will keep you fresh – warmed up," Nicole smiled up at me.

"My name is Martine," said the girl. She held out her hand; I shook it. I said, "I'm Gwendoline, and this is Nicole."

"May I?" Martine reached a hand toward my brightly lacquered nipples, still tight and even more erect. I nodded, "Yes, go ahead, Martine. I'm public property."

She touched my breast, running the tip of her finger around, softly, in a circle, caressing, massaging, the glands, and then gently, squeezed, increased the pressure, and twisted the stiff nipple. The sensation, voluptuous pain, almost made me rise on my toes. Martine ran the tip of her tongue along her lips and bared her teeth in a wicked little smile.

"I think we will eliminate Gwendoline's stockings and garter," said Nicole. "Would you help me, Mademoiselle Martine?"

"Of course."

Martine knelt and removed my shoes.

Then she stood up, and I felt her fingers, delicate, warm, and caressing, against my skin as she unclipped the garter belt. She stared at me and blinked, and then she knelt again, and, while Nicole watched, she rolled down the stockings and removed them.

I was once again naked

The fitting for clothes began.

"This perhaps is just what is required. Just the right thing." Nicole held out a short skirt, it was red, and shiny, and it looked like it was made of latex. I reached out and touched it. It was, in fact, made of latex or rubber; it had stiff pleats.

It fitted nicely, and flared halfway up my thighs, and it had, I noticed a built-in belt with adjustable notches, making for an adjustable slit down one side – it could be a narrow slit, or a wide slit, or a very wide slit, baring one whole thigh. Hmm ...

Then I was outfitted with those perfect black stilettoes.

Martine and Nicole both offered comments.

Nicole took a black silk jacket out of a cupboard, and I slid my arms into it. It was very thin and very light; it had one button to fasten it.

So, there I was, outfitted with a black silk jacket, closed with one button, and the short pleated skirt, made of red latex, that rode high up my thighs, stilettoes, and, of course, no panties.

I went out between the curtains.

James approved. And so did Martine's man. He gave me a long appreciative, and pleasantly friendly stare.

I returned to the change room to help in the preparation of "Mademoiselle Martine."

Nicole unlaced the corset. I stood very close. Martine smelled nice. Nicole opened the corset, and Martine wiggled, let the corset drop down around her ankles, and she stepped out of it.

"Gwendoline, perhaps you could help Mademoiselle Martine and prepare her for her new dress."

"Okay," I said. I guessed this must be part of the training.

"A little powder will help," said Nicole. The powder was skin-colored.

"Use your hands, Gwendoline."

"Okay."

I smoothed the powder over Martine's back.

"Go ahead, go ahead. Don't be shy."

"I like your touch, Gwendoline." Martine blinked at me.

"You do?" I smoothed the powder over her breasts and buttocks, down her belly, and over her thighs. It quickly became invisible, leaving only a glistening sheen.

"I think that, before we put on the dress, we should emphasize the nipples and areolae," said Nicole.

"Really?" said Martine, looking down at herself.

"Yes, I really do." Nicole pinched one of Martine's nipples and ran the whisk up and down her body.

"You are clearly the boss today, Madame Nicole," said Martine.

"I think black is your color, Martine."

"Black? Black nipples?"

"Yes, that is my thought."

Martine glanced down at her breasts, and then at me, and then looked Nicole in the eye. "Well, as I said, you are the boss, Nicole. I submit."

"I am merely here to serve, Mademoiselle Martine," Nicole said, narrowing her eyes, and brushing the whisk, with an imperious gesture, over Martine's breasts and belly, and then she turned to me. "Here, Gwendoline. You shall, for this occasion, be Martine's keeper." She handed me a small bottle with a fine brush. It looked like an ink bottle, with thick Chinese ink, something that a scholar of Confucius might use to draw elaborate Chinese characters on an ancient poetic scroll.

I dipped the brush in the little pot.

I began to paint the black lacquer onto Martine's breasts.

"Careful, now, Gwendoline, just the nipples and areolae."

"Yes, of course." I concentrated. "How much?"

Nicole showed me, "More – thicker."

The black paint dried quickly. I applied more and more, layer upon layer. Martine watched me throughout this exercise; a very nice, friendly smile hovered on her lips. Her nipples were anthracite black, standing erect, swelling, engorged, like mine.

"Wonderful," said Nicole.

"Yes, wonderful," said Martine; she mimed, giving me a kiss, nicely puckered up, and very sensual. Her eyes had a bright cool blue sparkle, like diamonds.

"Now, let us find the right dress for Mademoiselle Martine." Nicole rifled through a number of hanging dresses and catsuits, and finally pulled out a white elastic latex dress. Nicole handed it to me. Between my fingers, it was slinky like wet oiled silk latex. The material was ultra-thin. It looked like it was transparent.

Holding the dress, I knelt at Martine's feet.

"Thank you, Gwendoline." Martine caressed my hair.

As I held the dress, she stepped into it. I pulled it up as she shimmied into it. I had to help her pull and tug and smooth it, running my hands over her body, and stroking the material. The dress was ultra-tight, creamy white, and almost transparent; the material was so thin, it looked like Martine was naked, or dressed in a skin-tight wet elastic T-shirt. The black nipples and areolae were visible, starkly outlined; the latex sculpted and molded the erect nipples in stark and suave white and black.

Nicole provided stilettoes, exact twins of the black stilettoes I was wearing. As instructed, I knelt humbly at Martine's feet and buckled them up.

I stood up, and Martine turned to look at herself in the swing-out full-length mirror. The dress went up and enclosed her neck, but it bared her shoulders and her back down to her waist. Her collarbone, nipples, and breasts were delineated, as if coated in a glossy patina of milk, and her belly button, and her hips, and her thighs were as if sculpted in paint. Underneath, of course, it was quite clear she was naked.

"You are beautiful," I said. I swallowed. She was, in fact, stunning, utterly desirable, and adorably vulnerable.

"Thank you, Gwendoline." Martine turned to me; her blue-eyed gaze sparkled, so clear, so bright. "And you, dear Gwendoline, are luscious, appetizing beyond belief." She licked her lips, as if she were going to devor me on the spot.

Nicole watched over us as if we were two of her favorite protégées. She took a long hard look at me. "Now, I think we should perhaps add something extra for Gwendoline." She opened a drawer, and brought out a collar. It was a thick black leather collar with a sort of black filigree, lacy, ruff-like fringe on top and bottom. "Perhaps you would do the honors, Mademoiselle Martine."

"With pleasure." Martine took the collar and turned to me with a sly smile of sadistic anticipation, her perfect teeth gleaming between her perfect lips. I was beginning to think that this casual encounter was a piece of theater that Martine and her man – his name was Philip I had discovered – were part of, in fact, I was sure that it was all a little plot that James had concocted. I didn't care. I wanted to see where it was going and what would happen next. And, above all, I was eager to take James back to the apartment and make love, or perhaps make love under a bridge, or in a park, or in Saint Peter's Square under the obelisk – which would surely get us arrested.

"Do you like it, Gwendoline?" Martine put the collar under my nose so I could sniff the rich, polished leather smell; she turned it over in her hands and showed me the large metal ring attached at the front of the collar. Over the ring was a coat of arms, and in bright, embossed red letters, "Madame de Sade," with a cameo of the Marquis de Sade himself. Martine licked her lips and gave me that sly mischievous look that seemed to be one of her specialties. Yes, they intended to brand me.

I nodded. Do it!

Martine moved close. I felt her breath against my cheeks. She opened the collar, slid it around my neck, closed it, tightened it, and locked it. It made a distinct, definitive, click. The lacy frills tickled; they were designed, I figured, to make me continuously aware I was wearing a collar. Never forget your servitude! The collar was high, even higher than the panther collar, forcing me to hold my chin up, my head erect.

"Fetching ... perfect!" Martine stepped back and looked me up and down. She put her finger in the collar's ring and tugged, pulling me toward her. I tried to give her my mutinous from-under-the-eyebrows look, thinking, she is so extremely attractive and tempting, but what exactly do I want to do to her, or what do I want her to do to me? The tip of her tongue ran along her lips; she leaned forward and kissed me, lightly, on the lips, a soft sweet flickering kiss.

It was in that instant that I realized who Martine was. She was Martine Aubin, a French actress, a rising star. I'd seen her in at least two films. One was about two young women who go on a road trip from Paris to the south of France and who make love on a beach and then meet two young men who are intent on robbing a bank – and in a shootout, everybody gets killed but the Martine character. Filled with regret for all the death, and for the loss of her friends, she escapes, all alone, and disappears forever. The other film told the story of a young woman who was a professional killer with a heart of gold, sort of like Luc Besson's La Femme Nikita in style – chic and fast, sexy, and funny. I returned her kiss.

For a few minutes, Martine and I goofed around, flirting and touching up our makeup, under Nicole's stern and friendly supervision.

"Now," said Nicole, "I think the gentlemen are ready. They may indeed be getting impatient."

Stifling our giggles, Martine and I put on very serious faces, and we returned to the salon to be displayed as Nicole's latest creations, and to see if our masters approved.

James approved.

Philip approved.

Nicole offered us a choice of drinks, and because of the hot weather, everyone chose a gin tonic. We made small talk, and Nicole showed us some of her other products – some of which James bought; they went into the box with the catsuits and with my clothes. Nicole said she would arrange for everything to be delivered to our flat.

James said, "It is time, I believe, for dinner."

I glanced out the window. It was already growing dark, displaying that delicious, sensual, late, drowsy Roman summer twilight, with the golden light bathing everything for hours in warmth and tapering off and dying so slowly, as if with infinite regret.

"So, where are we going?"

"I thought Alfredo's might be appropriate." James took my hand and kissed it, and then looked up, giving me his best, most irresistibly charming smile.

Oh, dear, I thought. The remnants of my prissy cautious Boston-based me woke up from their slumber. Once again, my reputation would be shot. But, to tell the truth, I don't know why I kept thinking that. In fact, my reputation was certainly already completely shot; and had been for a long time. At this moment, did I really care? In fact, I was really enjoying this little theater of naughtiness – for that's what it was, it was theater. I was a fallen woman, already fallen! Alas! Even the good Carabinieri colonel and his faithful lieutenant knew I was a high-heeled, night-prowling, plastic panther in a catsuit, and on a leash. But, now, at Alfredo's, crowded as it would be, with everybody there on a beautiful summer evening ... Oh ...

How would I ever eat lunch there again?

Well, I would simply show up, shameless hussy that I am, and eat lunch. That's what I'd do.

"And our new friends, Philip and Martine, will come with us," said James, "If they are interested."

It seemed they were.

"James, is this a plot?"

His eyes twinkled. "It might well be, Goddess. It might well be! "

Alcide was waiting for us at the end of the little cobbled street. He was standing by the car, with his chauffeur's cap, and his blue suit, and his distinguished gray mustache and his perfect tan.

"Alcide," I said, "Aren't you hot in that suit?"

"I'm used to it, Signorina Gwendoline. And I see you have been buying clothes."

"James has been buying clothes. I'm merely a model, or maybe a clotheshorse."

"Well, it all looks quite wonderful. I am going to suggest, Signorina Gwendoline, that my wife consult with you on fashion." Alcide gave me a very courtly smile as he opened the door.

We got in. I was to sit in front, next to Alcide. James, Martine, and Philip were in the back.

The cobblestones glowed. Suddenly, it was night.

≈

We stopped at the edge of the little piazza where Alfredo had his kingdom. The restaurant terrace was crowded. I stepped out of the car. The short scarlet rubber skirt flared halfway up my thighs in a bouncy elastic way, and the black lock-on stilettoes made my bare legs feel much too long. My body felt utterly naked and exposed. I stood, teetering, hesitating, on the glowing cobblestones, feeling, with a delicious, trembling anticipation of shame, that, already, I was making a spectacle of myself. The audience I wished for was James and James alone.

What are we doing here, with these strangers, Martine, and

her handsome man? I wondered. I wanted James to hold me. I wanted to be back in our apartment. I wanted to press myself to him and feel his lips on mine. I wanted to feel his desire. I wanted him pressed against me. I wanted to make love. I desperately wanted to make love ...

Actually, dressed as I was, it felt as if James was already, at this very moment, making love to me, and not only him but the whole piazza, even the walls and vines and cobblestones and the air itself. Each glance was a greedy caress.

James was, indeed, my Master. My sense of myself had been redesigned – by him and just for him. I was, I blush to admit, excited. This would certainly be embarrassing – and, therefore, it would be exciting.

Martine came around the car and joined me. Philip was just behind her. People's faces turned to glance at us and then stopped to stare. We did look, well ... Provocative, I suppose.

My face was a bright white mask, my lips scarlet, my eyelids and eyebrows turquoise and black, and splashes of scarlet marked my cheekbones. The high leather velvet-fringed collar held me in a vice of steel and, at the same time, tickled in a feathery way. The ivory cameo of the Marquis de Sade would be interesting and revealing, I suppose, for anybody who truly examined it. The thin black silk jacket, buttoned with one button, a red handkerchief flaring out of the vest pocket, was a flimsy barrier between the world and my skin. I was not wearing a T-shirt or a bra; that was clear. The short pleated high-flaring scarlet rubber skirt with the hidden slit was very revealing, and under it, no stockings, and no panties. The lock-on high-strap black patent stiletto heels cantilevered my body into an interesting and provocative pose. Yes, I might as well have been sketched out in scarlet neon. Oh, boy! I sighed.

Martine appeared like a demi-goddess. The sheer white elastic dress was semi-transparent. It looked as if she had been dipped in a sheen of skimmed milk, and it was suggestively opaque in just the right places, making the effect even more titillating. It so precisely sculpted her body, her breasts, and her nipples – stark black and erect – that it made it seem like she was naked underneath, which of course she was.

"Oh, no." I saw a photographer approaching.

Martine put her arm around my shoulder and swung us around.

"Face them and smile," she whispered.

The flashbulbs flashed.

Martine held me tight. She turned and kissed me on the lips. It was so fast I didn't have time to react. The kiss lingered. It was very, very nice – soft and perfumed and somehow subtle, communicating, in a quick little apercu, a world of feelings. The kiss ended. I blinked.

The flashbulbs flashed.

"Martine," the photographer shouted, "just another shot with your friend!"

"Of course," she said.

We hugged and mugged for the camera. I put on my best smile.

Several other photographers had appeared, as if from nowhere and the flashbulbs flashed in various directions and other people – sitting at tables on the restaurant's terrace – had taken out their smartphones and were snapping pictures. It looked like it might turn into a circus.

Two hefty waiters came and began gently to shoo the paparazzi away. "Off with you! Off! That's enough! Bye-bye!"

As the paparazzi headed off or jumped on their Vespas, they shouted, "Thanks, Martine, thanks!" They favored me with special waves, lascivious grins, and winks. Martine Aubin was obviously an old hand at this, but I certainly was not.

I sighed, almost melodramatically, while still clinging to Martine. She patted my arm, and I mumbled to myself: Oh, boy, what have I gotten myself into? Now I am truly undone; now I am the shameless moll of a French starlet. My infamy is infinite. What will the mathematics departments at Oxford and Cambridge and MIT think ...?

Well, Alfredo's was a restaurant, as I well knew, where the provocative was normal. And in fact, over there, on the terrace, was a young woman in what looked like a gold catsuit and I saw another woman – with a famous soccer star I think – who was wearing a skimpy leather skirt, and wide brightly colored suspenders that covered her breasts, and nothing much else.

Okay, I thought, we are just part of the show. Martine will certainly focus all the attention. I can be an invisible masochistic mouse, a bit player in her show. Then I glanced around ...

Oh, my God ...!!!

Oh, my God ...!!!

My eyes opened wide. It couldn't be! Professor Rupert Harrington-Smyth the Third! With his wife, Professor Cynthia Parker!

Oh, my God!

Rupert Harrington-Smyth the Third was the President of the University! He was one of the most prominent mathematicians and scientists in the US. Oh, my God! And he had just been named special adviser to the President of the United States. Harrington-Smyth and Cynthia Parker were deep in conversation with a Chinese gentleman and his wife, who were standing there, and seemed about to leave.

Engrossed in the conversation, it seemed Harrington-Smyth and Cynthia Parker had not seen me yet. Maybe they wouldn't recognize me!

Oh, God, how embarrassing!

This was fatal!

Perhaps I should pray – but to whom? To the Marquis de Sade?

At the same time, strangely, it was exciting. Philip was talking to Alcide about something – I think about where the car was to pick us up; or something like that. Martine was standing next to me, her arm still linked in mine. James, who had my purse, came up and put his arm under my arm, and, held me close: I was a prisoner between the two of them. Martine rubbed her body against mine, like a cat, almost opening up the moveable slit in my pleated latex skirt. Hmm, I thought, this French girl is truly a wicked girl.

This really could be my total and absolute downfall!

Professor Harrington-Smyth's wife Cynthia looked in our direction, and stared. Her face lit up in a smile, she made a timid little wave. Oh, God! She's recognized me! Harrington-Smyth stopped talking and turned to look at us.

I pretended I hadn't seen them. I felt sweat beading on my back. The Chinese couple moved past us on the way to their car, which had just pulled up.

Then – thank the Deity! There was a welcome distraction: A waiter – no, it turned out it was the owner of the restaurant, Alfredo, had come up to our group. He shook hands with James and then with me, "Ah, Signorina Gwendoline," he said, "Even more beautiful than usual!" Releasing my hand, he kissed me on both cheeks – carefully, so as not to muss the makeup. "You look like a goddess, Signorina Gwendoline."

I introduced Martine and Philip. It was clear that Alfredo had not met them before, but he knew who they were, and he was always delighted to have celebrities dine on his terrace.

Alfredo was about to lead us to our table when we were stopped by Professor Harrington-Smyth, who stood up and waved. His wife was still staring straight at me.

I pretended I had just now seen them, and smiled my broadest, most idiotically surprised smile. I was about to open my mouth and introduce everybody – while feeling I wanted to die – when Professor Harrington-Smyth reached over and shook James by the hand, saying "James, it has been so long, it has been too long!" Then he turned to me, blinked quizzically, hesitated, blinked again, and said, "Gwendoline? Gwendoline Clermont! You and James know each other?"

"Yes," I said, startled, and I wanted to say – yes, we know each other, and how! Just let me describe what we did the other night!

Harrington-Smyth kissed me on both cheeks – the most contact we'd ever had was when I shook his hand once at a graduation ceremony – and he turned to James and said, "James, my God, look at you! It has been too long! How did you discover Gwendoline?"

This was like an ambush! I was dying for us to get away, and park ourselves at the farthest possible point away from Professor Harrington-Smyth the Third. At that instant, out of the corner of my eye, I noticed that by some horrible diabolical coincidence, the table next to theirs had just become free – room for us.

Oh, no, no, all the gods! No! I tell you no! While I was making this inner prayer, Harrington-Smyth was saying, "Join us! Join us!"

"Delighted!" James beamed at them. He gave me his most wicked smile. He obviously knew Harrington-Smyth, and knew him quite well. Philip and Martine seemed pleased, too, for some reason.

I wondered who had planned this ambush. I was thinking it might be a good idea to turn paranoid. Did all these people know each other? Was I the unique and solitary ignoramus, the fetish model patsy? I thought I was going to die. I had naively believed I could keep my different worlds – and my different selves – apart, compartmentalized, but, no, it appeared I definitely could not. All my worlds were colliding, right here, and right in front of me.

I sighed. This was going to be terribly embarrassing. My chalk-white doll-like face, the scarlet lips, and the turquoise eyelids and eyebrows, the clownish splash of scarlet in my cheekbones: all of that was already bad enough. But, when I sat down, I could feel the seat through the latex, imprinting itself clearly on my bum. The rubber skirt had a strange skin-like effect, as if it wasn't there. It felt like I was naked. So there I was, Gwendoline Clermont, mathematician extraordinaire, virtually naked, a painted sex doll, sitting right across from the very eminent – indeed famous – Professor Rupert Harrington-Smyth the Third.

I swallowed and looked around: next to me, on my right side, was James. On my left side, was Philip; Martine was across from Philip and sitting on Harrington-Smyth's right side; Harrington-Smyth's wife, Cynthia, was on his left, facing James.

Alfredo appeared and leaned over the table, next to Martine, and asked us whether we would like to look at the antipasto buffet, where all sorts of goodies were displayed. It was just inside the restaurant. Martine said she would indeed love to look at the antipasto buffet, and she gave me a look that indicated I should too.

≈

So, carefully trying to keep my rebellious bouncy flaring red rubber skirt under control, and desperately trying to avoid a quasi-total striptease – the ultra-thin silk jacket was threatening to unbutton and open up wide – I cautiously stood up.

I felt dozens of eyes – like eager little laser beams – following us, as Martine and I went into the restaurant, our stilettos declaring themselves, and drawing almost universal attention, by beating out a clickety-click tap-dance rhythm on the cobblestones.

Inside, spread out on the buffet table, the food looked over-whelmingly scrumptious – tuna, smoked salmon, potato salad, dozens of types of frittata, plates of pasta, and... Yummy!

I forgot all my troubles; I forgot who I was and where I was. Yummy! I was looking to pile up everything, absolutely every-thing, and gobble everything up and stuff myself. Among other things, a full stomach would calm my nerves. I picked up my plate, and felt my mouth just watering in anticipation. Yummy!

"Dressed like this, we can't eat anything that bloats," said Martine, looking thoughtful. I glanced at her. The milky white latex transparency of her dress positively glowed; her body was the body of an icon, a divinity.

Several gentlemen, who were serving themselves from the buffet, stopped and stared in perfect awe. They almost looked afraid. A waiter went by and bowed a quick grinning homage.

"Oh, gosh, bloating." Damnation, I thought. "Right, so what do you suggest?"

"Farting is also an absolute no-no." She was licking her lips and picking up a plate. She poked me with her elbow.

"Really, farting? Do you think ...?"

"Absolutely. It is especially to be avoided with the camera run-ning, in love scenes, you know, where you are naked, with you limbs all sweaty and entangled, all steamy, during hot sex and so on."

"I imagine. Has it ever happened? I mean ..."

"Oh, boy, I can tell you some tales ... There was one time, and the leading man was very glamorous, you know, that famous Ital-ian, rather fastidious, really, and ... Well, I guess we had better dis-cuss this later. Meantime ..."

"We must eat."

"Right."

"So, what do you suggest?"

"To avoid swelling and flatulence, my dearest Gwendoline, I suggest that we both choose the very austere cucumber salad, and those tiny thin itsy-bitsy sections of avocado, not too much mind you, and that frittata, over there, a thin, thin slice, and perhaps those grapes with a tiny splash of that yogurt."

"Hmm, okay." I was not happy. In fact, I was furious. I wanted to yowl. I was starving; I wanted to gorge myself; I could eat a horse.

Martine leaned close and whispered. "By the way, there will probably be paparazzi when we leave the restaurant." She laid her hand on my arm.

"Oh, boy."

"It's always like this. It can be fun. The key is just to relax. They have to make a living too. It's part of the gig."

"Did you know James and I would be in that shop?"

"No, I had no idea. But it turns out Philip and James are old friends, so I think we were both ambushed, my dear, dear Gwendoline."

"Wait till I ..."

"Yes, revenge will be sweet. We'll think of something. We should organize something special, together, when they least expect it – Wham! Bang! Bullseye! Once, after we'd had a fight, I locked Philip naked outside his cottage in Normandy, but then I relented and let him in. He stood outside in the moonlight and serenaded me, yodeling like a mountain goat, and using bananas as horns, so I had to surrender."

We had filled our plates.

We were, I noticed, being watched by quite a few of the diners inside the restaurant; well, Martine was right: We were part of the show.

We went back to sit down. The others were already drinking and had ordered their first course – pasta dishes for most of them because, unlike Martine and yours truly, they were not almost naked, and they did not have to keep their tummies tight. They could probably even fart, if they spread their cheeks and were careful.

As I was cautiously lowering myself onto my seat – using one hand to keep the bumptious latex skirt from flipping up and revealing a naked depilated gold-painted pubis and scarlet labia, Harrington-Smyth was beaming across the table at me. "Congratulations, Gwendoline."

I stared at him blankly.

"You don't know?" he said

"She doesn't know," said his wife. She smiled, laid her hand on mine, "Gwendoline, you really don't know?"

"No, I don't know. What don't I know?" I swallowed, and cleared my throat. James had put his hand under the table and on my thigh, and he opened the slit in the skirt, and began edging the skirt upwards, so I was now really naked. Martine somehow realized what was going on. She looked at me and winked and licked her lips and for some reason, I felt a tremendous surge of desire: I would like to kiss her, to hold her down, and kiss her, and I'd like to run my fingers over that transparent dress, and I'd like to lick that honey-gold, sweet, slight swell of her ... I would like James to stand by and give us instructions. What was happening to me? Maybe Nicole's gin tonic had gone to my head.

"So you don't know," said Harrington-Smyth.

"No, uh, I don't know." I had no idea what I didn't know, and I felt extraordinarily stupid and excited, and at the same time, I felt I was blushing, but nobody seemed to notice. Anyway, I almost never blush, and if I did blush now the white ceramic-like lacquer foundation that covered my face –the fond de teint, as Nicole called it – would probably hide any blush, however shameful, from view.

"Gwendoline, congratulations! You've won the Neumann-Williamson Fellowship!"

"I've what ...?" My voice was going to break. James' fingers brushed my labia, and one finger captured my clitoris. I thought: I am going to kill James. And I'm going to have an orgasm, right here, right in the middle of the restaurant. I've won the ... I was damp, wet, excited, I swallowed, and I said, "I've won the Neumann-Williamson?"

"Yes. It was announced about an hour ago."

James released me from the unbearable tension. He said, "Well, you must accept it, Gwen, and right away," and he kissed me. He handed me my purse. "Send an email right now," he said.

"Yes," said Harrington-Smyth, "that is a very good idea."

"Gosh!" I slipped the phone out of my purse and searched for the email that informed me of the Neumann-Williamson, and there it was.

"We wish to congratulate you ... Confirmed!"

I began to type out a rapid reply. Meantime, Harrington-Smyth was ordering more wine, a waiter was hovering, and James' hand was resting on my naked thigh, where he had peeled the skirt away on one side, up to my waist. I was breathless and concentrating – all at the same time.

Harrington-Smyth called for champagne. I typed what I thought was a perfect but succinct answer. Leaving the peeled skirt perfectly peeled, James had now put his arm around me.

"What do you think?" I showed the draft to him.

"Perfect, darling, perfect."

I showed it to Harrington-Smyth.

Harrington-Smyth said, "Perfect, very adroit. They will be very, very lucky to have you."

I checked the message over once, twice, a third time, and then I pushed "Send." Off it went; I knew that my life from that instant would be different – now I was considered to be in the top rank of my field.

"That is an interesting choker," said Cynthia, "And the cameo is very ..."

"Yes," I said, steeling myself and thinking that offense is the best defense, "It's the Marquis de Sade."

"Yes, the Stanford image," she said, "You know, from the collection of Albert Lefebvre."

And then I remembered that Cynthia taught French literature at Princeton and that she had written on the Marquis de Sade and also on the libertine novel, Dangerous Liaisons, and, even, I think, on The Story of O."

"You wrote about his years in prison, didn't you?" I said, fishing in my memory, and keeping my smile and gaze steady, focused on her; James was now resting his hand on my thigh, just touching with the tips of his very active and artful fingers my naked pubis and labia. I was trembling with pleasure, and I wanted to hit him over the head with my purse or something heavier.

"Yes, yes, I did."

"You said he was a true revolutionary." I was glad Kate had briefed me one night when we were drinking wine and talking about books and how they contained locked up inside them, some of them at least, some explosive forms of desire. Kate knew – almost by heart – The Story of O, the works of the Marquis de Sade, and Marcel Proust, and Colette, and Anais Nin, and Henry Miller.

"Yes, I did." Cynthia was smiling, returning my gaze, focused on me. She was delighted, I think, to be recognized. She was a very good-looking woman and reputedly a brilliant scholar, but Harrington-Smyth was a very expansive man, an academic politician, and powerhouse; he occupied all the space; he would not be an easy partner or husband, not even for an accomplished, articulate woman like Cynthia Parker. She had a forkful of fish and pasta – the white flesh gleaming with olive oil – halfway to her mouth, but she paused and said, "The Marquis stripped away all our illusions, rather like Nietzsche, or that was what he thought he was doing. If there was no God, then everything and anything is possible. And absolute egoism, he thought, was, therefore, the only philosophy worth following – and that, for him, means torturing and enslaving other people, particularly women."

"Very interesting chap, the Marquis de Sade," said Harrington-Smyth. His face was a bit red. He was pouring us more wine.

James was eating, delicately, with one hand; the fingers of his other hand were playing a mischievous little melody on my pubis: knock-knock, who's there? "Do you think de Sade was right?" I asked Cynthia

She smiled again and began to explain that, no, in her opinion, de Sade was not as free of religion as he thought, that his fantasies and cruelties were a form of revolt against beliefs that, for him, were still very important and very real. Many of his erotic practices involved blasphemy, which is a sort of back-handed tribute to the power of religion, to the power of God or the idea of God.

"But surely there was a purely sexual drive behind his philosophy; it wasn't all ideology," said James.

"Yes, his sexual sadism must have been strong, overwhelming, something he couldn't control," said Martine, "He had to act it out."

"Yes, absolutely, you are right," said Cynthia, turning to look at Martine. "It was nor purely ideological; his hatred and sadism were pathological as well as social."

"He probably wanted to kill the mother inside him," said Philip, "Or his own mother and all the women who were proxies for her. Many serial killers are really trying to assassinate a part of themselves, the female part, or the maternal body they have internalized, and their victims are proxies, playing a part in buried, continually re-enacted traumatic dramas."

"Yes. That, I think, is definitely part of it." Cynthia nodded.

"Didn't his mother want to have him locked up?" said Martine.

"Yes."

"Dostoevsky saw himself as a sort of anti-Marquis de Sade, didn't he?" said Martine, "I mean in his Notes from the Underground, he explicitly confronts de Sade's concept of evil, of arbitrary cruelty and unfettered egoism, and tries to transcend it."

I could see Cynthia look at Martine with new interest. The girl was a starlet, her dress was as transparent as if she were painted in a varnish of sperm, her breasts were starkly outlined, with areolae and erect nipples painted black; and she had put on a show for the paparazzi, and she was very young, but it was clear she was not a bubblehead. "You are right. I think Dostoevsky as a Christian, felt obliged to confront the Marquis de Sade's ideas head-on. You're absolutely right."

Harrington-Smyth filled my glass. I thanked him and took a quick drink. James was happily eating. He had peeled my skirt almost entirely away, sliding it along the belt, and it was only because we were crowded so close to each other at the table that my nakedness was not apparent to all. I wondered about the waiters. Could they see my nakedness? I turned to James, kissed him, and whispered. "You are a very bad boy, and I, your goddess, shall punish you. I shall be your very own Marquis de Sade."

"Ah!" His smile was of pure pleasure.

"And James, how did you meet Gwendoline?"

"Running." James beamed. "Running is an interest we share."

I almost blushed. I thought, yes, running – me covered in shit and vomiting all over his Mercedes and all over his shirt and him lifting me, naked, up into his arms, ruining his Hugo Boss ..."

"You know, Rupert," said James, "Gwendoline did something remarkable for me the other day."

Oh, no, I thought, what is he going to talk about? Blowjobs, me pretending to be a sodomized cabin boy on the bounding main, the nighttime panther catsuit prowl, or me naked blind-folded and bound on the bed, or making love in the rain, or me stripping him naked in the stairwell ...?

"She did an extraordinary analysis of the growth prospects for that new Finnish biotech company, Enogerm, I'd been looking into. She took apart the assumptions underlying their business plan and their research program; her analysis was much deeper and more sophisticated than anything my people had done, so when I met the CEO and the owners – and the scientists – I knew exactly what questions to ask."

Whew!

He patted me on the pubis. Good Girl! Good Pony!

≈

At the end of the meal, we all stood up. I avoided total exposure by frantically pushing, pulling, and smoothing the flaring skirt back into place, and by managing, just barely and just in time, to close the mobile side slit and click it shut. Cynthia and Rupert had an early flight, but they told us we had to look them up – in Boston or in New York, or visit them in their place on Cape Cod, all of us, but the invitation was directed particularly to James and to me. Cynthia said she was often in Paris where she had a pied-à-terre – and she would love to get together, and this, she explicitly aimed at Martine and me. "I think we three girls might have quite a time, alone, in Paris," she said.

We both said we would be delighted.

She gave us both her card.

Then, when Cynthia and Rupert had driven away in a cab, James suggested we take a stroll and have a nightcap. He knew a little bar, which he was sure we would like.

True enough, as Martine had prophesized, several paparazzi were lying in wait for us.

Martine insisted that she and I pose together.

She did the kissing thing again – which meant I was probably going to end up in People magazine or in the Daily Express as the new – lesbian – squeeze of Martine Aubin. I found the idea rather pleasing; it made me feel all warm and fuzzy, deep inside.

The paparazzi drifted away, satisfied.

Martine and I walked just in front, and James and Philip strolled behind us.

Martine slipped her hand around my waist. It felt nice – as long as she didn't unclip the skirt. She knew how it was attached, and she knew she just had to snap open one button – Et voilà! I'd be naked. I whispered, "Don't you dare!"

"I think it would be fun!"

"Really!" I whispered.

"Yes."

"Well," I tightened my lips in a prim little grimace. "I ..."

"Yes, I'd love to strip you naked, dear Gwendoline Clermont. I saw how you looked at me back there. You were undressing me with your eyes."

"I didn't need to undress you," I said, giving her my special fierce look from under my eyebrows, "And I don't need to undress you now. You're already undressed."

"True, so true," she said, with a thoughtful, comically wistful pout. Her hand was now inside the slit in my skirt, and her fingers spread, possessively intimate, on my hip. It was exciting, dangerous, and very pleasurable.

I moved my hand down to her bum, and let it rest there,

stroking her lightly. Her buttock was smooth as silk, perfect, perky, and proud. I suddenly had a funny little image. "I'd love to give you a spanking," I said.

"Really, Gwendoline, I think that would be very nice. Let us arrange it sometime – and soon." She patted my hip, a series of neat little slaps.

"To the right, ladies," said James from behind us.

"Yes, sir," we said in unison.

We went under a small archway and into a very narrow little cobblestoned street, and then turned left through a still narrower archway and street, really an alleyway. We came to a tiny courtyard. It had trellises with thick green ivy running up the walls, potted plants, and overhead wrought-iron gas lamps. Tables and chairs were set out on the cobblestones, and two people, a man and a woman, were drinking. Oh, no, on second thought, and on closer inspection, the man was a woman – yes, the mustache was false, and the woman, dressed in a 1920s flapper dress, was a woman. The girl with the mustache was dressed in a tuxedo; her jet-black hair combed down slick and thick across her forehead; she glanced at me with charcoal eyes. I smiled. She nodded curtly, without a smile. So, I thought, carnival time, beautiful tempting carnival time.

James and Philip gallantly pulled out chairs, and Martine and I sat down side by side; James and Philip sat opposite us.

Martine leaned over and kissed me, then glanced at James, with the implicit question: Is this okay?

"Gwendoline?" He smiled, raising an eyebrow.

"Yes, yes, of course."

"I think we'll get a bottle of Chablis," said Philip, "If everyone agrees."

"Absolutely," said James.

Martine slid her hand through the skit and under my skirt

and let her fingers rest on my pubis. I kissed her. I didn't know quite what she was doing or what we were doing, but her fingers were skillful, and her lips were soft and sweet.

James and Philip watched us. I blinked at James, and, interrupting the kiss, I stuck out my tongue; he laughed. I went back to kissing Martine. James and Philip began to talk about French and Italian politics, and they hardly paid any more attention to us.

"While they talk, we do," she said.

"Right," I said, a door opening in my head.

She unbuttoned my jacket and slid her hand over my breast, softy touching it, just with her fingertips, timidly caressing. Then she twisted and pinched the stiff, lacquered nipple, but nicely, softly. I gazed at her fixedly; then, I kissed her again. I slid my hand up her thigh, between her legs, and I pushed the skin-tight latex-sheen white dress up her thighs. She kissed me back, now, fiercely, quickly, in a quick, hungry series of kisses – again, and again, and again; I pushed her dress up until, from the waist down, she was naked – not even a garter belt or stockings, soft damp naked thighs and belly and pubis – all mine!

The waitress arrived and took the order from Philip – for a bottle of Les Clos Chablis Grand Cru – but I was barely aware of her.

I glanced at James. He nodded his head, smiled, and silently mouthed, "Naughty girl!"

I lazily blinked and nodded my agreement returned to kissing Martine. She closed her eyes, tilted back her head, so I kissed her on the neck and shoulder. I caressed her, opened her, gently, slowly.

It is a truth universally acknowledged, or so I am told by those in the know, that many distinguished gentlemen, perhaps the most exclusive types of distinguished gentlemen, take great

– indeed excessive – pleasure in watching two women make love. Why this should be so has remained mysterious to me. When we got home, I intended to grill James, in the friendliest way possible, on this interesting psychological quirk, which has certainly been present from ancient times, and perhaps existed when we were furry creatures living in trees, two girl monkeys getting it off while the patriarchs in a state of high excitement gazed sagely on. And I would also, I thought, ask James about precisely how this afternoon and evening's adventure had been organized; quite clearly, it had been deliberately designed to get us to the point where now we were.

Meanwhile, it was exciting.

The waitress – who was dressed, I noticed, in classic 19th Century French waitress style – arrived with the chilled bottle; it was in a sparkling silver ice bucket, pearled with humidity. She made a cute little performance out of pulling out the cork, while giving us all an appreciative once-over, before handing the bottle to James, and disappearing back inside the café.

Martine was wet with desire; her intimate sheen was rich on my fingertips; I deepened my caresses; in synchrony with her caressing me, and I felt desire rise within me, a sweet tidal force of yearning and trembling. "Oh," I sighed, "oh ..."

James was carefully pouring our drinks from the bottle.

"Ladies," said Philip, "To your health!"

Martine and I hesitated in our caresses. We slowly stopped kissing – delaying it with little return kisses, our eyes closed, at least mine were. And we kissed, and again we kissed, slowly withdrawing, slowly more tentative, and it was amazing, I thought, how we were communicating with kisses alone. The message was this: We two are going to keep on kissing, and keep on caressing. We are going to stop slowly, in stages, in tantalizing, titillating little installments, and then, and only then, having made them wait, having made them watch, having tarried within our own private female world of mutual pleasure, only then will we turn out attention to our two gentlemen. And we knew, too, and we somehow communicated this to each other, that the gentlemen would be amused by this our arrogant little Sapphic delaying tactic. They would not be annoyed – unless, of course, we went on too long, and totally stripped, and began to make mad passionate love on the cobblestones, ignoring their patriarchal power, oblivious to their attentive male gaze, throwing away the script, casting off their masculine appeals to reason and decorum, and compromising their male dignity. But even then, perhaps, they would not be annoyed, for it is amusing to see children play at passion, and women, in some senses, are only children, are they not? As well as goddesses, mothers, partners, sisters, mistresses – and whores, and Eve and Jezebel, and Cleopatra, and Helen of Troy, of course.

"Ladies, to your health!" said James, softly echoing Philip. I could tell from the tone of his voice that James was quite satisfied and enjoying himself; we had indeed traveled a long road – and in such a short time.

I kissed Martine deeply, and I pushed her elastic dress up even further. I wanted her to be utterly, totally, completely naked. I had a brief glimpse of me, holding a leash, and leading Martine, who is wearing only a collar, not wearing a stitch, barefoot and disheveled, across Piazza Navona. We are walking through the bluish light of evening, when all the lamps are lit, all the fountains bubbling, and all the cafés open and when all the respectable bourgeois strollers are taking the air. Or perhaps it is I who am naked and Martine, wearing the see-through white latex dress, is leading me, collared and attached to a leash and tottering along on stilettos. We get to an apartment overlooking the piazza and its thronging populace. We make love, standing together in the window, our bodies interlaced, our hands, lips, and vaginas hugging, and then we do it on the balcony, in sight of all; and then we are all alone, just we two, making love in a big, flat, hard-surfaced, austere bed, no covers, just us in the sultry bluish twilight.

The kiss ended. We separated. She looked at me through half-closed eyes and smiled, and we turned out attention to our men.

"Gentlemen, to your health!" I said.

"Gentlemen, to your health!" Martine echoed.

We clinked glasses, all four of us.

Martine's hand was still on my breast, and my hand was still between her legs. "So, what is this place?" I asked.

Philip explained.

James mentioned a similar club that he knew in Paris. He added that there was a very interesting gay and S&M club in Testaccio, a bohemian and lower class, but newly gentrified, part of Rome that we might visit the next time we went out.

"I like that idea," said Martine, "Maybe next week if you are here. Philip and I are filming at Cine Città for the next few weeks. So we'll be here."

"Martine has rehearsals tomorrow," said Philip.

"Oh, my God, yes," Martine rolled her eyes, and she pinched my nipple. "We are filming a life of Lucrezia Borgia. I make love to everybody, give huge parties, and poison loads of people. I have dozens of babies, and die, in great agony, giving birth to the last of them."

"That's about it," said Philip, "that's the plot in a nutshell." I had gathered, from hints and from bits and pieces of memory from things I had read, that Philip was Philip d'Este, the famous French-Italian film director.

We talked a bit more. Then Philip said it was time for him and Martine to get some sleep. James said that Alcide could drive them home since they were at a hotel near the film studios outside town but that – and he glanced at me – perhaps he and I would walk home, as it was not far.

I nodded. I did want to walk across Rome with James. It was now about two o'clock in the morning. "Yes," I said, and looked around. "Alcide is here?"

"Yes, I called him."

"Poor fellow."

"Oh, it's double pay, overtime, and he has friends in an all-night café around the corner. I don't think he's unhappy."

I withdrew my hand from Martine's thigh. She gave my nipple a last sweet, gently twisting pinch and pulled her hand, slowly, from under my jacket. We both stood up.

She slowly tugged and pulled the skin-tight dress down, covering her nakedness: she smoothed it over her tummy and thighs. She was truly an apparition, a milky sheen of skin and muscle and tendons, perfect breasts and hips and abs: a body to die for! I blinked at her and swallowed. I felt my desires were careening wildly off in all sorts of new directions.

"Oh, Gwendoline, Oh, Gwendoline," she said, "We shall meet again, and soon, oh, sweet Gwendoline!"

She kissed me, fully, deeply, on the mouth, and she whispered, "And don't you dare do up that jacket button. You should be as naked as you can be."

≈

James and I saw Martine and Philip to the car. Acide saluted, bowed, and smiled, and waved. James turned to me. "So you're really up for a little nocturnal ramble.

"Yes, Master." I reached up, kissed him, and held his face between my hands and kissed him again.

He kissed me back. "Gwendoline, you are too beautiful."

"Yummy." I unbuttoned his shirt down to his waist.

He adjusted my jacket, leaving the button undone, and he reached down and opened the slit in my skirt, so that it was about three inches wide, one thigh almost totally exposed.

"Oh," I said.

"Let's go."

We began our stroll, hand in hand.

My heels made that click-click-click sound in the empty streets.

We walked through a tangle of little streets, then we walked along via Margutta, past buildings with artists' studios, with trellises of flowers, vines, and ivy stretching up the ochre and burnt sienna walls; past restaurants and bars, which were now closed, all the shutters pulled down; we came to Piazza di Spagna, which was empty of people and cars. We had the glorious stage set all to ourselves. The stairs soared up, in magnificent sweeping stages, toward the façade of the church at the top, Trinity of the Mountains, which towers over Rome; the cobblestones of the piazza glittered; the facades of the buildings glowed with a serene, warm glow, and not a soul was to be seen anywhere.

We sat for a minute on the edge of the Fountain of the Little Boat, which is just at the bottom of the Spanish Steps.

Feeling like mischievous kids, we climbed into the fountain, which, strictly speaking, was illegal; it was a hot night, of course, so I splashed water on James, and he splashed water on me until we were both soaked.

We sat on a lower level of the Spanish Steps. I felt the night air and the cool stone of the stairs directly against my skin. It was as if I were truly naked. We were both still dripping wet, rivulets running off onto the steps of stone.

I leaned against him. His arm was tight around me. He began, in a sort of dreamy voice, to talk. He told me how he'd been orphaned when he was twelve – his parents died in a plane crash in Africa; how he'd gone to private schools; how he'd inherited his parent's money; how he'd invested the money to create his business; how he'd always been fascinated by adventure – physical adventure, and sexual adventure. He told me how he'd found in me, and purely by accident, an unlikely fellow spirit, a fellow adventurer. He kissed me, and then he opened the jacket, and kissed my breasts. I looked into his eyes and kissed him on the forehead, on the end of the nose, and then on the lips. Yes, I was truly dripping wet, in every sense of the word. And, yes, I was his companion, his fellow adventurer.

We walked up the Spanish Steps, to the very top, and looked down on the city, on Piazza di Spagna directly below us, Via Condotti, the shopper's paradise – if you were a millionaire – and beyond, the rooftop gardens, the terraces, and towers and steeples and domes, the churches and palaces, of the eternal city.

We continued along the hilltop road, which, strangely, is called Piazza Trinità dei Monti – though it's not a piazza, it's a road. We came to a beautiful fountain – it was round, like a vast flat stone cup, with a flat surface of water barely rippled by the night breeze. We stopped. James began to kiss me. He carried me – well, almost carried me – to the stone balustrade in the shadow of the trees behind the fountain.

I lifted off his shirt and folded it on the balustrade; he lifted off my jacket and folded it on the balustrade. He kissed me and pushed me against the balustrade; he unclipped my skirt, lifted it off me, and folded it over the balustrade. "Ah, dear sir, dear Master," I sighed. He kissed and caressed me. Then he was on his knees, kissing me, and burying himself in me. I backed against a tree trunk. I held onto the tree, gripping the bark with my fingertips. I felt I was going to cry out, to scream, in pleasure.

He kissed my breasts, he kissed my tummy; my back was against the rough bark of the tree. My Master was opening me, with his lips, with his fingers. I bit my lip, I clutched the tree bark, I swallowed, I closed my eyes; I opened them.

A car went by, swishing past in the semi-darkness, and the lamplight reflected on his hair. "Oh, you, you, you," I whispered.

I knelt, opened his belt, and unzipped the zipper. I reached in to help him step out of his jeans and underwear. He was naked.

I licked and caressed him to prepare this phallic god of mine for entry – though I was already totally liquid and more than ready.

I stood up, he lifted me up, he bent me back, and he entered me. I flung my arms around him, and I kissed him, and I tensed and held him, my legs locked around him, and I wanted to hold him like this forever, so he would be part of me, one with me for all eternity. We kissed. Around us, the city of Rome, the eternal city, slept; the moon, I noticed, had come up, a pale sliver of a silver shadow in the sky gazing down on us.

I tensed my thighs willing myself to make him come, to subdue him, and he was thrusting into me, gently, slowly, and kissing me, and our kisses merged into one long kiss; he filled me and fulfilled me; I was one with him and then ... we came ...

We came.

We came in a scream and a shudder and a cry and a whimper of joy.

And, then, for a time, we just stayed there, clinging to each other.

"You little devil." He laughed and scooped up a handful of water from the fountain and put it in my hair and coated my breasts, and then he licked and drank from my breasts, sucking drinking, and licking.

"You, dear Master, I worship you!"

"Oh, Gwendoline," he breathed.

Slowly, we put our clothes back on – a very simple operation in my case, and we walked back to the Church of Trinità dei Monti and down the Spanish Steps.

The slit in my skirt was now about three inches wide, a big open gap swinging from my right hip.

I felt I was walking in a new way, swaying, acutely conscious of my buttocks, my belly, my breasts; it defined me; I had become this new way of walking, this nonchalant, devil-may-care, sensuous amble, everything tingling, every inch of skin, every tendon, every muscle, aware and self-aware; and everything alive.

My hair was still wet, and my jacket too, so water was dribbling between my breasts, and down my belly. James' shirt was open. I wrapped my arm around his waist; I couldn't keep my hands off him.

"That was very cute," I smirked, "with Martine and Philip."

"Are you angry?"

"On the contrary, dear James, I have discovered within myself resources I did not know I possessed."

"Ah," he said, "and so ..."

"I adore the golden girl, and, I trust that, with your permission, of course, dear Master, Martine and I shall meet again."

"That would, if you wish it, be very fine," he said; he took my face in his hands, and he kissed me, and he pushed aside the unbuttoned jacket, and he kissed my breasts.

"Oh, Master," I said. "The night watch is coming, I believe."

"Ah, yes," James said, and he allowed me – for a moment – to pull my jacket shut.

A patrol car passed us slowly. I saw the oval face of a cop, a woman, looking at us, lively eyes, nice teeth. She wasn't frowning.

We walked down Via Condotti, past the Café Greco and all the high fashion shops; there was no one else to be seen – not anywhere.

We finally got to Campo de' Fiori.

The market was just beginning; the vendors were setting up their stands.

We bought two navel oranges.

We peeled and ate them.

One of the cafés was already open, doing business for the vege-table sellers and the fishmongers.

"Want an espresso, darling?"

"Yes, Master, that would be fine."

"I think we perhaps should sleep in this morning."

"That, Master, is a fine idea."

"Then, perhaps, we could go to the beach, in the afternoon."

"The beach? That, too, Master, is a fine idea."

We sat and sipped the espressos, not talking, just holding hands, and watching the market come alive, and the sky over the city become lighter and lighter.

≈

We climbed up the stairs. The building was quiet. It was a Sun-day, so nobody would be appearing, probably, at the Institute for Global Studies for Progressive Economic Policy. James stopped on the first landing, and kissed me and lifted off my jacket.

"You are very gallant, sir," I said.

"This is only the beginning of my gallantry," he said.

He kissed me again; he licked my lacquered scarlet nipples; he bit one gently, kissed it, and sucked it. I took a deep breath. Naked skin, in some circumstances, seems to create one single enormous erogenous zone. Even the air was a caress. The drafts and breezes in Rome, particularly in this enormous drafty old building, with all its moldy smells, had a particularly perverse, in-sinuating, sensual, sexy quality.

The city, all around us, was slowly waking up. In this big old staircase, large enough and gentle enough for horses to ride up, little breezes and drafts touched the skin. Strange musty and musky odors floated and teased and whispered of secrets, of promises, of life, and of death. The smell of old stone, the waxed wooden doors of the ancient elevator, the musty smell of the basement storerooms far below us, the oily brassy smell of the elevator itself and the heavy, greasy coppery smell of the swaying elevator cables, all these sensations pressed in on me. The elevator, responding to the drifting air, creaked in its lattice-like tower.

So many sensations and so much desire! I thought I would burst. As we went up to the next landing, my heels clicked, amplified, and echoing in the empty space. Old statues of ancient serious stone gentlemen in togas in stone niches gazed blindly at us. I was not sure whether they were envious – or disapproving.

"Lift off your skirt," James said.

"Yes, Master, this is revenge, I suppose, Master, for the other night."

"Yes, boy, roles are reversed, for a time at least. So – undo that skirt!"

"Aye, aye, Captain." I saluted. I reached down, snapped open the skirt, and lifted it off. I bowed and handed it to him. Looking down, it was strange, seeing my naked pubis, exposed, no thick dark protective Bermuda Triangle, but merely painted labia, bright scarlet areola and nipples and a dusting of gold, between my legs and on my breast. Non-smear indeed! The paint had resisted all its trials and tribulations very well. "Oh, Master, I desire you, and I need you, and I want you." I kissed him and pushed him against the wall.

An ancient bust, some Stoic philosopher I imagine, stared with blind lofty disapproval.

I pressed myself into him, and felt his – very reliable, I must say – erection straining at his jeans. Like a good butler, like Jeeves, it appeared, attentive and at attention, whenever it was called for.

"It appears you might burst at the seams, Master," I whispered.

"Yes, boy, you do something to me ..."

I took it up, "Yes, Master, you do something to me, something that ... mystifies me ..."

We danced Cole Porter style – Ginger Rogers and Fred Astaire – up the last steps to the door, and without breaking the rhythm, or hardly, James twirled around, and unlocked and opened the door. He entered, and then stood blocking the door, grinning at me.

"Are you going to leave me out here, naked on the landing, Master?" I struck an abashed pose, bent in shame, knock-kneed, my hands pressed between my legs. He laughed hesitated, pretended to close the door, and then opened it wide.

"Not on your life, Gwendoline." He swept me into his arms, carried me through the entrance, and closed the door behind us.

≈

When we were inside, James carried me through the apartment and out onto the terrace, lolling in his arms, and he said, "Wait here." He went inside. Whew! It had been a long night.

I collapsed, naked, onto a deckchair. The air was taking on the lively milky quality of dawn; the sky was beginning to display a delicate tinge of blue. The birds were twittering.

"This water will be warm in a few minutes." James had reappeared, wearing only a white towel, wrapped neatly around his waist; he turned on the garden hose.

"Hot water from a garden hose?"

"All the comforts." He screwed a shower nozzle onto the hose, and he hooked the showerhead to a bracket on the wall – and we had what looked like a perfect outdoor shower.

"That looks delicious," I drawled; I didn't want to move; I felt luxuriously lazy.

"Right," he said, and let his towel drop.

"Am I to join you, Master?"

"Of course."

"I should like to pee and poop first, Master, begging Master's permission, of course."

"Of course, Gwendoline, permission granted. Go forth and poop and pee mightily to your heart's content. Spray excrement everywhere, deposit dung on all the walls, paint every surface with your own sweet, sweet poop."

"I shall try to restrain myself, Master." I honored him with a quick kiss, and I headed off to my very own bathroom where I accomplished all the necessary acts and rituals quite quickly, though I did manage to read ten paragraphs of a story in The New Yorker, while sitting on the very fine toilet.

The terrace shower was luscious – and the experience even more so, outside, in the rising sunlight, with the fresh dawn smells, in the midst of the flowers and plants, on the top of the building, in the middle of Rome, our feet bare on the tiles, and we soaped and washed and scrubbed each other and toweled each other down.

Finally, after dawdling for a bit, we turned off the shower and headed to the Master's bed, where we fell in a tangled heap, in each other's arms, but not before I noticed that my nipples and labia were no longer scarlet and that all traces of gold dust and Nicole's artwork were gone.

James smelled of soap and shampoo, and I suppose I did too. The bed and his body were so comfortable that I disappeared in an instant into a deep and dreamless sleep.

CHAPTER 6 – SEA & SAND

The sun was in my eyes and the wind was in my hair.

We were driving toward the west, toward the sun. I was wearing skin-tight black spandex short shorts that James had bought me, and a loose black cotton tank top. James was in blue jeans and a blue shirt, and he had put a small backpack – with cooler – in the trunk.

He had rented a car, a Porsche convertible.

"There's a nice beach just south of Ostia," he said.

"Ah," said I.

"And then there are some fine beachside restaurants, farther north, in the fishing village Fregene," he said.

"Ah, more eating!"

"Yes, we must fatten you up."

"For sacrifice ...?"

"Indeed, Gwendoline, for sacrifice."

I stretched in pleasure. It was sublime, the sun shining into our eyes and hot on our skin, and the breeze from the sea rippling through my hair.

We didn't talk. We were just together. I was beginning to think this was the natural state of the universe and of my life, this feeling of comfortable sensuality, of being together with him, of total, natural, relaxed ecstasy and unity. I was beginning to think it could last, which, of course, was a mistake. As it turned out, it was a very big mistake.

We turned south onto a rough, bumpy paved road that went along the dunes, the forests, and the coast. The asphalt was ancient, cracked, and drifting apart into bumpy islands. Ribbons of yellow sand stretched across the half-shattered roadway. There were no houses or buildings, just high dunes that rose up on both sides of the road; then, the landscape on our left – inland – changed to a thick pine forest. It seemed to go on forever. To our right, toward the sea, were more dunes, but they were lower, and marked with scattered clusters of sagebrush. Through the dunes, I caught glimpses of bright dark blue – the sea! Cars were parked here and there, as if abandoned, along the side of the road, their hoods and roofs glittering in the sun, but nobody was in sight. We drove past the parked cars, going more slowly now.

"Lift off your tank top, darling."

I lifted it off, held it up, let it wave in the wind, and tossed it into the back seat.

"And wiggle nicely out of your shorts."

I obeyed and tossed them into the back seat. I wasn't wearing panties. So, there I was – his naked young trophy, and quite happy. I closed my eyes and let the sun and the breeze take hold of me and carry me where they would. The sun, already low in the west, was hot.

We drove another mile. Then James pulled over to the side of the road, on the ocean side, and made a U-turn and parked on the far side of the road, with the car facing north. For a minute, we sat silent, and just listened to the breeze, the sea, and felt the heat.

"Here we are."

"And I get out?"

"And you get out."

"And you leave me here, wearing scarlet flip-flops, and nothing else."

"And I leave you here, wearing scarlet flip-flops."

"So, I can hitchhike naked back to Rome."

"Absolutely. I'll have dinner prepared." He smiled. "After the painted artifice of yesterday, we have nature in its naked purity today."

"I see. Okay. How philosophic! It's a deal, Master." I kissed him and got out of the car. The sun was warm, and the breeze was sweet. Nobody else was in view. A few cars were lined up along the side of the road, which was merely a stretch of rough broken asphalt sweltering under the blazing sun. I walked across the road and turned to look at him. I was beginning to think it might be quite an adventure, trying to get back to Rome, alone, naked, equipped with nothing. A car went by. James was sitting there, looking at me.

"Well, Master, what are you waiting for?" I said, "Aren't you going to drive away and abandon me to the elements?"

"Ah, Gwen." He got out of the car, walked around and opened the trunk, and said, "Would you like to help me undress?"

"Yes," I said. I walked back across the road. Even if it was late afternoon, the heat was stunning, vibrating up, blinding, from the pebbly melting tar. The air was like melted gold. The cicadas were deafening, rasping, pulsating. I unbuttoned his shirt.

"I really like this shirt," I said.

"Yes, it's nice."

I lifted his shirt off, and I put it, neatly folded, in the trunk. I almost forgot I was naked.

A car pulled up behind us. Two women got out. One was a blonde, the other a brunette, both deeply tanned and wearing enormous white-framed sunglasses, and identically skimpy black bikinis. They glanced at us, but then ignored us and concentrated on getting a bag out of the trunk of their car; they crossed the road and disappeared into the dunes, heading toward the sea.

"Will they arrest me?"

"Probably not," he said.

"Oh, that's disappointing." I unbuckled his belt, and kneeling, I removed his jeans. Underneath, he was wearing a slick black wet-look speedo-type bathing suit. "Not this," he said, putting his hand on my head and stroking my hair.

"Okay," I said, "But that is a very small and snug bathing suit, James, you might as well be naked." I folded his jeans and put them in the trunk. He put his arms around me, held me close, and stroked my sides; and, slowly, deliberately, he kissed me

I pressed against his chest, feeling my nipples harden and feeling the delicious strength of his muscles, the dark energy of his body, the steely resolve of his desire, forcing its way into mine, tunneling into my mind, into my soul. A flame of yearning consumed me. The breeze was so hot it was like we were standing in an oven. The heat was blinding; it vibrated off the asphalt. He kissed me again, and the scorching breeze mingled with our kiss; he kissed me yet again, harder, deeper this time, and his hand went down to my belly, caressing, soft, and then between my legs.

"Oh, Oh, Oh," I said, the excitement rising. His fingers had found the magic place, and he brought me, as so often – right to the edge. Then, slowly, with little return caresses, he retreated, and left me eager, panting, a tamed animal, and his concubine, standing naked in my scarlet plastic flip-flops, pressed against him, beside the dazzling, dusty, boiling, fragmented asphalt.

He kissed me again, and tugged at one of my earlobes, and smiled, and said, "Well, let's go!"

"You, Master, are truly evil." My voice was foggy with suppressed excitement. I cleared my throat.

He lifted the cooler-rucksack out of the trunk and shut the trunk, put up the top, and locked the car.

I realized that I was truly losing my heart, losing my heart to this man who was – so I had been warned – deathly afraid of love. I was in love with a man who was afraid of love. Oh, oh, oh!

Okay, I told myself, live for the moment, Gwendoline! Be brave! Be shameless! Hitchhike naked along the roads to Rome, if he asks you to! Wrestle naked in a mud puddle with a Burmese python, if he asks you to! Cover yourself in chocolate, make love to an actress, do a striptease in the middle of Saint Peter's Square, make love to a naked girl tourist in the Trevi Fountain, walk naked up Oxford Street in London or sidle up Broadway in your birthday suit, whatever he desired, I would do it.

Besides, these little imaginary scenarios felt like fun. Gwendoline, I am truly afraid you are becoming shameless – the lesson, I suppose, is this: When you leap into the bottomless pit, there is no end to it.

He kissed me again, his hand between my legs, bringing me right up to the edge of orgasm, and then keeping me suspended there, vibrating like a violin, and then easing away, only to bring me back again, and again, and again.

And so we stood, on the edge of that rutted and broken seaside road, kissing, and making love, my hand – since I needed some return leverage – having slipped inside his bathing suit, was teasing, stroking, and twisting him, keeping him right on the tense edge, as close as I could. I don't know how long this little tableau lasted – but it was a long time. A few cars rumbled past, but I hardly noticed. I felt like a nymph who had arisen out of some fountain or forest and who was being greeted and embraced and teased by a merciless god. I had a strange fantasy: I thought, so many men and women must have made love, over thousands, tens of thousands of years, near this spot, so many men and women must have stood or lain together and made love, just as we were making love. And, suddenly, I saw us, as if we were two figures embracing, one-dimensional and hieratic, stiff naked figures in a faded ancient fresco or mosaic, on the wall of some ruined villa or temple, and tourists would come and gaze on us, from beyond the glass, and wonder. We were mere players, vessels of an eternal life force, vessels of desire, enacting our roles in a pageant that went back into times before history began. Our passion, I thought, is truly eternal. The truth is – I was in love. My inner voice repeated: Watch out, Gwendoline! Watch out, Gwendoline!

I looked up at him. "What is this place?"

"You'll see," he said. Reluctantly, we detached ourselves from our little exercise in ecstasy. We crossed the road, climbed over a sagging, rusty barbed wire fence half-buried in the sand. We churned our way up the soft sand of the dunes, and then we slid down into a dip in the dunes; my flip-flops kept getting stuck in the sand; the sand was burning hot – even though midday was now long past. We were in a cup or little valley in the dunes, walls of sand on either side, and the sun and sky above, and nothing else. Blue sky, and golden yellow sand, that was our whole universe. He took my hand and kissed me, the heat roiled like an oven; my skin pearled with sweat, glowing all over.

We climbed up the other side of the dip. Suddenly we were on the crest of the dune, standing amidst a line of aromatic scrub that straggled low along the ground, as green as spinach. The vista opened up, breathless, immense, and naked – a wide beach, stretching off in both directions, north and south, and the sea, rank upon rank of small waves marching toward us, and the blue-cobalt-azure water reaching off to the hazy horizon, a light breeze coming landward, and not a cloud in the sky.

Hand in hand, we zigzagged our way down the steep sand slope toward the beach. There weren't many people. Some were naked, some had skimpy bathing suits, most of the women wore bikini bottoms. The sea was a vast empty horizon except for what looked like an oil tanker drifting lazily, a shadowy, smoky blue mirage, on the vague, distant smudge separating sea and sky.

"This is a nudist beach," he said.

"Oh. So, I am only one among many." I stuck my lower lip out in a pout. "Nothing special, just one naked body among naked bodies."

"Nudity is optional. In any case, you are and will always be exceptional – unique – absolutely one of a kind."

"Well, as long as that is settled then, that I am absolutely unique in the whole wide world, whether dressed or not! Let's go!"

Setting off a minor avalanche, we traipsed down the last few meters of the hill of sand to the beach.

We selected a spot, right at the edge of the water.

Not far away was a small hotdog and ice-cream stand made of bamboo, with a small row of flags fluttering above it, and some young kids, in shorts, were kicking a ball back and forth.

James spread out a huge towel – more than enough room for both of us to lie down. The man thinks of everything!

"Oil," he said, "And cream."

"Oil what?"

"You all over."

"Really?"

"Yes," he said, pulling a bottle out of the cooler-rucksack.

"That, Master, is a very fine, very sticky, very oily idea. If you wish to oil me, I am eager to be oiled."

I lay on my back.

"I think we'd better protect your eyes," he said.

"I see."

He pulled a blindfold out of the rucksack, and I sat up, and he slipped it over my head and adjusted it. The world went black, a silky, hot, vibrant black. The heat, the smells, the sounds, the lapping of water, the distant shouts, the flapping of the flags on the hotdog stand, and the touch of his hands on my skin – that was what I was reduced to, that was what I became. My master had turned me into a world of surfaces, of sensations, of pure, intense ecstatic presence, no past, and no future. The man does think of everything!

"Lie back," he said.

I did.

It was thick, creamy oil.

He began with my feet and ankles and worked his way slowly upwards. He smoothed the oil over me, all over and everywhere, every inch, every centimeter, and I lay there, on my back, supine, and just concentrated on the sounds of the beach and sea and on the touch of his hand on my body. "Open your legs." He was massaging me carefully between my legs. Smoothly he entered me, carefully opening me, and massaging my inner self.

"Oh, oh," I murmured. "This is, I see, a total massage." His fingers were so strong yet so sensitive. They seemed to be everywhere at once. The Bermuda Triangle was merely a memory, almost mythical by now. I wondered if it would ever return.

"Turn over, on your tummy, please."

"Tummy," I said, "it's such a cozy, domesticated, old-fashioned, sitting-by-the-fireplace type of word."

"Yes, it is."

I sat up blindly and then got on all fours and lowered myself down onto my tummy. Even blindfolded, I could feel the smile in his voice. There were the sensations, the pure naked wordless sensations: the cream going on, smoothed on, his palm flat, against my bum, up and then down. "I like this little curve here," he was saying, "And this dimple here. And this little valley here."

"You are being very intimate, sir," I murmured

"Sodomy," he said. He was oiling me, inside and out, very juicy.

"Hmm," I murmured, "You use me ill, sir. Sodomy indeed." I was dissolving into pure liquid, everywhere. I was dripping.

This was interesting. Yes, I was a cabin boy cast upon a foreign shore, and the pirate captain, a Hook for a Hand and a facile jolly Yo-ho-ho on his glib sunburnt lips, and a Bottle of Rum, has thrust me down, naked, helpless, bound, and blind. He was preparing to bugger me here on the beach not far from the fluttering flags of the Imperial Spanish Navy's hotdog stand. Rather exciting, actually. "That's a lot of oil," I said.

"Yes, lubricant," he said, "like Vaseline."

"You mean, it's not just suntan oil?"

"No, there's an extra bottle, greasier."

"Oh, boy, oh, boy."

This went on for a bit, and then he said, "You're done."

I turned over and sat up. "Can I take off the blindfold?"

"Maybe not just yet."

"Oh."

He put a bottle in my hand. "Perhaps, as a good servant should, you could oil my back."

"Blindfolded?"

"Of course."

"Okay."

He patted me on the bum. "But no funny business!"

"I promise, Master. Absolutely no funny business."

"My dignity as a man would not survive it."

"I totally understand, Master. The Phallic Kingdom is fragile and sacred, and one must treat it with the utmost respect. Any girlish mischief, and it would totally disintegrate."

"Indeed, Goddess, you totally understand." He guided me. I lowered myself down and straddled him, feeling myself dripping wet and dripping oil, and liquid with grease. I massaged the oil into his back. He turned over, and I did his chest, shoulders, and arms, though he made it difficult to concentrate because I was riding on top of his erection – imprisoned nicely in his bathing suit – and because he insisted on caressing and teasing my – dripping, oily – breasts.

"Thank you," he said, "Now, if you wish, Gwendoline, you can take off your blindfold – or I can take it off for you."

"You do it, Master. I am but a helpless maid, cast upon a foreign shore, knowing not what I should do or how to do it."

He loosened the blindfold and lifted it off carefully. I blinked. The light was terribly bright. Then I looked down at myself. I was glistening, soaked in oil – and so was he.

I slipped off him, and we lay for a bit on the towel.

We held hands.

He kissed me.

Our kisses tasted of perfumed oil and salt.

People on the beach – and there were not too many people – passed by. Some of the people were naked – men, women, children.

We went for a swim.

A family – mother, father, and two small children, a boy about eight or nine and a girl about six or so – sat down and set up their large colorful striped umbrella not too far from us, about twenty feet away. They waved at us, and we waved back.

We drank a bit of wine, in plastic cups, from the cooler. Then we nibbled on the sandwiches James had prepared.

"We might want some ice cream," he said.

"Where are we going to get ice cream?"

"That hotdog stand over there."

I squinted at it. It was about one hundred yards away, with little flags and banners fluttering from flag poles, and there were kids playing football close by. "You want me to go there?"

"Of course." He handed me a few bills.

"Yes, Master, I am your errand boy. I spurt, I fly, I gallop, I leap, I go – I shall return!"

He slapped me on the bum, a nice affectionate slap.

I blinked at him, stuck out my tongue, and set off.

I walked over to the ice-cream stand. A young girl in a flowered single-piece bathing suit was serving. She didn't blink at my nakedness at all. The flags fluttered and snapped in the breeze. They really did serve luscious hotdogs too, I saw; there was a little grill, and the smell of burning charcoal and sizzling grease drifted toward me in wafts of smoke. I licked my lips.

A woman came up to the stand; she was wearing a sleek one-piece bathing suit. She gave me a look from behind her dark glasses and then a big smile. Another woman came, wearing a bikini bottom. She gave me a careful once-over, and I looked back at her and smiled. She nodded and said, in Italian, and with a smile. "You're a foreigner?"

"Yes," I said, "Yes, I am."

"You are very beautiful," she said in English.

"Thank you, so are you!"

"Thank you, but, you know, children, giving birth." She patted her tummy, which, to my eyes, looked perfect. "I think you are perfect," I said, "Don't let anyone tell you otherwise."

She laughed. "I shall tell my husband you said so. You are a saint."

I walked back with the two ice creams. "Hurry, eat before it melts." I handed him his.

"Lick yours," he said, "don't bite it. Lick it slowly."

"But, it's already melting." My fingers were all sticky, and there were gobs of chocolate on my breasts.

"Come," he said. "Down on your knees."

I got down on my knees. He got down on his knees and faced

me – and I leaned back, and he leaned over me, and he licked the chocolate from my breasts and kissed me. I was still desperately licking the cone, when my mouth was free to do so; and he was licking his, between kisses. Our mouths were cool and sticky with ice cream.

≈

My Master – aka James – asked the family that was picnicking not far away, right on the edge of the water, if they would watch our stuff.

They said they would, they were staying until dusk, so we should not worry about anything. James gave me big dark, glamorous sunglasses with a thick white frame and a straw hat with a ribbon. We waved to our guardians and set out.

We walked along the beach. A soccer ball came bouncing along toward us. I kicked it back toward the people who were playing. The men and women kicked it back to me. I kicked back again. Some of the women were topless. Otherwise, they were wearing bathing suits.

"Play," my master said. He took my hat and my glasses. "Go," he said. I left my flip-flops, glasses, and the big straw hat behind and, while he watched, I skidded around in the sand, kicking the ball, receiving, kicking it back, splashing sand up, and then down, falling once or twice on my backside or sprawling down in the molten hot sand, which stuck to the oil on my skin. For a naked novice soccer player, I was not at all bad. I even scored two goals. Cheers greeted my efforts.

"Phew, I'm covered in sand," I said, as I returned to my Master.

"You are a statue of sand," he said. He took my picture with his smartphone, and then took a quick series of pictures.

My new soccer friends waved and shouted, "Ciaò," and we waved back and shouted, "Ciaò!"

We left the game behind, and we walked for what seemed like miles, and then, finally, we headed back – walking in the water, or on the shore, and sometimes swimming, sometimes splashing.

We got back to our big towel and rucksack spot. Everything was just as we had left it. The family had guarded our treasures. I thanked the little boy who was, I think, about eight or nine. He said he liked my hat.

"Grazie," I said.

He gave me a huge grin and ran splashing into the water, dove under, and came up, grinning and looking at me.

James and I went for a swim to get rid of the sand and just to cavort, and, out there, where it was just a foot or two too deep to stand, we made love. I wasn't quite sure such a thing was possible, but it was, though it involved a lot of splashing and groping and improvisation.

Hand in hand, we waded our way back to shore and lay down and just snoozed. With my eyes shut, I listened to all the lazy distant sounds of the beach; the children shouting, the waves lapping, the hotdog stand flags flapping, the whispering of the grass on the dunes, the seagulls cawing. Then I sat up; the sun was low in the sky, almost gone. "Time to leave, I think," said James.

We bid farewell to the family – mother, father, two little girls, and the little boy – and we walked back toward the car. I blinked at the wonder and beauty of it all. The light was now soft – it was evening; the world was turning beige. It was twilight time.

When we got to the car, James had a new costume for me – a large sheet of very fine white silk. He wrapped it around me. "A pareo," he said.

We drove along the coast, with the top down. I had just the thin white pareo wrapped around me. It fluttered in the breeze. "We need a shower," I said.

"Exactly, a shower." James glanced at me; it was a mischievous glance, and I could see he had already concocted some new plot.

The air was vibrant with heat. The rasping, violent music of the cicadas was sensual, a sound like the strumming, shimmering, blinding sea, the baking, vibrant sun.

≈

James pulled the Porsche off the road near some wooden shacks that stood on short stilts on the dunes over the beach. The grass was long and golden, and the light was slowly fading into a burnished, whispering amber.

We got out of the car. James asked me to take off the pareo. I unwrapped and opened it, and handed it to him. He took it from me and stored it in the trunk.

I looked down at myself. I was naked and coated in streaks of fine golden sand. "Itchy," I said.

"Golden girl," he said.

"Yeah," I pouted, looking up at him, giving the coal-black glance from under my eyebrows, "Itchy Golden Girl."

"Goddess!"

I stuck out my tongue and, standing in the middle of the ancient broken asphalt, truly feeling like a goddess, I pivoted around on tiptoes. I was drunk with the sun and the sea and the soft evening air. I was drunk with my Master's gaze. He took out his smartphone and began to fame me. I felt like a fashion model doing a cover shoot. He took a few photographs, in quick succession.

"Are you satisfied, Master?"

"I am delighted."

"Then, I too am delighted."

"Now a shower," he nodded. "There is a shower down at the end of this path." He pointed to an opening in the dunes.

"Good," I said, "Finally."

"Go," he said, and slapped me on the bottom.

I headed down the narrow path between the long grass and the dunes with James following, just behind me.

The shower was at the end of the path. It was all by itself, an isolated stand-alone open shower, consisting of a water pipe, a shower nozzle, and a three-sided plank-and-bamboo stall where there would be room for both of us.

"Disrobe me, please, goddess."

"Yes, Master. Your every wish is my command."

I got down on my knees on the sandy path – I adored adopting this worshipful position – perhaps I am a natural idolater.

I set to work and pulled down my man's slick little black bathing suit. He stepped out of it, and, still crouching, I handed it to him.

"Thank you."

"You are welcome, Master."

I stood up, and he kissed me.

He hung the bathing suit and the smartphone on a hook outside the shower. We stepped into the shower enclosure. He took me in his arms, pressing my sandpaper, sand-coated body against his warm, oiled muscles; he kissed me, and the kiss went on and on, the two of us standing there, locked together, in the small wood-bamboo box that smelled of cedar and sun-warmed pine and bamboo and the long sunburnt grass of summer.

"Get ready," he said. "This water will be cold at first, then hot."

He turned the rusty daisy-wheel handle. It squeaked. Then the water came.

"Oh, ice cubes! Oh!" I curled up. I hugged myself. I jumped, laughing, out of the shower. James leaped behind me, grabbed me in his frozen arms.

"Coward!" he laughed. "Ah, coward!"

Beads of ice-cold water covered his body, and his skin was ice-cold. He pulled me to him. Caught in his arms, I pretended to fight and squirm.

"You bugger," I whispered.

"You, luscious darling," he laughed.

I was trapped, his prisoner, enfolded in his strength.

"You are a cruel, hard man." I bit his lip, and licked it better

His skin was already warming. He looked into my eyes, plunging deep. "You are a remarkable creature," he said, "wild and never to be tamed."

"And you?"

"Oh, me, I'd like to be wild, but I'm not – you're my proxy."

"Ah," I said, "Projection and possession – such Freudian depths!"

He smiled his most enigmatic smile. He had such fine lips. The lowering sun caught glints of gold on his cheeks and chin. We shared another kiss. He murmured, "The water will be warm now."

"Okay, I believe you, maybe I believe you, but you go first."

"Certainly," he walked back into the shower. Steam rose.

"Oh, nice, you are all steamy." I stood and watched. I loved the effect as the water steamed up around him, turning him into a dark mysterious stranger, and I loved how it streamed down his chest, making patterns in the black hair, glinting on the shiny muscles.

"Step in, Goddess." He reached out his hand. I took it and stepped into the hot, thick cascade.

"Oh, boy, oh, boy ..."

"Now, Princess, I'll do the scrubbing. Lift up your arms."

I tilted back my head and obeyed, stretching my arms straight up. I surrender! Oh, yes, I surrender. This may not last, but I surrender. I surrender totally to you, my love; I surrender to now, to

the moment, to this. The golden coating of sand was, by now, almost all gone.

"Soap," he said, "You, filly, now I soap you for the show."

"Yes, sir, do, sir, please, sir!"

When he had done with me – and he was very thorough, I
soaped him down. "Oh, you man, you man, you, I will explore
every part of your, every nook, cranny, every mountain and valley
and plateau." And I did.

≈

Then we were outside the shower, dripping wet.

He turned the water off.

There was a sudden silence – and the sounds were reborn: the
cicadas, the breathing murmur of the surf, the cawing of seagulls,
the breeze rippling in the long, straw-like grass, and the whispering of the light, dying on the golden beach and the dark, dark sea.

Naked, we walked hand in hand down the last few yards of the
path toward the view over the beach, letting the air dry us. The
view opened wide – a few faint clouds, gold with the dying light,
lay on the horizon, and a container ship rode high, just a shadow,
and there were a few dark silhouettes of people, kneeling, walking, and playing at the water's edge.

"So, darling, let us eat." He put his arm around me; we were
Adam and Eve, and this was paradise.

"This has been a long day, Master, and I suddenly discover I do
have a considerable appetite. I'm famished!" My saliva rose at
the prospect of a cool glass of wine, a luscious slice of grilled fish,
some scrumptious antipasti, and perhaps a big wedge of chocolate cake.

We strolled slowly back to the car. My master had a tied a neat
little towel around his waist; but I, as per usual, being the animal, the femme, and the catamite slave boy, was naked, and quite

happy in my nakedness. I think part of me wanted to be arrested and carried away in a paddy wagon, housed in a cell, naked, with some drunken prostitutes. Let's see ... the cell would be very dark, and the girls would be all tricked out in splendidly garish ...

We got to the road. There was the Porsche, obediently waiting for us.

James opened the trunk. "Please hand me my underwear and jeans and my shirt," he said. "And would you be kind enough to dress me, Jeeves?"

"Yes, your Lordship. Where would your Lordship desire me to begin – bottom, or middle, or top?"

"The boxer shorts would seem a good beginning, Jeeves."

And so it was that I, his Lordship's very own naked and un-adorned Jeeves, dressed his Lordship – striped black-and-gold boxer shorts, blue shirt, open down to the collarbone, blue jeans, crisp and pressed, with a wide black leather belt, and black leather sandals.

Now he gazed at me. "Now, I have just the thing for you. Let's see, where is it?

He pulled it out of his backpack.

It was a sheer black catsuit; it went from the tip of my toes to high around the neck.

I held it out. "I'm supposed to dine in this? In a seaside restaurant?"

"It's very cool," he said.

"Cool, it is, indeed, Master!"

"Try it on."

I was by now entirely dry, wearing only my scarlet flip-flops. I was also entirely free of gritty golden sand. The air was warm and drifting in from the sea. I glanced back at the little shower. A few people were walking along the beach, far away, tiny silhouettes, glimpsed and framed, as if in a painting, by the narrow path, shadowy beings at the edge of the water darkly glinting water.

"Okay. Let's see how exposed I shall be." I pulled it on carefully; it was open at the back, with a minuscule almost invisible zipper

"See," he said.

I looked down. It was skin-tight and almost entirely sheer, but it was opaque in exactly the right strategic places where it was just barely opaque and somehow gave the impression of not being opaque. My breasts were clearly delineated, and areolae and nipples, but my 'Heart of Darkness' was shadowed, as if by a fine mist of dark silk.

"And then there is this."

It was a skimpy, wet-look, moiré, black silk jacket.

"Okay, I guess I'm rehearsing for a part, eh?"

"You've already got the part, darling." He fitted a velvet collar around my neck and locked it; it had a large ring, of course, that was just under my chin, so he could attach me to a leash.

"Yes," I sighed, "I suppose I have."

Then, of course, I was equipped with black, high-heeled pumps.

I was again a goddess, a prisoner goddess, a fetish goddess, but a goddess just the same.

As for James, he looked eminently respectable and normal and perfectly repressed with his healthy he-man blue shirt, his deep tan, his crisp blue jeans, and his perfect black sandals. The only slight touch or suggestion of cruelty was the thick black belt and the large buckle – very dominant, masterly features, and which made me think for some reason of the black-and-red cat o' nine tails in Nicole's shop window.

We got into the Porsche and drove along the dusty little road that ran parallel to the beach, just behind the restaurants and seaside dunes; after ten or eleven kilometers, he pulled off the road and parked, and we got out. We were in a small fishing village, with some wooden cottage-like houses and dusty palm trees on the inland side of the road, and, on the seaside of the road, restaurants whose terraces gave onto the beach and the sea. The streetlamps projected garish white light over the road, and over us.

"You like these second-skin things, don't you?" I put my hand on his chest.

"Yes. I like to see you wrapped up like a present on display." He stroked my flanks.

"It's funny, but I do too. I like them too." I kissed him.

The restaurant had a terrace facing the beach and the sea and the setting sun. We walked through the interior and out onto the terrace. The owner, Salvatore, a solid, handsome man with a broad, tanned face and fierce-looking handlebar mustache, greeted us as if James were his long-lost brother. James introduced me as Gwendoline, a math prodigy and winner of the famous Neumann-Williamson Fellowship.

I am sure this meant nothing to Salvatore, but he very kindly pretended to be impressed and feigned interest and was perfectly gracious, ushering me forward and kissing my hand. "Welcome," he said, and he accompanied us to our table, which had been reserved, out on the terrace, facing the beach and the sea.

I was ravenous. I decided that I would let my tummy swell if it was going to swell, and let it show if it was going to show. Martin Aubin was not here to give me advice, and I didn't see any paparazzi.

≈

I went to the antipasto table and pigged out by piling my plate with prosciutto and mozzarella, salad, creamy coleslaw, and pickled mushrooms and slices of parmesan, and piles of bruschetta, and several different versions of frittata, plus a mountain of sardines. Several of the women and men who were collecting their own food glanced at me and then at my plate, and one woman, who was standing next to me, said, "Doesn't he feed you, dear?"

"Never," I said, "He keeps me locked in a cage, and I can only eat when I am allowed out – which is extremely rare."

"Well, we can't have that, can we?" She laughed and forked up a thick slice of the frittata and dropped it on my plate, on top of the mountain that was my booty.

"Thank you," I said.

"You are welcome. Just shout if you need to be rescued."

James looked at my plate, crossed his eyes, and stuck out his tongue.

"I am planning to become extremely, spectacularly fat." I sat down primly. "Fat is beautiful. This will mean I shall have to change my wardrobe every two weeks. You must feed me, fill the trough and allow me to grunt and wallow and slosh about and eat 24 hours a day. The bill for fodder will be immense."

"I shall be delighted to provide the fodder, Goddess."

Looking at him, and smiling, I blinked – to chase the moisture away from my eyes. I wondered: how could any man be so absolutely, so utterly handsome.

We ate, and we talked. We drank some fine dry wine. It was – from somewhere in the Aeolian Islands, so Salvatore told us. It had a snappy sulfurous volcanic taste, a suggestion of earth and sea and salt sea breezes and elemental telluric forces. It evoked deep sources far underground, an echo of ancient gods and goddesses, and Greek and Roman galleys plowing through the salty spray.

James clinked his glass against mine, and as if he had picked up an echo of my musing, he said, "I thought next week, we could take a week off, Gwendoline, if you can spare the time, and go out to some of the volcanic islands in the Tyrrhenian Sea, the

Aeolian Islands. A friend of mine has a house on one of them. We could visit her there. I think you will find she is a very interesting person."

"That sounds wonderful."

A photographer came by and asked if he could take my photograph. I glanced at James. He nodded. I said, "Yes, of course," so I stood, and let him take a couple of shots – front on, and sideways, and flirting with the camera, tilting my head this way and that, posing beside the antipasto table and all its treasures. Salvatore and the waiters stood grinning, and all the diners watched. The photographer thanked me and gave me his card. I vaguely recognized the name. He was famous, I think. He would send me an email, he said, with the shots.

"You will probably get a modeling contract out of this." James gazed at me through half-closed eyes. He seemed pleased. His trophy, his possession, his other half, me, was drawing attention – but he seemed oblivious to the attention of others; he didn't seem to notice anyone else; he only had eyes, as the old song goes, for me.

"Well, that would be sweet," I leaned down and kissed him, and then I sat down in front of him and concentrated on eating. It was a damp, warm evening with a very light breeze, and the breeze carried evocative suggestions of sea and sand and suntan oil and grilling fish.

As I tucked into my mountain of goodies, James began to tell me about his woman friend, the one with an isolated house in a little bay with a sandy and pebbled beach, on one of the Aeolian Islands; she was in her late seventies, he said, famous as a journalist, and not always easy to get along with, so ...

"So, she may be a challenge," I said.

"Precisely, darling, she may be a challenge. And I'm not sure, she will ..."

"... approve of me ..."

"There is that danger," he said, narrowing his lips, rather primly, I thought; I wondered why we were setting ourselves up for such unpleasantness trapped out on an isolated island in enemy territory; but if the lady was a friend of his, well, then, come hell or high water, I would try to make her a friend of mine!

Then came the main course.

I looked at the sea bass. It was magnificent. It came with a luscious salad and a small serving of rice. Now that I had something in my stomach, my feeding frenzy was slowly grinding to a halt. I looked down. I patted my tummy neatly wrapped in the transparent silk catsuit. Yes, perhaps there was a small swelling; but I rather liked it; it made me feel all fertile, and feminine, and maternal; I would make sure James kissed it before we fell asleep.

I held the cool wine glass against my chin. The wine smelled delicious, a suggestively sulfurous and sinful bouquet, and the cool icy feeling of the glass was a titillating contrast with my sun-sensitized skin and the sultry humidity of the air. The wine radiated a primitive power like that of that resinous Greek wine, Retsina, or so, at least, it seemed to me. It made me think of the glaring midday sun, the pine needles, the bare rocks, the glittering sea, and the rasping chorus of cicadas, and all the old gods, nymphs and satyrs, dancing and fornicating in the sun and under the moon.

After dinner, we drove down the coast a few miles, and we stopped on the side of the road, again, near a strange building, sticking out above the beach. It looked like the stern of a stranded ocean liner from the 1930s.

"Are we going skinny-dipping?"

"No."

"Am I to run naked along the beach?"

"That would be pleasant, but I thought, darling, that we might dance."

"Oh, well, then ..." I stepped out of the car, thinking this might be romantic – but I didn't see a dance club.

"Leash," he said, holding it up.

"Of course, Master."

He came around the car. I offered my neck to him, and he clicked the leash to my collar. I purred.

"Here we go, darling." He led me under an arch with sparking, blinking letters, colored, flashing lightbulbs, *Cabiria Ballare*, and down a path under a vine-covered trellis and lined with oleander and rose bushes, and we arrived in fairyland.

≈

It was a strange club, with a circular dance floor, open, outside, under the stars, and overlooking the sea. The restaurant overlooking the dance floor was shaped like the stern of an ancient ocean liner, with portholes, and decks, and a giant funnel painted white and blue and which soared up into the dark blue starry sky. The dancing couples were older, in their 50s and 60s, at least. The men were dressed in slacks and shirts, and the woman in cotton dresses.

The small orchestra, seemingly conjured up from some past time, consisted of old men, with chalky pale faces, all wearing the same faded blue jacket, with dark lapels and white shirts and black string ties and tiny black mustaches. They were sitting on the stage of a cute little bandstand. They looked like a miniature orchestra, a toy orchestra. They played music from ancient times – from the 1930s and 1940s, and sometimes, being very daring, from the 1950s. Lots of it was big band dance music – swing music.

"This is a time warp," I said, "Have you transported me into the 1940s, James?"

"Indeed, I have."

290

We had a reserved table, it seemed, a tiny round table, at the far end of the dance floor. There was something miniature and Lilliputian about the whole place. After leading me on my leash across the dance floor to our table, James unhooked me, and coiled the leash on the table; we sat down, and James ordered a bottle of wine from a young waitress who suddenly, miraculously, appeared.

"Let us, dance, Gwendoline," he said.

"Yes, Master." I stood up. My Master reached out his arms to take my jacket. I glanced at him and said, "Oh?"

"Yes," he said and gallantly lifted off the thin silk jacket and put it carefully over the back of my chair, leaving me naked except for the dark moiré semi-transparent sheen of the catsuit, the collar, and the stilettos.

"Displaying his prisoner, Master is being naughty," I whispered.

"Of course, he is." He took my arm. We stepped onto the dance floor, and we danced.

Wearing the sheer catsuit looked and felt like being naked. The sensuality of being in his arms as he held me tight, and as we slowly danced our way around the dance floor was utterly delicious and perhaps a bit risqué. But, aside from a few not unfriendly glances, none of the old couples paid any attention to us, though when we sat down, between dances, the couple at the next table, they must have been at least in their late seventies, leaned over and told us about themselves. Under Mussolini, their great grandparents had moved here from the Vento region. "We are celebrating our sixtieth wedding anniversary," the woman said. "I only hope you can be as happy as I am, my dear," she said, laying her hand on my arm. I thanked her. James bought a bottle for them, and a cake with six candles, and we drank to their happiness and to their anniversary. We returned to the dance floor.

"I could dance forever like this, Master," I said.

"And so could I, Gwen, so could I."

About an hour later, when we left the club, James neglected to put me on the leash, but once we were outside on the street, he again attached me. After a long and very passionate kiss, we went for a little walk along the road. No one was about, so the show had no public except we two, but still, I thought, it was worth it. I am dangerous enough to be kept on a leash, I thought, indulging in my own fantasy – I am a panther. The Great White Hunter has tamed me.

"Yes," he said, as if reading my thoughts, "You are dangerous, Gwen." We kissed and groped and caressed, there on the side of the road, in the light night breeze from the sea, as if we were two oversexed teenagers.

Finally, we drove home to Rome, left the car in the underground parking lot that was its home, and caught a cab back to home base, and we showered, and tumbled into bed.

That one weekend had felt like a whole lifetime.

CHAPTER 7 – SEA SPRITE

The following week was calm, all work, and a very domestic life, dining at home, or at Alfredo's, and I was dressed, except at home, in civvies. No magic striptease, no corsets, no painted labia or nipples, no catsuit extravaganzas, just jeans or shorts, T-shirts or tank-tops, and sandals, or, at home in the heat of midday just panties or nothing at all.

≈

I must admit I was nervous – about the upcoming week, which we were going to spend on the Aeolian Islands with the older woman friend of James.

I googled her: Oh, this will be intimidating! She was, as James had told me, in her late seventies. She had been famous, first as a model and photographer, and then as a reporter and writer, doing in-depth, first-hand battlefield stories on wars and crime; she was a woman who had risked her life many times – often under fire – and she had won almost all the awards a journalist could win.

This, I thought, is going to be a challenge.

I brought along my iPad loaded with math and a small book on Einstein that I had been meaning to read, plus a biography of the woman herself – Lauren Lockhart.

We took the early morning train to Naples, and then we took a six-hour hydrofoil trip out to the islands – roaring over sparkling waters – and, finally, we met Ms. Lockhart in the marina of the little island port where she kept her boat.

James waved at her, and then he headed straight to down to the dock to stow our things on the boat, leaving me alone, to introduce myself to the lady. I wanted to shout, "Hey, help! James! Don't leave me!"

Lauren Lockhart was wearing big wraparound dark glasses, and she had a loose-limbed lanky way of walking – a quick, aggressive stride – which clearly showed she'd been a model used to sauntering arrogantly down a runway and impressing everyone who saw her. It was a very stylish gait, vaguely masculine, almost threatening.

She glanced at me, quickly and askance, and shook my hand, in a casual limp-wristed, but muscular and rather arrogant off-handed way, as if to dismiss me even before we'd met.

I took careful note. Her fingernails were unvarnished, clean, and cut short; her hand was bony and strong, with long sensitive, distinguished-looking fingers; and her deeply tanned hands were mottled with age marks and sunspots. She'd lived a lot outdoors; she had high cheekbones and thin, finely delineated, almost masculine lips, but, when she did smile, it was a startlingly beautiful big frank smile. She took off her glasses to submit me to closer inspection.

Her eyes slanted up somewhat, giving her a wicked impish look, with black satanic eyebrows. She was the very epitome of elegance.

"So, you are the friend of James."

"Yes," I said.

"And you are some sort of prodigy, I hear."

"I wouldn't say that," I said.

Her smile flickered away. She now raised an eyebrow and examined me, frankly, as if I had crawled out from under a stone or perhaps from a sewer.

I tried to figure out what she despised. Was it because I was his lover, or because I submitted to his games – which I'm sure she knew about – or was it because I was young, too young for James, and much too young to know anything about life, or love, or about anything at all? Was it because I was young, and she was old?

"And what do you talk about?" She gave me a smile, which was meant, I think, to be openly condescending – a glove thrown down, a challenge.

"She may be difficult," James had said, "but you will overcome her, I'm sure." "Well, I'm not sure," I had said, "that I'll overcome her, I mean." By that time, in the train heading to Naples, I was reading her biography, so I knew quite a bit about my rival and enemy.

"So, what do you talk about?"

I narrowed my eyes. She was beautiful, I decided. She was wearing a broad-shouldered jacket, and a T-shirt under it, and white trousers.

"So, what do you talk about?"

"Hmm," I said, "well, we talk about sex – sometimes but not really that much – and we talk about art and about politics, about business – his business – and about – you won't believe this – but we talk about math."

"Of course, James is very brainy, very cerebral. He could have been a scientist." She looked at me with a bit more interest.

"Yes, he is – and his curiosity ranges everywhere," I said, "Our conversations are fun, but it's sometimes like sitting for an examination."

She gazed at me and then said, "I must change." She went

away to the marina's clubhouse; ten minutes later, she came back in denim shorts and a shirt tucked into the denim shorts, and under the shirt, there was a bra, and she was wearing nice plain leather sandals.

"This more like it," she said.

"You look perfect," I said.

She just looked at me.

We went down to meet James at the dock.

≈

Lauren's boat was a small yacht that could be crewed by one person, or better, by two. It could sleep four people comfortably.

Sailing close under craggy cliffs, and using the motor, not the sails, it took us only about twenty minutes to get to her villa, which was an isolated house, just up from a solitary cove, in a very rocky part of another island in the group.

Immediately after leaving our luggage in the villa, we set out for some rocks that stuck up out of the sea – the tip of part of a sunken volcano, which was far from any real land. We would picnic and snorkel and laze about. It was already getting on late into the afternoon, but the sun was still high, and hot.

So, twenty minutes after leaving the villa, there we were, out on the rocky ledge of nothing – just cliffs and ledges of volcanic stone – with the boat anchored in shallows about fifty meters away.

Lauren and I were left on the reef while James took the inflatable dinghy back out to the yacht to get the food and wine and make some complicated telephone calls he had to make.

He was negotiating a difficult takeover deal in India, and the Indian company had some complicated but promising entanglements in East Africa, and the values on some of the properties were vulnerable to political and terrorist risks. I had used my math and hacking skills – and cryptographic skills – to help James research these risks and how to evaluate and price them, and how best to insure against them. Doing the work, I'd spent many hours on the phone with my old friend, his New York assistant Allison, and she'd helped me with the background research. The more I talked to her, the more I liked her.

Lauren had taken off her shorts. She had tanned, sun-mottled skin, and she was wearing a skimpy flowered bikini with the open cream-colored shirt loose over the bikini top.

She took out a cigarette and lit it, took a couple of deep puffs, and then set it down in between the rocks.

"Well, we'd better take advantage of what little sun there is," she said. She took off her shirt, and then stood up and took off the bottom of her bikini and then the top. So, there she was, a naked, deeply tanned seventy-eight-year-old woman standing on a low and cragged reef of stone in the middle of the immense blue of the sea and sky.

She looked at me and smiled. She had a very bold unapologetic smile, of the Katherine Hepburn type, and so I said, "Yes, I guess we'd better take advantage of it," and I lifted off my bikini top and then the bottom, feeling extra naked in front of this intimidating woman.

My Bermuda Triangle had not yet reappeared. The waxing had been very thorough, and I didn't even sense any prickly feeling yet, though I was eagerly waiting for it. I was worried that perhaps I was going to remain waxed, smooth, and naked forever. Lauren took another puff from the cigarette. "You're shaved," I see.

"Waxed," I said.

"Total," she said.

"Yes."

"Men like that," she said, "some men prefer an Amazon forest – or a tailored French garden."

"And some men like both," I said, "or all three."

"Yes, some men like both," she laughed, "or all three." She took another puff of the cigarette. The bluish smoke curled up, then dispersed.

I looked at her closely: she had a tangle of blond-gray pubic hair, thin now, from age I guess, sparse desert sagebrush; it looked interesting, a little forest, a contrast to smooth and naked me. She also had, I had noticed, with a bit of surprise, no breasts – or little caves or craters and scars where her breasts had been.

She saw me looking.

"Surgery," she said, "I really shouldn't smoke. Or be in the sun. But, you know, at my age – who cares ..."

"I guess, if it gives you pleasure."

"It's like most addictions. I'm not sure that pleasure is the right word." She stood up. "Do you want to feel?"

"Ah, yes, sure." I stood up, stepped closer, and felt where her breasts had been, I could feel a bit of hardness where I suppose the suture lines had been, and lumpiness. It felt interesting – vaguely arousing in a weirdly pleasant sort of way. I explored with my fingers.

"Maybe you could put a bit of oil on this old body," she said.

"Certainly," I said.

She lay down on her stomach on the towel and little fold-out mattress on a flat patch of stone, and I knelt beside her; I poured oil into my hand, and I began to smooth the oil onto her back. There were mottled bits, and there was one very smooth patch of olive-colored skin where it looked like the skin was transparent and that I could look into the whirling smoky depths.

"What is that?" I said, touching it.

"That? Oh, radiation, they burned away a growth, many, many years ago. That's what I am, a sinking ruin covered in barnacles, marked by signs, stigmata of age."

"They're interesting signs," I said. "This one is beautiful." I kissed the smooth olive-colored patch; it was a swirl of mystery, like a precious stone; you could stare deep into its silken smooth intricacy.

"Life is strange," she said.

"How so?"

"Well, you are young one day, then the next day – suddenly and without realizing so many years have passed – you are old. And when you are young, you think, Oh, what a horrible thing to be old."

"If you think about it at all," I said.

"Yes, you're right, if you think about it at all. And then suddenly you are old and, actually, aside from a few little aches and pains, it's not that bad – if you are lucky that is." She took another puff of her cigarette. "I've had fun all my life." She stretched out one arm.

"But you worked pretty hard – and you took risks."

"Yes, I did, but that was fun too!"

I smoothed the oil over her backside – nice and firm, actually – and down her legs. The varicose veins made an interesting pattern.

She turned over. "Do me all over, except the face," she said, the cigarette dangling from the side of her mouth, looking a bit like a villain or a seductress in an old French movie.

I started with her shoulders and worked my way down, slowly, concentrating on her breasts. Well, where her breasts had been – and her belly, which had neat little sag lines, nothing much really.

I messaged the little sag lines. I took my time. Each centimeter was intriguing. I returned to where her breasts had been, lightly massaging, sculpting the whorls and scars.

"Do you mind? Is this okay?" I asked; I was intrigued; it was interesting, and rather arousing.

"It's perfect, Gwendoline."

I concentrated. I liked it. The more I massaged her, the more I put the oil on, the more beautiful I thought she was – every little detail of the body, and different shades and imperfections of the skin ...

"I'm like these craggy volcanic peaks," she said, "all ruins, mostly sunk and invisible, just a bit of me remaining above the surface."

"But beautiful," I said.

"Look at us," she said, "you, chalk-white, young, perfect, a northern nymph risen from shadowy forest and mountain brook, and me, a weathered sunburnt old wreck, barely afloat, masts and spars swept away, holes and scars on the hull. But still, we sail on, both of us."

"Yes, both of us, we still sail on." I poured some more oil into my hands and then began to move down her lower belly.

"What is that?"

"Appendicitis."

"And this one?"

"I was shot once."

"I didn't know."

"It was at a demonstration in Cairo. A long time ago." She breathed out some smoke. "Everything is a long time ago."

I was now messaging her lower belly, and her pubis.

"Ah, my dear," she said. "Now, you're talking!"

I became bolder, and I wondered what it would be like, and so I caressed her, opened her lips, oiled them, and touched her deeper and deeper, and she lolled her head back, closed her eyes, and took a long puff of the cigarette, and murmured, "Oh, don't stop, nymph, don't stop."

I loved the way her body, lean and rugged and laden with experience and time, was at my mercy; I adored the feeling that I was giving her pleasure, that this important woman, who had written so many articles and books, who had risked her life so many times, was now in my hands. I pressed harder, and harder, and opened her more and more, and she began to sigh, "Oh, oh, this ... is ... this is ... this is hardly dignified!"

"Oh, yes, it is," I said, "it is perfectly dignified."

"Oh, oh, oh," she said, "don't stop."

"Don't worry," I said, and I continued, and then I kissed her, and then I knelt close, and using my tongue, I entered her. By now she smelled like sun oil, and it was a nice coconut smell, and I nuzzled her and caressed her and then, she came, it was in convulsions, like sobs, like a prayer, like a long sigh, and then she screamed but pulled my arm to her so that she could bite my hand and stifle her scream. Luckily, the bite was not too deep.

My hand was free again, and I kissed her sex once more, and her pubis, with a little farewell lick, and I began to massage her thighs. She was still lying back. She lit another cigarette.

"I want to kiss you," she said. "I want you to lie next to me and let me kiss you."

I crawled next to her and lay down on my side, and we kissed – it was quite a nice kiss, slow, and gentle, and soft and smoky and smelling of tobacco. It lasted quite a long time.

"This will make James jealous," she said.

"I don't think so." I touched her lips with my finger.

"He loves you." She was looking into my eyes. She traced the side of my face with her finger. "I think he truly loves you. I fear ..."

"Yes, but ..." I didn't dare finish the sentence; James feared love; Allison had warned me; even James had warned me.

Lauren nodded and kissed me. "You are strong, Gwendoline," she said. "Remember to be strong."

We sat up, alerted by the hollow clunky sound of wood oars being put into their oarlocks, then by the splashing and dipping that echoed across the calm, calm water. James was on his way, rowing the dingy over to us. Behind him was Lauren's yacht, which was a beautiful boat; it seemed suspended in the air, everything was so still; it drifted in its own reflections, between the smoky blue sea and tender blue sky, caught in a world of mirrors. I stood up. James waved. He was standing in the dinghy as he steered it toward us. It looked as if he was walking on water.

James stepped off the dinghy and waded to the rocks. He stood knee-deep in the water, little wavelets radiating around him, ripples and loops of light reflecting on his lean, tanned body, and tied the dinghy's anchor rope to a rusty crooked old steel construction rod that stuck up from a smear of cement where someone had tried to build a pier. "I see you two have become well acquainted," he said, his smile bright, his hair slicked back, and his eyes invisible behind the dark glasses. "I have brought some chilled white wine and some sandwiches."

He waded back to the gently rocking dinghy, lifted out the supplies, and came over, laying out his treasures, and sat down with us; he took off his glasses and kissed me and said, "You are an angel."

"Yes, she is," said Lauren. "She is an angel."

James opened the bottle, got out the plastic cups, and spread out the sandwiches on a towel.

Lauren – like me – was still naked; her whole body glowed with oil. She lit a cigarette, glanced at me, and squinted against the light and wisps and tendrils of bluish smoke that curled up against her eyes.

She exhaled. "Your nymph is a marvel, James. She is wise and compassionate and very forgiving of the foibles and weaknesses of age."

"Yes, she is," said James, "I should know." He gazed at us as if we were a picture, a painting perhaps by Gaugin or Monet or

Cezanne, two naked women, one young, one old, stranded on a rock in the middle of the hovering, mirror-like, gently breathing sea.

The sun was by now quite low. The air turned a paler blue. Shadows, like departing ghosts, faded and disappeared, leaving everything foreshortened and dreamy. We were drifting in a sort of one-dimensional glowing world of water and stone and sky. And here we were, three tiny humans, sitting on the edge of a ruined volcano that went down at least two kilometers into the dark and alien depths, and below that, somewhere, maybe five or ten kilometers down, was a huge chamber of magma, just waiting for the right moment. It gave me a shivery little feeling, all that immensity and violence, lying right under us.

We drank the wine, swam, snorkeled, ate, and swam again, and then we got on the boat and headed back toward the island and Lauren's villa.

The rock of much of the island was fragile, friable volcanic rock that shattered easily; it was unstable and rose up in steep crags and cliffs. People couldn't build there – only in little outposts near the shore. Lauren's villa stood alone, all by itself, in a cove far from the main village. The villa was white stucco, two stories high, crouched against a rock cliff, and had a covered and sheltered terrace that overlooked the sea and the cove.

The cove was so quiet it seemed, in a way, to be Lauren's private little cove, though there was a small bar, serving coffee and wine, on a rocky ledge overlooking the beach. The cove and the beach were sheltered from the sea by outlying rocks and by two small promontories. Lauren's yacht was the only boat anchored in the cove. Only one path, which wandered along the edge of the cliff, linked us to the one village of the island, about twenty minutes away by foot. At night, you needed a flashlight to go anywhere.

The villa didn't have electricity, so we used kerosene lamps. Even after dark, the cicadas were still making that thrilling rasping sound.

I was naked – but wearing my thick black leather collar – and I was in the kitchen making pesto sauce.

When Lauren realized I was going to be walking around in the kitchen without clothes – James had stipulated this – she took hers off too. "Gwendoline is an untamed animal," James had said, "She doesn't need clothes. Clothes are too constraining."

"Well, then, I shall try to be an untamed animal too. If you do not mind, James?"

"Not at all," James was pouring a drink, "delighted."

Lauren pulled her T-shirt up over her head and stepped out of her shorts and panties.

While I prepared supper, James and Lauren sat in wicker chairs in the gathering shadows near the porch and the – unlit – fireplace. Beyond them, out in the darkness, was the sea. I could feel it even if I couldn't see it, a vast salty, gently breathing presence.

Lauren was smoking, and James was drinking a whiskey. They were discussing some war she had been in, some fights he had seen, and some skirmishes he had fought in. And they were arguing about how the new troubles in that particular country were like a repetition of the old, how the patterns of tribalism and religious hatred could not be evaded or ignored, and how there is nothing new under the sun, and, plus ça change, plus c'est la même chose.

I listened idly. Their talk was the talk of people who had lived through decades; it was talk informed by so many anecdotes and events from the past, by so much wisdom – but they were still eagerly curious about today and about the future. I was happy, listening passively, naked, acutely conscious of my youth and energy, pleasantly aware of the collar around my neck, a seal of possession and belonging, and enjoying the sensual thrill of the warm terracotta tiles under my feet, in the warm atmosphere of the large, open kitchen, with the water boiling in a big pot. I had read the instructions on the pasta package carefully, and I was going to make the pasta just right – al dente. I had also prepared what I reckoned would be a splendid salad, with lettuce and arugula, and tomatoes and onions and anchovies and capers and tuna.

I succeeded: the pasta was just right – al dente, and James and Lauren declared that the salad was a masterpiece, which was perhaps an exaggeration.

We sat on the terrace, overlooking the invisible sea, and ate by candlelight.

I was thinking that this was a perfect moment, that it was a pagan paradise, and that it couldn't last.

Lauren looked beautiful, a tangle of gray-blonde hair over her forehead, her hands lit up by the candles. With her long fine fingers, mottled with decades of sunlight, and her bare and bony shoulders marked by time, the scars and cavities where her breasts had been, she was like a weathered and ancient monument that has lived so long, and that bears the marks of having lived so long.

"People make too much of a fuss about being naked," she was saying. "It should be the most natural thing in the world. Shame is an illness and not a very productive emotion." The darkness surrounded the terrace, and the lamplight was very low.

"Yes, I agree," I said, "I think people make too much of a fuss about a great many things."

"Some more pasta, please, darling," said James.

I stood up and served.

James looked at me with his eyes half-closed, and he smiled. It was an enigmatic smile, possessive and distant, mysterious, and intimate. He poured all three of us more of that wonderful white wine that carried tangy and sinful suggestions of the sulfurous volcanic fertile pagan land where the grapes had grown.

≈

That night, in bed, James whispered to me that I had made Lauren very happy.

"I wanted to do it," I said. "I loved it. And she looked so beautiful, and alone, and enticing, and a bit angry too, inside."

"It's not easy to grow old when inside you are still young," he stroked my hair.

"I guess not." I was lying against his side and running my hand over his chest, and then down his belly, to his sex, and I played with it, gently, teasing it just a little bit, soft up and down strokes, gentle little twists, and immediately it was hard, and he signed and said, "You really are a dangerous girl, Gwendoline."

"Yes, Master, I agree – sometimes, I am dangerous. Let me kiss it and comfort it and make it better."

And so I did. It was very slow-motion and sweet, and then I curled against him again. Such comfort …

There was a gentle little knock at the door.

It was Lauren. She peeked in. "I'd prefer not to sleep alone," she said, "I promise not to smoke."

"Come on," James said, "It's a big bed, and it's your bed, after all."

"Come," I slipped out of the bed. "Let's make room."

I lay between the two of them. It was sweet and intimate in a way that I think people used once perhaps to know – along with squalor, violence, strong acrid sweaty smells, and dirt – when they were hunter-gatherers, or peasants, or workers in some demonic factory. There they would be, all piled into one cave, or one room, or one bed – submitting to forms of casual, violent and tender intimacy that most of us today, at least in the rich, privileged parts of the world, have never known, separated, as we are, each dozing in a privileged, isolated, little cubicle.

I wrapped my arm around Lauren, and James wrapped his arm around me, and kissed me on the nape of my neck, tickling the loose strands and small fringe of hair.

Where was the jealousy in all of this? Where was the pain? For the moment, there were none of those things. I fell into a deep and dreamless sleep.

The rest of the week was equally relaxing. We swam, we snorkeled, we visited isolated beaches and volcanic outcroppings lost in the middle of the sea. I gave Lauren several of my very special massages.

James and I made love, in a relaxed and amusing way. I think he was pleased that I was giving some pleasure – and some love, for it was love – it was sex and it was love – to his old friend.

I think we all realized – or knew – that earthly paradise is a rare and fragile thing; that our attachments would not last; that all things pass – and so that we should, therefore, be gentle and passionate and compassionate and generous to each other when we could.

As the ancients used to say, Carpe Diem, seize the day, cultivate the instant, for tomorrow ...

≈

Lauren stayed on, alone, in her villa on the island when we left. We took the hydrofoil back to Naples, and then the train from Naples to Rome. I felt as if I had plunged into something like ancient pagan Greece and was now being transported back – in a single afternoon – into the 21st Century.

≈

Two days later, I was sitting on a towel on the terrace of our Rome apartment, with a ballpoint pen and spiral notebook, and naked as I had been told I should be, except for the high collar, its ring, and my leash. I was working, concentrating, rather hard actually, on a mathematical problem: on refining my research program, for the Neumann-Williamson Fellowship. At the end of the fellowship, I had to deliver a major speech in New York to an audience that would include some of the world's greatest mathematicians. Just the idea made me break out in a pearly sweat.

When I concentrate, I forget where I am or how I am dressed. I would be quite capable of jumping up, walking through the flat, and answering the door without putting any clothes on.

James came out onto the terrace – dressed splendidly in jeans and a shirt and sandals – and announced that he had to leave for Paris in two days. He would need to stay there for an indefinite amount of time. I was free to remain here if I wanted to, but he was hoping that I would go to Paris with him.

"Hmm, there are some very interesting mathematicians in Paris," I said, pretending, for a mere second, to be coy, "Well, Master," I stood up and kissed him, "I would be delighted to come to Paris."

I immediately emailed Kate. "I'm coming to Paris, and I want to see you the instant I arrive. I have lots of news and lots of experiences to report!"

The reply was instantaneous: "Oh, darling, I am leaving for Africa tonight. There is an outbreak of a new strain of Ebola, and they think they need my skills in detective work to track down the source and predict how it might develop next. I am taking some of your epidemiological math-based computer programs with me, and your statistics shortcuts. So, you will be with me, in more ways than one. I shall think of you being sinful on the Left-Bank! My darling! Keep me informed of your adventures."

Tears and a sudden void welled up; I hadn't realized how much I missed her. But I took a deep breath and immediately put on a cheerful face: "Oh, Kate, darling, be careful! I'll drink a toast to you. And, when you can, keep me up to date with what's happening. Be very, very careful! I love you!"

CHAPTER 8 – PARIS

James and I did the old-fashioned thing and took the train. It was an overnight train, and it was lots of fun, the two of us competing acrobatically for space in one of the two bunks of our suite, and ending up in a very intimate tangle in one bunk where it did seem that, for most of the night, our bodies had truly become one.

James' flat in Paris was an ultra-modern, large, two-story flat with a nice terrace in an old building on the Left-Bank, not far from the Sorbonne, and not far from the Seine. Just around the corner were scores of little art galleries, and food was everywhere.

I loved it.

And I did make a few appointments with some mathematicians I had corresponded with and met them in one of the Left-Bank cafés, the Café Flore or Les Deux Magots, or for lunch at one of the little cafés on the Place de la Sorbonne or one of the restaurants on the rue des Écoles.

James and I ate out at a number of restaurants; James was quite busy, but he did tell me in great detail what he was doing – mainly dealing with some French investment banks and looking into a small French start-up pharmaceutical company that did some cutting-edge biotech work and owned several promising but, he thought, under-exploited patents.

"What do you think of this French company?" He put down a thick wad of studies.

"Really?"

"Yes, really."

"Okay. But I'm not a geneticist. I'm not a biologist."

"But you do understand statistics and modeling experiments," he said. "And you understand the limits of various methodologies; that's one of your strong points."

"Yes, Master, I do understand some of those things."

I spent the next two days happily combing through company reports and lab reports and scientific papers, and I reported in detail what I thought I had discovered. Several of the company's patents were maybe of doubtful value – the scientists had hedged a bit, and some academic journals had expressed doubts – but there were five ideas, and patents, that were possible breakthroughs, though the scientists and experts were still uncertain about them. The upside on an investment was, potentially, very big. I detailed all the reasons I had come to my conclusions and the methods I had used to reach them.

"You are a marvel," he said, and he rewarded me with a deep, lingering, and very tender kiss, a truly romantic kiss.

I noticed that James was looking at me, from time to time, in a very intense way that made me nervous.

"What?"

"Oh, nothing," he said. He looked guilty.

"You are having deep thoughts, Master. Do you wish to share them?"

"No, it's nothing."

"Really," I frowned.

"Yes, really," he said.

"Okay," I said brightly. I did not want trouble; I didn't want to rock the boat; I was determined to be Little Miss Sunshine.

"Let's go out," he said, as if relieved by my quick retreat into bright cheerfulness.

So, we went out. And what was interesting and delightful, but unsettling was this: our conversations were getting deeper; we talked about everything; our "games" became less elaborate, less fetishistic, less bondage and domination, less sexually aggressive; we held hands more and more, like true lovers. This made me uneasy. Something was not right. James, I think, was in love with me. In the bathroom one night, I leaned into the mirror: "Gwendoline," I said, "All is not well in our little paradise. A storm is in the offing, Gwendoline. Get ready to trim your sails."

It all became a romantic haze, with only a few little perverse interludes.

We walked along the edge of the Seine. He took me to some business dinners, the other men had wives, or perhaps a boyfriend, and the women who were the presidents of companies brought their husbands, or, in one case, girlfriend. James had me – and that seemed to work. I was confident enough to get along in French. Thanks to Claudia, reinforced by Kate, my French was fluent. James spoke like a native, and I spoke well enough to chatter away with CEOs and their spouses and with experts – I was particularly good, James told me, with scientists. Always, of course, I was dressed in an alluring, but not scandalous style.

"You are definitely an asset," he said.

"An asset!" I laughed

"Yes." He was looking at me with that strange, uneasy intensity. I got up, came over, kissed him on the eyes and on the lips. "You're getting serious," I said, "You're making me nervous. Let's go out and eat at the Flore or La Coupole, and I'll dress like a floozy."

"You couldn't be a floozy if you bet your life on it."

"Oh, I don't know."

Doing my best to be a floozy, I dressed in a new wet-look black catsuit he'd bought for me. We had found it when we were rummaging around in a shop near les Halles, the site of the old 19th Century meat, fish, and vegetable markets. The place is now an underground shopping mall – much more boring than the louche and glamorous 19th Century version – but young people like to hang around there.

I slipped a black velvet jacket over the catsuit and wore high heels to complement the ensemble. We ate at La Coupole in Montparnasse and walked back through the Parisian twilight, arm in arm, and then holding hands.

This is getting dangerously romantic, I thought. Of course, I was right, and, of course, I was in love.

One night, James tied me down on the bed. The bed was hard and wide, and the cuffs on my wrists and ankles were attached to cords that stretched to the steel bedposts at the four corners of the bed. I was naked and spread-eagled facing upwards toward the ceiling lamp.

James was very careful, very considerate. He almost seemed in awe. He moved his hands over my breasts; he kissed my nipples, and then he kissed my forehead and my lips. He moved down, kissing my belly, and, slowly, oh, so slowly, moved down further, kissing the inside of my thighs, while his hand explored my pubis and entered me, teasing, touching, withdrawing, entering, withdrawing, while his other hand twisted my nipple.

He kissed me, between my legs, hard and deep, and his tongue! Oh, his tongue was magic!

He made love to me slowly – to me with a blindfold on, and then me without the blindfold, but still tied down to the bed.

"Oh, oh, oh," I sighed.

He silenced me with a kiss.

≈

One balmy night we went out to a dance club. I wore the black latex catsuit, but without the hood and mask. We danced until quite late, and then we walked out into the warm Parisian night, and we headed along the Seine, heading home. It was the new version of the catsuit, the one Nicole had provided with the little flap at the crotch. We took advantage of the flap, down by the Seine, on the quay below the retaining wall, in the shadow of Notre Dame.

Martine Aubin was on a break from filming. She and Philip would shoot the rest of the film about Lucrezia Borgia later in the autumn at Rome's Cinecittà, but she was now in Paris and phoned to say she would love to see me. "We have to catch up," she said, in a sly, insinuating voice.

Martine and I had a demure lunch at a rather splendid restaurant in the old Jewish quarter, Le Dôme du Marais; but, while talking of books, films, and life in general, we did exchange a few delicate, tentative kisses, and we agreed that we might quite enjoy doing more. But, being sage little girls, we decided we would ask for the approval of our men first, which approval was duly accorded. "Now, we just have to find the right moment," said Martine. "We will," I said.

≈

James knew an artist who specialized in leather and latex, and fabric designs, and who used a lot of sadomasochistic imagery in her portrayal of power relations in sexuality.

"She needs a model," he said. "Would you be interested?"

"If it doesn't take too much time," I said.

When I went to meet the artist, Martine came as my chaperone. The woman was surprised to see the two of us, more surprised still that I was with a talented, well-known actress well on her way to becoming a big star.

The artist explained her concept of feminism and art – "re-appropriating the male gaze" and "deconstructing the ideologies and iconographies of sexual power" and "empowering the female narrative" – and how it fitted into art history.

"Taboos are important," she said, "And it's important to destroy taboos or transcend taboos, to appropriate them for our purposes, for our liberation. Women will not be free unless they liberate their desires and recognize their ambivalence. We are not angels or Madonnas or saints."

She talked about the meat dress, first developed by Jana Sterbak; she talked about Sterbak's "Remote Control" a sort of crinoline metal skirt frame on rollers and piloted by remote control, about Madonna's use of SM and Fetish gear, about Lady Gaga, and Miley C's fetish SM performance videos. "We have to manage the transition from being object to being subject," she said.

"Without losing the advantages of being an object, I hope," said Martine, with that sly little smile she had.

"Precisely! Eroticism is power, and being an object and a subject, simultaneously, is our destiny," said the artist, "as it is the destiny of everyone, even the most macho of men depends on his image for his existence."

"Hegel," murmured Martine, "the dialectic."

"Precisely," said the artist, giving her a glorious smile.

≈

I posed naked for a series of photographs that she would use for an installation. They showed my body only, so I presumed, as we had agreed, that I would be anonymous.

So, she created images of my body, wrapped in ropes, and strapped in leather and latex, or crucified on a sort of cross-like thing. At the end of the session, she asked me if I would agree to be a model, a living work of art, at the opening.

Martine thought this would be exciting. What would I have to do? I asked. Well, you'll be chained, and in latex, and so on ... so and you'll be hooded, nobody will see who you are.

I asked James.

He said, "Of course. Then we'll go to dinner afterward."

"With Martine and Philip, as part of the group?"

"Of course, that would be splendid." He seemed genuinely happy.

Meantime, days went by, and I visited the gallery from time to time – usually with Martine if she was free – for more photographs or measurements. The artist made a body cast, which took up quite a bit of an afternoon. Otherwise, I worked at home, or in several of my favorite cafés. I like to migrate when I work, using one café and then another. I like working in a public place – it helps me concentrate.

All sorts of art people attended the show. The artist had turned the body cast of me into a headless and armless statue, a bust, re-worked so that it looked as if it had emerged from an archeological dig in ancient Rome or Greece.

There were photographs of my body all over the walls – fetish photographs of various kinds with texts from theorists of art, of sadism, of bondage, and of masochism, the sort of theories of perversity the French are so good at. Each text had a feminist gloss or interpretation and critique from the artist.

There was a black-and-white period-piece-look photograph of Martine and me in La Coupole, obviously spooning, the sort of photograph Robert Doisneau or William Klein or Jeanloup Sieff might have taken.

Then, as a centerpiece of the show, there was me – the real me, in flesh and blood, a performance "art object."

I was on my knees, chained, my arms pinioned behind my back, encased and hooded in skin-tight ultra-revealing silver latex, with only my heavily made-up eyes and scarlet painted lips showing. It was not a particularly uncomfortable pose and, since we had decided I would not remain anonymous, I was there to answer questions.

The art object talks back.

We had rehearsed some of the answers to probable questions, but an aspect of the performance was that I would be spontaneous. I would express my own thoughts, not only those of the artist.

People asked me why I did it, what I was feeling, what the latex felt like, what did the various photos on the wall mean for me.

To some of the questions, I gave the artist's point of view and then juxtaposed it with mine, as she and I had agreed.

At first, people were shy about approaching the living art object. But then they started, and soon there was a group, five or six people sitting on chairs, and some of them squatting on the floor, quizzing me, as I knelt shackled and chained in front of them, and other people gathered behind them, listening, and adding questions.

Sometimes they began to argue among themselves. I felt like a politician – or a philosopher. Perhaps I was like an ancient oracle, masked and kneeling, in a sacred artistic space, making gnomic pronouncements

"Marvelous," said the gallery owner afterward.

"You're a star," said Martine.

"It surpassed what I thought it might be," said the artist and kissed me full on the lips.

James took me in his arms and embraced me.

The artist decided that, during the dinner afterward, I should remain in the silver latex, including the hood and mask; and so it was. It was a lively dinner table. I felt strangely present – because it was so intense – but I was also absent, masked, an exotic object, a "creature," not really me.

James that night was even more affectionate than usual. We made love just as lovers have made love from the beginning of time. He held me in my arms, and when he fell asleep, I listened to the night sounds for a long time; about two o'clock in the morning, it began to rain, and, far away, I heard thunder and saw vague flashes of lightning light up the Parisian sky.

Why can't I sleep? I turned on my side and lay against James' body, my arm over his chest. I want this to go on, and on, and on! I want this to continue forever.

"I love you," James said, when his eyes opened, "I love you so much, Gwendoline, I truly love you."

He insisted on making breakfast and bringing it to me – with wonderful steaming hot coffee – in bed. There was a new softness, a new attentiveness about him. It made me more and more uneasy – but I only understood why in retrospect, looking back.

CHAPTER 9 – ABANDONED

Three days after the vernissage, I left for Cambridge. I had to give a talk and then hold two seminars. I flew to London and then took the train to Cambridge. The seminars were fun, and the talk seemed to go over very well.

One of the professors who introduced me, Gerald Skinner, explained that I was known not only as one of the most brilliant mathematicians of my generation, but also as a performance artist and member of the Parisian avant-garde. If I knew how to blush, I would have blushed; and I did have to answer a few questions about Martine Aubin and the Performance at the Quantum Pixel Gallery.

After the seminars, I phoned James to tell him how Cambridge had gone. How eager I was to be back. How I missed him. How I loved him.

His phone didn't answer.

His voice mail didn't kick in.

I texted.

No answer.

I emailed.

No answer.

Suddenly, I was worried sick.

I had a terrible premonition.

I felt I was going to throw up.

I caught an early flight from London back to Paris. Summer was ending. Paris was achingly beautiful. The taxi took me along the Seine and up Boulevard Saint Germain and left me off at the corner of our little street. I walked down the street. The baker just below our building shouted out, "Hello, Mademoiselle!" I answered, "Hello," and, on a sudden impulse, I went in and bought four croissants of the kind I knew James loved. I went up in the elevator. I got out at our landing. Everything seemed normal. I opened the door to the flat. I entered. It was deadly quiet.

"James?"

"James, darling?"

"James, I've brought some croissants – the chocolate ones with the almonds ..."

Dead silence. I walked through the rooms. James was not there; there was a strange feeling of emptiness, of abandonment.

I went into the kitchen.

Propped on the kitchen table was a letter, addressed to me, hand-written, in James' script. I tore it open.

Dearest Gwendoline,

I am gone.

I have fallen in love with you, which is something I cannot do. Please forgive me.

This apartment is yours, darling. The papers have been signed and are with the concierge. The transfer of property is irrevocable.

Stay in Paris, as long as you wish, or go to Oxford or Cambridge. As I said, this apartment, and the funds to keep it operating in perpetuity – taxes and so on, are all in your name. The concierge will help you with anything you might need.

Wherever you are, you will always be in my heart.

Again, please forgive me.

James.

I sat down.

I was paralyzed, sick, stunned.

I was going to throw up.

I rushed to the bathroom and knelt over the toilet bowl.

Nothing came.

I stood up. I was hollow inside, empty, dizzy – all the blood draining away. I put my hand against the wall, the cool ceramic wall.

Then I thought, this must be a joke. "James," I shouted. "James!" I walked around the flat. I opened all the cupboards. "Are you playing hide-and-seek? Is this a joke? This is cruel, James! This is not funny!"

I went out on the balcony. I went into his washroom and into the separate bedroom, which he had never used as we always slept together; rarely, when we were in the flat, were we far from each other.

Every sign of James had disappeared. No clothes hanging in the closet. No toiletries in the bathroom. No computer. No charger for his cellphone. He was minimalist as it was, but ...

"You coward, James, you bloody fucking coward! You could have just told me to my face; you could have ..." I sat down. I was shaking; my teeth were chattering; I couldn't control my body. Tears were streaming; I let them stream.

No, maybe he couldn't have told me. Maybe he couldn't have faced me. Maybe he couldn't have stood it, seeing me like this.

My heart was gone; a chasm opened up; I was falling into a hole, an infinitely deep dark hole, with no bottom and no end to it.

I stood up. I walked back and forth.

I swore – by all the gods and all the devils! James!

I went downstairs to the concierge.

The concierge and her husband said, "Sit down, dear, sit down, Mademoiselle, here are the documents. Yes, it is all signed. You own it. Only your signature is needed – then it is final."

"I don't want to sign it."

"Here, let me make you some coffee," said the concierge.

"He's a strange man, that one," said her husband.

"Put some Cognac in the coffee," said the concierge.

"Yes, yes, Cognac," said the husband.

Sitting in the concierge's lodge, I tried James's cell, again, and again. It rang and rang. Yes, he'd turned off the voice mail.

How could he do this?

I raged. Then I calmed down.

I called the New York office, Allison's number, her cell. "I'm sorry, Gwendoline."

"You warned me."

"Yes, but it doesn't make it easier, does it?"

"No, but thanks, Allison."

I sat stunned.

As I drank the coffee, the concierge and her husband fussed around me. "Will you be alright? Do you want someone to stay with you?"

"I think I'll take my time and look at the papers," I said.

"Yes, I think that would be absolutely the best thing to do," said the concierge.

"Absolutely," said her husband, pouring me more coffee, and pushing a thick piece of chocolate cake toward me. I looked at it: thick gooey chocolate. Yes, what the heck! I began to eat. "This is delicious," I said. "Did you make it?"

"Yes, I did," the concierge grinned. She was delighted; at least somebody was happy.

Kate was in Africa, and she had enough on her plate and no need to listen to me whining.

My cellphone rang. I held my breath, hesitated, said a little prayer, and finally dared glance at the screen. It was Martine.

I answered.

"Hey, Gwen ..." Her voice was bright and cheerful. Philip was away, she said. Did James and I want to do anything? Maybe the three of us could go to a restaurant for dinner. A new place had just opened in –

I told her.

"Oh, my God! I don't believe it! How could he? How utterly stupid of him."

"Yes," I said. My lips were numb. "Yes, it is stupid."

"You can't be alone, Gwendoline, not now."

I hesitated. Part of me wanted to stay in the flat and wallow in misery; part of me wanted to take off instantly for Cambridge or New York, or Boston; most of me wanted to be alone, just alone. But being alone was a bad idea, definitely a bad idea. I took a deep breath, "Yes, let's go to dinner."

"Excellent idea," she said. "I'll come and pick you up."

So, Martine and I went to dinner; it was an intimate little bistro, in a tiny alley on the Isle Saint Louis, and, since Martine was a star, they give us a VIP table, isolated and safe in our own little alcove; during dinner, we talked. I tried not to whine; we talked about films, books, then, of course, about James, about love, about the fear of love, about men ...

Then, when we were hovering over dessert – crème brûlée for her and gâteau basque for me – Martine, lifting a dripping spoon to her mouth, looked at me through half-closed eyes, and said, "Do you want to sleep at my place tonight?" She paused. "I think you should."

I blinked at her. She was so warm, so beautiful, so giving. But in my mind, I had a heroic picture of myself. I was waiting in the empty and desolate James-Gwendoline apartment, alone, and then James came in, got down on his knees, and confessed that he had been a fool, that I was his true love, that we would never be separated, not ever; and that we would live forever together, happily ever after. This little fantasy of reconciliation was a dream. It was masochistic, sadistic, and hopeless – a feathery, sugary sequined confetti dream: a fantasy. If I stayed in that flat, I'd be miserable; I'd be hopeless. No, I'm not going to wait for him, I decided. I'm not going to run after him. I'm not going to be bitter. He is who he is, and I have to accept that – it was our implicit agreement that we were both free and to be free – well, sometimes you have to fly away; and sometimes you have to close a door you'd like to keep open; and you have to let the other person fly away too. Goddamn it! Goddamn it! Goddamn it! I curled my fist and pressed my nails into my palm, hoping to make the skin bleed.

"Yes, I'd like to stay at your place," I said.

"So, it's settled then, darling." She got up, crouched next to me, and kissed me on the lips.

We left the restaurant, but not after a few paparazzi shot pictures of us at the door. "You don't have to smile if you don't want to," Martine whispered.

"I'll smile," I said.

Somehow, I did.

≈

After that, I had a year of hard work and commuted between Cambridge and Paris and London – occasionally going to Oxford and Toulouse – and then I had to go back to New York to give the big talk, the results of my research, my thesis.

I was satisfied. I was sure I had done a decent job, and my

supervisors in Cambridge and at MIT were ecstatic, or so they said, which was kind of them.

Before signing the ownership papers for the flat, I had examined my conscience – it was a huge gift; but, I thought, I could always give it back. I consulted with Claudia, and she put her French lawyers onto it. They said if I didn't accept the gift of the flat, it would end up in limbo and might just be taken over by the city. They advised me to sign the papers, to keep the flat, and to rent it out on short-term rentals, which I did through a very respectable agency; that way it generated quite a neat income – which I carefully reported to French tax authorities and the IRS – and I paid the concierge and her husband for looking after it and managing it. It also meant that if I was going to be in Paris for a long time, I could keep it for myself. Generally, I stayed away from the place. I loved it too much, and it held too many memories, too many associations.

When I was in Paris, I usually stayed with Martine. She and Philip were lovers, and they worked together, but they led quite separate lives, and they didn't live together. Philip seemed to consider me one of the family and he was more than understanding of my relationship with Martine – which he knew was amorous. He occasionally made very nice, and sensitive, jokes about what a nice couple she and I made. I had the keys to Martine's flat, and even when she was not in Paris, I was to treat it – and I did treat it – as my home.

Sometimes the three of us went out together; and, through Martine, and Philip and my philosophy and mathematics friends, I met a great many artists and actors and filmmakers, I became part of a sort of Paris artistic and intellectual "scene," with lots of people to see and gossip with, in cafés and restaurants, when I was so inclined.

Every day or two, Kate and I exchanged emails. She was

fighting the good fight against new forms of the plague – and all the teaming viruses that threaten to bring civilization crashing down. She was there, on the front line of a war than never stops. Her articles were widely cited in the scientific press, and BBC television and CNN and even Fox News interviewed her several times.

She regularly consulted me on statistics and mathematical models on the spread of the epidemics. The UN and the Aid Agencies were applying some of my ideas about how to trace – and predict – the spread of these pathogens. The trouble spots and failed states of Africa and the Middle East were proving fertile breeding grounds for new epidemics, and also the so called wet markets in Asia, where live animals are sold for food, were also sources of possible pandemics, so using math to predict their behavior was crucial not only locally, but also globally; a repeat of something like the 1919 flu pandemic was becoming more probable every year. Kate was in the frontline of humanity's fight to save itself from catastrophe.

CHAPTER 10 – SHAME

I was back in New York. The day had come when I had to present my year's work – which was a summary of all my research for the Neumann-Williamson Foundation – before an elite academic and scientific audience; many of the world's best young researchers would be there too.

I was nervous about the lecture.

What if my stutter came back?

An hour before I was to go on stage, Martine, who was also in New York for a series of interviews and photoshoots, rang on my cell phone. "Hi, darling, there's trouble. You'd better look at these. I've emailed you the photos and links. Have a look."

I did. Attached to her email were pictures of me, naked, in chains, blindfolded, and – a close-up – of me naked on my knees, giving oral sex: a blowjob. "They are all over the Internet, darling," she said, "Quite exciting, really. Very photogenic, I must say."

"Oh, boy!"

"Did he do this?" Martine asked, "I can't believe he would."

"No, I'm sure it wasn't him. He wouldn't hurt me – ever."

"You're sure?"

"Yes, I'm as sure as I am of anything. It's probably a guy who lived down the street in Rome. He must have had a telephoto lens. And, as you know, there were a few paparazzi chasing us around in Rome and Paris. That's me on the balcony, handcuffed, with the leash. Some of these could have been taken by anybody. All you need is an iPhone or whatever. That's me on the beach, naked, that's me streaked with sand, and that's me splashing around, and that's me in that catsuit. Whew. And that's me, kneeling, naked, and giving James a ..."

"... a blowjob," said Martine, finishing my sentence.

"Yes." I felt sick, and yet strangely elated; each picture brought back a floodtide of memories.

"There's a photo of you and me too," she said.

"Oh."

"Use it if you have to – you and I, darling, are no secret!"

"Yes, that's right. We aren't." My mind was spinning.

"What are you going to do?"

"I'll think about it."

"Okay, my dearest sweetest darling, I'll see you after the lecture. You'll be great! Don't worry! And, these photographs, these days it's just part of life! Nudity and chains and blowjobs are nothing to be ashamed of. All part of the human comedy, all part of life!"

"You're right, Martine. It's just part of life!"

"Big hug! See you later!" She hung up.

"Just part of life ..." I frowned. Maybe that was the answer.

It was half an hour before the conference. Grandmother Claudia came into the hotel room, where I was making last-minute adjustments to my lecture. I explained.

She glanced at the photographs. "Those two are rather fetching," she said. "You look cute with a collar and leash." She flipped to the next one. James standing, me kneeling. "He's a handsome man, I must say that. And your submissive posture is very becoming."

"Yes, he is, handsome, I mean," I said, my throat going dry. I licked my lips. Damn it, and Damn it, and Damn it!

Claudia flipped to the next photo, a close-up of me on my knees, wearing the collar, of course, delivering first-class fellatio, too close for James to be identified.

She smiled. "And, this one, well ..."

"Hmm," I said. "Fetching or not ..."

"Well, you know what I always say," she said, giving me her most radiant grandmother smile.

"Yes, I know," I said. "Bite the bullet!"

"Precisely, darling. And a very appropriate expression in the circumstances, I might add."

"Very funny! Now, darling Claudia, I'm busy. Get out of here." I kissed her.

She gazed into my eyes, smiled, blew me an extra kiss, and left the room.

I frowned. Oh well, I'd asked for it; it was inevitable. In questions of sex, America could be a very unforgiving country. I would have to resign myself to oblivion; my career was about to go up in flames. At this thought, a hot flush spread through my body, a cold shiver ran down my spine, and sweat broke out everywhere. Oh, well. I squared my shoulders, and downloaded the photos onto the PowerPoint system, checked it on the computer. Yes, okay, everything was set up as best it could be set up.

I took a deep breath and walked down to the Congress Hall, where I would have to sacrifice myself on the altar of my supposed wickedness.

I waited in the wings. I walked up and down, and then I walked into the hall with Professor Ho Chan Lee, who worked in Shanghai and San Francisco and who was going to introduce me. He was a brilliant mathematician.

I said, "I am going to do something a bit different, Professor Lee."

He smiled. Whatever I did, he said, he was sure would be okay.

You bet, I thought.

Grandmother Claudia was in the front row next to Mrs. Neumann, the widow of the Nobel Prize laureate who had given his name to the prize. Professor Rupert Harrington-Smyth was there, also beside Mrs. Neumann, with his wife, Cynthia, who was sitting on grandmother's left. They all smiled.

Prof Ho Chan Lee made a brief introduction. It was very flattering.

I stood up and walked to the podium – suddenly alone in front of more than 800 people, the leading lights of mathematics, and many ambitious young graduate students and tutors.

I stood and looked at them all. I looked around. I said, how honored I was to have received the fellowship; I thanked all the people who had to be thanked. I cleared my throat. I could feel sweat pearling down my spine.

I could see a bit of a stir in the back of the auditorium. Younger people were receiving the images or had spotted them. Again, I cleared my throat. I would have to do this fast.

"I used to have a stutter. I hope I don't stutter now."

There was uneasy laughter.

"Now, I am going to do something unusual. I hope you will forgive me. Before you here, now, ladies and gentlemen, I am going to do a striptease. This is so we can get my body and my sexuality out of the way. Give me just a moment. I hope you will not run screaming from the auditorium."

Eyes opened wide. People perked up.

"I owe an explanation for those of you who may not be aware of what has just happened: pictures of me without any clothes on have been circulating on the Net – in the last few hours. In some of the pictures, I am not just naked, but I am wearing a collar and other trinkets. In one photograph, I am indulging in sex – well, it depends on how you define sex, but in my opinion, it was sex. It will be graphic. Any children should leave the room, or their eyes should be covered during this part of the show."

I scanned the room. No children.

"So, given that the images are out there, accessible to anybody and everybody, I thought that to satisfy everybody's curiosity and get any sniggering and prurience – my own as well as other people's – out of the way, I think we'd better have a look."

I took them through the images.

"This is the first shot – It's me on a beach in Italy. It's a nudist beach. As you can see, I'm naked, splashing in the water, it was a great beautiful warm day, and I was there with the man who was then my lover and whom I loved very much. We had a wonderful time, and I ate some vanilla ice cream, and we made love later, in the dunes, which you can see up there in the background of the second image.

"And here I am playing a sort of game of soccer, mixed team, on the same beach; as I said, it was a nudist beach. I'm not the only player who is naked, as you can see – for example – there's that girl in the background with the arm cast.

"This one is full-frontal," I used the electronic pointer here. "And you can see my pubis is waxed. There it is! And in this next slide," I again used the pointer, "It isn't.

"And here I am on a balcony and terrace. That man – you can see his back – he was my lover, and he and I are about to make love. You can see that I am in handcuffs and wearing a collar and a little chain – a quite nice silver-colored steel chain – or leash. That was a game he and I used to play, and we had a lot of games like that – and I liked them; in fact, I loved them.

"For me, they were fun and exciting – and very sexy – because I trusted him and loved him, and I still trust him even today though we are no longer together.

"And here I am in a catsuit – pretending to be cat woman – in

333

a street in Rome. You wouldn't know it is me because of the hood and mask, but it is.

"My friend took me that night – and dressed that way – to a very interesting gay and lesbian and trans bar, and I met some fabulous and wonderful people who felt, strangely, compelled to confess many of their problems to me. I guess the catsuit and mask conferred a sort of anonymity which made me trustworthy – as in a confessional.

"So, we played games, infantile and silly perhaps, but, as I said, for me they were fun, and very exciting. Like cops and robbers or hide-and-seek.

"And here is an example of what is called oral sex, or fellatio, or, more in popular parlance a 'blow job.' All very mysterious – what it means, and I seem to remember that whether this practice is to be defined as sex or not may have been a central point in what amounted to a constitutional crisis in the United States back when Mr. Clinton was President. So that's that."

I paused and looked around.

"Here's the essential point. All of this was consensual on both sides. I never did anything I didn't want to do. I was quite invent- ive in creating our games, or so I flatter myself. And my partner never forced me – or tried to force me – to do anything I didn't want to do."

I paused and looked straight at the audience. "Non-consen- sual sex of any kind is I think one of the worst crimes one can commit, one of the worst violations of another person's integrity and very being. It's an attack not only on the body, but on the soul."

A few people clapped, but it was hesitant. Oh, they are going to lynch me, I thought. Okay, this is the end – well, so be it. I had bitten the bullet! I am doomed. Onward!

I took a deep breath. "And, lastly, here's a picture of me with my friend Martine Aubin, the French actress, and we are kissing. Martine said I could show you this picture, by the way, and she has seen all the others."

I took a deep breath. "This is not just about me – or Martine, or my male friend. I think there's a general lesson here; when people try to shame us, and when we have done nothing wrong – that is, when we have hurt nobody – then I think the answer to the forces of shame and shaming is to be shameless.

"We have to be who we are and have the guts to be who we are. We have to declare war on shame. We have to declare war on those who would shame us. So, I am declaring, here and now, that I am in this regard, shameless.

"Okay, that's it: if you find any other pictures on the net – of me – then you can send them to me, and I'll add them to my collection, which will be available online, in a special separate website, for which thanks. My email is on the program for tonight's talk.

So ... now, let's get back to math." Well, I thought, now I've done it. I am done for – but, bite the bullet! I half expected shouts of "Take it off, you bitch, take it off!"

There was a hushed silence, and then there was a single cheer and then whistles, and then a few people stood up and clapped, and I inclined my head. The tide, perhaps, was turning.

Rupert Harrington-Smyth started to get up. He looked very serious. I saw Mrs. Neumann put her hand on his sleeve; she stood up too; Rupert Harrington-Smyth hesitated, but Mrs. Neumann nodded that he should accompany her, and together they headed toward the stage.

Grandmother Claudia gave me a tight smile and a timid encouraging wave. Cynthia Parker, her head tilted to one side, glanced at my grandmother, who was sitting beside her, and then added her wave, to which she added a big open smile. She leaned toward Claudia and began to whisper to her. Claudia nodded, smiled enthusiastically. So, there is hope, I thought. At least not everybody hates and despises me!

But I was about to be executed, of that I was sure; I had, after all, desecrated the memory of a Nobel Prize Laureates, no, two Nobel Prize Laureates – Neumann and Williamson.

Mrs. Neumann came toward me. She was a beautiful and severe-looking lady, wearing a wide-shouldered charcoal suit with vertical white stripes, and she was famous as a philanthropist and as an expert on butterflies and their evolution. I had never met her.

She was I think in her mid-80s, and I thought: Oh, now I'm really done for. A woman of her background, and her age, will never, never forgive what I have done – I have dishonored the memory of her husband, I have dragged the fellowship's name down into the mud, I have …

She came straight toward me, stopped, stared at me for just an instant, with a rather forbidding look of eagle-like intelligence in her gray eyes, and she stepped forward and opened her arms and hugged me.

I hesitated for a moment, and then I hugged her back. I felt, under the fine suit and the proud demeanor, the bony fragility of her elegant old body. For just an instant, I was transported back to the moment on the rocky volcanic island when I was holding Lauren Lockhart in my arms, kissing her, making love to her, comforting her.

Mrs. Neumann turned to the public, adjusted the microphone, and said, "I think – and I am sure Rupert agrees – that we have with us not only a supremely talented mathematician, but a wonderful, beautiful, kind – and very brave young woman."

She turned to me and kissed me on the cheek, and then she continued. "Gwendoline has just said what I have often thought but didn't find the right words or the courage to say. We have all been naked sometimes – actually quite often – once a day or more – and we have all, or many of us, played games, hide-and-seek, peek-a-boo, I'm the servant, you're the master, and such like, so let's accept it, even rejoice in it. And we have all practiced various forms of sexuality – well, I hope we have anyway." She paused and, over her glasses, favored the audience with a quizzical glance. Her timing was impeccable.

People laughed.

"Many powerful people – and many wicked institutions – and many miserable, hypocritical, sanctimonious jerks too, if you will allow me the expression – have tried to shame women – and not only women – and in many ways. It is time this stopped."

At this point, there was applause, first a ripple, and then it was thunderous.

"We must embrace our freedom, and our sexuality, in all its variety, and we must embrace our quirks, and we must not allow ourselves to be intimidated or shamed. False shame is the enemy of freedom, dignity, and honesty. False shame is the enemy of virtue, false shame is the enemy of wisdom and generosity, and I am convinced it is the enemy, too, of compassion, of desire, of tenderness, and it is certainly the enemy of love." She paused and turned to me. "Thank you, Gwendoline, thank you!"

She kissed me on both cheeks.

Professor Harrington-Smyth stepped forward, adjusted the microphone, glanced at me, and turned to the audience. "As a man, I feel a bit intimidated in saying anything, but you, Gwendoline, and you, Ms. Neumann, have said all that I could have said – and, obviously, much better. So, I will just add this one word. I have known Gwendoline for quite a few years now, and she is, I think, one of the bravest and most moral and principled people I have ever known – as well as being a very fine actress and a very ironic and funny person! Thank you, Gwendoline." He kissed me on both cheeks.

They stood on both sides of me, their arms around me, Professor Harrington-Smyth and Mrs. Neumann. It was hard to keep my tears back. Everybody was standing now, and clapping.

≈

Then I told them about the math ...

It was a forty-minute lecture with slides and some dynamic graphs. Some of the ideas came from my conversations with Kate, of course, but also with James – from all the problems of theory and practice he faced in making big investment decisions.

Then we had almost forty minutes of questions, none of them, miraculously, about my sex life or the photographs.

Martine joined us for dinner – Mrs. Neumann, Cynthia, Rupert, and Claudia, and Professor Ho Chan Lee and his wife, me, and two young mathematicians, one a woman, the other a man.

Martine was treated by everyone as if she was my date, which in a way she was, and which she found entrancing, and so did I.

"Do you want to sleep alone tonight?" she whispered.

"No," I said, "I don't."

Martine had several times joined me sleeping at Claudia's, so this was no problem at all. Claudia had adopted Martine as a second granddaughter, treating her as a delightfully glamorous and incestuous sister I had discovered in exotic Rome and brought home as booty one day. Sometimes I thought Martine was closer to Claudia than I was. Like Kate, Martine and Claudia were steeped in French culture and worldly-wise in a way that I am not and probably never will be.

When we three got back to Claudia's flat, there was a big bouquet of flowers – it was from James, the first time I had heard from him. I sat down and looked at it, and I wanted to throw it out. "Into the garbage, it will go," I said.

"But you love him, don't you," said Martine. We were sitting in Claudia's living room, on the divans that were in front of the fireplace. Claudia had served us nightcaps – hot chocolate.

"And, whatever he has done, I'm sure he loves you," said Claudia.

"Well, that's what he said," I said, "when he stabbed me in the heart."

"He does love you. Keep the flowers," said Martine, glancing at Claudia.

Claudia nodded and said, "You know, he has his own problems to deal with."

"Yes," I said, "I suppose he does."

I accepted the flowers. I even sent a hand-written thank you note to his New York office. I didn't receive a reply, though there was, separately, an email from Allison. "You are glorious, Gwendoline," she wrote, "I don't think we have seen the last of each other."

≈

The lecture was pretty much a sensation. There were front pages, in some countries with photographs. Headlines: Mathematician bares all. Naked Prodigy Startles Elites. Girl Einstein Strips Naked. Sex lectures from the podium of the Neumann-Williamson Fellowship ..."

I got a few complaints – the Catholic Bishops, of course, declared that I had set a bad example for youth and besmirched the idea of womanhood. I thought of many acid retorts to the honorable bishops – involving child-abuse, cover-ups, illegitimate offspring of priests abandoned to their fate, women and boys mistreated, etc. But I decided that such polemics were useless. Besides, through James, I had met some very nice Catholic priests and prelates, and one or two brilliant Jesuits, and the Catholic Church in some ways had been very kind to me. And one Jesuit father, a mathematician I had met several times in Paris, wrote a very nice note complimenting me on my Neumann-Williamson lecture, and saying I was an "honor to the profession of mathematics." I wrote back thanking him, and we began a very interesting correspondence, which then extended to several other Catholic scholars.

I had ongoing very creative and interesting correspondence and friendships with several Muslim mathematicians, teaching in Cairo and Paris, which were not interrupted at all by my notariety. We even shared a few jokes about it.

An imam somewhere pronounced a fatwa. I wrote him a polite letter. I said that I disagreed with covering women up, but that I would never attack them for it. And, though I didn't advise people, or myself, to run around naked in the streets, I thought that a bit more exposure, a bit less shame and a bit more respect and kindness for each other would be a good idea. It didn't matter whether one was naked or dressed, with a hijab or niqab, or wearing a bikini. We should be kind to everybody – whatever they believed or didn't believe. Just being polite and considerate might go a long way to making people better and happier and more accepting of each other's beliefs. I did not get a reply.

From time to time, some of the math prodigies – and even strangers – sent me photographs – me making out with Martine, my hand snaking up her skirt while we kissed, me standing tiptoe naked in a formal French garden, me performing in chains in the Paris art gallery. The photos came, for the most part, with friendly notes, like, "Hi Gwen, I really like this one. It's for your collection!"

There were, of course, the usual idiots, almost always anonymous, the scurrilous cowards, sprinkling obscenities and threats, but they were a tiny minority, and they didn't bother me – not very much at least. Mostly, with such people, I felt I would like to sit down with them, have a coffee, and ask them what was wrong with their life, what was lacking, why they were angry, what were the real reasons for their anger; and ask if I could help, and so on. This scenario of reconciliation was, of course, a fantasy. Some people are addicted to anger, whether it is righteous or not.

≈

Two weeks after the Neumann-Williamson speech, my cellphone rang.

It rang, and rang, and rang.

I'd turned off the voice mail.

It rang and rang and rang. I watched it: the number indicated a landline in Moscow.

I let it ring.

Finally, I picked it up.

"Hello," I said.

To receive a free book or novella
And to get notes on writing and other topics:

Sign up at

https://gilbertreid.com

Please write a short review!
Just two or three lines.
Post it to Goodreads or Amazon
or any other book group you may belong to.

And send it to Gwendoline:
gwendolineclermont305@gmail.com
or to: **gilbert@gilbertreid.com**

GILBERT REID is the author of two short story collections: *So This is Love: Lollipop and Other Stories* (2004, 2019) and *Lava and Other Stories* (2019). He also co-authored, with Jacqueline Park, the historical novel *Son of Two Fathers* (2019). He has written extensively for television and radio. Most notably he researched, wrote, and narrated two five-hour radio series: *Gilbert Reid's Italy* and *Gilbert Reid's France* for CBC's flagship radio program IDEAS. His many television series include *Paths of the Gods*, *For King and Empire*, *For King and Country*, and *Sir Peter Ustinov in Burma: Road to Mandalay*. After thirty years in Europe working as an economist, university lecturer, diplomat, script doctor, journalist, and adventure travel guide, Gilbert now lives in Toronto.

https://gilbertreid.com/